I0542276

IRREPARABLE
DEEDS

A NOVEL

SLOANE
KADY

BLACKWEALD

PRESS

This book is a work of fiction. Names, characters, businesses, places, events and incidents are either the products of the author's imagination or used in a fictitious manner. Any resemblance to actual persons, living or dead, business establishments, or actual events is purely coincidental.

Copyright © 2015 by Sloane Kady

All rights reserved. This book or any portion thereof may not be reproduced or used in any manner whatsoever without the express written permission of the publisher except for the use of brief quotations in a book review.

PRESS
Published in the United States by Blackweald Press, Seattle.
91 S. Jackson St. No. 4321
Seattle, WA 98104
www.blackwealdpress.com

ISBN 978-0-9862790-0-3

Printed in the United States of America

Cover Design by Keri Knutson of Alchemy Book Covers and Design

10 9 8 7 6 5 4 3 2 1

First Edition

This is for my amazing husband and our beautiful girls, who each own a third of my heart. None of these literary shenanigans would've been possible without your unwavering support and unconditional love. Your faith in me is the only reason this book came to fruition. Thank you doesn't seem like enough. But I'll love you for eternity. And I'll always love you more.

IRREPARABLE
DEEDS

Prologue

One of my earliest memories is of my mother sitting beside me on my bed, looking down at me with the strangest expression. Even as a young child, I knew that expression meant something, but it would take years to realize exactly what.

I was sick. I remember throwing up so many times that my thighs ached, my ribs burned, my entire body throbbed. I couldn't even take a sip of water to soothe my raw throat, and I could barely lift up my arms to hold myself over the toilet to puke, so my father put a bowl on the floor, next to my bed.

I still remember the look in my father's eyes because it was so much different than my mother's. Standing together, they looked like yin and yang. He was scared. I think he thought I was dying. Later that day, he looked so relieved when I didn't vomit up what must have been a half-gallon of water he made me drink. That's when my mother took over, relieving him of his duties so he could make dinner. He was always the one who cared for me when I was sick, until I got older. Then I took care of him.

That's when my mother sat beside me, looking down at me with that odd look. I remember feeling scared, but I didn't understand why. My mother never had a loving, maternal glow about her. She usually looked pained, discontent. But this look was different. She pulled the covers off me, exposing my arms and legs, covered in goose bumps. She offered to rub my belly, and I happily nodded. I wanted my mom to nurture and love me. She brushed her fingertips over my skin, sending a chill down my legs. Her hands were always so cold, I remember that. But I thought it was nice, even if it didn't make me feel better.

My door was just cracked open, and my mother pointed her toe, extending her leg to close it. I looked up at the closed door and asked for my father. That's when she put both hands on my stomach, lightly pressing into my belly. When I made a little sound, thinking she couldn't know she was actually hurting me, she raised one finger to her closed lips, shushing my whimpers. I always did what I was told, especially when she was the one doing the telling. I had learned that lesson early on.

She pressed harder, kneading deeply. I started to cry, but I didn't say a word. Like working a ball of dough, she kneaded and squeezed. I thought I was going to throw up from the pain. This went on for several minutes, and the whole time, she looked down at me with that same expression: cold, blank, icy, just like her hands. It was an expression I came to know as just my mother's face.

I bent over like I was going to vomit and she pulled her hands away, watching me, waiting. I'd never messed myself before. The sensation felt strange. That's why I didn't know what was happening. I grabbed my stomach and rolled into a ball as a warm gush of fluid pooled under my bottom, soaking my sheets, filling the room with a sick stench. My mother sat on the bed for what felt like an eternity, watching me as I just lay there, scared and cold. She never took her eyes off me. It wasn't until my father came in to tell us dinner was ready that I finally got cleaned up. Of course he cleaned my mess—my mother certainly wasn't going to. I remember him walking into the room, the look on his face. I was so embarrassed. He cringed until he realized I was the source of the smell, then he smiled at me and told me it was okay.

He bent down and scooped me up while giving my mother a look of utter hatred. Before he walked me out of the room and down the hall to the bathroom, he looked over his shoulder and asked my mother a question. I couldn't see her face because I had my own buried in my father's chest, but I never forgot her answer. That's one thing my mind never blocked out.

"What happened?" he asked. The tone in his voice made me think he really wanted to say, "What did you do?"

In a flat voice, my mother replied, "She's black inside, William."

As a child, I used to wake up dripping in sweat. The nightmares were so vivid. I'd wake up screaming, only to realize that I'd never really woken at all, because the nightmares were merely a reflection of my reality. There was no solace, not in the darkness of night, nor in the light of day. My real life played out in my dreams, leaving me with so little space to move and air to breathe that I often thought the fear would find its way into my heart in the middle of the night and stop it from beating. The saddest part was, I wasn't all that afraid of dying. Sometimes I wished for death. I even prayed for it. The corners of my childhood home were like the distorted mirrors in a funhouse.

Everything was morphed and ugly—disfigured pictures of a family whose demons and secrets kept each member locked in a kind of prison.

The nightmares eventually stopped when I drank so much that I couldn't remember them. Sometimes I'd wake up with the residual grime of a nightmare and I'd run to the bottle. Poof! The feeling was gone, replaced with the miserable but content haze of a drunken stupor. That stupor came to be my best friend, my bandage for all my failures.

The long drive home was more painful than I let on. I should have slammed on the brakes and turned around, driving as far away as I could get. Burrowing through the center of the Earth and coming out the other side wouldn't have been far enough away, but I would have done it, just to escape into the blackest depths of the Earth's womb. Because what I didn't know was that there was much worse lurking in the darkest corners of my history.

Chapter 1

Fall of 1976

Danlyn sat on the dingy bedroom floor, running her fingers along the worn wood panels, listening to the screams coming from the living room. It was the first bedroom she had called her own, and she had rarely left it during the six months she lived here. It wasn't perfect. It was a mere suggestion of what most girls' rooms looked like, but that made no difference, because it usually meant a quiet place for her to be alone.

Danlyn looked up at the window, longing for the day she would be old enough to walk out. But for an eleven-year-old, that felt like a lifetime to wait. She looked around the room she'd been prepared to leave since the day they arrived, and she began to cry. The bedroom door didn't meet seamlessly with the frame, leaving a thin crack through which she could see a sliver of the living room. She scooted across the floor, placed her ear against the crack, holding her breath and listening closely, willing Paul not to talk about her. A warm flush of fear spread to her fingertips.

She stared back at the window, out into a world she thought might be more forgiving than her mother. But crawling out the window and running away would take courage she didn't think she had, because she couldn't move, as though invisible chains held her locked in place. She wasn't brave. She was a pathetic wimp. Only pathetic wimps huddled against a door—a sloppy pile of scrawny arms and skinny legs—waiting for the big bad wolf to swoop in and eat them alive. She leaned her head against the door and closed her eyes, tired but edgy, emotionally spent but amped up on adrenaline. More than anything, she wanted quiet. But that wasn't going to happen because adults were fighting, and when they fought, their world stopped and no one else existed. It was just them and their screams, and somewhere beyond that was Danlyn.

Danlyn's ears pricked to life like finely tuned instruments, honing in on every sound and every word. She pressed her ear more firmly against the door.

~

"Are you ashamed of me, Paul? Or are you just such a coward that you can't be a father?"

"Dammit, Laura. Look at what you're doing to Danlyn. You're a monster. I took pity on you because you had a little girl. I guess I should say I took pity on her, but I can't do this anymore "

Laura stood toe-to-toe with him. "You never wanted me here? Fine. But I didn't see anyone holding a gun to your head when you were fucking me."

"This wasn't going anywhere. You and I both know that." Paul backed away. "I gave it all I had, but look at you. You're not the woman I thought you were when I met you. I've been "looking for a way to rid myself of you and your problems, and now I've got one. "

They glared at each other, as if waiting to see who might throw the first punch. Laura could push any man to violence. Even a man like Paul.

"Rid yourself?" Laura finally said. "You think this will just go away? You'll pay for this baby for the rest of your life."

"No, Laura. The only person who will pay is that baby. Just like Danlyn's paying now." He stormed into the kitchen, poured himself another stiff drink.

"You're one to judge," Laura said, standing behind him. "What is that, an entire bottle in the last twelve hours? Or should I say since finding out I'm pregnant? Yeah, some father you are."

"I have no way of knowing if that baby's mine," Paul said, looking over his shoulder and sniggering. "Why the look, Laura? Thought I didn't know about that? You screw some asshole from the bar and want me to take responsibility?" He tipped his head back, drew in a long, steady sip, wincing as he swallowed. "Well, sweetie"—he wiped the drool from the corners of his mouth, slammed the glass down—"that's not gonna happen."

He picked the bottle back up, pouring another glass, and didn't see the attack coming. Laura grabbed the glass ashtray off the dining table and chucked it at his back. Paul's glass shattered on the linoleum floor, and he spun around, closing in on her so suddenly she had no time to get away. "I'm not your daughter!" He grabbed her shoulders, dug his fingers in. "You won't lay your damn hands on me. This is why you'll get rid of that baby. Do you hear me? You're a fucking drunk. Hell, you're drunk now. I won't watch you abuse another one of your kids."

Laura tried to pull away, away from his words, away from the truth, but she wasn't strong enough. And it didn't matter that he was right, because in the life of an addict, there was no room for honesty. Her eyes moistened, she looked deeply into his, searching for compassion. "Please stop saying these things."

"You need to hear them. Maybe if someone's finally honest with you, you'll get the damn point." He held her closer. "What gives you the right to treat people this way? And Danlyn... Jesus, Laura, do you even see how you are with her?"

"Let go of me."

"No. Listen to me."

"This is all bullshit," she yelled. "Just shut up."

Laura pulled away, Paul pulled her back. She twisted her neck down and opened her mouth, hesitating for a split second before digging her teeth into his wrist.

"Fuck," Paul screamed. "What the hell's wrong with you?" He grabbed his wrist, pressing on the wound.

Laura staggered back, stunned that she'd really done it. "I...I'm sorry, but you wouldn't stop."

He moved away, eyes wide. "You're out of your fucking mind."

"You're not the authority on raising children, Paul. Hell, you're too afraid to have your own. At least I'm trying. And this *is* your baby. I know I screwed up with Mark. I shouldn't have let him kiss me, but I didn't sleep with him. You have to believe that."

Paul's eyebrows creased. "I tried to help you, Laura. You and Danlyn. What hurts the most is that I couldn't. I'd settle for just getting you to see that you're fucking up that kid in there." His voice was softer now. "You're damaged, and you're ruining her. She's a sweet kid now, but how long do you think that'll last? She doesn't deserve this. No one does."

Laura's shoulders slouched forward. The raging fire that burned in her tempered into a yearning to salvage any morsel of their tattered relationship she could. If baring her soul could fix this, if meeting him in an honest place could save them, it was worth the pain it would cause.

"You know this isn't me," she cried. "I'm going to stop. I'm sorry I couldn't handle it last night when I found out about the baby. I just got scared. But I'm done drinking. I promised myself I wouldn't put Danlyn through what I went through, and I swear to God I won't." She paused, searching for something to say. "I went a whole week without a drop before. Remember how good it was?" Wiping the tears from her eyes, she pleaded, "When it's good, it's better than good. It can be like that from now on, but not if you end it."

"You're right, Laura." Paul took several steps back. "I thought I could love you. The sober you. The beautiful, intelligent woman I met the day I helped fix your car on the side of the road. I think I did love you then. But how many good weeks did we have before your drinking got out of hand? We've had some good times, but when it's bad…" He shook his head. "You're like Jekyll and Hyde, and I can't balance the two anymore." He looked away. "Even I'm afraid of you."

Laura flinched.

"How pathetic is that?" he asked, not waiting for an answer. "No. I'm done, sweetheart."

Laura walked to him, leaned her head on his warm chest, but he moved to the other corner of the dining room and pulled open the top drawer of the desk.

"Here," he said, pulling out a large envelope, holding it out to her. Covered in sweat and with blood seeping from his wrist, he looked like a man who had been through battle.

"What is that?"

"Just take it and leave."

This was not an unfamiliar situation for Laura, being left by a man. But no one had ever presented her with a parting gift.

She snatched the envelope from him, pulled open the flap. "What the hell is this?"

Paul walked past her and opened the front door, leaning against the frame, arms folded in front of his chest. "If this is what it means to be loved by you, I want no part of it. If I were a decent man, I'd have that little girl in there taken away from you. Luckily for you, I'm not that decent."

Laura's breaths came in short bursts.

"I went out this morning while you were sleeping. There's a thousand dollars in there. That should be enough for an abortion and even a little extra to move you out of my house. I pulled from every bit of savings I had, but I think it's a good investment for my future."

Laura threw the envelope down. "I don't need your damn money."

"You haven't made enough in tips working in that hellhole. Just take it. I don't want you showing back up, accusing me of not taking care of my responsibilities. Take it and get out."

The look of finality in his eyes was like a dagger to Laura's heart. Bearing a menacing look of hatred made just for him, she called Danlyn. "After two miscarriages, this is what you ask of me?" she whispered. "Well, you'd better have the balls to explain that to her." It was a desperate act, cheap and unfair, but it was the only tool left in her arsenal.

Danlyn slowly crept into the living room, looking to her right, where Paul was standing. Her eyes widened when she saw the blood on his arm, but he quickly covered the bite mark with his other hand. She stopped in front of Laura and looked down at her shoes.

"Paul has something to tell you." Laura could hear the hesitation in her own voice, but her anger and drunkenness overrode any logic that lay in the background of her mind, trying to squeeze its way through. "Don't you, Paul?"

"Don't bring her into this, Laura. Spare her that much."

But Laura was working on autopilot, fueled by heartache—the worst kind of accelerant. She knelt down in front of Danlyn, held her hands. "I'm pregnant, Danlyn. You're going to have a little brother or sister. Would you like that?"

Danlyn kept her eyes on the floor, didn't say a word. She gave a slow, hesitant nod.

Laura had to look away. Something in the way Danlyn obliged her made the break in her heart sting. "That's nice," she said, swallowing the lump in her throat. "But maybe you need to explain that to Paul. See, he wants me to—"

"Enough, Laura," Paul shouted. But the words spilled over Laura's lips, too fast to catch before they could do damage.

"—have an abortion."

Paul balled his fist, punched through the wall beside him. Danlyn jumped back, yelping. Laura watched in shock as he ran into the bedroom, grabbing what he could of their belongings, and threw them out the front door. This was it. No going back. Laura picked up the envelope and yelled at Danlyn to get their last few things.

As the two of them gathered their belongings, Laura watched Paul walk back into the kitchen and pour himself another drink from the bottom of the bottle. One she knew he thought was well-deserved. She couldn't help but feel jealous. He was going to that place she fought to leave, amid a dreamy world where bright colors washed into dull, soft tones and pain existed on a realm so far removed that it might as well not exist at all. She looked away when he grabbed a new bottle from the cabinet.

When Danlyn's arms were full of clothing, Laura grabbed the last duffel bag and draped it across her shoulder, the money clutched tightly in her hand. Paul came into the living room just as they were about to walk out.

"I'm sorry, Danlyn," he said with a heavy sigh. "I really am."

Pain and animosity rearranged Laura's features. "Let's go," she yelled at Danlyn, who hadn't so much as looked at Paul.

They picked their littered possessions off the lawn and carried them to the trunk of their rusted, yellow wagon, cramming clothes wherever they could find space. Laura opened the door, dropped herself in. Her hands felt clumsy as she worked to find the ignition.

"Come on, you stupid piece of shit. Start."

Laura could feel Danlyn beside her in the passenger's seat, watching her take out her rage as she beat her fist into the center of the steering wheel. With every punch, the horn screamed, and with every honk, Danlyn jumped and tears streamed down her flushed cheeks.

Laura's screams turned into sobs. She leaned forward, resting her forehead on the steering wheel, pleading with a God she hadn't spoken to in years. "God, help me."

Danlyn's soft voice filtered in, "Please, God."

Laura lifted her head, reeled around in her seat. "Did I ask for your help? If it weren't for you, I wouldn't be in this damn mess. Get out. Now!"

~

Danlyn quickly plopped her feet in the wet gutter, slamming the heavy door closed behind her. She walked a few yards away and sat along the curb. The streetlight above reflected off the pools of rainwater in the grooves in the asphalt, and that's where Danlyn tried to focus, so that her bravery wouldn't leave her alone on the side of the road, just like her mother. But the pool of tears collecting at the bottom of her eyes made it too blurry to see much of anything. All Danlyn could hear and see and feel were Laura's screams from inside the car, and she wondered why every day had to hurt so much.

Danlyn blinked hard. The contrast of her warm tears gliding down her icy cheeks felt strange. She pulled her oversized sweater over her knees, poking her fingers through the neck, wiping her tears away. Small, quaint houses lined the other side of the road, filled with families. Mothers and fathers, sisters and brothers. Something Danlyn had never known. Looking at each home, she searched, trying to spot one family whose shades were open and whose lights were on. If she could catch a glimpse of normalcy, she could focus on that small view into a world she wasn't a member of, and maybe that would be enough to get her through this moment. But it was a cold autumn night in a small town in Massachusetts, and no one appeared to be home. If they were, they were tucked away behind the warmth and privacy of their walls. The darkness and isolation only deepened the loneliness Danlyn felt, leaving the next five minutes feeling like five hours.

~

Laura began to shiver, her jaw chattered. How could her car give up on her now, like it had planned it? Rusted out pile of crap. She wanted to drive her fists into the dashboard, even if it left her knuckles bloody and pulped. But exhaustion was making its inevitable appearance. The four drinks she had prior to the fight with Paul had almost worn off entirely, leaving in their place fatigue and the unrelenting nag of clarity. The sober hours that followed a binge were the most brutal. That's when Laura understood the full impact her actions had on Danlyn, and she had always hoped the unforgiving sear of reality would lead her to higher ground, to resolutions and productive life changes. But these painful moments only enveloped her in a shroud of guilt so impenetrable that it almost smothered the life from her. Liquor had proved a selfish but effective tool with which to cope. But now the events of the evening were coming through too loud and bright. Soon the guilt would eat her alive.

Laura leaned her head back against the seat and closed her eyes, smacking away her tears. "I'll count to ten," she whispered. "Then, you piece of shit, start."

As she counted back and steadied her breathing, the cold air sank in, creeping up her sleeves, wrapping around her neck. Her eyes shot open, her heart hammered in her chest. She looked behind her, out the back window, at Danlyn. Sweat beaded on her forehead. She gripped the seat like an anchor that might keep her mind from spiraling. She watched her little girl sitting alone in the cold and thought her heart might tear in half at the sight of her. Regret drenched her heart, her mind. She could almost taste it, and she wanted nothing more than to take back all the wrongs she had committed. Laura had once been that innocent child, sitting alone in the dark. Had she known back then that she was destined to play the role of the monster, she would have ended her pitiful existence years ago.

She rolled down the window. The icy air filled her lungs. "Get in the car."

Danlyn hesitated for a moment, then pulled herself up and walked to the car, slowly opening the door. But she didn't get in.

"I'm sorry," Laura said.

Danlyn sat down, cramming herself against the door. It was all Laura's fault. She'd forced her daughter into a rabbit hole, afraid to poke her head out. She could still remember doing the same when her own mother had put the fear of God in her.

Laura closed her eyes and turned the key. When the engine started, she finally breathed.

Chapter 2

Laura opened the door to the motel room and slowly walked in out of the rain. The smell of cheap pine-scented air freshener hit her nose. The walls were a stained shade of beige, lined with darker tones of tobacco-brown along the floorboards. Danlyn filed in after and looked around, crinkling her nose. A strange, unforgiving place to end a strange, unforgiving day of driving.

Laura sighed, "What else is new."

"Not as bad as the one we were in last night," Danlyn mumbled.

Laura would have to take her word for it. After the meltdown at Paul's, she had been too distraught to notice the first motel.

"And there's not another ugly tiger painting over the bed," Danlyn added.

Thunder struck not far off and a splash of light bounced off the walls.

"Curtains," Laura snapped, dropping the bags on the floor. "Close 'em." Her overtaxed nervous system couldn't handle the light show, not without setting off another migraine. Her body buzzed and her mind hummed with the unrelenting cruelty of withdrawal. Every sound and smell and sight hammered at her skull, and her drained body fought against her, clawing her down with gravity. She shivered under her damp, sweaty clothes, her eyelids hung heavily over her bloodshot eyes. She was so spent that maybe sleep would come easily, though history told her otherwise. She needed to escape the deserted little town out the window, kept in business by people who, like her and Danlyn, needed a cheap place to rest their heads, or to hide something, or maybe even someone. Judging by the rust-colored stains on the carpet, maybe someone had.

Laura turned around, looked at the full-size bed in the corner. "My back can't handle another night on the floor, so don't hog the bed." She slowly lowered herself onto the edge of the mattress and sat very still, staring at the door in what appeared to be a trance.

~

Danlyn dropped the other bag on the table while watching her mother, still unsure what to say or how to approach her. The usually unpredictable Laura was all the more unpredictable. Laura spent the whole day driving, and when she wasn't doing that, she was pulled over, puking on the highway. This was a bad one, Danlyn knew. She had seen this before, had watched her mother writhe in pain, being tossed about on a sea of hysterical emotions whenever she stopped drinking. And Laura had promised too many times that she'd sober up for Danlyn to believe her. She hadn't promised anything this time, though.

She had barely said a word all day. But Danlyn could see something in her mother, something raw and terrified and determined, right under the surface. She looked fierce and crippled all at once.

Laura's eyelids fluttered, her arms shook. Danlyn walked to the other side of the room and sat down in an old green chair. A small cloud of dust plumed up around her. She crinkled her nose against the sour stench.

"Mom?"

Laura's head clumsily swiveled around, head tipping to the side. "What?"

Danlyn had gone all day without asking. She'd been a good girl; she'd done what was asked of her.

"Where're we going?"

Laura lay down, eyes closed. "Not now, Danlyn."

Danlyn unleashed a heavy breath. When was she going to be part of the equation? When were her feelings going to matter? Where would they wind up living once Laura found another guy who was willing to put a roof over their heads in exchange for a few loud nights that would keep Danlyn awake with a pillow over her head? Or would things magically be different? As far as Danlyn could tell, anything was possible. Laura had always bounced between a drunken, animalistic monster and a rueful mother, but she never wore either hat well. Now, her current state fell somewhere in the middle, or maybe way outside both extremes, and Danlyn didn't have a roadmap to guide her though this new territory. All she knew was that the fear she had seen all day in her mother's eyes seemed to fit like an old, worn-in pair of shoes.

When Laura's breathing slowed to an almost peaceful rhythm, Danlyn leaned forward, watching the gentle rise and fall of her chest. After a few minutes, she got up, stood next to the bed, her forehead wrinkled. She knelt down, placed her hands on the edge of the mattress, and rested her chin on them. Their faces were so close, Danlyn could feel the warm, humid air from her mother's breaths. But she didn't smell anything. No beer, no liquor. Nothing but the leftover scent of the banana from the gas station.

She couldn't remember ever being so close to her mother. Of course, she must have been, when she was a baby, when she needed to be, but she had no memory of such things. She bent down lower, inspecting every unfamiliar line and wrinkle. The way Laura's eyes angled upward at the far corners, how her upper lip formed a perfect heart. Laura's usual grimace was gone, smoothed away. She looked so close to lovely that Danlyn could almost imagine she was happy, like all the moms on TV. The ones she always wished for. Long, dark, chestnut hair, perfect cheekbones, piercing green eyes. Truth was, Laura really used to be lovely, and probably could be again. At one time, she could have played the part of the trophy wife and bouncing mother. But she didn't look twenty-nine. Time had been unforgiving, and Laura's reckless lifestyle had eaten away so much of her beauty. Her eyes were masked by the sunken circles encasing them, and her ashen skin gave away her addiction.

Danlyn's eyes fell to the floor, her shoulders slumped forward. The problem was, Laura wasn't like those moms, because those moms weren't going to wake up, drenched in sweat and shaking from head to toe because they needed that special something to take the razor edge off with. If only Danlyn could wake her and ask all the questions that had gnawed at her for as long as she could remember. But that wasn't possible. One day without drinking didn't mean Danlyn could venture into uncharted territory.

Danlyn dropped to her bottom, along the side of the bed, brushing her long blonde hair behind her ears. Her hazel eyes filled with tears as she looked up at her mother's face, feeling a strange mixture of hope and sadness. She heard her own voice break, a soft whisper. "What happened to you?"

Sobs built in her chest, working into her throat. She swallowed hard, keeping them at bay, whispering so quietly that her words sounded like soft breaths. "Maybe things will be better and you can have the baby. I hope you have the baby."

Danlyn felt everything right along with Laura. She carried her mother's pain and sorrow and burdens as her own, and they were growing too heavy. Danlyn's throat tightened at the thought of her next question, but she needed to ask it, even if her words got lost amid Laura's dreams. She got up, bracing herself on the bed. "I don't think you like me very much. But you do love me, don't you?" There was no movement; no fluttering of Laura's eyelids to register that she had heard anything. Danlyn almost felt disappointed. On some level, she wanted her mother to hear her, to know that all the years of pain added up to one conclusion: Laura didn't like her much at all.

Danlyn leaned forward and placed the smallest kiss on Laura's cheek, then got up, wiping away the last of her tears while looking around the room. She looked behind her at the green chair, then back at her mother. "What scares me the most is being like you," she whispered, her normally angelic features hard, far too worn for any eleven-year-old girl. She plopped her lanky frame down on the green chair, sending another plume of dust billowing through the air. She closed her eyes and whispered, "I love you, Mom."

Chapter 3

Things could have been worse. At least, that's what Laura told herself. She could have got no sleep at all, or she could have run to the bathroom all night to dry heave into a filthy motel toilet. That's not to say the opportunity hadn't presented itself, because it had, about every hour. But her head pounded so fiercely and her heart raced so wildly that she couldn't get up, because maybe her heart would burst, right here in room fourteen of the Lazy Days Motel, and what a way to go that would be.

Sometime in the middle of the night the rain had finally stopped, and now the morning sun glared through the torn curtains. Laura could barely open her eyes or make sense of anything around her. Her head was still pounding and her skin itched all over. She ran her hand across the bedspread, and the rough, vinyl-like fabric sent a message through her flesh and back to her brain to scream. There was no one beside her. No thin, warm body. Her eyes shot open, she bolted upright. Panic rushed into her lungs instead of air. "Danlyn? Danlyn?"

She was on the chair, asleep. Laura finally exhaled, only the tension didn't leave her body. Danlyn's frame was silhouetted by the bright light coming through the window behind her. Laura squinted, fighting to keep her eyelids from closing. "Holy shit."

She grabbed the side of her head. She had to get up, had to get in the car and make the final trek back to a place she wanted to run from—not run to. She hung one leg over the bed, then the other, and slowly felt the swimming in her head stop. That was good, but the headache had to go. As she stood up, gaining her bearings and making sure she didn't topple over, every muscle in her body felt as if it were on fire. How the little person growing inside her could survive this, she didn't know. She was barely breathing. At least it felt that way.

A warm batch of tears filled her eyes. "Not now," she said out loud. "Don't go there. Don't even think it." The baby had to be okay. She could handle whatever aches and pains withdrawal threw her way, but the baby had to be okay because if she lost it now... God, if she lost it now. For reasons she couldn't emotionally afford to debate, she wanted this baby more than anything. Danlyn and the baby were what got her through yesterday, and she was counting on them to get her through today and tonight. Shit, tonight.

Danlyn's legs were tucked up under her sweater, her arms wrapped around them. Laura pressed the button on the wall heater beside the chair. Nothing. She smacked it with the palm of her hand, "Piece of crap." But it didn't even try to gurgle to life. She walked back to the bed, holding her aching stomach, and peeled off the bedspread.

~

The warm shower got Laura's blood pumping and her limbs moving. As she toweled off, making sure not to step on what appeared to be dried semen on the floor—which made her all the more thankful she hadn't hung her head over the toilet to puke—she heard Danlyn moving around in the room.

"You up?"

Danlyn slowly opened the bathroom door and abruptly looked away. "Yeah." She rubbed her eyes. "Thanks for the blanket."

"Sure." Laura slowly twisted her hair in the towel. "Take a quick shower. We've gotta move. And don't…" Laura looked down at the floor, but her head fought back, like a punch to her skull.

"You okay?" Danlyn asked.

"I'm…fine. It's just a headache." She saw both hope and fear in Danlyn's eyes. "And no, I didn't drink. I feel like I'm going to die, but I didn't drink."

"I'm sorry," Danlyn backed away. "But I'm happy. I mean…because you didn't—"

"I get it," Laura sliced the air with her severe tone, frustrated and tired and pissed off at the whole world. "Just get in the shower. And don't step on whatever that is." She pointed at the spot on the floor.

Danlyn moved past her, staying against the wall. Laura followed her eyes as she finished toweling off, noticing how Danlyn tried to hide the quick glance at her stomach. She wasn't showing yet. Not even close. But Laura knew Danlyn was waiting for signs that the baby was still alive, hoping against the same devastating outcome they'd both come to expect.

~

The day was chilly, but the sun felt soft and warm and filled the sky with a buttery glow. As was their habit, Danlyn and Laura both stared at the ignition as Laura slid the key into place. When the car started without hesitation, Danlyn hoped it was a break in their bad luck. With one crisis averted, Danlyn watched her mother, waiting for her to send the car in any direction at all, but she only sat motionless.

"You okay, Mom?"

"Glasses. Glove compartment."

Danlyn reached in, handed them to her. "You don't look good."

"That's because..." Laura slowly worked the glasses over her ears, easing them onto her face. "I'm not okay. I need you to just be quiet."

Danlyn's eyes reddened. "All right."

"Listen, Danlyn. I don't want to hurt you. I'm not trying to. I just..." Laura looked down at her shaky hands. She gripped the wheel, took several increasingly shallow breaths.

"Mom, what's wrong?"

Laura slowly turned to face her. "This happened last time. My heart...it feels like it's going a mile a minute."

"You're okay," Danlyn told her, really feeling just as hopeless as her mother looked. But if Laura was going to be brave, Danlyn could, too. "You're okay," she said again. "It's bad right now, but you'll get better. That's what you said last time, remember?"

"That's not it."

Danlyn frowned. "What is it, then?"

"Anxiety. Looks and feels scarier than it is. I'll be all right. But I've got to tell you something, Danlyn." Laura hesitated. "And please don't ask questions, because I can't get into it right now. I'm telling you this because you need to know where we're "going, and I need you to be prepared to leave as soon as I get my shit together." Laura rubbed her forehead. "I think I need to say it out loud, because it still doesn't seem real."

Danlyn leaned in.

"We're going to…we're going to Rome, Georgia. Where I grew up. To my mother's house."

"What?" Danlyn hadn't meant to shout. "Your mother's? My…"

"Yes." Laura looked like she might be sick. "You knew you had a grandmother."

"Well, yeah. But you only mentioned her…" Danlyn looked into her mother's eyes, and there it was. She would never forget the look on Laura's face when Paul had asked about her mother. She had looked so horrified. She couldn't even talk about it. She had poured herself a drink and spent the rest of the night in the bath.

"You only mentioned her once, and you looked…like you do now," Danlyn said. The momentary hope she had felt now vanished. "Why do you look that way?"

Laura shook her head. "Today's not the kind of day to dig around in that closet, Danlyn. Having the kind of discussion you deserve requires a lot of…" Laura paused. "I just can't. Not right now. I'm already scraping the bottom of the barrel, kid."

"Then why are we even going there?"

Laura faced forward, pushed her foot down on the gas pedal. "Because I'm out of options."

Danlyn quietly sat back, watching Laura brace the wheel so tight that her knuckles turned white. Then they pulled onto the highway, away from the only life Danlyn had ever known, and back to the place where both their horrors had come to life.

Chapter 4

The porch was a faded shade of yellow, much like the rest of the house, which had somehow maintained its beauty throughout the years of use. The large wraparound porch made a grand entry into a large, modest farmhouse, and it was still Vivian's chosen spot.

Placed upon nineteen acres of land sat Hallows' Farm. It wasn't much of a farm anymore. Corn hadn't sprung from the ground, reaching for the skies in decades, and cotton no longer dotted the western edge of the property. But it was still known by the people of Rome as Hallows' Farm. It didn't take much to get noticed in a small town, and the Hallows had given ample reason to get noticed. Their sad story was told to newcomers, and from older siblings to younger siblings. The Hallows' past had even spurred schoolyard ghost stories. There were no real ghosts in the Hallows' past, but not all scary stories need ghosts. Sometimes living, breathing monsters are far more terrifying than ghouls and goblins.

Despite the gossip, Vivian Hallow walked tall and with an air of confidence. Gossip meant nothing in her world. Chattering behind backs was meant for swine, and anything worth repeating in hushed tones wasn't worth repeating at all. The town knew about the Hallows' past; they pointed and stared, they crept behind corners in the market and aimed fingers, like loaded weapons. But Vivian never apologized. Whether the residents of the town respected or feared her made no difference, so long as they kept their usual distance. Vivian came up with a remedy for the few incessant pigs that wouldn't keep away. She stopped leaving home altogether. The solitude fit her well, because people were messy and useless, and quiet was underrated.

This morning was like every other. Being a creature of habit, Vivian woke at five a.m., showered—despite having taken a bath the night before, as she always did—and then read her Bible for precisely one hour while sitting in the same chair in front of the same window in her bedroom, the one that looked out over the barren fields that used to be so rich. Then, making her way downstairs and into the kitchen, she walked to the stove and placed her teakettle over the fire. Next was the fireplace in the family room. Vivian adored the feel of it. Even in the hot months of summer, smoke rose from the chimney. She flicked the match and threw it into the pile, watching the flames bloom while reaching her hands out to warm them.

The day was chilly, the leaves were dazzling with fall colors, the sky displayed deep gray October clouds. Vivian peered out the window that looked onto the front porch. She knew by the look of the trees and sky what the temperature was, just like she knew the inner and outer workings of the home she grew up in. She walked back into the kitchen just as the teakettle screamed to life, breaking the tranquil silence.

With her knit sweater in hand, she took her tea to the front porch. No matter the weather, she sat on the porch swing, sipping her tea and watching the trees sway in accordance with the wind. This was her time, and it wasn't meant for reflection into the past or planning for the future. She didn't care for either of those things, but she also didn't avoid them for the same reasons most people did. There was no fear of an emotional breakdown or the emergence of regret. Vivian avoided such things because wasting a moment on them was pointless. She saw things in black and white. Steps A, B, and C had brought her and her family to this point, and there was no going back. Maybe if she was like everyone else and could cultivate the emotions required to feel guilt or shame, she would. But in all her years of living, such frivolous things had evaded her. Besides, why should the strong bring themselves down to the same level as the weak? No, there was no playing into people's games, into their emotions. Not when there was here and now: the cold, brisk air and a hot cup of tea.

A bitter gust of wind swept by, carrying with it an earthy scent. Vivian gripped the mug tight, filling her lungs with the sweet smell of fall. A wave of detachment spread over her. She used to try to fight against it, pushing her way through the void, where emotion might be waiting on the other side. But with age, she had learned that such things didn't exist for her. She had been this way for as long as she could remember, and she wondered if it was possible to have been born without the ability to feel, especially for people—always there, prodding and pestering and needing, needing, needing. Damn heathens. Damn fools.

But there was Frank. There was only Frank.

Vivian stood, walked down the front steps. Under the comforting blanket of the heavy sky, she turned, facing her home. The day was so quiet and soft that she could feel the wind envelop her. She looked to her left, to the giant elm tree that had been the home's ever-steady companion, then to the wrap-around porch, cradling the house. On the second story were two windows, one that looked into her bedroom, and one that looked into a life she had never wanted. A life she was content believing never existed. But together she liked those windows. Watchful eyes, looking out over the land, protecting the home and its contents. Vivian adored her home, maybe more than anything. The construction of ordinary lumber and hardware had become her safe haven, where she had come into this world and where she'd probably leave it, and where, once tucked inside, she could pretend nothing else existed.

She turned around, facing the long dirt driveway that met the lone road that led to town. Her heart quickened. She began the same internal dialogue she always ran through before having to leave her home. Life was cruel, and even it couldn't respect her, couldn't allow her to be left in peace. She walked back up the steps and stopped in front of the door, tensing against the horrible sensation. Tiny insects, all over her skin, crawling and burrowing—that's what it felt like to leave home and expose herself to the world.

Her face hardened, her eyes narrowed. With her shoulders set firmly back, she took one deliberate step into the house and walked back into the kitchen, setting her mug in the sink. She closed her eyes while bracing herself on the edge of the counter, then slowly raised both her hands and delicately ran them along her salt-and-pepper hair, tucking in the strands that had managed to escape her rigid bun.

The sound of gravel crunching under Frank's tires carried to the kitchen. When Vivian heard the truck come to a stop, she walked back to the front door but didn't open it. She wasn't ready for this—not this appointment, not this day, not this trip into town. If she had any sense, she'd cancel. But Frank was there. He was the only reason she'd agreed to this in the first place. She could do it for him, because she thought that what she felt for him was the closest thing to love she'd ever known. But mostly she needed him, in the way a child needs a parent. Either way, it didn't really matter. Life without him was unimaginable.

Vivian pulled her purse off the hook, placed her hand on the doorknob, and waited. When the crawling sensation eased, she opened the door just as Frank was about to walk in.

"You ready, sugar?" he asked.

"I suppose."

"Well, let's get it over with, then."

~

Vivian watched the side mirror, and with every bit of distance that grew between her and her sanctuary, her home looked smaller and smaller until it disappeared from sight and her detachment grew, coating her in an almost impenetrable sheath of protection. She had found the void that she hoped would allow her to receive whatever news might come her way today.

Frank looked at her sideways. "You gonna be all right?"

Vivian folded her hands together, placed them in her lap. "Of course," her voice monotone.

He gave a quick nod and turned onto the road that would lead to Vivian's doctor.

Chapter 5

Rome was a small town that sat at the base of the Appalachian Mountains in Georgia. It teemed with captivating beauty. The sprawling hills and lush greenery extended beyond what the eye could contain. It was enough to please anyone's senses, but as Laura drove into the tiny town, nothing but fear registered. A two-lane country road led her closer to the places and people of her past, and when she approached Clock Tower Hill, it leapt at her like a blazing omen, screaming for her to turn around. She pulled the car onto the shoulder of the road.

Shivering, she wrapped her arms around herself. *What the hell am I doing here? What's wrong with me?* She'd lost her mind. What else could explain such an incomprehensible decision?

A wave of screams sat behind her pinched lips, and it took all of her willpower not to weep. Rome was right there, in front of her, waiting to receive her like a human sacrifice. She looked up at the rearview mirror; it was the only view she could tolerate, and though it was nearly dark now, it shed light on her heavy heart. She could turn the car around and take Danlyn as far away from Georgia as she could get. She could run, as she had ten years ago, and never look back. But where would they go, and when would the drinking stop?

Danlyn lay asleep in the passenger's seat, conked out long before they reached Rome. Laura looked at her daughter and felt everything too strongly. She remembered in painstaking detail the last year she and Danlyn had lived in Rome. She remembered the hell and terror and death. It was her love for Danlyn and her need to protect her that had pushed her to flee all those years back. Now, it was that same love that brought Laura back, because maybe this time Laura was the very person Danlyn needed protection from.

Laura reached over, nearly touching Danlyn's hand, but her own hand only hovered there, shaking and clammy. Her stomach recoiled. Rolling down the window, she let the cold air run down her neck. But even the air smelled eerily familiar. Nothing was right. The whole damn picture was upside down and scrambled, and hidden within it were ominous shadows. Laura tried to remind herself that most of the demons lived in her past—not Danlyn's. She could do this one small favor for her little girl—if she could just muster up the courage to put the car in drive.

Laura leaned forward, braced the wheel. She shook her head, trying to rattle her screaming conscience, and pulled back into the lane, avoiding the street where her father had last lived. And where he died.

~

The whole world had decided to pile on Vivian today, like some mean bully. As she sat at her small breakfast table, holding a glass of water in her hands and listening to the wind blow around the house, she fought the urge to break the glass, so that it would match her. Shattered. Useless. Damn the universe to hell for taking away the only thing she cared about: her independence, her dignity. She stood up, braced herself for another wave of vertigo. As it came, she looked around the kitchen, around the home that seemed to have troubling memories in every corner. *And now this?*

Vivian widened her stance while waiting for her brain to stop rotating in her skull. She couldn't risk another fall, or fainting only to wake on the kitchen floor. It wouldn't be the first time, and what scared her more than dying was having the kind of accident that would land her in the hospital, full of the sick and wasting excrement that passed for patients. With any luck, her illness would just kill her, but the incessant dizziness and headaches and forgetfulness cropped up every day, reminding her that her road might not be so quick. The damn doctor, giving her so many numbers and so many odds and so many orders. *Don't do this, Vivian; Don't do that, Vivian.* And Frank, having to open his mouth, blabbing about her leaving the burners on that *one* time. So what if it had been all night? It was her house, and if she wanted to burn it to the ground, so be it. But in truth, that was why she went to see the doctor, because she didn't want to burn her house down and she didn't want to rely on others and she didn't want Frank angry with her. She was as prideful as they came. For a woman like her, such a diagnosis was more than scary—it was inhumane. Her apathetic nature was being tested today, and that alone was enough reason to feel a new emotion: anger.

Slowly making her way to the living room, Vivian gently lowered herself onto the sofa. "I'm only fifty-two." Her voice was bitter. She stared into the fire Frank had started before leaving, and looked at her hands, fisting them into hard knots.

"Only fifty-two." She yanked the crocheted afghan off the back of the sofa and flung it over herself. Even the brilliant flames couldn't wash away her thoughts or squelch the cold seeping into her body. She rolled the yarn, and one of her fingers slipped through a space between the stitches, and then another, and another, until all of them poked through, wiggling, squirming. Peering closer, she inspected her fingers by the amber firelight and closed her eyes, bracing for the sting of recollection. Her defenses were down, and God help her, she wasn't guarding herself.

Her nine-year-old daughter's laughter and her husband's low, husky voice echoed in her skull. They were laughing endlessly.

"Zombie fingers! Zombie fingers! Coming up from the grave!" William bellowed. "Zombie fingers, looking to feed on the toes of little children!" William pushed his jagged, bent fingers through the afghan and sent them lurching for his daughter's feet.

Through her vivacious laughter, she happily pleaded, "No, Daddy! No!" as William pretended to devour each one of her toes with his gnarled fingers.

Vivian's eyes shot open. She tore the blanket off her body, throwing it toward the fire, narrowly missing it. "I won't have this. It can kill me, but I won't have this."

Where were her walls? Where was her uncanny ability to feel nothing, to think of nothing, to remember nothing? It felt like an old friend had abandoned her, leaving in its place a filthy mess.

She stood up, staggered to the fireplace. She breathed deeply, one hand on her forehead. She wouldn't be sick. She wouldn't allow it. She squeezed her eyes shut, allowing the last remnants of the memory to fall away. Maybe this was nothing a warm bath and some good sleep couldn't remedy, and so she grabbed the checklist Frank had made her and started about the house, checking off each item. The stove was off, the lights were off; she would let the fire die out. Then she walked to the front door and checked that it was bolted. She turned back around, walking toward the staircase when it occurred to her that maybe she'd be okay. Yes. If she kept enough lists around, and with Frank's visits, she'd be okay.

Vivian was halfway up the staircase when she heard a car coming down her driveway. Cocking her head to the side, she listened. It wasn't Frank's truck. The throaty rumble wasn't there. This was someone else, and certainly no one Vivian had invited. She hurried back into the living room, pulling back the sheer white curtain just in time to see a vehicle creeping toward the house. Its lights were off, and the moon provided too little light for her to see anything. As the car came closer, Vivian's heart galloped. She could turn around and call Frank, and the rifle was... Where was the rifle? She couldn't remember. But she didn't run to the phone or search for a weapon. She remained at the window. When the car came to a final stop, Vivian nudged her face against the glass, holding her breath.

The unlatching of the car's heavy door was loud, and with a squeak of its hinges, it swung open and the silhouette of a woman appeared. Vivian pulled the curtain back further, and when the woman walked closer, turning toward the porch, a sliver of dull moonlight splashed across her face.

"Dear God," Vivian gasped, clasping a hand over her chest. She was going to faint or have a heart attack. And her legs...she tried to move them, but they felt numb. Maybe this was a bad dream. Maybe the whole day had just been a nightmare. But it couldn't be. This moment burned too clearly to be a dream, and the sudden pounding behind her eyes was too violent to be anything other than real.

When Vivian's legs finally obeyed her, she slowly crept to the door. Quietly, she placed her hand upon the knob. In that single moment, with her adrenaline at a peak and the world spinning around her, something snapped back into place: her void. Just like that, her apathetic friend came home, and everything that had just been forced to the surface had eerily descended back into the dark place where all of Vivian's memories, emotions, and dark secrets lived. A small smile spread across her lips as the sweet sensation bled into every cell in her body. She could handle it now. She was ready. She waited for a knock.

~

As both women stood on opposite sides of the door, they hung suspended, one still drenched in fear, the other waiting calmly—present but not really there.

~

The knock was timid, mirroring Laura's fragile state. She dropped her hand, waited in the cold, doing all she could to not turn around. Laura couldn't remember being this scared since she was a child and lived in this very house. When the knob began to turn, she gulped loudly, certain no words would come out. Then the creak of the old door broke the night's silence.

After what felt like an unnecessarily long unveiling on her mother's part, Vivian stood before her wearing a stony expression, not a trace of enthusiasm or curiosity to be found.

Laura looked into her mother's eyes, but she couldn't speak. Her lips moved—only a fumbled attempt.

"So you're not dead," Vivian finally said, looking Laura up and down. "I assumed you were dead."

With nine short words that cut like a knife, Laura had been reduced to tears.

"Where is she?" Vivian asked.

"In the car. Asleep. It's been a long day."

"Why're you here?"

"Because we've got nowhere else. I wouldn't be here if we did. I'm sorry."

Vivian lowered her voice. "What does she know?"

"Nothing at all."

Vivian stepped forward, placing her face just inches from her daughter's. "You'd better tell me now if that child knows anything, Laura. Or by God, I swear I'll—"

"I would never."

"Fine. It better stay that way." She slowly backed away, opening the door wider. "Stay if you must, but keep out of your grandmother's room. And don't bother me. I'll be in my bath."

Chapter 6

The next morning the mood in the kitchen was constrictive. The three of them sat at the small dinette table, Vivian staring blankly at Laura, Laura keeping her eyes trained on her cup of coffee, Danlyn's eyes bouncing between them. The night before, Laura had quickly ushered Danlyn into a pink room with pink blankets and pink walls. Laura's old room. Danlyn hadn't met her mystery grandmother until earlier this morning, and Laura guessed that Vivian made as little sense to Danlyn as a pink room did for her.

Laura dared a glance around the kitchen. Everything felt surreal. The eager morning sun gleamed through the large window, bringing images from her childhood vividly into focus. Everything was the same. The same sage-green cupboards, the antique stove, the ancient teakettle Vivian had acquired from her mother, Rose. Sheer white curtains still hung on every window, and the walls were the same shade of beige, only aged. The kitchen counters were still bare butcher block, holding only the few essential items her mother had used decades ago. The room was the same empty shell it had always been, absent of personal expression. The quaint style of the construction was its only redeeming quality. Even the same stagnant stench of history wafted through the air—a profoundly unsettling odor. The only difference was Danlyn. Danlyn was here, in her grandmother's kitchen. The more Laura thought about it, the more she wanted to crawl out of her own skin just to get away from this place.

Laura kept her focus on the room, on Danlyn, on her coffee—anywhere but on her mother. The silence was swelling beneath them. Laura knew it was coming.

"Stop tapping your fingers on the mug like that, Laura. It's obnoxious," Vivian finally said.

Laura moved the coffee away, out of reach. "Sorry." That wasn't what her mother really wanted to say, but it was a start.

"You shouldn't be drinking that vile junk."

"It's just coffee, Mom."

"It's horrid. And it smells." Vivian cringed. "I'd rather drink vinegar."

Laura thought of her father, but she couldn't feel him here anywhere. The smell of coffee used to remind her of him because he loved it, drank it in abundance, but it didn't have the same effect anymore. "I wouldn't have made it if I had remembered. Sorry." Two apologies down, one thousand more to go.

"Why do you buy it, then?" Laura didn't really care why. She just needed something to say.

"Frank," Vivian said.

"Frank?"

"Yes. Frank. He drinks it. I tell him not to, but he insists."

Laura's eyes rounded. "Um, all right. Tell *Frank* I said thanks for the coffee."

Vivian laid her own mug gingerly on the table. "You can thank him yourself. He'll be here shortly."

"Oh. Well, we didn't mean to intrude on you and—"

"Enough, Laura," Vivian warned, a sudden edge in her voice. "Besides, surely you remember Frank?"

Laura gave her a blank stare.

"Frank Roland? He's an old family friend."

Laura remembered nothing about any family friend. The Hallows didn't have family friends. "No, can't say that I do."

"Well, that's neither here nor there. He's an old friend. And no, *Laura*, you didn't intrude. Your suggestion wasn't lost on me."

Laura and Danlyn exchanged a nervous glance. "Okay," Laura said, biting her lip, pulling her mug back in front of her. "Good. We didn't intrude." She needed to stop while she was ahead, but her frayed nerves had other plans. How could anyone deal with Vivian without drinking? Before she could stop herself, she said, "So, Mom, how long has Frank been keeping his *coffee* here?"

"Go upstairs," Vivian ordered, suddenly leering at Danlyn. "I need to speak to your mother in private."

"Go ahead," Laura said when Danlyn didn't move.

Danlyn reluctantly pushed out her chair and left the kitchen, tiptoeing up the staircase.

Laura slowly raised her eyes, looked at Vivian. She nearly looked away when she saw how the anger rearranged her face. Laura had never seen such emotion from her before.

"You tell that child that if she's to stay in my home, she'll mind me as she does you. Do I make myself clear?"

Laura nodded once. "Crystal."

This familiar picture sent a pang of dread through Laura. She was alone again. Alone with her mother and her ability to rattle a person to their very core with her relentless stare. She felt exposed, vulnerable. She could almost feel her mother's eyes boring into her. It was unnatural, Vivian's focus. Such penetrating concentration, like her soul had checked out but failed to send the message to her eyes. Laura couldn't take the silence anymore. Just as she pushed her chair back, Vivian spoke.

"How far along are you?"

Laura slumped back in her seat, plopped her hands on the table.

"I heard you in the bathroom this morning. Danlyn heard you, too. Does she know?"

"About two months along. And yes, she knows."

"Does the father know, or is that why you're here? He knows but doesn't want it?"

Laura spoke through clenched teeth. "Yes."

"Yes, what?"

"Yes, he knows, and no, he doesn't want it."

There was cold and mean, and then there was Vivian, with her vapid smile and oversized ego.

"You do know who the father is, don't you, Laura?"

"Of course I know who the father is."

"Who is he?"

"Does it matter? He's gone. It's over."

Vivian cleared her throat, straightened her back. "So, you're pregnant, the father doesn't want it, you've got nowhere to go, probably no money—"

"I've got some. I was working."

"—and no job. You show up here with Danlyn, after ten years, wanting what? Money? Sympathy? Just a place to stay? Tell me, Laura, did I miss anything?"

Laura told herself that right now was about getting through one second, and then one minute, and then one hour without a drink. It wasn't about crying over Vivian's cruelty.

"No," Laura said, resenting her need to always be honest. An admirable quality alcohol had masked. "You didn't miss anything. I've made a mess of things."

Vivian perked up when she heard Frank's truck coming down the driveway. "Straighten your face," she demanded. "I'll not have you making a scene in front of company."

The last thing Laura wanted was to meet her mother's boyfriend. Not that Vivian would ever admit to such a thing, with her religious hypocrisy. Laura took a deep breath, tried to look natural. She heard the sound of a car door shutting and looked at her mother. "So do you want us to leave?"

Vivian opened her mouth to speak but stopped when she saw Laura's hands, the way they shook, the way her whole body trembled. She squinted, tipped her head to the side.

Laura didn't pull her hands away or hide them. She didn't cower or look away. This was what she'd come for. This was what would make tolerating Vivian worth it.

Vivian stood up, walked around the back of her chair, bracing against the slatted back.

"You all right?" Laura asked. Vivian suddenly looked ill.

Vivian's lips curled back, she threw the chair into place. "Why did he leave you? The father. Why doesn't he want the baby?"

Laura closed her eyes, dropped her hands in her lap. "I think you know why."

Vivian nervously looked over her shoulder, dropped her voice. "You two need to stay here, fine. But I expect it won't be for too long. That being said, make no mistake that when I say "this, I mean it wholeheartedly, and you will leave my home if you find it too difficult to abide by this rule."

Laura nodded.

"I lived with your father for way too long to not spot a problem when I see one. What you do with your body and that baby is your business. I don't much care. But if you're under my roof, you'll not take another sip. You hear me, Laura? Not so much as a drop. I've seen all this before. You're too much like your father as it is, and I won't live with your version of him."

Despite it being what she wanted and needed to hear, Laura felt even smaller. "Yes, ma'am."

"Look at me when you address me."

Laura met Vivian's eyes. "Yes ma'am."

The front door opened and a man's voice boomed through the house. "Viv? Where you at, sugar?"

"In the kitchen."

Frank strolled in and stood behind Vivian. Laura rose, waiting for her mother to make introductions, but Vivian didn't move or speak or even seem to be breathing. She just stood there, again holding onto the back of the chair, trying to squeeze the life out of it. Laura was so focused on her mother's tension, she hadn't noticed Frank moving toward her.

"Oh," Laura said, startled to find him by her side. "Frank, I take it?" She reached out her hand, but he hadn't so much as noticed. His smile was generous, emphasizing the deep lines on his sun-spotted skin. He was a tank. Tall, like Laura's father had been, but thicker, and round around the belly.

"Viv!" he said, far too excited. "Look at her. She went and grew up on us. As pretty as ever, though. And where's the little one?"

Vivian finally let go of the chair and took a place beside him, but something in her posture told Laura it still wasn't safe to relax. There was something about them, their expressions, their voices that didn't add up.

Laura pulled her hand back, slid it into her pocket. "She's upstairs." She waited a moment. "So my mother tells me you're an old family friend. You'll have to forgive me, but I don't recall having met you." Frank's eyes were a bluish-gray, with specks of brown and zero familiarity. His hair was peppered with silver. He had to be in his late fifties, but Laura couldn't place a younger version of him, either.

Frank chuckled, a hard, throaty laugh, and gave Laura a friendly slap on the shoulder. "No need to apologize, sweetie. I knew you wouldn't remember me. You were a tiny thing last time I saw you. It's just nice to have you back. It's about time."

"Sure." Laura offered up a polite smile while slowly pulling her shoulder away from him.

Vivian cleared her throat. "Laura and Danlyn will be staying here for a short time. Just till Laura gets on her feet."

"Glad to hear it," Frank said, with a smile that never quit. "But"—he took a step closer to Laura—"you might just decide on stickin' 'round. Gorgeous land, good schools for the little one."

Vivian nudged his shoulder, forcing her way between them. "That's quite enough." She tried out a smile that looked even more peculiar than her last expression. "Laura has made up her mind. She's eager to get back out on her own. She never liked being looked after. Isn't that right, Laura?"

Laura nearly laughed. Where was all the looking after Vivian had ever done? "That's right," she said. "We'll be leaving as soon as possible."

Frank's disappointment was evident. "All right, then. But I'm tellin' you, good schools, safe place."

Laura waited, then said, "Well, it was nice meeting you. I'm going to go check on Danlyn. See if she's hungry." She quickly turned on her heel and was nearly out of the kitchen when she heard her mother whispering something about homeschooling Danlyn.

No. That wasn't part of the plan. After a week of homeschool with Vivian, Danlyn would be an alcoholic, too. Another wave of nausea clenched Laura's insides. She turned around, took a step back into the kitchen.

"Are you sure?" Laura asked, sounding sheepish. "I mean, maybe it would be good for Danlyn to make some friends."

Vivian slowly walked toward her, arms crossed over her chest. "Surely you aren't suggesting that Danlyn be tossed about in the school system?"

"No." The word shot out too fast. "But I thought—"

"You thought what, Laura?"

Laura calculated the risk. This wouldn't end well. "I was just thinking out loud. Forget what I said. Sorry." She couldn't believe those words had just come out of her mouth. In one hour, her mother had her resorting back to her scared inner child.

"You know," Frank offered, leaning back against the counter, "your mama used to tutor some local kids. It's not a bad idea."

Laura raised her hands up. She was out of options and had no desire to argue. "I said okay. I'm going to check on Danlyn now."

She turned around, hurried up the stairs, taking two at a time. The kitchen felt toxic, and Frank and Vivian together were about all she could handle. Laura reached the top of the staircase when she heard Frank's baritone voice.

"Hey. Send that child down here. I've been waitin' to meet her."

Frank seemed friendly enough, bearing all the charm of a traditional southern gentleman, but something was out of place. Maybe it was jealousy. Maybe seeing another man in her mother's home was enough to make Laura dislike him, but that didn't seem quite right, and when Laura heard his laughter follow her up the stairs, her annoyance blossomed into anger.

~

Danlyn's head popped up when Laura came in the room and fell back on the bed, letting out an exhausted breath. She needed to sleep and wake up in a different house in a different town and with a different mother.

"How're you doing with all this?" Laura asked.

Danlyn looked surprised. "Me? Well...I don't know. She hasn't even talked to me. It's weird."

Laura sat up. "I know, kid. Sorry. It's just her way. It's nothing personal." The letdown on Danlyn's face was too much. "I really am sorry. I wish I could snap my fingers and make everything better. I'd have done it a long time ago. But really, try not to take it personally." Laura worked to keep her expression neutral. "Frank, her boyfriend—don't call him that—he wants to meet you. He's downstairs in the kitchen."

"Do I have to?"

Laura gave her an apologetic look. "Yeah."

Danlyn lowered her head. "Can I ask you something first?"

"Sure." Laura felt the weight of Danlyn's words. Something heavy was coming.

"He's obviously not my grandfather. So who is?"

Of course that was coming. Danlyn had met her grandmother and had to have wondered whether there was a grandfather to go with her.

"Danlyn, my father's name is…was William. William Hallow."

"Was?"

"Yes."

Laura's eyes stung with tears. Danlyn had no way of knowing that she hadn't talked about her father in years, how it broke her heart to even think about him.

Danlyn frowned. "What happened to him?"

The third day of sobriety wasn't meant for questions like these. This was one of those big steps that required a circle of recovering alcoholics waiting to hand you a coin for all your bravery.

"Listen. I will tell you about my father, but not today. I'm trying my best, and considering everything, I'm doing better than I thought I would. But give me time. I loved my father with all of my heart, and you deserve to know who he was. But not until I figure out how to explain things to you. It's just very complicated."

"I know you're trying hard, Mom. It's okay. I can wait."

Laura was about to speak when she saw it. Danlyn had placed her hand next to hers. There was no touching yet. Laura understood why. Such things would have to be worked toward because, though there was love, there was little trust. But Laura imagined how sweet it would be to hold her and never let go. But she saw the look in her daughter's eyes, how it begged for kindness but feared what might follow. Laura had hurt her too much, and she'd have to hurt her again, when the day came for Danlyn to learn the truth about her family. A truth Laura couldn't even face. Would Danlyn be so quick to forgive her for coming here, for bringing her world down another notch, and all because Laura was too weak to fight her addiction without Vivian's threats looming overhead? So selfish. So essential.

Laura inched her finger closer to Danlyn's but stopped. Danlyn smiled, small and delicate, and just like that, Laura broke. Her shoulders collapsed and her whole body seized with each gut-wrenching cry. Laura knew it wasn't time for this discussion, either. She hadn't proved herself worthy of such words, but there was also no holding them back.

"I'm sorry, Danlyn." Clutching her chest, she quietly wept. "I'm so, so sorry. For the rest of my life, I'll be sorry."

Laura's chest heaved, her heart ached. She thought she might never stop crying. The seal had cracked, allowing her to feel all of the regret she had covered with years of drinking. Her mind was clear, despite needing sleep, and her mistakes were boldly staring her in the face. The immense weight of her failures was too much, the pain too great, and she wondered what that meant Danlyn had felt all those years.

When she thought she couldn't take another moment of clarity, she felt it. Danlyn placed one finger on her hand. The touch was sweet and subtle, soft like a whisper, but its effect was monumental.

In that one precious moment, Laura thought her heart might burst, not from pain, but from love.

"I love you, Danlyn," she cried. Her exhausted mind and broken heart were overwhelmed by this all-encompassing moment "God, I love you."

And God forgive me for bringing this little girl back here. Forgive me for what I've done.

Chapter 7

Two long weeks had passed since Laura and Danlyn's impromptu late-night appearance on Vivian's doorstep, and every day had proved a learning experience as much as a re-acquaintance with the past. Almost everything was the same: Vivian's schedule, the food she ate, the tea she drank, the way she stared into that damn fireplace Laura hated so much. Every day ran like a well-oiled machine, and somehow Vivian managed five hours of homeschool with Danlyn each morning. But some things had changed. Vivian's new emotions were steadily becoming the elephant in the room, and her relationship with Frank the thorn in Laura's side. The way she clung to him, obeyed him. He even made her laugh once, though she fought to hide it.

Laura was changing as well. The first week was a special kind of hell she hadn't known could exist. The withdrawal actually made Vivian look like a walk in the park on a beautiful spring day, if that was possible. Laura lay in the room, shaking and puking and sleeping for days on end, oblivious to everything, fighting through every unbearable minute. And she would have drank. Had it not been for her baby, even Vivian wouldn't have scared her enough to stop. But she'd made it, and this last week was the first one that left her feeling some trace of normalcy, or at least a new kind of normalcy. That's why Laura thought she might have imagined the changes in her mother, just a manifestation of her overly sensitive mind. But it was no manifestation. Differences were there, whispering from beneath Vivian's hard exterior.

~

"Here," Laura said, standing beside Danlyn, taking the large wooden spoon from her hands. "If you stir it this way, you get less lumps."

Danlyn smiled. "I still can't believe you're so good at this."

"I cooked dinner every night when I was a girl. It's like riding a bike. You never forget how to do it."

"What do we put in the potatoes?"

"Salt, pepper"—she snapped her fingers—"garlic. Always garlic." Danlyn made a face. "Trust me, it tastes like heaven."

"Any luck with the job search today?" Danlyn asked.

"Not yet, kid. Small town, not many jobs. But it'll happen. How was school today?"

Danlyn leaned in, whispered, "Boring. I'd rather be in school. She makes me—"

"Danlyn," Vivian interrupted, almost gliding into the kitchen. Even her voice seemed light. "How would you like a break from making dinner? I'd like to show you something, but we have to go upstairs to your great-grandmother's room."

Laura's head whipped around, eyes alert. Vivian never let anyone in there. Ever. The place was off limits, like a tomb.

Laura had only been in there a few times, none of which she liked to think about. What the hell was Vivian up to?

Vivian cleared her throat. "If you're about finished with that, Laura, you may come with us, if you'd like."

"What?" Laura nearly dropped the bowl.

"Yes or no? Dinner can wait. But I'm not asking again." Was Vivian actually smiling?

"Um," Laura looked around, waiting for the punch line. "Yeah. Okay."

~

The air in the room was stale, much more so than the rest of the house, and when Vivian turned on the lamp, the gentle glow lit just one corner of the room. Walking through the door was like traveling through a time warp. Nothing had changed since its last inhabitance. The walls were dreary and aged. The floral wallpaper was barely discernable through the dust. The furniture had a primitive feel and looked as though it might crumble into fragments if touched, and an ancient braided rug covered the floor. The colors had probably been vibrant at one time, but now they were muted and depressing, much like the rest of the room.

The three of them stood still, but Danlyn's eyes darted around, finally falling on a table in the corner, upon which a silver frame with a black-and-white photo of Rose sat.

"Go ahead, Danlyn. You can pick it up. But be gentle," Vivian told her.

Danlyn slowly walked to the table, studied the photograph. "That's my great-grandmother?"

Vivian and Laura's eyes met for an instant. "Yes. That's my mother, your great-grandmother. Beautiful, wasn't she? I wish you could have met her."

"Did you ever meet her, Mom?" Danlyn asked.

Laura slowly nodded. "I don't remember her, though."

"She's not alive, either?"

Before Laura could formulate an answer, Vivian slowly turned around, leering at her.

"Either? Who else are you referring to, Danlyn?" Vivian asked without taking her eyes off Laura.

"Mom told me that…" Danlyn turned around and fell silent when she spotted the standoff. "I don't know. She just said that my grandpa died, too. I'm sorry. I didn't mean to…"

Vivian perched her hands on her hips, making her narrow waist look even smaller in her navy blue dress. She turned, facing her granddaughter, still moving with a fluid ease, but with fire in her eyes. Her words came out sharp. "Danlyn, this room is very special. Aside from this having been my mother's room, this is also where you were born."

The blood drained from Laura's face and pooled in her feet.

"You know, Danlyn," Vivian went on, "maybe your mother can tell you the story. What do you say, Laura? Would you like to tell the story? That might be special for your daughter." One corner of Vivian's mouth pulled up into a grin as she looked back at Laura.

Vivian was insane, evil. What had Laura done to make her own mother hate her so much?

Vivian walked to the edge of the bed and sat down, patting the spot next to her. "Sit, Danlyn."

Danlyn moved cautiously, her expression hesitant.

"Well, go on, Laura. Tell her," Vivian ordered.

It probably wasn't possible to hate anything in life more than Laura hated her mother in that moment. Poor Danlyn, just sitting there, waiting to hear a story Laura didn't know how to tell. She tore through her memories, deciding what to extract from that day so that Danlyn wouldn't know how tragic it was—so that she wouldn't know that this moment was intended by Vivian to hurt both of them.

Laura walked to the old rocking chair behind her and sat down. She didn't care if it broke. Everything in this house eventually broke: Laura, William, and maybe now Danlyn. She sat uncomfortably straight and looked into her daughter's eyes, avoiding her mother's because they might turn her to stone. "You were born at seven twenty-two on a Tuesday. It was a really hot day. I still remember, it was the hottest day in nineteen sixty-five."

Danlyn's eyes grew eager with curiosity.

She deserved so much more.

"I was only in labor with you for a few hours. It wasn't very long. I remember your cry…how beautiful it was. You were such a content baby, so happy."

Using all her focus to not dare look in Vivian's direction, Laura went on. "It wasn't supposed to happen here, in this room," she lied. "When I went into labor, we all thought I'd have more time. But before I knew it"— Laura managed a smile—"I was walking out with the most beautiful gift in my arms. It was only your grandmother, your grandfather, and me. It was…special." That last word caught in Laura's throat. She pointed to a spot on the bed, behind where Danlyn sat. "Right there. That's where you were born."

Danlyn turned around, lightly brushing the spot on the bed. Laura silently watched, allowing time for the moment to soak in. The room came to a still silence when Danlyn's face didn't light up but became solemn. She looked up at her mother. "That's strange. I was born right here."

Danlyn turned back around, stared at the center of the bed. This time, a small smile finally showed on her face.

~

Laura sat on the porch swing, feeling a hungry ache in her stomach, but there was no way she could sit for dinner with Vivian. It was cold outside, and the wind in the trees filled her with an eerie sense of dread. She wrapped her arms around herself, completely drained, and closed her eyes, listening for the front door to open, prepared to wait all night, if that's what it took. But it didn't. When she heard a squeak from the rusted screen door behind her, her palms began to sweat, her temper flared. She had to keep it together.

"What are you doing out here?" Vivian asked, carrying her mug, from which plumes of steam rose. She looked down at Laura, waiting for her to move.

Laura got off the swing, leaned against the patio railing. "What were you doing up there, Mom?"

Vivian said nothing. She blew into her tea, sending another cloud of steam into her face.

"Seriously, have you lost it? Putting me on the spot like that, making me tell a half-truth. You were the one who made me swear never to tell. Do you want her to find out now?"

Vivian got to her feet, nose-to-nose with Laura. A fiendish rage passed through her eyes. Laura forgot to add her mother's new emotions into the equation, but she didn't much care. Vivian's little stunt had pushed her past her limit.

"What were you trying to achieve?" Laura stiffened her body. She wasn't going to give Vivian the satisfaction of knowing how afraid she still was of her.

Vivian's face turned red, her hands shook. She panted heavily, nearly growling. There was something strange in her eyes, something hazy and vacant.

"Mom?" Laura said.

The mug slipped from Vivian's grip and shattered on the floor, sending tea all over. Vivian finally blinked and staggered back, sloppily reaching behind her for the swing. She slapped her hands over her ears, pinched her face up. "That sound." Heavy breaths poured from her lungs, and when she found the swing with the back of her legs, she dropped, almost falling off the edge.

"Mom? Mom? You okay?"

Vivian yanked herself back, slapping at Laura when she saw her bending down to assist her.

"Jesus. I'm just trying to help you." Laura backed away.

Vivian hurled her weight off the swing and came to an unsteady stop on her feet. Laura stayed close, reaching her arms out in case she needed to catch her.

"Get …away from me," Vivian spat.

Something wasn't right. Laura saw nothing but the whites of her mother's eyes as they rolled back in her skull. She lunged forward, catching Vivian under her arms just before she collapsed.

She lowered her to the porch. "Mom!" Vivian's eyes lazily opened and she started to thrash. "Stop fighting me. I'm just trying to help." Feeble punches found their way into Laura's shoulders, her ribs, her face. "Dammit. You just fainted!" Laura pressed her weight into her, trying not to break one of Vivian's thin bones. "Stop fighting me."

Vivian opened her mouth, gasping like a dying fish. "Get off!"

"I will when you stop," Laura demanded.

When Vivian's limbs went slack, Laura lifted herself off the heaving slop of arms and legs and bent over, regaining her breath. "You don't want my help, that's fine," Laura panted. "I'll stay out of your way, and next time I'll let the ground break your fall. But don't you ever put me and Danlyn in a position like that again."

Laura turned around, pulling the squeaky door open, and heard Vivian's shallow voice. Looking over her shoulder, she saw Vivian trying to get up, but her arms only danced under her. She gave up and dropped back down on the porch. It was so pathetic, Laura almost felt bad for her. Vivian had always appeared so strong. Now she looked weak, old, angry.

"I don't know what came over me up there." Vivian held her head. "You just keep your mouth shut, and I'll make sure that never happens again."

"I've always kept my mouth shut. I've never even suggested that—"

"Stop," Vivian yelled. "I won't let it happen again. I've had some difficulty lately with..." She waved her hand through the air. "I'll keep myself in line."

Laura knew her mother would rather die than start spilling family secrets like blood from a severed artery. So what was going on?

As though reading Laura's thoughts, Vivian said, "I need you to drive me into town tomorrow. I need to see my doctor."

"You don't want Frank to take you?"

"Of course I want him to, Laura. But he can't. He'll be here later tonight, but he's got to leave first thing in the morning so those idiots on his crew don't fall apart because "their contractor's gone. Otherwise I'd never dream of asking you."

"He'll be here later tonight?"

"Yes. He's a good friend. He checks in on me."

"Right," Laura said, resisting the urge to roll her eyes. "This isn't the first time you've collapsed, is it?"

Vivian slowly got to her feet, sat back down on the swing. Laura couldn't see her face anymore, but the spike in her tone was enough to tell her she was right. "That's none of your business."

"It is if Danlyn's going to be alone with you during the day."

"I get migraines," Vivian shot back, glaring at Laura from the corner of her eye. "That's all. I need to change medications. That's why I need you to drop me off at my doctor's office tomorrow. So don't question me with Danlyn. It's just migraines."

"That's why Frank practically lives here? Because of your headaches? Seems excessive."

"Laura!"

"Never mind. Just forget I said anything, Mother. Let me know what time tomorrow. I'm going to bed."

~

Laura paused halfway up the stairs and looked over at the front door, where another one of Vivian's little notes was taped, reminding her to lock it. Laura was beginning to think they weren't strewn about the house for Danlyn's sake, as Vivian had claimed.

Laura climbed the rest of the stairs. If her mother didn't make it in, so be it. She could sit out in the cold all night and wait for Frank. He had seen behind the curtain and had apparently liked what he saw. All Laura wanted was to get away. Away from Rome, away from Vivian, away from Frank—her dear, old family friend.

Chapter 8

The day was gorgeous, like most crisp November days in Rome. The clouds left brushstrokes of pale white across the cool, blue sky. The trees were nearly bare, dropping their decaying leaves, shedding their former life to the ground. Laura understood the feeling of being stripped so clean.

Danlyn giggled from the backseat when she heard Laura's stomach rumble. "Maybe the baby's hungry, Mom. Can we eat after Grandma sees the doctor?"

Laura never knew she could be both hungry and nauseated all at once. "Yeah," she said, looking over at the passenger's seat, where Vivian sat. Being in Rome meant growing, and by God, even if it killed her, Laura would give it all she had. She opened her mouth, trying to work the words out. "Would you like to join us for lunch?"

"I can eat when we get back. No sense in wasting money." Vivian lifted her chin, staring straight ahead.

Danlyn leaned forward and grabbed the back of Laura's seat. "Cheeseburger with fries and a shake? Please? Pretty please?"

"No," Laura said. Vivian gave a quick nod of approval. "'Cause I got you beat. How about cheeseburgers, chili fries, and a banana split?"

"Oh! Can we?" Danlyn squealed.

Laura gripped the wheel, waiting for Vivian's protest. "We'll see. That diner I tried to get a job at had some stuff like that. Maybe we'll go there."

Vivian cleared her throat. "On what planet is that a proper meal for a child?"

"Well..." Laura searched for something amicable to say. "We won't make a habit of it. It won't kill her this once."

"Certainly don't wait for me, then. Just go eat while I see the doctor."

"We can wait. It's no trouble." The high road was getting narrow.

"Don't." Vivian straightened her sweater, pressed the wrinkles from her long skirt. "Just drop me out front, and when you're through eating whatever it is you two eat"—she swallowed back the sour look on her face—"you need to stop by the market and pick up some basics. Milk, eggs, bread—"

"I know what we need, Mom." Vivian's raised eyebrows suggested otherwise. "You've been eating the same thing for the last twenty-plus years. I know what you keep in the house. I've got it. Really."

"Fine," Vivian said with one arched brow. She popped to attention, pointed at the curb ahead. "There. Drop me off right there."

Laura looked at the buildings nestled together, all bearing signs too small to read. She pulled alongside the curb. "I can "drive into the parking lot. It's no trouble." But Vivian already had the door open before the car came to a complete stop. "Or not," Laura said, pressing on the brakes.

Vivian got out, leaned her head back in the car. "Here, in one hour. Can I trust you to do that?"

Laura looked back at Danlyn. "I don't know. Can she trust me?" Danlyn pursed her lips, then smiled. Laura leaned over, looking up at Vivian. "I can handle it, I promise." She looked at her watch. "It's ten fifty-eight. I'll be back at noon. Right here."

Vivian slammed the door shut and walked across the lawn in front of the buildings. Laura waved, wearing a strained smile. "God, that woman's strange." That was one word for it, and probably the nicest she could muster.

"What do you mean?" Danlyn asked.

"Your grandmother is acting stranger than normal."

"So she wasn't always like this?"

"Like what?" Laura looked over her shoulder.

"Uh...she's not very..."

Laura laughed. "Don't strain yourself, kid. I know what you mean. And yeah, she's always been this way. But she's been extra special lately." Laura grabbed the wheel. "Hey, you wanna crawl up here with me? I'm starting to feel like garbage. I could use the company."

Danlyn nodded enthusiastically and climbed over the seat.

"Cheeseburger first or banana split?" Laura asked.

"Banana split!"

"Didn't even need to ask, did I?"

"Nope."

Chapter 9

Vivian walked into the dreary office, with its eggshell walls and cheap baby-blue vinyl chairs. She gave the secretary her name, then looked from corner to corner, choosing her seat wisely. Sitting too near another patient might be mistaken for interest. She'd rather have her teeth pulled than hear someone's sob story. She rigidly stepped her way through the makeshift aisles created by the chairs, studying each person's peaked appearance while holding her purse tightly to her chest. They had dark circles under their eyes; their skin was a sick shade of gray. And how on earth some women wore those cheap, ugly scarves on their heads, Vivian didn't know. They looked like fools, advertising their illness with tacky floral prints in tawdry colors. That wouldn't have been her, even if chemotherapy had been an option.

She sat in a seat in the corner, as far away from the other patients as possible, and stared from wall to wall, patient to patient. Frank should've been here with her. Damn him for not prioritizing. Vivian's mind spewed thoughts that threatened her resolve, and the inescapable sense of death that dominated the room forced fear to the forefront of her mind. To her left was a middle-aged man. He was thin and pale. Blue veins shot through his arms like a roadmap. His hair was gone, but he was too young to be balding. Sitting beside him was an elderly woman who Vivian guessed to be his mother. To Vivian's far right, five chairs down, was another elderly woman and her adult daughter. What a pair they were: a sick, dying mother and an obese daughter. Vivian cringed, thinking about all the cheeseburgers and banana splits she must have eaten. There was another older man sitting in the corner opposite her. His companion must have been his wife. Her bright pink cheeks and rosy lips contrasted with his ailing appearance. He was the stark, black smudge in the middle of her glowing, white world. The man saw Vivian staring and he pulled down his sleeves, hiding the bruises left by too many blood draws. Vivian suddenly wondered if she was the black smudge mucking up Frank's world?

Everyone had someone with them, holding their hand, handing them those awful magazines with recipes for the perfect Thanksgiving dinner. It wouldn't always be this way, though. One day, Vivian would be just like the rest: too sick to come without a chaperone. A lump formed in her throat as she thought of Frank again. He was all she had. She certainly couldn't draw from Laura's sympathy, and with any luck, Laura wouldn't be around much longer. Vivian tried shutting her eyes, to close out the room and the people in it, but she couldn't peel away. Her future was looking her boldly in the eye.

"Vivian Hallow, the doctor will see you now."

Chapter 10

"This place hasn't changed at all," Laura said.

"It's small. What's that smell?" Danlyn asked.

Laura faced away from the register as she and Danlyn walked into the market and headed down the first aisle. "It's Rome. It always smells that way." She looked at a box of cake mix. "Even the aisles are the same." Laura stopped in front of the bread, leaned against the shelf. The bright lights from the low ceiling reflected off Danlyn's big eyes. She looked scared.

"What's wrong?" Laura asked.

"You just..." Danlyn scratched at a small scab on her hand. "You look mad. You seemed okay at lunch, but now you look like you used to. And your hands..."

Laura didn't need to look. She could feel them shaking. "Things don't get better that fast. But I'm not mad. I just don't feel well." She wiped sweat from her forehead. "To tell you the truth, I can't always tell why I'm feeling the way I am. Being pregnant has thrown me. But I promise, I'm not upset." Laura searched Danlyn's eyes for understanding, but all she saw was apprehension. "What I'm trying to say is that you can't…we can't go around thinking I'm ready to blow up all the time. I know why you're afraid, and I don't blame you. But sometimes I'm going to feel like crap." Laura stood on her toes, looking over the aisle at the cash register. "The guy at the register, the old guy, he's been working here since I was your age. I'm just not in the mood to talk. I'd drive to another store if there was one close enough, but we've gotta get your grandmother soon. You want to help me?"

"Sure."

"Go get a basket from up front. I'll grab the bread. Meet me two aisles over, next to the milk." She squeezed Danlyn's hand. "I'm okay, I swear."

Danlyn walked away, half smiling, half frowning. Laura knew the road would be long, but for now she just needed to get out of the store, but the next aisle over was almost directly in front of the register. She reached in her pocket, pulled out a crumpled-up receipt, then grabbed a pen from her purse and was about to scribble the grocery list on the back when she dropped the pen. "Shit." She bent down, reaching under the shelf.

"Laura, is that you?"

Dammit. It was just a friendly old man…who happened to know her entire family.

Laura turned around and saw Danlyn coming around the corner, carrying a small hand-basket. Just behind her Mr. Donaldson stood, waving.

"Hi, Mr. Donaldson," Laura said, still on all fours behind the Wonder Bread. She got up, pulling Danlyn close to her side. "Here," she said quietly, while writing fast. "Can you read this?"

Danlyn grabbed the paper. "Yeah."

"Good. Go get these and meet me at the register."

Danlyn strode off while returning a friendly wave in Mr. Donaldson's direction.

"Oh boy! Well, if you ain't grown into a woman. Gee, Laura, what's it been? Nine, ten years?"

Laura put her hands in her pockets and looked over her shoulder to make sure Danlyn was out of earshot. She walked to the counter. "Something like that."

"And the young lady, she your little one?"

"That would be her."

Mr. Donaldson leaned against the counter, getting cozy. Bad sign. "I never see your mama. How's she doin' these days?" He didn't let her answer. "After your old man passed, it seemed like all the Hallow women up and disappeared."

Laura's smile faded. Small-town people came with their own unique senselessness. "You'll have to forgive me," Laura said, looking over at Danlyn's head bobbing up and down the aisles. "But I'm in a hurry."

"Oh, sure. 'Course." Mr. Donaldson looked a little put out. He drummed his fingers on the counter, looked in Danlyn's direction. "She looks like you. Pretty girl, just like her mama."

"You're far too kind, Mr. Donaldson."

Danlyn jogged up to the register, lugging the small basket at her side. "Okay. Got everything. You sure this is enough?"

"That's plenty." Laura threw the items on the counter.

"How old are you, young lady?" Mr. Donaldson asked.

"Eleven." Danlyn smiled.

He snapped his fingers, grinning. "That's right. You were just a wee thing when y'all were living over at the—"

"I'm sorry," Laura said. "But we've really got to get going."

"Right, right." He rang up the few items and bagged them, wearing a slightly wounded look.

Laura grabbed a wad of cash from her pocket and tossed it on the counter, giving him the kindest smile she could. "Keep the change." She grabbed the bags. "Have a nice day."

"Okay, then. Hope to see you girls again soon."

~

"That guy knows you?" Danlyn asked when they stepped outside.

"He knows everyone. Nosy but nice." Laura rushed to the car. "You get him talking and he'll never stop." She opened the door, handed Danlyn the eggs. "Sit in the back and hold these. Her head will blow up if they break."

Danlyn scooted across the backseat and sat in the middle, perched where she could see everything.

"Here. One more." Laura leaned in, handing her the bread. "Don't smash that, or—"

"Her head'll pop off."

Laura smirked. "No. The Hallow women's heads don't pop off. They—"

"Blow up."

"Now you're gettin' it, kid."

Laura shut Danlyn's door and was about to get in the car when she heard a familiar voice coming from behind her.

"Holy mother of God! Is that really you, Laura?"

It was like hearing a voice from another life. Laura almost couldn't turn around. Fear and happiness walloped at her insides, and just when she thought she found her voice, her lips felt numb and her legs turned to Jell-O, like her bones had evaporated along with any intelligent thought.

"Wow...Jackie," she heard herself mutter.

Jackie threw her purse on the hood of the car and her weight into Laura, hugging her. "Holy shit! It's you!" She pulled back, looked into Laura's eyes. "What on earth...? Why're you...? When'd you get back?"

Dodging Jackie wouldn't be as easy. There was too much history between them.

"I've been back for a couple weeks now. But everything's good." Laura tried her best to look natural.

Jackie let go, dropping her arms. "That's a load if I ever heard one. Seriously, why're you back?"

Laura adjusted her weight, letting one leg hold her up at a time. She crossed her arms in front of her, feeling guilty for already being upset with Jackie's ability to read her. "Really. Everything's good. I'm just back for a little while. I've been doing a lot of traveling."

"Traveling? Where?"

Laura sighed, then looked back at Danlyn and immediately regretted doing so.

Jackie looked over her shoulder. "Are you kidding me?" She nudged Laura. "Danlyn's so big! She's beautiful." Jackie waved. "And that blonde hair."

Edging her way to the door, Laura grabbed the handle. "Yeah, that's her." She slowly pulled up on it. "It was great seeing you, but I really am in a hurry. My"—she paused, already knowing what Jackie's response would be—"my mother's waiting for me."

Jackie wrapped her hand around the back of her ear. "I'm sorry. Did I hear you right? *Your mother*? You're staying with *her*?"

Laura nudged the door back in place, dropped her voice. "Yes, and I know what you're going to say—"

"Did you two make amends, or do you have amnesia?"

"No. Not exactly. We have an arrangement. But I have to run."

Jackie stepped back, looked her up and down. "So...after a decade, that's it? I never thought I'd see you again."

Laura couldn't think of anything to say.

"Okay. You've gotta go, but why don't you and Danlyn come over for dinner?"

Laura looked at her watch. She could almost feel Vivian breathing down her neck from here. But Jackie wasn't going to let her out of this. "Okay. Fine. Dinner."

Jackie gave a half-hearted smile. "That's wonderful. Good."

"Or not," Laura said after seeing the change in her expression.

"No, no. That's not it. Invitation still stands, of course. I just...I have something I want to tell you first. I probably should've started with this, but you know how my mouth gets me in trouble. Can I call you so we can talk?"

Nothing about that would work. Vivian's head really would blow up if she picked up the phone and heard Jackie on the other end.

"Probably not a good idea," Laura told her.

"So things haven't changed?"

"Just give me your number and I'll call you."

Jackie reached into her purse but stopped. "Ah, shit." She placed her hands on her hips. "You remember Steven's old number, right?"

Laura leaned back against the car. Her legs had really given up on her this time. "You and Steven?"

Jackie didn't say a word. She only nodded and held up her ring finger with an apologetic expression.

"That's great news, Jackie." Those words didn't sound like Laura's, they didn't even feel like hers, but somewhere in her mind, they made sense. They felt right. But that didn't mean the pill wasn't bitter. "I mean it, that's amazing."

Jackie hesitated. "Yeah? You sure?"

"Absolutely."

"I'm sorry, Laura. I wish it had come out better. I didn't even think before inviting you. I was just so excited. But you'll still come, right?"

Laura couldn't think about that now. Vivian was going to have her head on a platter.

"What about tomorrow, six o'clock?" Jackie steepled her hands. "Please say yes."

"Jackie—"

"Just wait," Jackie said. She took Laura's hand, either choosing not to notice that she tried to pull away or not caring. "I know you think it'll be weird, but the three of us were like family. Please come."

Laura had to do something, even if it meant agreeing to something she'd never actually do. "Okay. We'll come. But you have to warn Steven. I'm the last person he'll want to see."

"That was so long ago, and Steven doesn't resent you. We both still love you."

Laura gently pulled her hand away, looking thoughtfully into Jackie's eyes. "I remember everything. I think love is the last thing he feels for me."

"We were such good friends. It would be a shame not to put it all behind us," Jackie said. "I know Steven has. He's not angry anymore."

Things were going from bad to terrible, and now Danlyn was watching everything. Laura appreciated Jackie's words, but she was going to start crying, and then the whole damn world would come crashing down.

"Thank you, Jackie. You were always a good friend to me. Hell, you were more than that. But I really have to go."

Jackie took a step back. "Please come. It would make me so happy."

Laura gave a quick nod, then got in the car and rolled down the window. She waved goodbye while watching her best friend in the world cry as she drove off.

~

Laura tapped on the steering wheel as she headed back down the road to Vivian's doctor.

"Who was that?" Danlyn asked.

Laura waited a moment. "Jackie. She's an old friend. A really"—her throat tightened—"really good friend."

"Are you still friends?"

"It's been a long time. She doesn't know me anymore."

"Did I ever meet her?"

All the secrets weighed too much. The truth had to start somewhere. "Yes. But you were just a baby. Actually, you and I lived with Jackie and her parents for almost a year before we left Rome."

"Why?"

"Let's just say things weren't very good with your grandmother, so Jackie's parents let us stay with them. They caught a lot of heat for it, too. Especially back then. But they were there for us anyway. They're good people."

Danlyn stared out the window, looking thoughtfully at the clouds. "Were things ever good at home, with Grandma?"

Laura looked back in the mirror. She could tell by the look on Danlyn's face that she already knew the answer. "No, they weren't."

Laura turned the corner and from yards away could see the scornful look on Vivian's face as she stood waiting on the curb. She slowed down the car, already dreading the drive home.

"She's pissed," Laura said. "Listen, before she gets in the car. What I told you, about Jackie and her parents, don't repea—"

"I know. I'm not going to say anything."

"Thank you, Danlyn."

"No problem, Mom."

Chapter 11

Vivian and Frank passed peculiar glances across the table, deep in a silent conversation. Laura turned her focus back to making dinner.

"This is a bad idea, Laura," Vivian finally said. "Your relationship was inappropriate in high school and it's inappropriate now. Traipsing around their home. He's a married man. He's got no right ogling you." She slapped her hands down on the table. "I won't have it."

"First of all"—Laura dropped the knife and pinched her eyes shut, trying to stay calm—"I'm not asking for your permission." Why did Danlyn have to let it slip? "I'll go to a dinner I was invited to if I feel like it. Steven and I were together a very long time ago, but"—Laura turned around, glancing at Vivian—"we all know how that ended, don't we? And no one will be *ogling* anyone."

Vivian rose from the table. "Is there something you'd like to say, Laura? Because after the talking to you gave me on the "porch the other night, you'd do well to watch your step, you hypocrite."

Laura's lips thinned. "I'll keep my mouth shut. But I'm going to Jackie and Steven's." She'd planned on canceling, but she'd be damned if Vivian was going to exercise that kind of control over her.

Vivian passed Frank a look that Laura knew meant she wanted his assistance. He grumbled, got to his feet. Laura turned around, back to cutting up the chicken. He settled beside her, leaning on the counter, watching her work. Laura could feel him there, could smell the stench of cologne and cigarettes. Her fingers tightened around the handle of the knife.

"Hey." Frank grabbed her shoulders, gently turning her around to face him. "I'm sure you can manage more respect for your mama. I know I'd appreciate it. What do you say, sugar?"

Laura thrust her shoulders back, growled through her teeth, "Keep your fucking hands off of me." Her nostrils flared—the handle of the knife felt slippery in her sweaty hand. She blinked fast, stunned by her own reaction.

"Whoa." Frank brought his hands up. "Little jumpy, ain't ya?"

The look on his face made Laura feel exposed, and when he laughed, hatred bubbled inside her gut, with gnashing jaws and foaming jowls. She wanted to hide, not just from him, but also from her own feral rage. She looked over her shoulder at Vivian, wondering why she wasn't chomping at the bit, protecting her man and all that nonsense that used to be below Vivian Hallow, but what she saw was nothing short of eerie. Vivian sat motionless, with a blank stare and stone-like posture. She'd checked out. She was looking at Laura, right at her, but there wasn't even a suggestion of life in her eyes. If a corpse could sit up, perfectly erect, it would look something like Vivian.

"What the hell's she doing?" Laura asked, looking back at Frank and his amused smile. "Frank?"

"She'll be fine. Just give her a minute."

Laura began to walk toward Vivian. "Mom? Can you hear me?"

"I said to give her a minute. Such dramatics with you women." He raised his voice. "Viv!" A loud clap of the hands. "Snap out of it!"

Vivian slowly blinked. Her voice was silky, but with a steely edge that made it sound robotic. "Of course I'm all right." She blinked again, looked around the room. "Now get away."

Laura slowly backed out of the kitchen, keeping her eyes on both of them. When she turned around, Danlyn was standing behind her. "Come on," Laura told her, grabbing her keys off the side table, pulling Danlyn along with her.

"Just know that if you go tomorrow night," Vivian said from the kitchen doorway, "you'll be going against my wishes. And you'll be going alone. I don't want Danlyn around those people."

Laura grabbed their jackets off the hook, opened the front door. "Just so you know, you can forbid anything you want, but using Danlyn as leverage won't work. I've been raising her on my own, and that's not going to change now. You want us out, just say the word." Vivian's lips quivered with the threat of a rebuttal. "You let me know when we get back if we need to get out. I can have our things packed by tomorrow morning." And with that, Laura and Danlyn walked out, slamming the door behind them.

~

Vivian sat back down, following Frank's eyes, waiting for his reaction. He knelt down in front of her and spoke, his voice strong yet gentle. As always, his confidence pulled her mind from a dark corner. "I've got everything under control, Viv. There's nothin' to worry about. I'll see to it."

Frank held her hand tight, not enough to hurt her, but just enough to let her know that he wasn't asking for permission to tie up any loose ends. "And about them goin' to dinner tomorrow, let 'em go. There's nothin' to worry about."

Vivian nodded. She closed her eyes, allowing the ease of his promise to wash her worries away, and his deep voice to seep into her mind, turning all her muscles supple. But there remained that last thread of doubt.

"But what if they—"

"Sugar, look at me. I don't give a damn what those two think. It ain't an issue. I won't have you thinkin' it is." His face softened. "Haven't I always taken care of everything?"

Vivian didn't need to answer. Her silence was her way of relinquishing power, and always had been. Her silence was essential to their relationship, past and present.

Frank leaned forward, kissed her head. "That's a good girl, Viv."

Chapter 12

The door was the same shade of barnyard red Laura remembered, and quaint cream-colored window planters still hung under each window. The lush trees lining the quiet cul-de-sac kept hidden the last of the sinking sun. Laura stared at the peephole, thinking now might be the time for a quick getaway.

"Are you going to knock?" Danlyn asked.

Laura shook her head. "Nope."

"You want me to?"

Laura chewed her lip. So what if she really did want to see Jackie. And so what if she had missed her like crazy. Maybe Vivian was right about this whole thing being wildly inappropriate. On the other hand, maybe screw Vivian Hallow.

Laura nodded, gulped loudly. "Go ahead. Knock." Danlyn lifted her hand to the door. "Wait. Stop." Laura stepped back. "Don't."

But before Laura could turn around, the front door opened and there Jackie stood, with open arms and a warm smile. Once you got past her sailor's mouth, she was warm and gooey, the stuff of great preschool teachers.

"You came! I thought for sure you'd cancel." Jackie beamed. "I'm so happy." She wrapped her arms around Laura and pulled her into the house. "And you." She moved on to Danlyn, hugging her with the same exuberance. "You're so big. And gorgeous."

Laura watched as Danlyn hugged back, smiling happily, like she remembered Jackie from all those years ago. Laura looked around the room. Everything looked the same but somehow totally different. She could see touches of Jackie where Steven's mom used to be. And Steven, where was he? Laura's stomach flipped. Earning his forgiveness would mean slaying a much bigger dragon, even if Jackie had promised otherwise.

She never should've come.

"Can I get you something to drink? We've got red wine, white wine, ginger ale, martinis..." Jackie winked at Danlyn. "Shirley Temples. What'll you ladies have?"

"She'll have a Shirley Temple," Laura said, giving Danlyn a reassuring look. "And I'll take a ginger ale."

Danlyn's smile brightened, her shoulders relaxed. It was moments like these that made every hellacious step easier for Laura to endure. Even if her mouth was salivating.

"Let us help you with those," Laura offered, really just wanting to avoid a lone encounter with her ex.

"Absolutely not. You're my guests. But you two can keep me company."

~

They followed Jackie into the kitchen. Laura stood at attention behind her, hands in her pockets, head down.

"Danlyn"—Jackie grabbed four glasses from the cupboard and gave Danlyn a smile—"would you tell your mother to relax? She looks like she's waiting for her execution."

Laura shifted uncomfortably. "Sorry."

Jackie pulled bottle after bottle from the refrigerator, and Danlyn's eyes lit up when she set a jar of cherries on the island. "So, you have to tell me what you've been doing with yourself all these years." Jackie looked behind her at Laura. "Spill the beans."

Getting drunk. Shacking up with assholes.

"You know… Nothing too exciting."

"Oh, come on. Anything seems exciting to me. I've never really left this dinky town. We went to Atlanta last year, for Steven's cousin's wedding. It wasn't as fun as I'd hoped."

"Well…let's see. We were in Massachusetts before this."

"Massachusetts! Boston?"

"No. About an hour south, near the cape."

"Cape Cod? So beautiful. Well, from what I've seen in pictures." Jackie poured the soda over ice. "Did you ever see the Kennedys?"

"Yes, it's beautiful. And no"—Laura quietly laughed—"no Kennedys."

Jackie moaned, looking miserable with envy. "You lucky ass. I wanna go to Cape Cod. I'd settle for any beach. Don't get me wrong, the foothills are beautiful, but I've been looking at them my whole life. I'm thankful for everything, really. Steven and I are very happy. But this damn town, and the people…they're like hemorrhoids."

Jackie had no filter. It had always been one of the things Laura loved about her. She was real and honest, and so was Laura's laughter this time.

"Oops." Jackie covered her mouth. "Sorry. I'm not used to being around children. Hey! Steven just forked out the bucks for one of those remote controllers. You want to watch TV, Danlyn?"

"Sure!"

"Make yourself at home, sweetie," Jackie said, but Danlyn was already out of the kitchen. "I take it your mother still thinks TVs are possessed?"

"You know Vivian. She thinks everything's possessed."

"So how's that going?"

Laura grabbed one of the glasses, filled it with ice. "Um..." The TV came on, speakers blaring. "Sorry, Jackie. I'll go tell her to turn it down."

Evasion would be the theme of the night.

Laura turned the corner, into the living room. "Danlyn, that's too lou—" Her mouth went dry, her knees buckled. She couldn't remember what she'd come in the living room for. There he was, standing next to Danlyn, showing her how to use the remote control. Danlyn told him about her favorite show, and he said he really liked westerns and mysteries. But Laura could hardly understand their words, or why she was even here, in his house. Suddenly, the idea of dinner with Steven and Jackie was preposterous.

Jackie walked up behind Laura, grabbing her hand, "It's okay. I promise." Jackie slowly guided her further into the living room, and when Steven and Danlyn turned around, Laura fought the urge to duck behind Jackie.

"Laura," Steven said, sounding like the wind had been knocked out of him.

Laura forced herself to look at him. He looked the same. Exactly the same. Tall, lean, handsome. Even his dark hair hadn't lost its luster, and his eyes were still a stunning shade of blue. *I don't look the same.* And Jackie. Had Laura just not noticed that Jackie was the same beautiful brunette from high school— petite and adorable? Laura was suddenly aware of how much she stood out, like a dilapidated apartment sandwiched between two breathtaking colonials.

"My God," Steven said. "I can't believe you're here."

"Hi," was all Laura managed.

Steven reached out for her. Laura could feel his hands on hers, and then on her arms, and before she knew it, he'd pulled her into him and was hugging her. She nervously looked sideways at Jackie, searching for help or approval or...she wasn't quite sure what.

Smiling, Jackie moved back, allowing them space.

Steven's arms tightened around her, and finally, slowly, Laura reached her arms around him. Tears formed in the corner of her eyes, and when she looked back at Jackie, she saw that she was crying, too.

"It's so good to see you," Steven whispered into her hair.

"You, too."

In that moment, Laura remembered how much she still loved these two people, and just how much they still meant to her.

~

Dinner went as smoothly as possible. The conversation was light, the food heavy, the ginger ale flowed. Laura couldn't remember better spaghetti. They talked about days of old, politely dancing around the elephant in the room. Memories of high school were passed back and forth, and Laura was told funny stories about what had become of their fellow classmates. Danlyn told everyone about her big plans. She was going to be a doctor, or maybe a teacher, but only if she didn't become a singer first. As unthinkable as it had been at the beginning of the night, Laura felt surprisingly at ease. Welcome, even. Just like she had fourteen years ago. The house, the furniture, the music, the company, it was as close to home as she and Danlyn had ever come. And what a perfect picture Jackie and Steven made.

"Are you all stuffed?" Jackie asked. After everyone nodded and thanked her for the delicious meal, she stood up, pointing at Laura. "I've got something waiting for you in the oven. Are you too full for pumpkin pie?"

"You remembered."

"Of course I remembered."

Danlyn looked around the table. "Remembered what?"

"Let's just say that when we were kids, my mother didn't always make two pumpkin pies for nothing," Jackie said, arching her eyebrow at Laura.

When Laura laughed, she sounded younger, even to herself. "You're going to make me fat, Jackie." But Jackie was already in the kitchen, and when she returned and set the pie on the table, steam swirled up through a crack on its surface, sending the smell of nutmeg in Laura's direction. She swallowed, held her breath, but mind over matter wasn't enough to ward off the lurching of her stomach. Of all the times...

"Bathroom?" Laura mumbled, hand clamped over her mouth.

Steven pointed down the hall. "First door on the right." Laura was out of her seat, running to the hallway when he remembered she already knew where everything was.

~

Laura shut the door, took several deep breaths. Just getting away from the smell was enough to ease her stomach. She ran cool water over her face. "Don't throw up in Jackie's pretty pink sink." She looked at the floral hand towel and the poppy shower curtain. Everything about the room screamed Jackie. *Steven and Jackie Brenner's bathroom.* She laughed, muted and tired. It was hard to believe she was back here. The way she aimlessly moved throughout life, never finding any means to an end. It could get real depressing to think about where she'd be if she had been afforded what Steven and Jackie had. Good parents who offered a good upbringing. But she'd done that, dreamed of it, dared to wish for it, and look where that had landed her. Pregnant, single, and without any real home.

Standing was suddenly daunting. She staggered back against the wall and dropped to her bottom, laughing and crying all at once. It wasn't the first time she'd cried in this house. She used to escape here to find solace when she was just a girl. How many times had she come here? How many times had both she and Jackie come here together? Jackie would watch and sigh as Steven and Laura never tired of kissing and holding hands. Had it not been for those memories, Laura's childhood would have been devoid of any happiness. A mentally deranged mother and an alcoholic father didn't make for a Norman Rockwell kind of life, and Steven had understood that well.

"Fine young man" was what William had called Steven when they had first met. "Drunk, no-good gimp" was how

William was known around town, usually followed by a sympathetic smile or disappointed shake of the head. But Steven and Jackie had been kind enough to pretend they hadn't heard the same things, because poor William Hallow was a good man who'd been driven to drink. That was the excuse made for a drunk with too little room for change but plenty of room for his poison. William made room for Laura, though. Or tried to. She was the only one he allowed in, and God, how he loved her, and how she loved him, even when he was stumbling over his own feet and slurring his words. But even Laura had her limits, and when the sobbing and drinking got to be too much, she pulled away, to this very house or to Jackie's house, where solitude was found and comfort was offered. No one wanted to step foot on Hallows' Farm. Not after seeing behind the scenes. Steven had hardly believed his own ears when he heard the things Vivian said to Laura, and he didn't want another backstage pass. He wanted to rescue her. Any blow dealt to Laura was a blow dealt to him. That's how things had been so long ago.

"Jesus," Laura whispered. There was too little space in her mind for so much history.

The TV snapped back on. Laura heard Danlyn laugh. She got up and looked in the mirror. Bad idea. After a quick pinch of her cheeks and a swig of water, she opened the door. Danlyn was sitting on the sofa, watching TV and eating pie. Such a happy picture, a proper picture.

"You feeling better?" Jackie asked.

Laura walked back into the dining room and sat down at the table, looking at the pie. It had cooled off and wasn't exuding much of an odor anymore. "Yeah. I'm fine. I woke up today with a bit of an upset stomach. Guess I overate. But it was worth it. Best meal I've had in a long time."

"That's our Jackie. Regular Julia Child," Steven said, rubbing his wife's shoulder.

Jackie laughed. "You wish. And Laura, don't worry about the pie. It gives you an excuse to come over when you're feeling better. Can I get you some water?"

"That'd be good. Thanks."

When Jackie disappeared into the kitchen, Laura fiddled with her fork, uncertain of what to say. "So how're your parents?" A safe starting point. But Steven frowned, pushing the pie around on his plate. God, she was an idiot. Of course that hadn't been a safe subject. Here Steven and Jackie were, living in their old home. What had she thought happened to them?

"My parents passed away. My mom had lung cancer. Advanced by the time we found out. My dad had a heart attack shortly after she died."

The news stung more than Laura thought it would. "I'm so sorry, Steven. I should have known. Forgive me."

He shook his head, gave her a heavy smile. "Nah. It's okay."

Jackie sat a glass of water in front of Laura, then sat back down. Steven took Jackie's hand in his. "It was hard, but"—he looked at his wife—"she was here for me. We got through it together. Otherwise…"

"You two seem happy. Like, actually happy. I can't think of two people who deserve it more."

"Yep. We are," Jackie said. "Seven years this February, and I guess I'd do it again, if I had to." The look Steven gave Jackie told Laura that this was their regular banter. Jackie reached across the table, patted Laura's hand. "You know, you deserve happiness, too. More than anyone *I* know."

Laura glanced at Steven. Did he think so, too? If the sincerity in his eyes was any indication, he did. Laura ran her finger along the daisy print on the side of the glass. "Steven, I really am so sorry to hear about your parents. They meant a lot to me." She looked at Jackie. "You, too. Your parents were always there for me, and I know they paid for it. The whole damn town judged them for it, but they never let it show. Not with me, anyway. I just want both of you to know how much your families meant to me." Before either of them had a chance to respond, another horrible thought crossed Laura's mind. "Jackie, your parents—"

"They're great. Moved to Virginia, but they come visit a lot. I miss them."

"Good. I just wish I had been here to help after your parents passed away, Steven. After all you and your families did for me. . I should've been here."

Jackie squeezed Laura's hand three times—their old, secret way of saying *I love you.*

Steven cleared his throat. "It's okay. No one blames you for leaving, Laura. I mean, we didn't know if something else happened or if it was just that everything got to be too much. But we understood."

"You two…" Laura said, trying to hide the emotion in her voice. "You have no idea how much this means to me. I know I don't deserve your kindness. I just didn't expect you two to be so forgiving. But I should have known. Thank you. Truly."

"Dammit, Laura." Jackie grabbed a box of tissues off the shelf behind her. "You've got me crying now. You don't need to thank us. You, of all people, thanking us for forgiving you? You've had to forgive people your whole life."

Steven nodded. "She's right."

"Your childhood was…. You just…you had so many demands put on you," Jackie said. "You walked around every day with the weight of the world on your shoulders. I don't know if you ever realized this, but your kindness towards me, towards everybody, never wavered. Even when you were going through hell. I never got how you did that."

Laura shook her head. "I don't remember that. I was always in my own head. I never felt like I had time to consider other people's feelings, aside from my parents'."

"You were in your own head a lot, but you never failed to show us how much you appreciated everything. We knew you loved us. But how the hell were you not supposed to be in your head? I'm sorry, but it still pisses me off. What you were put through. What that woman did to you, to your father. How were you supposed to escape your own thoughts and fears and…shit, everything?"

Laura was suddenly so tired. She looked at the table, the pie, the dirty plates, anywhere that wasn't Jackie, because there was more truth there than she could take on right now. But she didn't want excuses made for her. Not by the people she had hurt most. And her damn tears. Jackie was cracking her exterior wide open, like a deep, gnarled fault. If they saw what was inside, they'd despise her.

"Is she listening?" Steven asked, gesturing toward Danlyn.

Laura checked. "She hasn't seen a TV in weeks. She's off the grid." She pressed her palms firmly on her thighs, bracing for impact.

"Why'd you leave like you did?" Steven asked.

Laura opened her mouth, then closed it.

"I know you and I weren't…speaking. But weren't you happy at Jackie's?" He shrugged. "I probably would've skipped "town, too, given everything. So no judgment. We've just always wondered. It was very sudden."

Words formed in Laura's mind, but none of them added up to what it was she wanted to convey. "I couldn't take anymore. My mother, my father's death. I couldn't handle it, and it seemed unfair to keep Danlyn around. Isn't the idea to give our children at least a little more than what we had? Besides, after my dad died, what did I have to stick around for? I know he had his issues, but I loved him. My mother certainly didn't want me here." She felt the sting of her own words and tried to fix it. "I mean, not that you weren't enough, Jackie. But how long was I really going to camp out in your room with a baby? It was time."

"We figured as much," Jackie said. "Your father was a good man. He had his issues, but he sure adored you. I know how hard you took his death. We just didn't know if something finally pushed you. You were there, then you weren't."

Laura fidgeted in her seat. There were too many exposed nerves. "I was always afraid his drinking would kill him, and then I'd be alone with my mother. I never thought it would actually happen, though. Not the way it did, at least."

"It was terrible, what happened with your father," Steven said. "I apologize for not being there for you during all that. I've never forgiven myself for that. I was too angry and immature, but I should've been there. When you left Jackie's, she was really broken up about it. You were like a sister to her. We both tried to work through it together." He rubbed Jackie's shoulder "She cried for weeks, and I blamed myself. I'm truly sorry I wasn't there for you. If I could go back and change that, I would."

The room was suddenly too small, and everyone's emotions were splayed out, like the jagged pieces of metal after a car crash.

Laura frowned. "You had every right to be furious with me, Steven. And Jackie, I never meant to hurt you. I had to get Danlyn and myself out of Rome. After I heard about my dad, I felt like I was going to lose my mind. I wasn't thinking. I just went on autopilot. I was so damn angry with him for allowing my mother to kick me out. I mean…you want to talk about guilt? I never spoke to my father after she threw us out. He tried but I refused, and then he was gone. How is a seventeen-year-old kid supposed to handle all that?" Laura asked, knowing no one had the answer. "I never meant to hurt either of you, and I missed you, too. I cried and cried. That's all I did for the longest time after I left. Then I found other ways to cope." She sniffed, wiped her nose with the back of her fist. "The day my dad died, he called your house, Jackie. Your mom kept giving me his messages, but I just ignored him. I was so pissed. Now I'll never get that chance back. Even when I drove back here, I couldn't bring myself to go anywhere near his apartment." Anger splashed across her face. "Such a stupid way to die. And had I been there, maybe I could've prevented his accident. I always took care of him when he was drunk. I'd kept him from falling down the stairs probably a hundred times. I could've stopped it. That's why I left so fast. I didn't even go to his funeral. It was my fault. I was selfish, and I didn't stop it from happening."

Jackie and Steven's expressions suddenly changed. Steven straightened in his chair as he glanced at Jackie.

Laura looked at Danlyn, still sitting on the sofa, quietly laughing at the TV, then at Steven. "What? What is it?" Laura had opened up too much, had exposed too much of herself, and now she needed to go, needed to give them back their peace. "I'm sorry. I shouldn't have said all that. Not here, when we were having such a nice evening. Listen, it's getting late. We'll get going—"

"No." Steven was louder than he meant to be. "Just sit. You didn't say anything wrong."

"Then what is it?"

Jackie gave Steven another look, then said to Laura, "You just…well…"

"I just what? You guys aren't very discreet. Something's wrong."

Steven lowered his voice. "You said your father's 'accident.'"

"Yeah." Laura shook her head. "I'm not following."

"No one ever talked to you after you left?"

"Talked to me about what?"

Steven reached his hand across the table, but Laura slowly pulled hers away. Her heart sped up as she searched his eyes. "Tell me," she whispered.

"Shortly after you left, there was a new…development in your father's case. They re-evaluated the cause of his death. I'm not even sure why." Steven paused for a beat. "They ruled it a suicide, Laura."

Laura went rigid, feeling suddenly as if she couldn't breathe. Her eyes darted between them.

"Please say something," Jackie said.

"No. No, no, no. My father was an alcoholic. He took painkillers for his knee, got drunk, fell down a flight of stairs. I don't know who told you something so stupid, but he never… No. That didn't happen."

"Maybe we shouldn't have told you tonight," Steven said. "But you had the right to know. I figured it'd be best coming from us, instead of your mother, or someone in town."

Laura wondered how Steven and Jackie had gotten this so wrong? Her voice softened, sounding almost dismissive. "I know you two are just looking out for me, but there's obviously been some kind of misunderstanding." She waited for them to agree. When they didn't, she said, "Suicide? Not William Hallow. My father thought that was weak. He had a friend who killed himself after they got back from Korea, and he always said how weak that was. He fell down a flight of stairs. Like I said, I kept him from falling at home all the time. I used to lock their bedroom door just so he couldn't get out when he was drunk." Laura paused. "And why would they re-evaluate an accident, anyway?"

"I have no idea," Steven said. "I'm not sure why things played out like they did. But from what I understand, your mother said she found a note...a suicide note in your father's apartment. This is where things get fuzzy. I don't know why they reevaluated the case. You know how information travels in small towns. Details are always left out, things always get twisted. But it definitely was ruled a suicide. I'm sorry, Laura. I wish I could tell you more. Maybe you can ask your mother?"

"So let me get this straight. My father overdosed, but then...supposedly threw himself down the stairs? On purpose?"

"We heard lots of rumors, but we don't know for sure. We're so sorry," Jackie said. "But Steven's right. God forbid you had heard it from Vivian, or even Frank."

"Frank?" Laura's voice was suddenly sharp. "You know Frank?"

"Laura, sweetie, we're here for you. If you just need time to process the news, it's okay—"

"Perfect." Danlyn turned around when Laura slapped the table. "Everyone knows about Frank. Everyone but me."

Jackie's expression strained. "If by *know* about him you mean his relationship with your mother, then yeah, that's old news."

"How long?" Laura's eyes smoldered as she thought of her mother and Frank. "How long have they been together?"

"About ten years," Jackie guessed. "It was pretty soon after you left that people started seeing them together. Not often, of course. Your mother keeps herself boarded up in that damn house as much as ever. But if we see her, we see Frank. Plus, he did some business with Steven. Just some orders and stuff." Jackie frowned. "I had no idea you didn't know any of this."

"If they got together after I left," Laura said, "why are they telling me I've known Frank since I was a kid? That he's an old family friend."

"I don't know why she'd say that," Jackie said. "I don't remember seeing him around here much until you left. You don't remember him at all?"

"No." Laura needed a drink. A drink she couldn't have. "But he's pretty damn sure I should remember him. I have no clue who he is, but he struts around, acting like we've been chumming it up since I was in diapers." She gave a brittle laugh. "This is perfect. I have no clue what the hell's been going on, and all the while Danlyn and I are living right under it." She stood up, walking toward Danlyn. "You two have been great, and it's certainly not your fault." She rubbed her head, brushed her hair behind her ears. "I apologize, Jackie. You cooked a wonderful meal and here I went and ruined it. I'm sorry. I gotta go. Come on, Danlyn."

"Is everything okay?" Danlyn asked. But Laura didn't hear her. She couldn't hear anything over the screaming in her head.

Jackie and Steven followed them to the door without speaking.

"Thanks for everything, you guys. And thanks for telling me about my father. But it's just not true." Laura threw her jacket on, got out her keys.

Jackie said, "We shouldn't have said anything."

Steven wrapped his arm around Jackie's shoulder and leaned in, grabbing Laura's hand. "Maybe you should stay. It's probably best that you not go home right now. Just give yourself some time to process everything."

Laura took a deep breath. God, she didn't want to take this out on them, and she did need time. But not here. Not with the only people in the whole world she cared about. "Thanks for the offer, but we can't stay. You two did nothing wrong. You've been the only ones who've told me the truth, and I'm sure I'll appreciate that later, but right now I need to be alone."

"No apology necessary. We get it," Steven assured her.

"Please come back, though," Jackie said. "Take some time, but don't stay away. We're here for you. You call any time, okay? And don't say anything to your mother tonight. Just give yourself some time."

Laura only nodded.

"Really, Laura. Promise me you'll leave it alone tonight." Jackie sounded just desperate enough to convince Laura that she ought to heed her warning.

"I promise," Laura said, and then, avoiding their worried looks, she walked out the door.

~

Laura ran as fast as she could to the car, with Danlyn barely keeping up. She yanked the door open and threw herself in. When the engine came to life after a couple sputters, she drove away but only made it a couple blocks before pulling over. She didn't want to do this in front of Danlyn, but it was coming, and not a damn thing could stop it.

Terrible sobs rose in her chest, her whole body shook. She wrapped her arms around herself and hung her head.

"What happened?" Danlyn asked.

But Laura couldn't speak.

Chapter 13

Monday morning was Danlyn's least favorite part of the week. It was the start of another five days of non-stop Vivian. She sat at the table in the kitchen, hands folded in front of her, ankles crossed, dark circles under her eyes. The morning started out as usual: five forty-five wake-up, bed made, teeth brushed, hair combed, teakettle prepped, all under Vivian's watch, who ran the day with the meticulousness of a drill sergeant.

Vivian made her tea while Danlyn silently waited at the table, straight as an arrow—no slouching. Vivian sat down, blowing on her tea, and then each of them waited in silence while the sun began to light the morning sky. Six thirty, on the nose, Vivian said, "Open the Bible to Matthew, chapter twenty-four."

Every school day started with reading aloud from the Bible. Never out of order. Danlyn yawned, fighting her eyelids. Vivian read for twenty-five minutes, then Danlyn read for twenty-five minutes. No explanations were given, no deciphering the complex words so that a child might understand them. The last ten minutes of the first hour were dedicated to prayer, and prayer meant repenting. Vivian repented for others, for Laura's sins, for her unborn bastard child, for her heathenism. Then she asked for the Lord to cleanse Danlyn's soul. Next it was Danlyn's turn, when she, too, asked for forgiveness. She didn't know how or when she had sinned, but what did that matter when there were threats of eternal damnation? Danlyn liked this part least. Vivian's God was scary, and when Vivian prayed, she was scary. By the end of the first hour, Danlyn was sapped of the strength required for the rigorous curriculum. And there wasn't even recess.

~

Laura untangled her legs from a heap of twisted blankets and sat up, looking at the clock. "Ah, crap." Oversleeping was bound to win her a lecture. She got up, stretched, knees popping, hips aching. She and Danlyn taking turns sleeping on the floor was taking its toll. She braced the side of the bed, heaved herself up. Additional aches and pains emerged. Her belly was growing, and accommodating to her ever-changing body proved to be a constant learning curve. When she got familiar with one uncomfortable sensation, another would sprout up.

"Pristine squares," she mumbled, foggy-eyed and fed up with Vivian's demands, but she folded the blankets to near perfection anyway. Danlyn's bed was already made. Pressed corners, seamless lines.

Laura sat on the edge of the bed, listening to the muffled voices coming from the kitchen below. She couldn't drag herself downstairs. After dinner with the Brenners, she'd kept her promise to Jackie and kept her distance from Vivian, spending the weekend driving all over God's creation, looking for work doing anything, anywhere. Now the town was wearing on her, and the lack of jobs was killing her hopes…and her savings.

She bent down, pulling her suitcase out from under the bed. Another *pop-pop-pop* from her back. She had been hiding her money in the same place for years, under a tear on the bottom panel of her suitcase. The secret compartment had served its purpose, keeping out prowling men, including Paul. One day she'd open an account, but that meant being in one place for longer than six months. One nervous glance at the door and then she counted and recounted. She sighed. "Fifteen hundred dollars." She shoved the money back into the hidden slot and saw the envelope from Paul. She factored that in, too. His one and only child support payment, and boy, wasn't he getting the easy end of the deal. She pulled out a change of clothes and tiptoed to the bathroom.

Laura was startled when she looked in the mirror. The reflection staring back at her was still unfamiliar. She thought she'd be used to the color in her cheeks and the extra weight on her frame, and how she even looked younger. But the woman she saw before her was someone else. She hadn't seen that shade of pink in her lips since she left home, and her eyes…they couldn't have always been that green. She hadn't paid back her sleep debt, though, and the circles under her eyes remained. She looked away from the mirror as she stripped off her pajamas. Some habits never die, and looking at her body—a body that had belonged to men who had used it for their own selfish needs—had been one of them. Even before she'd ever slept with a man, her body hadn't felt like her own, though she never knew why. She touched the small swelling of her belly, gently stroking her taught, smooth skin. Her body still didn't belong to her, but this was the first time in her life she didn't mind.

~

Laura paused at the doorway in front of the kitchen. She could just see Danlyn's back and her feet, silently tapping away on the floor. Poor kid needed a break. She tiptoed to the door, hoping Danlyn wouldn't notice and say good morning. She'd already made that mistake once, and Vivian had rewarded her with two extra hours of reading. Considering how touchy Vivian had been since their dinner with Steven and Jackie, the punishment would surely be worse.

Off on the job hunt, and then Laura and her daughter could spend time together.

"Viv!" Frank yelled from the family room. "I'm gonna fry up a steak, so don't get your panties in a bunch when I come in."

Laura froze in place, jaw clenched. She took her hand off the doorknob. Frank was usually gone by morning, but here he was, yelling, interrupting Danlyn's studies, all while Laura had to move around like a church mouse. Laura turned back around, trying to work the look of disgust from her face. Getting Danlyn out of there meant she'd have to play nice. Leaving her with Vivian was bad enough, but she'd be damned if Frank forced his way into Danlyn's life. This had been William's home, and he'd been Danlyn's family. If that meant Laura was jealous and petty, so what? Loyalty had to count for something. And if all that didn't matter, something in the fog told Laura not to trust Frank. Not to dream of it.

Frank's boots thumped across the dining-room floor and into the kitchen. Laura followed, moving in the other direction, to the other door leading to the kitchen, just in front of the stairs. She craned her neck and listened.

"Want a steak, sugar?" Frank asked.

Danlyn's feet stopped tapping.

"Quiet," Vivian hissed.

Laura held her breath, waiting to hear what the secret world on Hallows' Farm was like when no one thought she was listening.

"Shit!" Frank slammed the freezer door shut. "Where the hell are the steaks?"

Vivian's voice was as cool as ever. If she was angry, she hid it well. "I'm sorry, but you must've cooked them. I'll send Laura out to the market to pick some up later."

Laura's face twisted. An apology? Was this a joke? Frank had broken a handful of Vivian's rules, and *she* was apologizing? Laura shoved herself off the wall, walked into the kitchen, more curious than afraid. Frank was still standing in front of the refrigerator. Danlyn and Vivian were sitting at the table. All three of them turned around and looked at her. Only Danlyn smiled.

"What?" Vivian asked, not completely hiding her embarrassment.

"I was just going to make some coffee," Laura said. "Everything okay in here?"

Frank grabbed the urn off the counter and held it out to her.

Vivian straightened her back. "Is there a reason it wouldn't be?"

Laura shrugged. "Seems like a perfectly rational question to ask, especially considering your rules."

"Nothing that goes on in my home is any concern of yours. I don't believe Frank was talking to you. Did you hear your name?"

"Oh, I beg to differ." Laura stood behind Danlyn, placing her hands on her shoulders. "Danlyn is my concern, and if *he's* going to be yelling while she's trying to get work done, that is my business."

"Really?" Vivian leaned across the table. "Just like she was your concern when you were getting drunk every day?"

"Must you dredge up every mistake I've made, even when you can see that I'm trying so hard? You've got to beat me while I'm down?"

"Trying *so hard*? Not getting drunk every waking moment is trying *so hard*?" She looked at Frank. "Frank, poor Laura is trying so hard. Let's give her a medal."

"Don't worry, Mom. We all know what a terrible disappointment I've always been. But if you cut me a little slack, no one will mistake it for weakness. Jesus. A little compassion never killed anyone."

Vivian's finger shot out, aimed at Laura. "Don't you use that language in my home. You understand me, Laura Hallow?"

Laura threw her hands up. "Sorry. Okay? But if I'm working hard, staying sober—and yes, I am working hard—it's only fair that you back off. And maybe Frank here should follow the same rules. Danlyn doesn't need the yelling. I would know, because I used to do all the yelling, and the kid deserves a break."

Vivian slowly rose from the table and took a few steps toward Laura. Frank grabbed her waist from behind. "Sit down, sugar." He guided her to her chair, lowering her down with kid gloves. "Let me deal with her." He kissed the top of her head while she glared at Laura.

"You've got to be joking," Laura said under her breath.

Frank turned around, honing in on her. Danlyn looked up, watching them, her mouth hanging open like a trout's. Both Laura and Frank held their hands on their hips, squaring off. Laura stepped in front of Danlyn when he came closer.

Frank's voice was low. "I've been patient with you, Laura. I even stood up for you when you wanted to go to dinner with those people. But you're pushin' me now, girl. I'm glad you and Danlyn are here, but somethin' has gotta give. Your mama could use your help, but your mouth is another thing." Laura's lips parted, but he placed one finger in front of her face. "I said we don't need the mouth." He lowered his finger. "Now, let's get some things straight."

Laura clenched her hands into fists, feeling her anger take root and spread.

"First of all," he continued, "know your place. This is your mama's home, and I'll see to it that you respect her and me. Second, you'll leave it to your mama to decide what's best for Danlyn. You couldn't really manage that on your own, now could you?"

Hatred seared through every inch of Laura's body. Her heart beat furiously, like a ticking bomb.

"Last," Frank said, "if we're going to be a family—"

"Family?" Laura shouted. "We will *never* be a family." Her words bounced off the farthest corners of the kitchen. "You are no family of mine or Danlyn's, and my mother won't make any decisions for my daughter. She couldn't hack raising me, and she certainly as hell won't determine Danlyn's future."

Vivian's face turned screaming fire engine-red. Every vein on her forehead bulged, her eyes popped like orbs. She braced her hands on the edge of the table, pulled herself up. Her whole body eerily shook. Even her head seemed to vibrate. Hatred had a smell, and it was pouring from Vivian's flesh, stinking up the room.

Frank moved aside, opening up the space between him and Laura. There was no room to run and no time to do it in. Laura was planted firm. She had spoken up, and now it was time to pay the piper.

Vivian stopped in front of her. Her lips quivered, her mouth opened, but no sound came out. With the reflexes of a cat, Vivian raised her hand into the air. Before Laura could deflect the movement, Vivian drove a closed fist into her face, sending her knuckles rocketing into Laura's cheekbone. Danlyn screamed and leapt from her chair, racing to Laura's side as she dropped to her knees. Laura held her face with one hand and shielded her stomach with the other. Vivian had nothing on some of Laura's old boyfriends, but the blow still sent her brain bouncing against her skull, drowning her eyes and nose in that fuzzy, electric feeling that meant the lights had almost gone out.

"Don't hit my mom!" Danlyn screamed.

Vivian staggered back towards Frank.

Danlyn grabbed Laura's hand, prying it from her face. "Are you okay? Look at me."

"I'm fine," Laura whispered, reaching her arm around her shoulder.

"Your face," Danlyn gasped. "It's all red."

"Just help me up."

Danlyn grabbed under Laura's arms, helping as she gained her bearings.

"Why'd you do that to her?" Danlyn cried, staring at Vivian.

Vivian nestled into Frank's side, still silent, and there they stood, squared off at opposite ends of the kitchen: Frank and Vivian, Laura and Danlyn—glaring at each other while Laura caught her breath. Maybe it was the disorienting effect from the hit, but something breathed new life into Laura, and it felt good. With one punch, Vivian had disarmed herself, revealing the desperate woman behind the facade.

Laura pulled her shoulders back, raised her head, making damn sure not to shed a single tear. Her voice was cool, calm. "This is all you've got left," she told Vivian. "Your hands. Your fists. It's all you've got, because you've done everything else to me you could possibly do."

Frank tightened his hold on Vivian's shoulders. "That's enough, Laura," he said.

Laura glared at him. "And you. You told me you remember me as a child. If that's true, how can you stand here and tell me my mother should make decisions for Danlyn?"

"Your mama did her best. You were just such a strong-willed child. Your mama had to be just as strong."

"No, I wasn't. If you knew me at all, you'd know that. I was under her rule, completely. We all were. Strong-willed?" Laura laughed. "Is that what she told you?" Laura squeezed Danlyn's hand once, then took a small step forward.

"Our lives were centered around you," she said to Vivian. "You determined everything. Our happiness, our misery, down to the smallest things. You determined all of it. Dad and I…we existed to keep you sane."

Vivian growled through her teeth, "You barely remember anything. These are lies your father told you. He turned you against me."

"No, Mom. That man refused to say a bad thing about you. These aren't his memories. These are mine. Whether my memory goes back fifteen years or twenty-five, it doesn't matter, because it was all the same, every damn day. Whether you had locked yourself in Rose's room for months, threatening "to kill yourself, or managed to pull yourself out of bed only to terrorize us, it was the same. Every day with you was hell. We couldn't breathe in this house. You stifled the life out of everyone. You were a dictator. Happiness wasn't allowed, normalcy wasn't allowed, and Dad and I were never good enough. No matter what we did, we were always the cause of your misery, remember? You were going to kill yourself because God had cursed you with such a despicable child and unworthy husband."

"You wanna let it all out?" Frank said. "Come on, then. Tell us how bad you had it."

Laura ignored him, remaining focused on her mother. "You can hit me again, Mom. I don't care. You can go into your creepy world and pretend not to listen, but I'm not done. You owe it to me to hear me out."

Frank leaned back against the counter, dragging Vivian with him. "The floor's all yours," he said.

"What?" Vivian shot him a menacing look. "I'm not letting her speak to me like this."

"I think you've done enough here, Viv. Once she gets it out of her system, she'll pipe down. Then we can put this nonsense behind us."

"I have no interest in hearing this," Vivian spat, yanking herself out of Frank's arms. "I'll not have it. Isn't that what you just told her? That she's to respect my rul—"

"Jesus Christ," he yelled, yanking out a chair. "Sit down."

"Damn you, Frank," Vivian said. "You and Laura. Damn you both." She threw herself down in the chair.

"Now get on with it," Frank told Laura.

Laura's eyes bounced between them, thrown by the sudden shift. But she had Vivian where she wanted her.

"Why am I always the bad guy, Mom?" Laura didn't wait for an answer. "You remember what you did to us. Why the hell did we make you so miserable? Because I've thought about it. I used to spend most of my time trying to figure out what I did that was so wrong…what we could've done to make you happy." She paused, wishing Vivian would look at her. "But I never came up with anything. You were just a miserable, unhappy woman. You still are. You constantly threatened to kill yourself because you needed us to live in fear. You needed control. You locked yourself away, and when that got boring, you locked me in rooms, or in the basement. Remember that week, Mom? With me in the basement, begging to be let out? And now you want to take charge of Danlyn?"

"Once," Vivian said. "Just once. And you deserved it."

"How? You found a magazine in my room."

"Blasphemous garbage is what I found."

"Fashion, Mom! Dresses and clothes and makeup. That's all it was. Normal stuff that any fourteen-year-old girl would want to read about. But that was vain, right? And somehow I was going to find Jesus in all of your abuse. Funny thing though, I never found the Lord in a dark, cold basement. You pushed me away from God. You made him ugly. You made him terrifying. And all the while, there you were, with that emotionless stare. The same face I see right now. The same look, day after day. Because if life with you wasn't unbearable enough, there was that look on your face, letting me know that you felt no regret, that you hated me. We were dispensable. The family you were given to take all of your misery out on."

Laura had dug too deep, and maybe now she would cry because it stung and ached and burned so badly that she could barely breathe. But she wouldn't shed a tear for Vivian. She would cry for her father, and for Danlyn, because she loved them more than she could ever love herself.

"I raised myself. By the time you pushed Dad past the breaking point, I had learned how to care for myself. You never cared for me, and you certainly never made healthy decisions for me. So what is it you expect?" Laura looked back at Danlyn. Hearing all this couldn't be easy for her, but Laura needed her to know that everything would be okay. She gave her a smile, but Danlyn only cried when she saw her mother's battered cheek.

"What do you want from me?" Laura asked, looking back at Vivian. "'Cause I'll leave this minute if you expect me to see things your way. I'll never understand the liberties you take. The way you judge me, the way you hurt people. And I'll certainly never let you make every decision for Danlyn." She bent down, positioning her face in front of Vivian's. Vivian could zone out, but she was going to see her and hear her. "Isn't Danlyn my responsibility?" Laura placed her hand on her own chest. "*Mine*, and *mine* alone, right? Isn't that what you said the day you kicked us out?"

"Yes. She is *your* responsibility, and *yours* alone. But in my home, *I* determine the rules, no matter whose responsibility she is. If you don't like it, get—"

"Vivian," Frank said, lazily shoving off the cupboard behind him. "I know you haven't forgotten our little talk we had the other day, now have you?"

Vivian didn't look at him.

"You two had a bit of a spat," he went on. "But that's no reason for anyone to go runnin' off again. You need a place to stay, Laura. And you can use the help, Viv. You two need to just calm down and think about things."

Vivian stared ahead at Laura, looking like she was swallowing glass. "Fine," she said. "But you know my rules, Laura. You either live by them or you leave." Frank came up behind her, grabbed her shoulders. "You know my rules," she tried again. "You respect them and I'll—"

"Let us stay?" Laura looked at Frank. "Because you need us here, right? That's what all this is about. Someone's losing her grip and you can't do it alone. Otherwise our crap would be on the front yard right now, and the house wouldn't be plastered with little reminders."

Frank gave Laura a pleading look. Vivian was ready to erupt.

"All right, Mom. Luckily for you, I took after Dad. I'm not completely heartless. We'll stay here, help you out. And we'll respect your rules, within reason." Danlyn looked at Laura like she'd lost her mind. "But I have a demand of my own. You answer one question for me." Laura turned around, told Danlyn to go to her room. Danlyn grumbled something as she thundered up the stairs.

Fear and nausea bubbled up in Laura's chest, so much that she hadn't noticed how the mood in the room changed, how both Vivian and Frank tensed. But it registered, imprinting on her subconscious. "Why would Steven and Jackie say that Dad killed himself?"

There it was. Out in the open.

"Because he did," Vivian said, sounding neither mad nor relieved. Her posture eased.

"Dad never would've hurt himself."

"Ladies, I need to be gettin' on. I'll leave you to this," Frank said while walking out, winking at Vivian along the way. "See you two later."

Laura pulled out a chair and sat down. "How could you say that?"

"How could you say he'd never hurt himself? What do you call drinking a bottle of whiskey every night? Is that not hurting yourself? It's just a slower form of suicide, Laura."

"He wouldn't have taken his own life. Even you have to know that. Somewhere deep down, you have to know it doesn't make sense."

Vivian got up, walked to the sink. She grabbed a hand towel off the faucet and began wiping down the counters. "You loved him. That's why you can't fathom such a thing." She obsessively scrubbed at one spot. "Drunks do stupid, selfish things all the time. You, of all people, should know that. You always thought that man walked on water. You were blind." Vivian turned around. "Why the tears, Laura? It hurts knowing he wasn't so perfect after all, doesn't it?"

"I never thought he was perfect, but I knew he loved us. He always tried. I gave him credit for that. You're the one who was blind to any good he could do. Drunk or no drunk, it still makes no sense."

Wearing a disingenuous look of pity, Vivian made a *tsk-tsk* sound.

"Dad loved life. I know he drank, but when he was sober he loved life."

Vivian threw the rag in the sink. "Your father was overly optimistic. He didn't like to face reality, just like he never faced his drinking."

"He tried to be happy. You can't fault someone for that."

"He was oppressively optimistic, Laura. He was delusional. That man couldn't ground himself to the realities of life if someone had paid him."

Vivian wasn't wrong about that, but William's optimism was the only thing that had kept young Laura from spiraling into a depression all her own. Someone had to counteract Vivian's dark outlook.

"Exactly. He was overly optimistic, yet he killed himself? I mean, Jesus. Even in his worst, piss-poor drunken state, he would never—"

"Watch your tongue!" Vivian ordered.

"Fine. But don't you get what I'm saying?"

Vivian took a few steps closer, peering into her daughter's eyes. "Your father took his own life. You want to know why? You'll have to look elsewhere. I don't concern myself with that man or why he did what he did." She sat back down, opening up a textbook. "We're done here."

Laura was surprised Vivian had opened up as much as she had. But talking any more would mean talking to a brick wall. "Fine. I'll get Danlyn and we'll get out of here." Laura got up from the table.

"No one is hiring around here. You'd better think of another option. And you're not going anywhere with Danlyn. She needs to finish school."

"You're kidding, right?" Laura turned back around so Vivian could get a good look at her face. "I'm not leaving her here after what you did."

"Send her down, Laura." Vivian licked her finger, thumbed another page over in the book.

"I'm not leaving her alone with you. I don't care if that makes you angry."

The lift of Vivian's chin was smooth, her eyes icy.

"She's coming with me," Laura said. Then she lowered her face close to Vivian's and whispered in her ear, "You can fight me all day, but just know that the next time you hit, I'll hit back.

"And if you ever lay a finger on Danlyn, I'll kill you. I swear to Christ, I'll kill you. Those are my rules, Vivian Hallow."

Chapter 14

Jackie opened the door before Laura knocked. "Holy shit! What the hell happened to you?" She pulled Laura inside. Danlyn followed. "Shit, Laura. You promised."

"I didn't plan it. It just kind of happened." Laura brushed loose strands of hair out of Danlyn's eyes. "Maybe Jackie won't mind if you watch TV again."

"Of course not," Jackie said. "Go ahead, sweetie."

Danlyn hugged Laura so tight she could hardly breathe.

"It's okay, Danlyn. I'm just going in the kitchen. I'm fine, really."

Jackie rubbed Danlyn's shoulder. "We'll be right in the there. Just call if you need anything."

Danlyn reluctantly let go and sat in front of the TV, looking at the controller with no interest.

"She saw everything?" Jackie whispered, walking into the farthest corner of the kitchen. Laura nodded. "Because you asked about your dad?"

"No."

Jackie grabbed a bag of frozen peas from the freezer and placed them on Laura's cheek. "God, that looks awful. What the hell did she hit you with, an iron?"

"That bad?" Laura hadn't seen her face yet.

"How the heck did she manage this?"

"With her fist."

Jackie's eyes widened.

"We got in a fight about…" Laura had to think. "Frank, I guess. Everything, actually. Danlyn, Frank, the past…everything. Frank said something about us being a family and I went off on him, so she decked me. Put all one hundred and twenty pounds behind it, too."

"I can't believe she'd do that in front of Danlyn. Well, actually, I can, but… Since when does she care enough to stand up for anyone?"

"Since Frank's been leaving coffee at the house." Jackie looked confused. "She's been that way since I got back. You can't say a damn thing to him."

Jackie slowly shook her head. "The woman's insane, Laura. Do you have your things in the car?"

Laura had felt a lot of emotions that morning, but shame hadn't been one of them, until now. She looked away. "No. I told her I'd stay."

"What? Are you nuts?"

"Shh!" Laura pressed her finger to her lips.

"Sorry. But what the hell's wrong with you? You can't stay there. Especially not with Danlyn."

Laura knew that. Of course she knew that. But she needed a couple days. "She's sick, or something. I don't know what's going on, Jackie. She's got one hell of a temper on her now, but I can handle it."

Jackie laughed sarcastically. "Oh, yeah, clearly. I mean, it's written all over your face."

"No. I pushed it today. I won't do it again, and I definitely won't leave Danlyn there alone. But I can't leave yet. I need to…find some work." Jackie gave her that look. Laura hated that look. "She's not going to do it again, Jackie. I won't give her the chance. And stop looking at me like that."

"Fine. How should I look at you?" Jackie walked to the cupboard, pulled out a bottle. "Your face is pulped and you're sitting here looking like…like you're fine. How is that?" She shook the bottle. "Two or three aspirin?"

"None, thanks." Laura avoided Jackie's intense stare. "I'm okay because for the first time in my life, I spoke up. Even after she hit me, I didn't back down."

Jackie shook the bottle again. "At least take one. You're going to be sore."

"I don't want anything. My stomach is—"

"Still upset?" Jackie looked at her stomach, raised her eyebrows. "Okay, but when your face starts pounding like a damn jackhammer, you just let me know." She put the bottle back, slapped the counter. "So what's going on? I mean, really?"

"I don't know. All I do know is that she's crazier than she was before. She's…" Laura still couldn't place it. "Just not normal. Normal for her, I mean."

"You think she's going through the change? My mom went a little batshit when that happened."

The thought of Vivian succumbing to any natural process seemed odd. She was made of granite. Cold, hard granite with an evil vein.

"I don't think so. Who knows?" Laura tried not to let it show that her face was starting to hurt. "It doesn't feel that way, though. It's Frank. I've never seen her cling to someone like "that, or protect someone like she does him." She paused, thoughtfully weighing her words. "I hate him, Jackie. Like, deep down, ugly hatred."

"Don't get upset, but do you think it's jealousy? Because you miss your dad?"

"That's what I thought at first. Hell, I don't know. Maybe. But I'm missing something. Maybe I'm making things up in my head, but you always used to say to trust your gut. Remember?"

Jackie nodded.

"Well, something's not right with him. I can sense it."

Jackie seemed to consider this for a moment, then asked, "What'd she say about your dad?"

"Nothing." Laura flipped the peas over, gently placing them back on her cheek. "William was a drunk. William didn't appreciate life. Drank himself stupid. And in the end, killed himself." Laura tossed the peas on the counter. "Actually, she was pretty chatty about the whole thing. I figured she'd shoot me down before I finished saying his name. It was different. Like she felt guilty or something."

"She should feel guilty." Jackie leaned against the wall next to Laura. "She pushed him to—" she caught herself. "I'm sorry. I didn't mean to sound so casual. I just meant that—"

"It's okay, Jackie. I'm sorry for the way I reacted the other night. It's not your fault. I still don't believe it, though."

"Can I ask you something?"

"Go ahead." That didn't mean Jackie would get an answer.

"You never really said why you came back."

No. She wouldn't get an answer. At least not a full answer.

"As stupid as it sounds…" Laura hesitated. "I thought maybe things had changed. She's an old woman, for crying out loud. I didn't expect her to be Mary Poppins, but I hoped she wouldn't be so damn mean still. I overestimated her ability to "grow into something that resembles a human being. Plus, I had nowhere else to go."

"You can't blame yourself for hoping. There's nothing wrong with wanting a mother who loves you and cares about you."

"I guess. But I can feel like an idiot for hoping. I deserve everything I'm getting, and then some."

"Why would you say that?"

Laura shrugged. Jackie could never understand.

"Look at me," Jackie said. "The only stupid thing you've done is blame yourself. So you're human. You wanted your mom to change. That's not a crime, but you can't keep doing this, either. You and Danlyn are always welcome here. If you need a place to stay, don't hesitate, okay? I should drive out there and get your shit and hold you hostage here, but I'm trusting you to do right by yourself."

Laura couldn't shed another tear. She didn't think her headache could handle it, and her face was hurting so bad that the thought of tears gliding down her hot, swollen skin made her want to scream.

"You have no idea what that means to me, Jackie. I can't thank you enough for everything. But I would never do that to you and Steven. It would be—"

"It would be our pleasure. Just think about it, all right? The offer's there. And if she puts her hands on you again, or Danlyn, just leave. Come here."

Laura wrapped her arms around the woman whose love had kept her afloat for so many years. "Thank you for being my friend, Jackie."

"There's no need to thank me, silly. You're such a beautiful person. I love you."

"But I'm not beautiful. Whoever that girl was that you knew, that isn't me anymore. I haven't seen that girl since the day I left here."

"Laura, we've all done—"

"No." Laura pulled away. "You don't understand. When I left with Danlyn, things changed. They got bad. If you knew what I've done, the person I became, you wouldn't welcome me into your home."

"I know you're not perfect. None of us are. I believe you've made mistakes, but you need to hear me out. Don't take this the wrong way, but I don't know how you managed to stay sane in that house."

Couldn't Jackie see that she wasn't sane? She was a monster. A Vivian sequel in the making. Laura slapped, Vivian punched. Laura screamed, Vivian ranted. Laura drank, Vivian hated.

"I think any other child would've crumbled in that environment. If you can find me one person who's been through the hell you have and who's managed to be a model citizen, point them out. Until then, cut yourself some damn slack, Laura."

"But the things I've put—"

"Ah-ah-ah!" Jackie's hand went up. "Did you murder a village of children?"

"What?" Laura shook her head. Bad idea. Too much pain, too little aspirin. "No!"

"Did you take up running over puppies for sport?"

Laura tried not to laugh. "No."

"Were you the third gunman on the grassy knoll?" Laura rolled her eyes. "Okay. Clearly you didn't do anything so terrible that we need to call the authorities. I promise, I'll be there to listen, but first you're going to listen to me, you're going to let it "soak in, and when you're feeling a little better, we'll get out some shovels and start digging up your past."

Laura gave a half-smile. "Okay."

Jackie grabbed her hands, squeezing for emphasis. "You were bound to fall somewhere along the way, and from the sounds of it, you did. You had no one to show you how to pull off this whole mom gig. You're obviously remorseful for whatever you've done. Just know that we love you, and whatever you need, we're here. Take care of yourself and Danlyn." Jackie looked down at Laura's belly with an understanding smile Laura couldn't deny. "Take care of yourself, because you're no good to your children if you're putting yourself in danger."

Laura didn't argue. "Thank you so much, Jackie."

"Anytime, sweet cheeks."

"I actually do need something," Laura said.

"Out with it."

"After Steven's parents passed, did he get a copy of their death records?"

"Yeah. Why?"

Laura drew her shoulders back, took a deep breath. "I need to get my father's records."

"You sure? I mean, what if it doesn't help?"

"Doesn't matter. I need to see it, or I won't believe that he… I need closure."

Now Jackie was the one avoiding eye contact.

"What is it?" Laura asked.

"There were just lots of rumors about your father. We didn't say anything the other night because no one actually knew for sure, but…"

"But…?" Laura felt the knot in her stomach tighten.

"I suppose you'll find out when you track down the reports. From what we heard, your father didn't fall down stairs. It was a...a gunshot wound."

The words hit Laura like a hard slap. Nausea rose in her stomach.

"I just didn't want you alone, reading that on a piece of paper," Jackie said.

Laura looked dazed. "Where, Jackie? Where did you go for the records?" She reached into her pocket for her keys.

"Shit. I'm terrible at this. I shouldn't have... Just don't leave yet."

Laura pressed her. "Jackie, where?"

"At least let me come with you."

"Jackie?"

Jackie's shoulders dropped. She sighed. "Floyd County Hall of Records, right by City Hall."

Chapter 15

Laura and Danlyn entered a small building, and on the left was a door that read "Floyd County Hall of Records." Inside the office, everything was too small for such oppressive fluorescent overhead lighting. There was a long, gray counter, and behind it sat a very small, old woman with unnaturally silver hair that looked more blue than anything. Her red lipstick crawled up the deep wrinkles outlining her lips. She looked clownish, but her smile was warm.

The room was empty, aside from one other employee who sat at a desk in the corner of the small space. Laura couldn't see his face, only a balding head above the partition wall.

"Hi, doll," the old woman said, giving Laura a sympathetic look when she saw her bruised cheek. "How can I help you?"

Laura hesitated, then took one uneasy step forward.

The woman watched her for a moment. "You in the right place, honey?"

Laura looked around. "I…" The bald man popped his head over the partition. His nose was snout-like, his eyes were small and beady. Laura's mind switched back into gear. "Go sit down," she told Danlyn, pointing to the two chairs crowding the tiny waiting area. "I'm here to get a copy of my father's death certificate. Or an autopsy report, if that's available."

The old woman gave her a sad smile. Her deepening wrinkles made her look like a basset hound. "I'm sorry, honey. Let's see what we can find for you. What's the name?"

"William Daniel Hallow."

"I'll need to see your identification, honey." Laura pulled out her driver's license and the old woman said, "All right. You have a seat and I'll be right back."

~

Laura sat down in the chair opposite Danlyn's. "What're you reading?"

Danlyn lifted up a small pamphlet about the agricultural history of Floyd County. "Boring."

The corners of Laura's mouth turned up. "I'll second that. That's what your grandfather did before he left for the Korean War."

Danlyn switched gears, suddenly interested. "He was a farmer?"

"He was. He grew up near Rome, with his aunt and uncle. His uncle taught him everything about farming. That's why he married your grandmother. To save her father's farm."

"Hallows' Farm?" Danlyn asked. "What do you mean, that's why he married her? Didn't he love her?"

"God, yes. Very much. But that's not why they got married. They didn't even know each other when they got married."

Danlyn's eyes grew large. "How come they got married if they didn't know each other?"

If it hadn't been for Vivian holding their marriage over William's head every day, Laura would never have known the full story.

"When Vivian's father, Samuel Walker, died, it was just your grandmother and Rose on the farm. Their farm"—Laura nodded toward the pamphlet—"was one of the largest in Rome at the time, and Rose and Vivian couldn't do everything alone, especially since Rose was already really sick. Your grandfather's uncle Peter had done business with Samuel, and from what I was told, Peter and Samuel were friends, so when Samuel died, Peter figured he'd do the right thing and arrange for his nephew to marry Vivian. He could get the farm back in order and help Vivian and Rose. So…they got married."

"Wow," Danlyn said. "That's really weird. I wouldn't want to marry someone I didn't know."

"Same here. And apparently my mother felt the same way."

"She was mad?"

"Well," Laura looked back at the counter. Still no sign of the old woman. "Vivian never warmed to your grandfather. He tried and tried, but they were really young. He was only seventeen and she was fifteen."

Another shocked look from Danlyn.

"Between being forced to marry a man she didn't love and her mother being sick, my dad thought it was too much for her. She didn't talk much, wouldn't get close to anyone but Rose. But he always thought she'd come around. Little did he know that Vivian had always been that way. It was just her. Let's just say things got worse from there."

"Hey sweetie, you want to come over here?" the old woman asked from behind the counter.

A wave of sickening warmth hit Laura. "Be right back," she told Danlyn. As she walked to the counter, her eyes locked on the piece of paper in the woman's hand.

The old woman began reading as Laura reached her hand out to take the slip. "All reports pertaining to one William Daniel Hallow have been transferred to Polk County for re-evaluation." She handed Laura the paper, took the tiny glasses off her nose. "Are you sure your father lived here? Did he move before he passed?"

"I'm positive he lived here." Laura silently read the paper. "Less than five blocks from here." She shook her head. "I don't understand."

"Hmm…" The old woman pursed her lips. "I'm not sure why we don't have them, then."

"Aren't there any other reports at all? This makes no sense. He lived here, he died here. Why are his records in Polk County? And why did they need to be re-evaluated?"

"I wish I could help you, but I really don't know. They should be here. They were at one point. But if someone put this in his file"—she pointed to the paper—"that means they're at Polk County."

"Can you tell me why someone's records might be sent somewhere else to be re-evaluated?" She spotted a name on the slip. "It says his files were requested by Benjamin Day, at the Polk County Hall of Records. Do you have a phone number for this guy?"

The old woman turned around. "Hey, Bob, do you know if that young man Mr. Day is still working in Polk County?"

"I don't know," he yelled back from behind the partition wall. "He might've quit. That was a few years back. I'm not sure, though."

The old woman huffed, turned back around. "I'm sure you can go to Polk County and pick up his records. They should be able to tell you why everything was sent there. I'm real sorry, honey. There's usually more in someone's records, and it's pretty rare that things get shuffled around like this. All I know is they must've had a reason to transfer them."

Anger was taking over where apprehension had just been. "Might this have been at the request of a family member?" Laura asked.

"That'd be strange. But it's possible."

Laura folded the paper, shoved it in her pocket. "Can you please tell me how to get to the Polk County Hall of Records?"

~

Laura crept to a stop in front of the house. It was dark, but she could just make out the outline of Frank's truck. Dammit. She needed to get inside and to the phone. Her brain was buzzing with adrenaline; her thoughts were moving a hundred miles an hour.

Danlyn mumbled something, but Laura didn't hear her. She'd stopped listening to everything when they stopped for dinner in Polk County and she read the reports over a roast beef sandwich she never touched. She was lost in a whirl of words that made too little sense and results that didn't add up, no matter how she arranged them.

"Mom?"

"What?" Laura was rattled back to the present.

"I said I don't want to stay here."

The pain on Danlyn's face cut deep. "I promise, we won't be here too much longer. Just hang in there for me. Can you do that?"

Danlyn made a guttural noise. "I guess so."

"And please, Danlyn, don't say a word about where we went today. Just say I was looking for work."

Danlyn looked up at the house. "She's going to ask me."

"I know," Laura sighed. "But just let me do the talking."

~

Laura and Danlyn crept up the porch, opened the door, and tiptoed through the foyer while scanning the adjoining rooms. Laura didn't see or hear Frank. He was too loud to go unnoticed. Vivian, on the other hand, could be lurking anywhere.

"Go upstairs and shut the door," Laura whispered, switching on the lamp in the living room. But still there was no sign of anyone. The kitchen was empty, too. This was her chance. One quick call.

Picking up the pistachio-green phone off the wall, Laura punched in Jackie's number and huddled in the corner. On the third ring, she answered.

"Jackie, I got the reports."

"Laura? I can barely hear you." Jackie yelled at Steven to turn down the TV. "Okay, did you say you got the reports?"

"Yes, and none of it makes sense. To begin with, the records were sent to Polk County, and—"

"Polk County?"

"Yes, Polk County. And Jackie"—Laura's voice lifted with relief—"he didn't do it. He didn't kill himself."

"What? How do you know? What does it say?"

"The first report was inconclusive." Laura dropped her voice. "The second one, the one done in Polk County, says that it was a suicide, but that's not all…"

"Why don't you and Danlyn come over?"

"I can't. Not right now. I've got to figure this out."

"You can do that here," Jackie insisted.

"I would, Jackie. I want to. But—" The basement door opened and Laura spun around, gasping.

"Hey there, sugar." Frank, right there, in front of her.

Laura turned around, trying to speak in a casual tone. "Well, I'm glad everything's going well. It was nice talking to you."

Jackie whispered, "Is that Frank?"

Another casual answer from Laura. "Yep."

"Come by tomorrow. And stay out of your mother's way."

Laura could feel Frank standing over her shoulder. "Will do," she said, then hung up the phone, wearing a manufactured smile.

"Who was that?" Frank said, grinning.

Laura looked back at the phone, waving her hand dismissively through the air. "Oh, just a friendly woman I met earlier. She's pregnant, too." God, she was a terrible liar.

"I see. So…" He placed his fingertips on her stomach. "How's the little one doin'?"

Laura stepped back, guarding her stomach with her hands.

"Touchy, are we?" Frank laughed.

She looked around his shoulder. "Where's my mother?"

"She's tired. She's upstairs resting."

Frank came closer, moving in such a way that a chill ran down Laura's spine. "I'm going to bed," she told him. "Good night." She turned around, hoping it would be that easy, but nothing on Hallows' Farm was ever easy. She felt Frank's hand on her shoulder, and just as she spun around, promising herself that she wouldn't lose it again, he hugged her, whispering his hot breath in her ear.

"I'm sorry, Laura. You look like you've had a rough day. This stuff with your mama will blow over."

She pried her hands between his chest and hers, pushing him away without making a production of it. "I asked you not to touch me, Frank. Can you *please* respect that?" It nearly killed her to ask him so politely, but if she didn't want Vivian coming down, she'd have to play nicely with the other kids.

Frank raised his brows. "Guess all them hormones are makin' you sensitive, huh?" He pulled out a chair. "You're lookin' a little peaked. Why don't you take a load off?"

The guy didn't listen.

"I do not want to sit. I just want to go to bed."

Frank sat down in the chair instead, leaned back. "Well, hit the sack, then."

Laura walked away, more than happy to let him use her hormones as an excuse. So long as it got her away from him, she'd ride that train all the way out of this house and out of this town. She stopped halfway up the stairs, bracing herself on the banister. Her head felt so light, her legs so heavy. She heaved herself up another step. She was badly out of breath and her stomach was beginning to cramp.

"Good night, sugar," Frank said.

Laura turned around and saw him looking up at her from the bottom of the stairs. Screw fatigue. She jogged up the remaining stairs and disappeared into her room.

Chapter 16

Laura and Danlyn pulled up in front of the Brenners' house at eight in the morning. The sun was shining and white, bulbous clouds ascended into the sky. Laura knocked on the door, ready to see an eager Jackie on the other side, but Steven answered, sporting puffy eyes and a red nose.

"Laura?"

Shit-shit-shit. Laura turned away, hiding her bruised cheek.

"Hey. Is Jackie here?" Just like a child, asking if her friend could play.

Steven cinched his robe tight around his waist, rubbed his hands together. "No"—he moved aside—"but come in, it's freezing."

"Sorry. I didn't mean to bother you." She turned to leave. "I'll come back later."

Steven grabbed the hood of her sweater, gave her a tug. "I won't bite, Laura. Get your butt in here." He opened the door wide. "She went to get cough syrup for me. Just wait here."

Laura reluctantly turned around, allowing her sweeping hair to hide the bruise.

"Can I offer you some coffee?"

She stepped inside. "No thanks." She peered out the front window. "Did Jackie just leave?"

Steven shook his head. "You're worse than a kid, you know that? Just relax. And Danlyn, there's bacon and eggs in the kitchen. You're more than welcome."

Danlyn's eyes brightened. "Bacon?"

"Plates are in the cupboard next to the fridge. Eat all you want."

Danlyn thanked him and trotted off, leaving them alone.

Steven picked up his cup of coffee from the end table and took a sip, cringing as he swallowed. "She's not in school?"

"No. My mother was homeschooling her, but that's not going to work. I've got to figure something else out. She'll have a conniption fit if I put Danlyn in public school."

"Ah, yes. None of that pesky interaction."

"Yep. You know Vivian. Wouldn't want Danlyn picking up any nasty bugs from the other kids. Like social skills. Or happiness."

Steven laughed. Laura smiled awkwardly.

"Well," he said, "she sure is a sweet kid. She looks a lot like you, too."

"You think?"

"Oh, yeah. She's nearly as tall as you, too. I guess she didn't get that from you. Her father must've been—" he stopped abruptly.

Laura chewed her lip, looked at the floor.

Steven stepped back with a short sigh and set his coffee down. "I'm sorry. That was stupid." He shoved his hands in the pockets of his robe. "I don't want to make you feel uncomfortable."

Laura looked at him sideways. "I'm just glad it wasn't me. And besides"—she managed a small laugh—"you're sick, and you look like shit, so I guess you're allowed to fumble."

"That's no excuse. Leave it to me to put my foot in my mouth."

"It's no problem, Steven. Really. And thank you."

He clapped his hands together. "So how about that coffee? I was just going to get a refill."

"That's okay. I've got an appointment with my doctor at ten. Gotta get going soon." She swung her hair around again. It was starting to look like a nervous tic.

Steven lowered his voice. "Jackie told me everything, so you can stop hiding your face."

Of course Jackie had told him. That's what married couples did. Laura felt foolish. She turned around, exposing the eggplant bruise on her cheek.

"Jesus," Steven whispered, his jaw set. "She told me it was bad, but she didn't say it was that bad."

"It wasn't yesterday. It looks worse than it is."

"Jackie also told me she offered for you and Danlyn to stay here."

Laura looked away, embarrassed by the conversation and the damn bruise on her face and the pity on his.

"I just want you to know that it's not just Jackie's offer. It's *our* offer. After all these years, it still hurts to see you like this." He walked to the sofa, sat down. "I think I'll pass on coffee, too." He pointed at the chair next to the sofa. "Can we talk?"

Laura perched herself on the edge of the cushion. She felt like a pathetic dog, sitting in a pound, with big, weepy eyes, waiting for someone to rescue her. But did her ex have to be the one signing the adoption papers?

Steven leaned forward, resting his elbows on his knees. "I meant what I said. If there's any way we can help you and Danlyn, we want to. Please don't worry that it'll be weird if you stay here. When I actually sleep, my foot-in-mouth syndrome doesn't flare up so much." Now they both smiled. "I guess neither of us know what to say. I know that's why you didn't want to come here. You know, when Jackie first saw you at the market."

"You're right," Laura admitted. "I was uncomfortable. But, hell, who'd have thought we'd be sitting here, ten years later?"

"Not me. It's strange, isn't it? But there are no hard feelings. I can tell you don't quite believe that. I get it. A lot of shitty things happened back then, but that was a long time ago. I've had years to get over it. After you left, I think what bothered me most was that you thought I hated you. But I never did."

This was an opportunity for a conversation Laura had always wished for but never thought possible. She hadn't expected his vulnerability, and she wanted to meet him there, in the middle, but she'd hurt him so badly. What if she couldn't find the words to make it better?

"Steven, I feel so terrible about everything that happened. Always have. You had every right to hate me. I just couldn't bring myself to see you or talk to you." She dabbed at the corners of her eyes, then looked away. If she saw pain in his eyes, she'd fall to pieces. "I never meant to hurt you. I never would have. I mean…" Her voice faded into nothing, because there was nothing to say.

The lines on Steven's face deepened. "I was mad at you back then. But I was more hurt than anything. I'd never felt so confused in my whole life." He let out a tired laugh. "You never knew this, but before everything happened, I went out and bought a ring."

His words rang in Laura's head. She raised her hand to cover her eyes, because now she would cry.

"It was just this cheap little thing," he said. "But I was proud of it." He laughed again, but the weary look was back on his face.

Laura had to tell herself to breathe. Why would he tell her this now? She had had the same plans for them: marriage, a family, happily ever after, and she knew he did, too. But hearing it aloud… She couldn't bring herself to say more because if she did, she might never stop, and then everything might come out—every horror, every agonizing truth—the very truth she tried to drown every night in a bottle of liquor. All she could say was, "I'm sorry."

"There's something I've always wondered," Steven said, looking serious now.

Laura couldn't will herself to speak. She just nodded, slowly and uncertain.

"Why wasn't it me? You were always so serious about waiting for marriage, waiting for the right time. What changed?"

Steven was right. She had wanted to get married first, and he had waited for nearly four years. She had thought the idea was romantic; how special their marriage night would be. Only that never happened, and now nothing in the world could bring her to tell him what had really taken place all those years ago. She had made a promise never to tell, even if the thought of lying to him again broke her heart.

"It was a bad situation," she finally said. "All I can tell you is that I loved you. I loved you so much, and I would have done anything for you. I wanted it to be you. I wanted all of it. But things just…got mixed up. But you have Jackie now, and she's got you, and that makes me unbelievably happy. It really does. Just knowing something wonderful came from this."

"Can I ask something else? Did I know him, Danlyn's father?"

"No." The lie tasted bitter on her lips.

"How did you hide it? All that time we were together, how did I not know? Because I've convinced myself that I must've been the stupidest kid in the world. Even for a seventeen-year-old boy, how do you not notice your girlfriend's pregnant?"

"I promise you, you were never stupid. My mother made sure to hide it well. No one knew. Not you, not Jackie, not the school."

Steven took hold of her hands. He stood up, pulling her up with him, wrapping her in his arms. "I'm not angry anymore. I forgave you a long time ago. So if you need our help, don't hesitate."

Laura closed her eyes, sinking into his words. She didn't know how much she had needed his forgiveness until now. "Thank you, Steven."

The door opened and Jackie walked in, fumbling with her keys and the two bags in her arms. Laura backed away from Steven, like a kid caught with her hand in the cookie jar. The last thing she wanted was Jackie getting the wrong impression.

Danlyn turned around, waving happily. "Hi, Jackie!"

"Hey there, Danlyn. How're you, sweetie?"

"Good," Danlyn said with a mouthful of eggs.

Jackie rushed to Laura's side. "Thank God you're here." She placed her palm on Steven's forehead. "You're still hot.

"Sorry I took so long, but ol' Chatty Pants at the store wouldn't let me go. Thought you had malaria or something. Go lie down. I'll put these away and bring your medicine in soon." Jackie kissed him on the cheek; he ran his finger along her nose.

"I'm actually not feeling too tired," he said. "I'll put the bags away."

Jackie pulled Laura back down and sat beside her on the sofa. "Okay, tell me everything." She paused. "Wait… Did I miss something? You okay?"

Steven hollered on his way into the kitchen, "She'll be all right. We had a good talk. Then I hugged her. The shock should wear off soon."

"Thank God!" Jackie beamed. "I'm so happy you two hashed everything out. Now we can move on." Her smile abruptly fell flat. "But back to the report. What'd it say?"

Jackie wasn't wasting time, and Laura was still in a fog. From infidelity to engagement rings to her dead father.

"Um…" Laura patted her pockets. "Damn. I left the papers in the car." She looked at her watch. "Actually, I've gotta go, but I nearly memorized everything. Walk with me to the door. Oh, and"—she called Danlyn—"when you're done, wash your plate and cup. Don't just rinse. Wash. And clean the other plates off the table while you're at it."

Danlyn nodded while sluggishly getting to work.

"Okay," Laura said. "That bought us a minute. So—"

"Wait." Jackie called for Steven. When he strolled up beside her, the three of them stood huddled in front of the door.

"Geez, where to begin?" Laura thought for a moment. "First of all, I went to the Floyd County Hall of Records. To make a long story short, they told me my dad's records had been transferred to Polk County for re-evaluation and—"

"Yeah, I heard that part," Jackie said. "But why?"

"I still have no idea. No one could tell me why, and apparently there's no way to find out, either. Those people are inept."

"How could they not know why?" Steven asked. "They keep records of all those things."

"You'd think," Laura agreed. "But apparently there was a change in the way their records are kept. Something about switching to computers. I guess some of the records got lost in the process. Plus, the man who requested the transfer doesn't work there anymore. Hasn't in years. So there's no asking him. The guy I talked to said that if someone's remains are transferred it's usually because they need more advanced testing. Floyd County doesn't have the technology Polk County does. But the strange part, aside from there being no notes in his records, is that it doesn't look like his body was transferred there. There was a request for a transfer of the paperwork, but no request for a transfer of his remains. So unless someone lost that, too, just his records were sent there." Laura watched their expressions change from confused to bewildered. "You two look the way I felt yesterday. That place is ridiculous."

Jackie told Steven, "Remind me not to mysteriously die in Polk County. You'll never find out what happened."

"Yeah, well, that's not the worst part," Laura said. "I read all the reports, over and over. Nothing adds up, you guys. The autopsy report, the one done here, says that he died from a GSW. I'm assuming that means gunshot wound."

Steven nodded. "Right."

"But nothing about suicide. It also said a lot more. So much of it was written in abbreviations, but I made out most of it. It said he also sustained several significant wounds to his ribs, head, and wrist. Deep abrasions and possible bone fractures. It "said right on the paperwork that a blood and tissue analysis was needed on a sample taken from under his nails. Wouldn't that suggest there was something under his nails that sparked interest? Say...from a struggle?" Both Jackie and Steven frowned.

"But Polk County's coroner—the one who requested that the files be sent there—said that he died from a self-inflicted gunshot wound to the head. There are no pathology reports. No labs. Nothing." Laura paused, waiting for them to digest everything. "Two reports, one with proof of an autopsy, one without. Whoever did the actual autopsy, here in Rome, didn't think it was a suicide, or else it would have said so. Then the next guy from Polk County says it's a suicide, possibly without having even seen my father's body. How can two different coroners have such conflicting reports? And if the second examiner never saw his body, how the hell could he rule it a suicide?"

"Wait," Jackie said. "So the second report just said the first report was...what...inconclusive?"

"Not exactly. *Flawed.* The man who re-evaluated the findings said the report from Floyd County was flawed, and that the other wounds weren't consistent with the time of death. That they had been sustained prior to my father's death and shouldn't be factored in. Something like that. But the timing's all wrong. The request for the records transfer was sent four days after he died. The exam here was done within the first twenty-four hours after he died. If Polk County did do an autopsy and just lost the transfer slip, how's a postponed autopsy as reliable as the first one? And the request to test the tissue under his nails...it was never done. If remains are sometimes sent there for more advanced testing, why wasn't that done?"

Laura stared at the floor, still working the puzzle pieces around. She nodded once, now looking determined. "Someone killed my father."

That brought Steven to attention. Jackie's mouth went slack.

"There's got to be another explanation," Jackie told her. "You can't torture yourself like this, thinking these kinds of things. Polk County definitely fucked up, but I think you're jumping ahead of yourself."

"I'm sure Jackie's right," Steven said. "There has to be another explanation." But something in his expression told Laura he didn't quite believe that.

"What else am I supposed to think?" Laura asked. "Can either of you tell me I'm crazy for thinking this?"

"No one thinks you're crazy," Steven said. "If it were me, I can't imagine what I'd think. It's ridiculous that no one can give you any answers, but that doesn't mean it's gotta be the worst possible thing. I'm not saying you're wrong, but there's no reason to jump to a conclusion that severe. At least not yet."

"What do you mean *not yet?*" Jackie asked. "Not ever! There's no need to ever think that way."

"Yeah, maybe you're right, Jackie," Laura said. "But it's impossible to know for sure. I can't ask my mother. It went so well the last time." Laura took a deep, broken breath. The exhaustion was taking its toll. "Anyway, I'll let you know what comes of this. But I've gotta run. I have an appointment."

"We can watch Danlyn," Jackie said.

"That would be great, actually. I appreciate it."

Jackie rubbed Laura's shoulder. "Are you okay?"

"I'm fine. Just been feeling a lot of pain, and I've avoided doctors long enough." Laura rolled her keychain around on her finger. She paused a moment, looked at Steven. "Our talk meant a lot to me."

"Me, too," he said. "I can't tell you to leave this stuff with your father alone, but try not to drive yourself crazy with it."

"You're right. I can't leave this alone."

"I can at least drive you," Jackie offered. "You don't look so good."

"I'll be fine. Besides, you're helping enough by watching Danlyn."

Jackie hesitated. "All right. We'll see you when you're done, then?"

"Yeah." Laura called for Danlyn.

"Are we leaving?" Danlyn asked when she reached the door.

"Actually, how would you like to hang out here for a little while? Just while I go see the doctor?"

"That'd be good. But you won't be long, right?"

"Shouldn't be."

Danlyn hugged Laura goodbye before heading back into the kitchen to finish cleaning up.

"Danlyn really adores you two," Laura said as she opened the door to leave. Jackie and Steven beamed. "So do I."

~

Once Laura left, Jackie leaned back into Steven's arms. "God, I don't know what to say to her."

Steven spoke quietly, "All we can do is be here for her."

Jackie craned her head around and gave him a soft kiss.

"She's pregnant, isn't she?" he asked. Jackie looked stunned. "I'm not going to say anything, Jacks."

"Was it that obvious? She never actually told me. I implied it and she didn't argue, but she never actually said it."

Steven raised his brows. "Fool me once…"

Chapter 17

Laura walked into a small, quaint office. Two other women with bellies like globes sat in the waiting room, glowing and pink. Poster women for the happy, bouncing mommy-to-be.

"Do you have an appointment?" the woman behind the counter asked Laura, her cheery disposition matching the brightly painted walls.

"At ten, with Dr. Murray." Laura kept her face hidden.

The woman handed her a clipboard with several papers. "Fill this out and bring it back when you're called. And since we'll be seeing you again, I'm Janet. It's nice to meet you."

Laura felt like the new kid in school. She sat down on a small sofa next to the window, opposite the other mothers, and flipped through the papers, all so blank, all so intimidating, like some passive-aggressive interrogation. She nervously tapped the pen on the clipboard. Name of father? She jotted down Paul's name but left out his contact information. Ever received obstetric care before? Date of first menses? How long had she been sexually active? Had she received yearly exams? How many pregnancies? History of miscarriage? Alcohol abuse? Substance abuse?

Laura rubbed her temples. She looked around the room like a child trying to cheat off a classmate's exam, her pen still tapping away. She was failing before she'd even started the test.

"You nervous?" a young woman across the room asked. Her bulbous belly bounced along with each adorable hiccup of laughter. She had blonde, wispy hair, and a light breeziness filled the space around her. The morning sun pouring through the window reflected off her hair, making Laura think of lemonade.

Laura wasn't lemonade. She was black coffee.

"That obvious?" Laura asked.

"This your first?"

"No." Laura flushed.

"Why so nervous then?" The woman was cute and clueless and rubbed her belly in that precious way Laura only did behind closed doors.

"It's just been a while. Out of practice."

The young woman leaned forward as much as her belly would allow. "You'll be fine. Dr. Murray's the best. He's been my doctor since my first, and this is our third. Both boys. I'm hoping this one is my little princess."

"Lord." The woman didn't look old enough to have one child, let alone three.

"Yep," the woman laughed. "I met my Michael when I was fourteen and got pregnant with our first before the wedding. Got married at seventeen and have been having babies ever since. Already planning our fourth...and then maybe our fifth."

This young woman wasn't happy. She was clinically insane.

"But really, you'll love Dr. Murray. He's like Santa Claus, but with a shorter beard and not so fat. He's from California. Really open-minded. Not like a lot of the other doctors in Rome."

In fact, Laura did know he was from California. That's why she had decided to see him. He wasn't from here, he didn't know her family, didn't know Vivian Hallow. That meant Laura could tell all her truths.

The door to Laura's left opened and a tall, grizzly-looking woman holding a clipboard called her name. Laura got up, followed the nurse back into a hallway, full of more bright colors and cute pictures of babies. All the images, all the joy— none of these things reflected Laura's memories of Danlyn's birth. Her memories were not painted in soft pastels; there were no baby showers with plush teddy bears and pink balloons. There was only sadness and silence, then guilt and shame.

"Right in here, Ms. Hallow. Go ahead and sit."

Laura walked into a light blue room and sat on the edge of the exam table. The nurse took her blood pressure and weight, then scribbled down the information.

"There's a gown behind you. Take everything off. Dr. Murray's just finishing with another patient."

Laura waited for the door to shut and closed her eyes. Dear God, what was Dr. Murray going to think of her when he heard her story?

Chapter 18

The sun fell behind a thick layer of dark clouds, the air was heavy with moisture and the earthy smell of rain. Low thunder rumbled in the distance. Laura sped the car up. The silence between her and Danlyn was maddening. Laura knew why. She could see the question held captive behind Danlyn's sealed lips and the worry in her eyes. Was the baby okay? But Danlyn didn't say a word, and Laura was too preoccupied with Dr. Murray's warning. The baby sounded great. Everything seemed to be on track. But Laura was underweight and in great need of good sleep. Oh, and didn't she know she was under too much stress? He'd spent nearly an hour with her and had sent her home with lists and pamphlets and his personal number, just in case the cramping got worse or she found herself with more questions. But for the time being, stress reduction was key and good nutrition was a must. Luckily the woman in the waiting room had been right. Laura had felt more at ease with Dr. Murray than she had with any other man since her father.

When Laura turned left, bouncing along the driveway and rolling to a slow stop along the side of the house, her shoulders relaxed. Frank's truck wasn't there, and maybe that meant Vivian wasn't, either.

"Okay, kid. Get in there and wash up. I'll start making dinner. We're eating really healthy tonight. Doctor's orders."

Danlyn opened the door, looked back over her shoulder. Laura waited for the question that hung suspended in the car, but Danlyn turned away, shutting the door behind her. Laura followed behind, slowly taking each step up the porch, breathing in the sweet smell of impending rain. The trees gently swayed with the growing wind, the sky deepened, blending into gray-and-black milky tones. Everything was so calm. Even the thunder sounded like a serene chorus. Then came the rain.

~

"Hello?" Laura called into the dark house.

Danlyn moved past her, into the foyer, and disappeared up the dark staircase.

"Hello?" Laura called again. Still no answer. She flipped the lights on in the kitchen, filling the room with a dull glow. Thunder roared closer, breathing down the neck of the house. Just as Laura turned on the sink to wash her hands, the power went out and the kitchen went dark. Her skin instantly chilled.

Dark corners in a house of horrors.

Laura walked out of the kitchen, looked up to the top of the stairs. The second story stood out like a black abyss. One step at a time, she crept up the stairs. Deep, guttural thunder rumbled overhead now. She could almost feel the storm pulling in energy from around her, from the house, from the very steps she stood upon. Then she thought of her mother. Vivian was a storm; a raging force that gained strength from her surroundings and left ill prepared bystanders vulnerable to her destruction. Like a tornado that devoured everything in its path and left massive, jagged trails in its wake, Vivian had left jagged scars on Laura's childhood. At least a storm couldn't think, couldn't manipulate, couldn't strategize.

"Danlyn?"

Laura's breaths quickened as she reached the top landing. She couldn't see a thing, but she knew her grandmother's room was to her left. The room Rose died in. The room Danlyn was born in. The untouched room that stood as a testament to the home's history. She could almost smell the stagnant, musty air wafting from under the door. A mixture of dust and lavender and sorrow. Laura touched the cold brass doorknob, knowing it would be locked, bolted away with the rest of the Hallows' history. Memories of long days, weeks, even months when Vivian locked herself inside, promising that each day would be her last, lined the walls, seeped into the floor, clung to the curtains. Laura twisted the knob, slowly working it under her fingers. Then the door unlatched, opening a crack. Startled, she yanked her hand back, slamming the door closed.

She grabbed her chest and yelled, "Danlyn?"

"What?"

The bathroom door opened. Laura could see Danlyn's outline in front of her. The faint light from the bathroom window spilled in around her.

"You okay, Mom?"

"Yeah. I just… Nothing. Never mind." Laura turned back toward the stairs. "I'll light some candles in the kitchen and start chopping the vegetables."

~

Smoke rose in a swirl above the match. Small candles dotted the kitchen counter. Laura rinsed the carrots and spinach and got to cutting, and Danlyn sat at the table behind her, watching the shadows cast by the flickering flames dance along the walls.

"What're you thinking about?" Laura asked.

"Those boring history books grandma made me read. You know, people used to use candles all the time, before electricity. That's all they had."

"That's true." Laura looked over her shoulder. "Can you imagine?"

"No." Danlyn fell silent for a moment, then said, "And women used to have babies at home, without any help. Kind of like you did with me."

Laura put down the knife, turned around. "Do you want to talk about it? I can tell you what happened today."

Danlyn tilted her head to the side. "I don't know." She ran her finger along the edge of the table. "I do. But not if it's bad."

Laura tilted her head to meet Danlyn's eyes. "Would it help to know that you'll be meeting your little brother or sister on June fourth?"

Danlyn rushed from her seat and threw her weight into Laura, almost knocking her over. "Really?" she squealed.

"Really." Laura wrapped her arms around her, planting kisses on the top of her head. When Danlyn looked up at her, Laura saw something in Danlyn's eyes she'd never seen before. Trust. Without apprehension or doubt, Danlyn held tightly to Laura, their tiniest family member nestled between them. Amidst all the turmoil and pain and recovery, this moment reacquainted Laura with a hope she had barely remembered existed.

"The doctor thinks everything is okay. I just need to rest and learn to chill out."

Danlyn rested her head upon her shoulder. "I'm so happy."

"Me, too, Danlyn."

That was, until the front door opened and they heard Frank's voice. The sound of his engine must have got lost in the heavy rain.

"What're you ladies up to?" he asked, looking at all the candles.

Laura slowly untangled her arms from Danlyn's just as Vivian came in behind him.

"What're all the hugs for?" he tried again, and when no one answered him, Vivian said, "Did you get a job, Laura?"

"No," Danlyn piped up. Laura tensed. "The baby's okay." Danlyn's smile wavered when Vivian's expression failed to match her own. She glanced at Laura with an apologetic look. Laura patted her on the back. What to say and what not to say was too much for anyone to keep up with, especially a kid.

"I went to my appointment today. The baby's due in June. That's what Danlyn's excited about."

Vivian's eyes narrowed. "You went to a doctor today? Where?"

"Just a doctor I found while I was out looking for a job. He's new to Rome."

"And you're excited about this, Danlyn?" Vivian asked as she grabbed the teakettle off the stove.

"Yes," Danlyn said, looking confused. Then the lights came back on, but no one seemed to notice.

"What about?" Vivian's tone had a bite to it. A faint smell of gas filled the room when she turned on the burner.

"What do you mean?"

"I mean"—Vivian stood directly in front of her—"what is it you're excited about?"

Danlyn's mouth went slack, her forehead wrinkled.

Laura said firmly, "She's excited about being a big sister."

Vivian gave Laura a look of pity. "I certainly hope she gets what she wants."

Laura flinched, bit down hard.

"What seems to be the matter with you, Laura?" Vivian asked.

"Nothing. I just don't think using Danlyn's excitement as a way to get at me is fair. Just let her be happy."

Vivian lifted her chin. Such a small gesture, like hair rising on a dog's back. "Really, Laura? Are you censoring me now? Let's see. I can't school Danlyn. She's not even allowed to stay here with me while you're gone. Now you're telling me what to say in my home?"

"You know why I won't leave her here with you. Or did you forget how I got this?" Laura pointed at her cheek.

Vivian refused to look at the bruise. "What would've happened?"

"What do you mean?" Laura's energy was fading fast. Vivian was sucking up all the oxygen in the room.

Vivian folded her arms over her chest, took a step closer. "If she had stayed here, what would've happened?"

"Who knows? But it's my job to not find out."

"Does she look abused?" Vivian gestured towards Danlyn. "Have I done something to her? No. Nothing's wrong with her, but you ripped her from me anyway."

"Are you kidding? That's ridiculous." Laura rolled her eyes. "Ripped her from you? She's standing right here."

"Don't call me ridiculous."

"I didn't. I said *that's* ridiculous. You know what…I'm concerned, that's all. There's no need to fight about it. Maybe next time you'll keep your temper in check, and then I won't have to worry." She was pushing it. She could feel it, like a current beneath the house. She thought again about Dr. Murray's words and lowered her voice. "Let's not argue, Mom. Besides, you don't need the added stress of schooling Danlyn. And it's better that she's with me when you have your appointments."

Vivian gave an eerie smile. "I don't think that's best. I think the time together is good."

"Well, she's here right now. That's plenty of time together."

"You're right, Laura," Vivian spoke softly. "She and I spend enough time together, but she and Frank don't."

Frank nodded once in agreement. "That's right, sweet pea," he said to Danlyn. "In fact, I got a project we can start workin' on together. What do you say to helpin' me build a crib for the baby?"

All three of them shot Frank annoyed glances.

Laura knew what game they were playing. Vivian wanted to see how far she could push her, but Laura was scraping the bottom of the tank. Even so, she'd build a wall between Danlyn and Frank if it meant keeping him out of her life. Laura was late to the mommy party, but she was catching up. Mothering meant more than home-cooked meals and providing a roof over a child's head. It meant protecting them, and everything in her screamed to protect Danlyn from Frank.

"Well, Mom, I don't see the need for Danlyn to spend more time with Frank. All due respect, of course." She moved in the direction of the stairs, but Vivian stood firmly in front of her. Laura walked the other way, into the family room, ushering Danlyn in front of her.

"We're not done," Vivian said, trailing just behind her.

Laura turned around, almost bumping into Vivian. "What? Why do we need to fight about everything?"

Vivian quickly raised her hand. Laura blocked her face, waiting for the impact. But it never came. Through her splayed fingers, Laura could see her mother's face, and what she saw was far more chilling than an impending slap or punch. Laura slowly dropped her hands and a wisp of her hair floated away from her cheek as Vivian's hand softly landed upon it. Vivian brushed her jawline, then brought her hand to a gentle rest on Laura's neck. She cradled her jaw in her other hand and smiled.

"What's going on out here?" Frank asked in a cool voice, joining them.

"My dear," Vivian looked deeply into Laura's eyes. "I know you don't want Danlyn to have what you never had. Seeing her with Frank must be like a dagger in your heart. But Frank loves her, and he won't leave her like your father left you. Don't make Danlyn and Frank suffer because William killed himself."

Laura had stopped breathing. She needed her legs to move, she needed Vivian's hands off of her because her touch felt like acid and her words tore at her heart. But her body wouldn't budge, like she was broken. Finally, she swayed and stepped back, as far away from Vivian as she could get.

"My father didn't kill himself. I know he didn't kill himself." Danlyn scrambled to her side. Laura wrapped an arm around her shoulder. "Danlyn won't be spending time with Frank. He practically lives here, and she spends enough time with him as it is. He's not her father, and it's not up to you to determine who plays that role."

"She's my flesh and blood," Vivian hissed. "The girl needs a father of some kind."

"Maybe that's true, but who plays that role is up to me."

"And I suppose you think you can do a better job finding a father for her? You don't know what makes a good father. Yours was a drunk and a coward."

"Even when he was drunk, he was ten times the parent you ever were. And now, maybe you're not in the right state of mind to make decisions." Laura finally found her anger. "I'll enroll her in school tomorrow. It's obvious you've gone over the deep end."

"You will not!"

Laura's voice rose. "I make decisions for her. Not you. And I'm done protecting you." Laura had crossed the line into extraordinarily dangerous territory. "You don't want Danlyn in school because you don't want her hearing all about the Hallows. About how completely fucked up we all are."

"Watch your mouth!"

"Why? It's true. You don't want her knowing exactly what this town thinks of you. Of us. Just don't go on like you graciously agreed to school her out of the kindness of your heart. It's your secrets we're all guarding here. Not mine."

Vivian's skin flushed. "Two can play at this game, Laura. You want to dig up the past—"

"You dug up the past. You brought up Dad and his *supposed* suicide."

Vivian stepped back until she was at Frank's side. "You want an honest discussion?" she asked Laura. "Let's get some honesty from you, then. Why is it you really don't want Danlyn around Frank? Once and for all, tell us what your problem with him is."

Laura just shook her head.

"Out with it," Vivian roared.

Laura frowned. "Jesus, Mom. Look at you."

Frank finally broke his silence, pulling Vivian into his arms. "Come on now, Laura. I know you've been havin' a hard time since findin' out about your old man, but give your mama a break. It ain't her fault any more than it's mine. You gotta stop blamin' everyone."

Laura watched Frank's eyes, the way they seemed to search her, always roaming, like he was waiting for something. She looked back at her mother and saw nothing. Vivian had vacated at Frank's touch.

"How about it?" he asked. "Let's start puttin' all this behind us."

Laura didn't answer. Her fears were out in the open, shrouded in colors too bright to go unnoticed. Her mind was spinning, and her reasons for hating Frank flew around her head like debris. Maybe Frank was taking William's place. Maybe he was too pushy and too touchy and too feely. Maybe he was hiding something beneath that smile. Something darker than she had originally thought.

She had no proof that Frank was a monster, and maybe she had no good reason for hating him at all. Maybe she was losing it, and maybe she'd find herself in a padded room if she didn't slow down and find some balance. But she wasn't crazy. She knew she wasn't. Because something was there, beneath the murky waters, circling her. Something she had buried was waiting to welcome her home.

"Laura, I know you don't wanna hear this stuff about your dad," Frank said. "But he had problems. Maybe you were too young, but he was more messed up than you know."

"Remember that his daughter and granddaughter are right here, Frank. Show a little respect," Laura said.

"Daughter and granddaughter?" Franks voice abruptly changed.

Vivian's back straightened. Her eyes widened, like she had just woken from a deep sleep.

"Daughter and granddaughter?" he asked again. "Well, he took himself away from his daughter and granddaughter. And you want me to show him respect? Sugar, that ain't gonna happen. See, I'm being kind right now, but I assure you, my job isn't to show you or Danlyn respect unless I see fit. Now, I'm tryin' to be nice. Don't you wanna be nice?"

It took everything Laura had not to slap the smile from his face. But instead she said, "You and I will have to agree to disagree."

"That's more like it." Frank nodded. "We don't have to see eye-to-eye, but you're learnin' to settle that bark of yours."

Laura bit down so hard she thought she might crack her teeth.

"And you ladies, you're always jumpin' ten steps ahead. Y'all are gonna have to find a way to get along if we're gonna make this family work."

Laura saw Vivian's hands ball into fists.

"How about you take it easy and see how things go, Laura," he said. "And don't fret about the job search. Take all the time you need, 'cause I think your mama's wantin' to see that baby of yours. I know I do."

No one had to tell Laura how wrong Frank was. Vivian's expression said it all. Laura turned away. She wanted her father. She wanted him to hold her baby and to spend time with Danlyn. Not Frank. Frank wouldn't lay one gnarled finger on her baby.

"Are you okay, Mom?" Danlyn whispered.

"You go up to the room, young lady," Vivian ordered, but Danlyn clung to her mother's side.

"Go, Danlyn." Laura let go of her shoulder. "I'll be up to talk to you in a minute."

"You haven't answered my question," Vivian shouted. "And that child's not going to hear your version of our history."

"She deserves an explanation," Laura said, watching Danlyn run up the stairs. "I'm not the one who decided to tear this wound open."

"Answer my question," Vivian demanded. "I don't know why you hate Frank so much. After everything he's done for me, I can't imagine what reason you have to treat him so poorly. I'm giving you one last opportunity to speak up, Laura. Just one."

Laura's eyes bounced between them.

"You say it now," Vivian told her. "But then this stops."

"I don't know what you mean," Laura said.

"Last chance."

Laura felt something, like a tick, burrowing into her brain. It itched and made her feel sick. These people were fire, wild and untamed. Whatever darkness lay between them was the dominant presence in the room. She needed to get them off her back. Now.

"I don't know," she finally said. "But I just don't like him, okay? I guess…" Laura's mouth went dry. She was edging toward something she wasn't sure she wanted to discover. "I guess I just miss Dad. And I'm worried about the baby. I don't feel well."

Vivian's eyes seared into hers. "Are you certain that's all it is?"

Laura slowly nodded. "Yes."

"Well," Frank said. "I think we're done here." He gave Vivian's shoulder a squeeze. "Let's get you in bed. I've gotta get goin'. And Laura," he stood next to her, softly nudged her arm. "We'll be okay, you and me. We'll work past this."

Laura leaned away.

"Oh, and maybe you can run to the store for your mama, pick up her meds?" He grabbed his jacket, put it on. "Get yourself somethin' to eat on the way, too. You're lookin' a little green behind the gills. Need to put some meat on them bones."

That was fine with her. Laura needed to get out. A stone was still firmly packed in her chest. "Fine. We'll go right now."

"Can't you leave Danlyn here?" Frank used his kindest voice. "Your mama's had a rough day. I'm worried about her."

"Absolutely not."

"Please? She's not doin' well. She fell in the shower today. Banged herself up pretty good. Luckily, she walked away with only some bruises. I had to take her in for an emergency visit with her doc. He says she shouldn't be alone."

"No."

"She doesn't have the energy to hurt a fly right now. Twenty minutes and you'll be back. Besides, I won't be here. Gotta go to work for a couple hours. All your mama's gonna do is lie in bed. Just tell Danlyn to keep an ear out for her, just in case she falls. Is that too much to ask?"

Laura looked back at Vivian. She really was a pathetic sight. She probably couldn't swat at a cockroach, let alone hurt Danlyn, but still...

"Laura, come on now. I'll take her up to bed, but then I gotta be gettin' on."

Laura frowned. "I'll think about it."

"Good. I can't afford to get called away from work again because she needs help."

~

"Are you okay?" Laura asked Danlyn when she came in the room.

"I guess." She looked anything but okay. "My grandfather... Was all that stuff true?"

Laura sat down next to her. "No. Definitely not. Listen, we'll talk about it, but later. I have to run to the store to get her medication." Danlyn rolled her eyes. "I don't like it either," Laura said, "but she looks like she might really keel over, and I don't need that on my conscience, too. So get your shoes on quickly."

Danlyn looked up at her. "Mom, I did something I wasn't supposed to."

"What do you mean?"

Danlyn looked away, peeking at her from the corners of her eyes.

"It's okay," Laura assured her. "Go ahead."

"The last time I went with Grandma to one of her appointments... You know how I'm supposed to wait in the car?"

"Yeah."

"Well, I followed them. I was just curious."

"Okay. That doesn't sound so bad."

"It's doesn't? You're not mad at me?"

"Not at all, silly."

"*She* would have thought it was horrible."

"Yeah, my mother certainly would, but she also hates puppies and thinks kittens were put here to torture the innocent. She's really not the best barometer for bad behavior. Then again, I guess I'm not, either."

Danlyn smiled. "No one hates puppies."

"Oh really? You see any dogs around here?"

Danlyn's laugh was sweet.

"Seriously, though," Laura told her, "your secret's safe with me."

"Mom?"

"Yeah?"

"What's an oncol...oncolog... I'm not sure how to say it."

"An oncologist? Is that where your grandmother went?"

Danlyn nodded. "That's what the sign outside the door said. Why? What's that?"

It was strange how little Laura felt. Not that she had any reason to feel much. If anything, she would have guessed that relief might be the emotion of choice, but she felt nothing.

"That explains a lot," Laura said, more to herself than to Danlyn.

"Explains what?"

"The way she's been acting." Laura held Danlyn's hand. "It means your grandmother might...probably has cancer."

There was a hint of sadness in Danlyn's voice. "Is she going to die? I don't like her, but I don't want her to die."

"I don't know, kid."

Laura waited a moment, watching Danlyn for any signs of upset. "You look okay. Are you?"

"I guess. I mean, I'm kind of sad, but maybe because I'm supposed to be. It's not like we're super close or anything. And she's...she's—"

"I know. Trust me, I know."

Laura got up, paused for a second. "Listen. Can you do me a favor, Danlyn?"

"What?"

"I need you to stay here. I won't be long."

"You said you wouldn't leave me here alone. Just like how you said we wouldn't stay here long."

"I'm going to get us out of here. But I need to get her medication, and then—"

"I hate it here so bad. I don't believe you anymore. We're gonna be here forever."

"That's not true, Danlyn. Listen, I'm not just going to the store. I'm stopping by Jackie's, too. That's why I need you to stay here. Don't be obvious about it, but I need you to start packing our things so we can leave later, before Frank gets back. I'm going to let Jackie and Steven know we'd like to stay with them. So can you do that, can you get our things together?"

"Oh my God!" Danlyn beamed. "Promise?"

"I promise. But listen—and this is very important—lock the door and stay in here. Frank's gone and she's in bed. If you hear her fall or something, you can help her, but otherwise stay here. And most importantly, *don't* let her know what you're up to."

"Let me come with you. We'll grab our stuff now."

"We don't have time. And I want to give Steven and Jackie some warning. Besides, you might not get this, but I can't have my mother's death on my conscience, God forbid something were to happen."

"Mom," Danlyn moaned.

"I know. But just think, we won't even be sleeping here tonight. An hour, tops. So move fast."

Danlyn sighed, then gave in, looking like the weight of the world had been lifted off her shoulders. "Okay." She hugged Laura. "Just hurry back."

"I will. While they're getting her medication ready, I'll grab us some food from the diner you liked. Then I'll run by Jackie's.

"Warp speed. I won't even go in the house." Laura pulled a pen from her pocket and scribbled Jackie's number on Danlyn's hand. "If anything happens, call Jackie. But only if it's an emergency."

Laura kissed Danlyn's cheek. "I'll be back soon. And remember, be quiet."

"I will."

Laura quietly opened the door and whispered, "One hour." She winked at Danlyn. "Love you, kid."

Chapter 19

The hours Frank had spent away at the job site had done Vivian some good. Based off Frank's grim expression when he returned, the same couldn't be said for him.

Vivian sat at the kitchen table, watching him peel off his jacket and throw it over the chair. "What took you so long," she asked.

"I was only gone for a couple hours, Viv."

"You just went to work?"

Frank ignored her. "We need to talk. Right now," he said.

Vivian pointed above her, pressed a finger to her lips.

"What the hell were you thinkin' earlier, askin' Laura those questions?" Vivian turned away. "Viv, you'd better answer me. What're you playin' at?"

"I'm not playing at anything. I'm simply trying to get the truth out of her."

"No, Vivian. You wanna see what she remembers. But she doesn't remember. You're losin' it. I'm tellin' you, you're slippin'." He stood in front of her and bent over, bracing her shoulders. "You lose your shit and tell her somethin', you're gonna have a mountain of hell on your head, ol' girl. I'm warnin' you." He lowered his head so that his eyes were level with hers. "You're gonna start watchin' your step. You hear me?"

Vivian's stare was equally fierce. "I don't know what you're talking about. I'd never do anything to hurt you."

"It's not just me you need to be concerned with. You were there, too. It's time you remind yourself of that. You see her and you start losin' it, Viv. Happens every time."

"I said I would never—"

"You need to let me know you're hearin' me. I won't tiptoe around here, waitin' for you to crack. And I won't let you or Laura ruin this."

Vivian shot him a bitter look.

"Get up," Frank said.

Vivian slowly rose to her feet, eyes glued on his. He moved around her, pushing her chair out of the way, and wrapped his arms tightly around her from behind, pressing himself into her.

"Not now, Frank. Stop." But she knew what the look in his eyes meant, and there was usually no stopping him.

He pressed himself into her harder, then spun her around while walking her backward into the dining room. He groped her sides, her back, her breasts.

"Frank, I don't want to," she forcefully whispered.

He bent her back, pushing her down on the large farmhouse table, pressing the full weight of his body against her small frame. "We've been doin' things your way long enough, Viv."

He breathed down her neck, and when Vivian felt her body respond, she flushed with an angry heat. Things between them had always been done her way, but only because they were done Frank's way for so long before that. Now it was always in her bed, lights completely off, her nightgown on, head turned, eyes closed, as though the act was taking place to someone else, in someplace else. That made it easier to wake the next morning and fall to her knees and repent. But here and now, under the bright lights, with Danlyn right upstairs, she couldn't escape. There was no darkness to fall into.

Frank ran his hands under her dress, pulling it up to her waist. Vivian tried to yank his arms off, clawing at his flesh with nails too short. He grabbed her arms, pinning them down, using his thighs to pry hers apart.

"No. Stop it," Vivian whispered. "Not here. Please."

He tore her underwear off her body.

"Danlyn will come down if she hears us. Stop!"

But every time she begged, Frank pushed harder. He reached down with one hand, pinning her with the other, and unzipped his pants. When Vivian felt the warmth of his flesh on her thighs, her entire body went limp. She just lay there on the table, half-dressed, like a lifeless doll.

"What're you doin', Viv?" She looked up at him with a blank expression. "Fuck, Vivian!" he yelled. "Why'd you stop?" He pushed himself away from her. "What the hell'd you stop for?"

Vivian calmly sat up, pulling her torn underwear out from under her. She got off the table, dropping her dress back down, palming it flat while straightening her hair. "Put yourself away," she said. But Frank didn't move. He just stood there, exposed and sweaty. "Now!" she ordered.

"You really piss me off, Vivian." He tucked his shirt back into his pants. Just as he closed his zipper, Danlyn walked in, her eyes like giant saucers.

"Your arms," Danlyn said.

Vivian looked down, saw scratches and blotches covering her skin. She folded her arms in front of her, squeezing her underwear into a wad in her closed fist. "I'm fine. Now you mind yourself. This is no business of yours."

"She's fine, Danlyn," Frank said. "We were playin', is all."

"I'm really worried about mom. She was supposed to be back a long time ago," Danlyn said.

Vivian walked back in the kitchen. "She's fine, I'm sure. Now go take your bath."

"But what if something's wrong? She was supposed to be back over an hour ago."

Vivian looked over her shoulder, one loose strand of hair danced in front of her lips, floating up as she hollered, "Do as you were told, now."

"Not until I know where my mom is."

"Danlyn," Frank yelled from behind her. "Go!"

Danlyn ran up the stairs, slamming the door behind her.

Frank frowned, looking at his watch. "I didn't realize Laura wasn't here. Where is she?"

Vivian arched one eyebrow. "That's all you have to say?"

Frank didn't care about her at all. All he cared about was Danlyn and Laura and making sure they were happy. Vivian had given every bit of herself to him, and still, she wasn't enough. She waited for him to say something, and when he didn't, she shook her head.

"She won't be back for a while."

"What the hell'd you do, Viv?" his expression stern.

Vivian gripped the table, bracing for the twist of worry that inevitably would show on his face and the blame he'd surely pin on her. "I got a call a little while ago. She's in the hospital."

Chapter 20

Platinum overhead lighting burned through Laura's closed eyes. Abstract shadows moved above her, echoed voices spilled in from every direction. One of the voices was familiar, but she couldn't place it. There was beeping in her left ear. The smell of rubbing alcohol. She was lying down flat, but she couldn't move. Everything was getting brighter. Too bright. This had to be a dream, but the aching in her lower abdomen was too real. Her eyes shot open. She gasped.

"Laura? Can you hear me?"

Trails and vivid afterimages burned into her vision, making it impossible to see. She squinted, trying to lift her head toward the voice she recognized, but pain spread through her skull.

"Wh-what happened?" She moaned.

"It's okay. Just try to relax. You're going to be a little groggy from the medication."

Laura lifted her hands to her eyes and felt pressure in the crook of her right arm. *An IV.* She reached out, brushing her fingers against the person beside her. "Why's there…an IV?"

"Laura, can you see me? My name is Jonathan Tillsten. Do you remember me?"

"No." She fought to keep her eyes open. She swatted at a nurse to her left.

"She's just checking your pupils. It's okay," Jonathan said.

"Too bright."

"I know, I'm sorry. But it's necessary. You hit your head pretty hard."

The nurse moved away, allowing Laura a better look at Jonathan. Familiar. But from where?

As the seconds ticked by, her surroundings began falling into place. A hospital. She was in a hospital. Laura bolted up.

"You're going to be all right," Jonathan told her, lowering her back onto the bed. "You're in the hospital, but you're okay."

But it wasn't okay. Laura's mind was too hazy and nothing made any sense.

"How much did I drink?" Her eyelids fought against her, her lips felt like two iron bars.

"You didn't drink anything. It's the medication. It's helping with the pain. Do you remember anything yet?"

"My head…" She grabbed both sides of it, squeezing. "It hurts. It's spinning, like earlier, at the…the…"

"At the diner," Jonathan filled in. "Do you remember that?"

"Yeah. I tried to get up…but my head was…" She lifted up a finger, made one small circle with it.

"That's when you collapsed. Do you remember that?"

"Yes. Maybe. I don't know."

Jonathan sat on the edge of the bed. "Is that the last thing you remember, your head spinning? You came to in the "ambulance. You were able to tell us your name and your doctor's name. You don't remember any of that?"

Laura placed her hand on her stomach. "Is my baby okay?"

Jonathan looked away. "Let me go get your doctor."

"You're not my doctor?"

"I'm a doctor. I'm Dr. Tillsten. But I'm not your doctor. We met at the diner. You still don't remember? You were ordering...we started talking."

There were definitely remnants of the diner, and of meeting Jonathan. But too much was missing. Laura squinted, rubbed her eyes, looking closely at him, but her head felt like it was stuffed with cotton. "I think I remember a little. I'm so tired."

"That's okay. Once the medication wears off, you should start to remember more. Let me go get Dr. Murray for you."

Jonathan's smile masked something that, even in her semi-incoherent state, Laura could sense. Maybe pity, maybe sadness. She couldn't tell. She could barely tell up from down, and she'd barely noticed the nurse standing next to her, adjusting her IV, but there was a heaviness in his eyes.

Laura heard Jonathan's voice carrying in the hallway, and then a woman's voice telling him the doctor would be right in. He came back, leaned over the bed.

"How's your pain?" he asked.

Laura tried to sit up again.

"Do you want me to incline the bed?"

She whispered yes, and when he slowly brought the back of the bed up, her brain did another somersault. "Stop."

"Okay. Can you tell me how bad your pain is?"

Laura finally got a good look at the room. She yanked her arm away from the nurse, raised her voice. "Is my baby okay?"

Jonathan gently held her hand still for the nurse. "You fainted at the restaurant. You hit your head on the floor when you fell, but it's not looking too bad."

"Oh." Laura breathed deeply. "I think I remember more now." She closed her eyes, picturing the diner and a very overweight, unhappy-looking waitress with a nametag that read "Joy." Jonathan had made a joke about the irony. That's how they had got to talking.

When Laura opened her eyes, she gave him a suspicious look. She remembered now. He had hit on her. Kind and sweet, unlike all the other low-life sleaze balls she'd met. He'd been so charming, he'd rendered her nearly speechless. That much, she remembered. She remembered something else, too.

"Danlyn?" The panic was back in her voice.

"Your daughter?" Jonathan asked.

"I need a phone."

When Jonathan gave the nurse a short nod, she quickly left the room.

"We made some calls when we brought you in," he told Laura. "You kept asking for your daughter in the ambulance. Dr. Murray called your mother and told her what was going on. She wasn't able to…"

"She wouldn't come," Laura said. "Yeah, well, she's not vying for Mother of the Year, so…" she wasn't going to feel bad about Vivian. Besides, it was best this way. Saved Danlyn the pain of seeing her like this.

"Is there anyone else you'd like us to call? The baby's father? I'm sorry. I'm not sure what the situation is. Your fiancé? Boyfriend?"

"There's no one."

"Okay," he said, offering a polite smile. "I can stay with you if you'd like."

A tear rolled down Laura's cheek. "No thanks."

"It's no trouble. You shouldn't be alone."

"I'm fine. You didn't need to come with me anyway. You said you rode in the ambulance with me?"

"I did. But I'm a doctor. It's kind of my duty. But I would've ridden with you anyway. Also, my shift starts in an hour, so it wasn't any trouble."

Laura pulled herself up a little, looking mortified. "You didn't…work on me, did you?"

"No. I'm an orthopedic surgeon. Well, a resident, actually. You break bones, you come see me. Not this, though."

Not what? Laura wondered.

"I just thought I'd stick around while Dr. Murray gets everything together. It's a bit of a madhouse out there."

"How long have I been here?" Laura asked.

"Two…"—Jonathan glanced at his watch—"…no, three hours, almost."

The door opened and Jonathan turned around. "Dr. Murray, hello."

Dr. Murray nodded in his direction, "Dr. Tillsten." Then he walked to the edge of the bed as Jonathan moved aside. "Glad to see you're awake, Laura. Good thing Dr. Tillsten was there when you had your fall. I trust that he's kept you good company?"

"Do you know what happened?" Laura asked. "Why did I pass out?"

When Dr. Murray cleared his throat, Jonathan said, "I'll get going now. If you need anything, don't hesitate."

Dr. Murray waited for the door to close, then dragged a chair to Laura's side and sat down. She could almost see the words in his eyes. He looked tired, discouraged, much older than she remembered.

"Laura, do you remember anything from earlier this evening?"

"I remember ordering food at the diner, and meeting Jonathan. When they called my order and I stood up, I got really dizzy. I guess that's when I fainted, because I don't remember anything after that."

He looked serious. "You don't remember arriving here, or the ride in the ambulance?"

"No."

Dr. Murray pressed his palms together, rested them in his lap. His eyebrows creased together, creating an eave that shadowed his eyes. "You were conscious when you got here. You gave Jonathan your name. Luckily I was working tonight. I'm glad I could be here."

"What happened?" Laura's eyes widened as she braced herself for the worst.

"When they admitted you, Dr. Tillsten brought me up to speed. You had a pretty decent egg on your head." He pointed at the side of her head. "You'll be feeling that more once the meds wear off." He refocused. "You were complaining about your stomach. We checked on a few things and decided it was okay to give you something for the pain, which you agreed to. Luckily your head hit a soft booth before impacting the floor. We called your mother and—"

"I know," Laura said.

"Oh. Okay."

When Dr. Murray placed one hand on Laura's shoulder, she knew his touch was the kiss of death. She felt it, as though he were reaching in and ripping out her heart.

"Laura, when you arrived, you were cramping and bleeding heavily. I made you aware that it was a possible sign of miscarriage, and you agreed to an exam. After a very thorough "examination, I found that your cervix was dilated, and I couldn't find the baby's heartbeat." He looked at her thoughtfully. "I'm so sorry for your loss, Laura."

Laura's mouth fell open, lips quivering. "No. My baby's fine. It has to be fine. I stopped drinking. I did everything I was supposed to. I know my baby's fine." She gulped at the air, hyperventilating. "You n-need to check again. Please. It'll be there. The heartbeat will b-be there. Please."

Dr. Murray hesitantly pulled the stethoscope off his neck, placing the buds in his ears and the cold metal on her stomach.

Laura held her breath, waiting for the look of relief she was sure would wash over him when he realized there was still life in that tiny body still cradled in her womb.

He moved the stethoscope left, then right, up, then down. He listened for minutes, and when Laura began to cry again, he slowly wrapped the stethoscope around his neck and lowered her shirt. Laura put her hands over her face as terrible sobs tore through her.

"I'm truly sorry, Laura." He rested his hand on her arm, and this time, she didn't move away. "I know how difficult this is. If there's anything I can do—"

"Tell me my baby's okay. Just tell me it's okay," Laura begged.

When her hands dropped, limp and sapped of strength, she wore the face of a much different woman. This one was broken, distorted. A fraction of the woman she'd been only minutes ago.

"I can't lose my baby. Please. I want my baby." She pressed her hands into her stomach and rolled onto her side, silently screaming out. Then she cried aloud, again and again, "Why, why, why?" Because this wasn't the kind of pain that would be followed by the delivery of a healthy baby. There was just sorrow, and no doctor knew how to cure that.

Dr. Murray looked back at the door, then at Laura. Protocol was made for patients whose mothers came to sit by their side and whose husbands held them up when they had no strength of their own. And so Dr. Murray wrapped an arm around Laura, and there she poured her agony out, gripping them both in her heartache.

Chapter 21

Danlyn had snuck out of bed and was sitting at the top of the staircase. The fire in the family room crackled, breaking Vivian and Frank's whispers. Warmth from the fire wafted up the stairs and washed over Danlyn's toes and legs, but that did nothing to warm her icy fear and the bone-deep chill in the night. It was nearly midnight and Laura still wasn't home. But a new visitor had arrived. Something unseen. Danlyn could feel it. The mood was different. The droning existence of the old house had taken on a new life. The walls even seemed to buzz and whisper, like living wallpaper, dazzling with horrific possibilities.

Vivian's voice traveled up the stairs in sharp hisses: Laura this and Laura that. But Danlyn couldn't make any sense of it. Maybe Laura had left her. Maybe she'd moved in with Jackie and Steven, leaving her behind to rot away on Hallows' Farm. But Danlyn knew that couldn't be. Despite all the ugliness of their past, Danlyn knew her mother wouldn't abandon her. Not just because Laura could have left her behind a thousand times but never did, but because of what Danlyn always saw in her mother's eyes. Every awful night, every drunken mistake, every time Laura failed her so completely, Danlyn saw that same look: absolute regret and agony over what she'd done, and the desire to be a better person. Even if Danlyn had been too hurt to always admit it, she knew it was there. Tonight, she would hold on to the only truth she knew. Her mother loved her. For good or bad, her mother loved her more than anything.

Danlyn moved down a few more steps, cocking her head toward their voices.

"We don't need to figure it all out tonight. Laura's not coming home anytime soon," Frank said.

Anytime soon? Danlyn shivered, fear spread throughout her body. She moved down another step. She was furious. Furious at Vivian and Frank for not telling her where her mother was. Furious at herself for hiding on the stairs when she should demand the truth. They were finally going to be free. But now the future was shrouded in fog. Danlyn tucked her face into her hands, thinking of that night on the curb, sitting in the cold. This was so much worse. She couldn't be left with these people. She couldn't handle it, couldn't even swallow the thought. It would choke her to death if she tried.

Danlyn held her breath, finally stood up. She leapt down the last four steps, fast enough so she didn't have time to change her mind and run the other way. She tore into the living room, almost stumbling to a halt in front of Frank and Vivian, who were sitting on the sofa.

"What in God's name are you doing, racing down here like an animal?" Vivian asked.

Danlyn's mind went blank. They were the neighborhood bullies and she was the scrawny-limbed wimp.

"Answer me." Vivian stood up, spine rigid.

"Let it go, Viv," Frank told her. "Danlyn, just get back to bed."

Danlyn shook her head, silent, testing out the waters that already felt too deep.

"Get to bed," Vivian ordered. "Right this instant."

"Where's my mom?"

"You will do as you're told, or so help me."

"She said she'd be back. She promised. Something's wrong, and you're not telling me what it is."

"Well, I guess she broke her promise," Vivian said coldly. "Now, for the last time, go to bed."

"No," Danlyn shouted. "She didn't lie to me. You're lying!"

Vivian bent down, eyes boring into her granddaughter's. Frank got up, staying near.

"Little girl," Vivian said. "You're just like your mother. Barging in here, making demands. I've already raised one child, and I won't do this again with you." Vivian stood up, swayed a bit. "Get back to bed."

"Not until you tell me where my mom is."

"I don't see the harm," Frank said. "Just tell the girl and she'll pipe down. Won't you, Danlyn?"

"Yes. I just want to know if she's okay."

"You stupid girl," Vivian said. "She's her father's daughter, and the sooner you realize that, the better off you'll be. I thought she'd disappointed you enough. I thought you were smart enough to see your mother for what she is. A liar and a drunk. Just like William. You thought she would keep her word? You thought she cared enough to come back for you?"

Danlyn didn't cry. Instead, her mouth filled with so many hateful words, she couldn't decide which to scream first. "I do believe my mom! She wouldn't leave me alone with…with…"

"With *me*?" Vivian features sharpened. "Well take a look around, Danlyn. Go ahead!" She grabbed Danlyn's head, forcing her chin up. "Do you see your mother anywhere?"

"Let go," Danlyn cried, wriggling her head out of Vivian's skeletal fingers. "You're hurting me."

Frank flung Vivian behind him like a ragdoll. "For fuck's sake," his voice boomed. "I've had it."

Danlyn scuttled back until her feet hit the bottom of the stairs. She couldn't peel her eyes away from Frank. The last man who had looked that angry was Paul.

Vivian stood behind him, holding one hand to her head while grabbing his shoulder with the other. "I'm fine," she panted. "Just move out of the way."

"Not until you calm the hell down. I'm fed up with your shit, Vivian."

Vivian huffed. Her hair was disheveled, her skin pale, her eyes no longer wild. "Fine." She ran her hands through her hair. She took a steadying breath. "I'm all right."

Frank waited a beat, eyeing her. Then moved aside.

Danlyn crammed the back of her heels into the step behind her as Vivian came closer. At least now she looked more exhausted than furious.

"Danlyn, you can't fight me. I won't tolerate it," Vivian said.

Danlyn's voice was as fragile as glass. "I don't want to fight. I just want to know where my mom is."

"Your mother's not coming home right now. So whether you like it or not, we're all you've got."

Giant tears slowly crept down Danlyn's cheeks. No. Her mother was all she had. Not Frank. Not Vivian. But her mother. These people were no substitute. Not for a night, not for a lifetime.

"What happened? Where is she? I just want my mom."

Frank's lips thinned. "Dammit, Viv. Tell the child or I will."

"No," she said flatly.

Frank walked to the staircase, leaned against the railing. "Your mama's in the hospital. She's gonna be all right, but she's not comin' home tonight."

Danlyn wiped her eyes. "She's okay? Will she be back soon? What happened to her? How do you know she's all right?" She moved up one step, eye-level with Frank. "Is it the baby?"

Vivian placed her hands on her hips. "Did you not hear him? He said she's going to be fine. See, Frank? This is why you don't tell a child something like that. Look at her face. She's as white as a sheet."

Danlyn begged, "Please, Grandma. Tell me what happened. How do you know she's going to be okay? Can we go see her?"

"No. We're not going anywhere. She's fine. She'll be out soon. This is no reason to go to a filthy hospital."

"I'll do anything. Please let me go see her."

Vivian only offered a slow shake of the head.

Suddenly, Danlyn's tears stopped. "It's the baby, isn't it?"

Wearing a look of satisfaction, Vivian said, "It was only a matter of time. And without a baby in the picture, your mother's got no reason to stay sober. That means she can leave now, but I wouldn't bet on her taking you along."

Too many words had been said that couldn't be unsaid. Too many seeds of doubt were planted that couldn't be unearthed. Danlyn turned around, picking up one heavy leg, then the other, and started up the stairs.

Frank reached over the banister, grabbing her hand. "I'll come tuck you in tonight. How 'bout that?"

"No." He looked so happy, and all Danlyn wanted was to disappear. She tried freeing her hand. "I just want to be alone." But still, he held tight.

"Frank!" Vivian shrieked.

Frank spun around, wearing a startled look. "What the hell, Viv. What're you screamin' for?"

Danlyn froze. The room was teeming with tension. Vivian glared at her and Frank's entwined hands, looking spooked. Danlyn could feel her hand sweating under his.

"Well? You gonna say somethin' or just stand there?" Frank asked Vivian.

Vivian rushed up the stairs, ripping their hands apart. Danlyn's mouth fell open as her grandmother shoved her up to the top landing. "I'll put you to bed myself."

"I said I was gonna do it, Viv. You didn't have to walk up the stairs," Frank barked.

"Stop underestimating me. I can do more than you think I can."

Frank's expression finally caught up to hers. "I'm trying to help you. I'm trying to help Danlyn."

Vivian didn't move.

"Fine." Frank threw his hands up. "You don't want my help, that's fine by me. But you got somethin' else you wanna say, or should I just leave?"

Vivian's posture relaxed. "No. There's nothing more." Her voice soft, she added, "Don't go."

Chapter 22

The long nap the nurses promised Laura she'd have after Dr. Murray performed the D&C didn't happen. She bounced between a light, unsatisfying sleep and the agony of wakefulness. The drugs took the edge off, but nothing eased her pain.

Laura rubbed her eyes, trying to see through the bright haze of the morning sun. She was in a different room, with large windows that looked out over the foothills. She tried to sit up but only managed to get on her elbows. Across from her, on the far left side of the room, someone lay sleeping in one of the three other beds. A gray bushel of hair crept up the pillow, but the face was covered. Laura lay back down, holding her chest. Though she knew the gentle touch of her warm hand over her heart would do nothing to heal the unrelenting ache, she clutched tighter, wishing she could claw out the gnawing, black monster that had taken up residence there.

The heavy door to the recovery wing clicked open. Laura heard a soft voice to her right. "Ms. Hallow? Are you awake?"

Laura squinted, trying to remember the woman's face.

"I'm Nurse Montgomery. When we brought you back here after the procedure, you asked me to call Mrs. Brenner."

"I did?"

"It's okay. You were pretty groggy. But she's in the hallway. You want me to send her in?"

"Did you tell her what happened?"

"Of course not, sweetie."

Laura turned her gaze away from the nurse.

"Do you still want to see her, Ms. Hallow?"

Laura nodded. "Can I have a few minutes first?"

"Sure. I'll let her know."

Laura lazily pulled herself up. She looked at the windows again, at the bright, dreamy glow of morning light, and she thought of Jackie. There was either very little to tell her or everything to tell her. But there was no in-between, and Laura was so bogged down with sedatives—like wading through waist-deep mud—she didn't know how she'd manage.

~

"My God!" Jackie said.

Laura hadn't even heard the door open.

"What on earth happened?" Jackie took her scarf and jacket off and threw them on the foot of the bed, nudging herself into the crook of Laura's waist. "The nurse said you've been here since yesterday?"

Laura moved over, pulled the sheet up to her chest, clenching the fabric in her fingers.

"Are you okay? Was it something with the pregnancy?"

The question made it too real. It filled the room with realities too jarring for Laura's tender heart, and just like that, she fell apart, sending the broken pieces of her shattered soul everywhere. Her throat seized so that she still couldn't speak, and she wrapped her arms around herself, trying with all her might to fight the moment.

Jackie's hand slowly rose to her mouth. "My God."

Laura let Jackie pull her into her arms, and with each sob that escaped her, Jackie held her tighter, quietly crying into Laura's hair.

"I'm here," Jackie reminded her. "I've got you."

Laura's pain was the kind that only another woman could truly understand, and so she cried what felt like a thousand tears, and she held on to her friend, allowing Jackie to bear her weight, and even a little of her sorrow.

~

When Laura's cries finally turned into soft whimpers, she leaned back, forcing herself to make eye contact. "I need to tell you something. I don't really know where to start. But first let me apologize."

Jackie opened her mouth to speak.

"Please," Laura stopped her. "Let me do this. I left without a word, Jackie. After all you did for me, I left here and never called, never wrote. And Steven, my God. What I did to him…"

"This is the last thing you need to think about right now. The past is the past. We've been over this. Don't you believe that we've forgiven you?"

"I thought you would hate me."

"I could never hate you. I love you. So does Steven." Jackie wiped the tears from Laura's eyes. "I can't imagine what life was like for you. I mean, I know I saw it, but I didn't live it.

"What I did see, it was a complete nightmare. No one could ever blame you for leaving the way you did. But none of that matters now."

"No." Laura shook her head. "No. That's not it. You'll hate me, Jackie. If I tell you, you'll hate me."

"Tell me what?" Jackie frowned. "Where is all this coming from?"

"You're wrong about me. That person you keep describing…that strong, kind woman…that's not me. I told you that before, Jackie." Her voice turned hard. "I killed my baby. It's my fault. So go ahead, tell me what a good person I am now."

"That's the most ridiculous thing I've ever heard."

"It's true. Sure, maybe I fainted last night and hit my head and woke up with a doctor telling me my baby was gone. Just…gone, like it had never been there. But I caused it. I killed my b-baby."

"Laura, you said you fainted. That wasn't your fault. You can't go blaming yourself. You're not God."

Laura sat up straight, talking a mile a minute. "I collapsed at a diner last night. I stood up from a booth, and all I remember is getting really dizzy. Next thing I knew, I was here. When I woke up, my doctor told me the baby was… I didn't believe him, even though deep down I knew this would happen again. They did a surgery earlier this morning. They took my baby." Laura fell forward into Jackie's arms. "They just t-took it, and it's m-my fault."

"It is not," Jackie told her. "Trust me, I know. Maybe you didn't notice that Steven and I are pretty much the only couple in this town who don't have kids."

Laura stopped crying, looked up at her. "What?" she asked softly.

"I can't get pregnant. Steven wanted kids, but I couldn't give them to him. I know what it's like to blame myself. I did the same thing for years. It took me a long time to believe that I hadn't done something wrong to deserve what I got. Laura...you've been blaming yourself for every shitty thing that has ever happened. But you didn't cause those things, just like you didn't cause this."

Laura was tired of hearing the candy-coated version of herself that Jackie liked to tell. "That's what my doctor said, too. But I've done so many bad things, God—or whoever the hell's out there—is going to make me pay for a long time."

"What did you do that you think you had this coming? You've got to help me out. I'm not connecting the dots."

Laura shoved her trepidation deep down, where it couldn't sneak back up and strangle her voice. "This is my third miscarriage, Jackie. My other miscarriages happened right after getting pregnant, so I thought I was in the clear this time. I swear, when I passed the point when I miscarried the other two times and I still wasn't having any problems, I thought this was going to be different. My doctor said things like this just happen. No rhyme or reason. But this is payback."

"For what?"

Laura took a steady breath. "I'm an alcoholic, Jackie."

Jackie didn't move, didn't blink.

"I left with Danlyn, moved all over, stayed with any man who'd put up with me, and when I wasn't shacked up with some asshole, Danlyn and I lived in crappy motels wherever I could find some worthless job, because I was too drunk and heartless to give a shit about my kid's happiness. Before Danlyn was even five years old, I was my father. Except he wasn't mean and violent."

Laura's breathing picked up. She leaned back, eyes still wide, like she was hearing all this for the first time, too.

"I was a monster to Danlyn. I had her living in conditions no child should ever have to live in. I made her childhood into the same nightmare my childhood was, and all because I couldn't play the cards I was dealt. So I drank my pitiful life away and destroyed my child's happiness. I hit her, Jackie. I slapped her, screamed at her, called her names. I blamed her for every problem I had." Laura paused, waiting for Jackie to grab her things and leave. But she remained frozen.

"I deserve all of this. But my baby didn't, and Danlyn doesn't." Laura's face was lost behind so many tears, her words were barely coherent against her crying. "I can't even complain, because I caused it. I thought I'd been given another chance. I tried to do everything right this time. I drank the day I found out I was pregnant. I figured I'd lose the baby anyway. But since that day, I've not taken another sip. I wanted to make it work. I didn't know what the hell I was doing, but I knew I had to try, and that Danlyn and my baby deserved a shot. So I got in the car and went to the only place I had left. To a woman who wouldn't allow a drop of liquor in her home. I was trying to piece our lives together, and I never took another sip, Jackie. I swear, I did everything I was supposed to. Except coming back here."

Laura laughed, defeated and exhausted. "How stupid was I to think that maybe things might be different? That maybe my mother would show Danlyn and me the love she never could before? It's entirely my fault, though. I lost my baby because I fuck everything up, even when I try so hard. See Jackie, I'm a coward. I'm not brave. And I'm not loving or good or kind. I barely know how to love."

Jackie leaned forward, close enough that Laura could feel her breath on her skin. "I would've helped you, for Christ's sake. If it meant locking your ass in the basement and not letting you out, I would've helped you stop drinking. I want to be pissed at you, but how can I be? You did as you were taught. Times get hard, hit the bottle." Jackie sighed. "I can't be mad at you. I told you I'd be here when you were ready to open up. That hasn't changed."

"I know you would've helped me, Jackie. But I couldn't ask that of you. And we couldn't stay here. I left with Danlyn because I thought getting away would make us happy. I needed to get her out of this place, away from my mother, but Rome stuck to my skin and just…lingered on me. Everywhere I went, everything I did, was tainted by this place. I left here thinking I'd get an okay job somewhere and be the best mom ever. All I wanted to do was give Danlyn what I never had, and keep her away from the life I knew she would've lived had we stayed here."

Laura's face abruptly changed. All the years of hardship came to the surface, turning her green eyes a gloomy gray, like her soul was full of ash—the fire snuffed out.

"I love Danlyn so much," Laura said. "From the moment she was born and I first held her, I thought she was a miracle. I remember when she first looked up at me and smiled. I'd never seen that kind of joy. She didn't know how terrible she had it, you know? I remember my father smiling at me like that when I was little, but it eventually stopped. My entire childhood was full of looks of sympathy from other people. Everywhere I went…school, stores, church, everyone looked at me with pity. Not that I blamed them. I would've done the same. Hell, I did. It was the same look I gave my father when he'd polish off a bottle of Jack. I heard the rumors just like everyone else. I knew "people gossiped about the crazy Hallows and poor little Laura, stuck with a drunk for a daddy and a nut for a mother. I couldn't even defend myself by saying the rumors weren't true. But then came Danlyn. This perfectly beautiful baby who just looked up at me with all the love and trust in the world. When she smiled, it wasn't to placate me. When she laughed, it wasn't to lighten the mood. When she cried, it wasn't because she lived with a drunk and a sociopath. Because she didn't understand that yet. She was just happy, and I loved her for it. Such an innocent, beautiful person."

Jackie dabbed her eyes.

"That kid owns my heart," Laura told her. "But she's never known it. I stopped thinking about how much I love her, and that's when I ruined everything. But I swear to God, I'm not going backwards. If I have to fight till the day I die, I'll make it up to her. I've come too far to go back. By all accounts, I know this should push me right back to drinking, but I'll die before I do that."

"Jesus, Laura. You deserve to make it up to yourself, too. I don't know what to say. I'm trying to wrap my head around everything. But what I do know right now is that...yeah, you screwed up really bad. But it's how you're handling the situation now that counts. No one taught you how to be a mother and father all wrapped up in one. You had two of the worst examples in the world, and then you were thrown out with a baby when you were just a child yourself. It's not my place to judge you, Laura. I'd be the first one to whoop your ass into shape if you were still drinking, but you've made massive strides. I can see how much regret you carry around. I saw it long before you told me this."

Jackie sniffed, fighting back more tears. "You're going to be all right. I promise, Laura. You had it bad, and yeah, we all "knew it. But I never pitied you. I felt bad for you. But I never pitied you, and I never gossiped. I respected you for being the person you were. I always felt like you were beyond us kids. You had more wisdom than all of us." She brushed Laura's hair behind her ear. "And when I say I want to help now, it's not out of pity, either. It's because I have faith in you." She placed her hand over Laura's heart. "You're an amazing woman. Your mistakes haven't changed who you are…deep down. I love you."

"I love you, too," Laura said. "Thank you for not walking away. Thank you for loving me. But now you see I'm not the person you thought I was." Laura's head was growing too heavy to hold up, but her heart felt lighter.

"You stopped drinking. Bottom line. You gotta let go of the guilt. You just got lost for a while there. Shit happens."

Jackie looked over her shoulder, at the old woman in the corner, now looking bright-eyed and bushy-tailed. "Does she look familiar?"

Laura could barely keep her eyes open. "I can't tell. Who is she?"

"I don't know. Hey"—Jackie looked back at Laura—"did your mother bring Danlyn by to see you?"

"Of course not. My mother wouldn't be caught dead in a hospital. Besides, she knows about my drinking. If I know her, she's thinking I got what I deserved."

"Yeah, your mother's a fucking psycho. What else is new? But what about Danlyn? She's your daughter. She has a right to see you. Poor thing's gotta be worried sick. Do you think she even knows?"

"No idea. I just know my doctor called Vivian. I hate the idea of Danlyn being there with her and Frank, but I don't know what to do. We can't stay there anymore." Laura hesitated, trying to read Jackie's expression. "Actually, I was going to come to your house last night, before all this…to ask if, um, if we could—"

Jackie raised one hand. "You don't have a say in this anymore. You're staying with us. I demand it."

"Are you sure? After everything I just told you?"

"Shut up." Jackie gave her a look that was supposed to be stern, and would have been on anyone else. "What you told me changes nothing. If anything, I'm even more certain now. As soon as they cut you loose from here, we'll get your things and you'll check into Casa Brenner."

Laura's heart filled with the first signs of relief in days. "I can never repay you for this."

Jackie patted her hand. "Stay with us as long as you need. No thanking us every day, no feeling guilty, just stay. That's how you repay us, even though you don't owe us anything. Deal?"

"Deal."

Jackie got up, grabbed her purse. "I'm going to let you sleep for a while. How about I go get Danlyn? I can bring her to visit later. She'll be with us and you won't have to worry about a thing."

Laura's eyes opened wide. "No. You can't."

"I know you're worried about her being there. Frankly, so am I." Jackie tossed her jacket over her shoulder. "You don't need the added stress, and that poor thing doesn't need to be there with your mother and Frank."

"Really, Jackie, don't."

"It's not a big deal. I'll go right now."

Laura shook her head with renewed vigor. "Dr. Murray said I could leave tomorrow morning. I'll get Danlyn first thing."

Jackie wasn't listening. Laura knew she'd go get Danlyn, anyway.

"You can't go over there, Jackie."

"Why the hell not? Because your mother doesn't like me? Yeah, like I give a rat's ass."

"I appreciate you caring for Danlyn. I love you for it. But I'm scared. My mother's been particularly crazy lately."

"Which is why Danlyn shouldn't be there." Jackie didn't look the least bit swayed.

"You're right, Jackie. But you need to trust me. If you go out there, I'm afraid something far worse will happen. I don't know what she might do, and I can't explain it right now, but she won't let you take Danlyn. She'll do whatever it takes to stop you." The last twelve hours had been a whirlwind, and Laura had almost forgotten about what Danlyn had told her. "I think she's got cancer. She's been seeing an oncologist. She's just so unpredictable now. What I'm hoping is that one last night with them will be better than what might happen if you show up and ask to take her."

"There would be no asking. Danlyn's your daughter. If you want her to be with us, she should be with us. Besides, I'm not afraid of the old hag."

Laura grabbed her hand. "Please. They'll never let you in, let alone near Danlyn. If you go out there and they find out I'm planning on taking Danlyn to stay with you, they'll have till tomorrow morning to do what they want. Promise me you won't go out there."

"This is stupid," Jackie said. "But you look scared shitless, and now you're freaking me out. I should just barge in with Steven and take her. But I guess you're right. If anything were to happen because I showed up, I'd never forgive myself."

Jackie bit her bottom lip. "I should at least drive by, though. A couple times."

"That'd make me feel better. Not that it will tell us anything, but at least we'll know they're there." Laura reached her arms out for a hug. "Thank you for…everything. If I weren't so tired, I'd bow at your feet."

"Yeah, yeah. Get some sleep. I'll stop by the nurses' station, find out when you're getting released. I'll be here early to help you get ready. You want me to bring you dinner later?"

"No. Just check on the house. I'll be fine."

"Everything's going to be okay," Jackie said.

Laura slowly nodded, trying to smile, but her eyelids wouldn't stay open a moment longer.

~

After Jackie left, Olivia Boone sat up in her bed, peeking over at Laura. "Psst! Psst!" she hissed across the room, but Laura didn't rouse. "Psst!" Still nothing.

Olivia lay back, watching the hours tick by. Poor thing across the way needed her sleep, but Olivia didn't know if her conscience could wait. That's what she got for eavesdropping: a whole load of trouble.

Olivia reasoned that she could wait a few hours. It was probably best, anyway. If Laura was who Olivia thought she was, she'd need the energy, because she needed to get her little girl out of that house and away from those people—tonight.

Chapter 23

Frank drove down the long drive, watching Hallows' Farm come into view. The sun was setting and an orange glow lingered over the trees; the sunlight flickered, dancing between the branches.

Frank had never thought of this place as William's. Hallows' Farm had never really belonged to him, despite his last name donning the sign that still hung askew on the tattered post. It had been in Vivian's family since the turn of the century. In all the years that Frank had been coming here, there had only been a handful of times when he found it impossible to make the trek down the driveway. Those were the times when he felt William's presence here, when every corner of the home teemed with remnants of his life. Frank couldn't stand those times—hated them. And today, as he drew closer to the house, he could almost smell the cologne William used to wear, could almost hear his voice, as if he were sitting beside him.

Frank floored the gas pedal, trying to speed through the sinking feeling. Things were stacking up too fast, and he knew, deep in his gut, that everything was dangerously close to falling apart. He felt it in his bones, like his father used to say he could feel a storm coming.

He brought the truck to a halt, spraying rocks under the tire wells, and rushed to the front door, plowing through the feeling that he shouldn't be there at all.

"Viv, you in the kitchen?" He slammed the front door behind him, walked through the foyer, pausing just outside the kitchen. He wiped the sweat off his forehead, took one step forward. "Hey, ladies. You two gettin' ready for dinner?"

"Sure are," Vivian said, standing in front of the stove, sounding rather chipper. "Go wash up and have a seat," she told him.

"Not hungry." He stood behind Danlyn's chair, resting his hands on top of it, waiting for her to acknowledge him. When she moved a few inches forward, without so much as a hi, he gave her shoulders a light squeeze. "How was school today?"

"Fine," Danlyn answered. To the point.

Vivian snapped her fingers, pointed at the stairs. "You go wash up, too, Danlyn."

Danlyn pushed her chair back, hitting Frank.

A nervous sweat dampened his skin as Danlyn passed by, glaring ahead. After she disappeared upstairs, loudly slamming the door shut, Frank said, "Somethin' ain't right."

Vivian slapped the spoon against the big pot. "What's wrong with you? You're awfully sweaty. Are you feeling sick?"

Frank didn't know what to do with his hands or his feet or all his vexing thoughts. He picked the chair up a few inches off the floor, slammed it back down. "Laura knows somethin'."

"She does not."

"I'm tellin' you, Vivian. I've been watchin' them two. I don't know… The way they look at me, they're more than just angry. Last night, with that little stunt you pulled…"

Vivian rested against the counter. "Frank, my child has been angry with me since the day she was born. Is it really all that surprising that Danlyn turned out the same? Just last night she found out that Laura lost the baby. Were you expecting joy?"

"It started before the baby. It started the minute Laura saw me, and it didn't take long for Danlyn to catch up. Unless someone's been talkin', they've got no reason to hate me. You're the only one who's been runnin' her mouth."

"No one has told them a thing. You're getting paranoid." Vivian's eyes narrowed. "You've been drinking. That's where all this is coming from, isn't it?"

He lowered his voice. "How the hell are you so certain? You've been hearin' the same things from Laura that I have. You've seen the way Danlyn looks at me. You always said our tracks were covered. But what if they're not? What if she remembers?"

"What do you want me to do, Frank?"

"Nothin'. I'm gonna take care of it."

Vivian tilted her head slightly. "What's that supposed to mean?"

Frank looked above him. "The attic. I want everything that's up there."

Vivian shook her head. "Absolutely not. They've been up there for years. They're not going anywhere now. It's the safest place."

Frank's warning was written all over his face. His eyes smoldered, his voice dropped. "I'm not askin', ol' girl. I've been "sayin' for years that we need to burn them damn things. I'd say it's time, wouldn't you?"

"You're not taking them. I don't trust them being anywhere but where I can keep an eye on them."

"An eye?" Frank laughed. "You've been keepin' an eye on 'em? You never go up there. You have no reason to hold on to 'em, anyway. Hell, you never needed 'em to begin with. Jesus, Viv. Why didn't you let me get rid of 'em years ago? What the hell do you still need those damn things for?"

"That's my history, too," she told him. "Those stories are my stories. I'm not going to rid myself of them now."

"You wanna hold on to memories you hate? You want stories from a life you couldn't stand? I don't get you, Vivian. What if Danlyn or Laura find them? What if they already have?"

Vivian's laugh made Frank feel small.

"They haven't been up there, Frank. There's no reason in the world for them to. Even if they did go in the attic, that place is full of boxes."

"What happens if this thing gets the best of you, Viv? What happens if you die and Laura's here? You don't think someone's gonna go through all your belongings? I'll try to beat 'em to it, but what if I can't?"

Vivian looked stunned by her own complacency.

The anger in Frank's voice fell away, allowing Vivian to finally hear his fear. "Have you even read through all of 'em? Do you know how much is in 'em?"

Vivian folded her arms in front of her. She seemed to be contemplating. "Promise me you won't read them," she said. "Promise me you'll destroy them."

"I will."

Vivian reached up, held his face softly in her hands. "No good can come from your curiosity. Don't even open one. Promise me?"

Frank never had a problem lying to her before, and he certainly wasn't going to start feeling badly about it now. "I promise. Now, let me go put 'em in the truck while Danlyn's still in the bathroom."

"What else is wrong?" she asked.

He took her hands off his face, squared his shoulders. "Nothin'." But as he started towards the stairs, he asked, "When's Laura gettin' back?"

Vivian picked the spoon back up. "I told those people not to bother with calling, but a nurse called me again earlier. She had surgery late last night. She'll be out tomorrow morning."

Frank's posture finally relaxed. "Good."

Chapter 24

Olivia watched the nurses wheel another patient into the room.

"What's his deal?" Olivia asked, looking at the unconscious man they parked next to her. There were so many tubes and wires coming out of him, she couldn't tell where they started and stopped.

"Olivia, I'm going to move you to the other side of the room. Our patient here needs as much privacy and quiet as he can get." Nurse Hill gave her a coy smile. "And you know I can't tell you anything about him."

"Aw, hell. I know you can't. And I can walk myself over there just fine."

Nurse Hill laughed. "You've been here enough times to know that I can't let you do that. Now you stop being a troublemaker and just enjoy the ride."

Olivia reluctantly pulled her feet back onto the bed. "You all underestimate me. I could dance my way across this floor if you'd let me."

"I don't doubt that. At twice my age, you could probably outrun me and out-dance me, but rules are rules."

The nurse positioned Olivia's bed next to Laura, who was still sleeping. "Here," she said, closing the curtain between them so that Olivia could no longer see Laura. "Give you a little privacy. Let me just get you hooked up here and we'll be out of your hair."

"That woman," Olivia whispered. "That's Laura Hallow, isn't it?"

"You're gonna drive me crazy. I thought you knew everyone, anyway. What're you asking me for?"

"Come on, Hill. I'm an old woman without a lot of time. What's the harm?"

Nurse Hill wagged a finger. "Not telling. But you can always ask her when she wakes up. There's no rule against that."

Olivia huffed. "Get out of here and take care of your other patients, then. The ones who can't dance circles around you."

Nurse Hill clipped a new bag of saline to Olivia's IV, quietly laughing. "That's why we love you around here, Ms. Boone."

"Ha. I know it. And that's why I keep coming back. Just to keep you ladies on your toes."

"You want this shut?" The nurse grabbed the curtain in front of Olivia's partitioned space.

"Better not. Watching you two hook him up might be the most exciting thing I do all day."

"Thought so. I'll come back and check on you in a little while."

Olivia sat back and watched the nurses work. One hose here, another there, a machine under him, a machine above, and wires galore. Olivia knew she shouldn't be watching. Too disparaging for a lonely old woman to think about. That's why she didn't like hospitals. They brought to life all the realities of growing old. But it could have been worse, she supposed. Some of the nurses were nice, especially Nurse Hill. But that didn't make up for the loneliness and vacant roommates.

After Olivia's son died at just four years old, she knew she would never have another child. When her husband died, almost nineteen years ago, she knew she would never remarry. It seemed like people made a habit of dying on her. Objectively, she knew that neither her husband's death nor her son's had been part of some cosmic plan, but the heartache was too profound, so she swore people off. Keeping her distance was the easy part. It was not caring—once someone stumbled into her life—that proved impossible.

The nurses at the hospital were Olivia's only company, and while that seemed a little pitiful, it gave her control. Sure, they asked personal questions: *Have you eaten? Passed urine? Can you breathe? Have you had a bowel movement?* In many ways, they knew more about her than anyone else, but it was a dance of sorts. A mandatory concern, which meant no one was personally invested. No one here was going to be Olivia's best friend or her next husband. They were just a group of emotionally disconnected people with smiles on their faces and one general goal: to keep people like Olivia alive. While it left her lonely, the arrangement meant Olivia wouldn't have to experience another loss.

After having finished hooking up the man's elaborate station, which created a melancholy symphony of buzzes and beeps, the nurses finally left, affording Olivia another chance to wake her roommate. But just as Olivia was getting out of bed, she heard Nurse Montgomery's voice.

"Ms. Hallow? Sorry to wake you, but it's time to check your temperature and blood pressure. We need to get you eating and drinking."

Olivia heard a couple deep groans. Laura sounded like something dredged up from the grave.

"How's your pain?" the nurse asked.

"Not too bad right now. Is it the medication?"

"Let's see."

Olivia detected the scrape of a clipboard.

"No. We decreased your dosage while you were sleeping. It's your own body doing what it needs to. That's good. Now open up so I can get your temperature."

Olivia waited.

"Our biggest concern at this point would be infection," the nurse said. "But your temperature is perfect. Dr. Murray will be in to speak with you in a little while. He's been very busy today. In the meantime, we'll get you some dinner."

"I slept that long?" Laura asked.

"That's the way anesthesia works. You have to sleep it off at some point. We've been giving you fluids in your IV, but I'll bring you back some water, too. You've still got a short wait till dinner's served. Click that button if you need anything. I'll be back shortly."

~

As soon as the door closed behind the nurse, the curtain separating Laura from the bed next to her peeled back and she found herself staring at an old woman with kind blue eyes and a sweet face framed with blonde-and-silver hair.

"Can I help you?" Laura asked.

Olivia looked Laura over, gave one quick nod. "Well, there's no mistaking it. You're the spitting image of..." she stopped, shook her head. "Listen to me. I'm such a fool. I must sound like a crazy old bat."

Laura frowned. "I'm sorry, but do I know you?"

"Not exactly." Olivia paused. "Listen, sweetie. You'll have to forgive me, but I heard you talking with your friend earlier."

Laura looked away in shame. "I'm sorry. We didn't mean to disturb you."

"No, no. You didn't bother me. I get so damn bored in this place, I'm afraid I get a little nosy sometimes. Anyone's voice is a welcome gift."

"Oh." The woman's face was so innocent and her delicate southern drawl so charming, Laura couldn't manage to feel annoyed by the intrusion. "You heard everything?"

"Bits and pieces. But that's beside the point. I'm pretty sure I know who you are. That, or it's one hell of a coincidence. You're William's daughter, aren't you?"

If anything could have snapped Laura out of her despair, that was it. She sat up, kicked her legs over the side of the bed. "Yes. You knew him?"

Olivia let out a relieved sigh, but then her expression became serious. "Listen, I know this probably isn't my place, but hell, I don't have much time on this Earth, and I don't plan on spending it in silence. At least not when it matters."

"I'm sorry, but you've lost me. You didn't mention how you knew my father."

Olivia lowered her voice, looked at the man across the room, then back at Laura. "I heard what you were saying earlier, about not wanting your little one with your mama and Frank."

Laura's eyes grew wide. "You know Frank?"

"Not well. We were never friends. But yeah, I know him. I'm just someone who agrees that those two aren't fit to be in the company of any child."

"Why?" Panic rushed through Laura's body. Her lungs suddenly felt tight.

"I'm sorry, honey. I just get so damn frazzled sometimes and my mouth starts running in circles. I should've started by telling you my name. I'm Olivia Boone. And, yes, I knew your daddy."

Laura felt like she'd just walked out of a dense fog and into the dizzying sun. "How?"

"We were seeing each other the last year of his life. Well, almost a year. He died about…" Olivia drummed her fingers on the bed. "Let's see here. I met him about ten months before he passed. I take it you never knew?"

"No."

"I figured as much. Sorry for springing this on you right now."

"It's fine. I'm glad you said something. I have a million questions I'd like to ask you, but what does this have to do with my daughter?"

"That's what I've been waiting all day to talk to you about." Olivia brought her hand to her chest. "Pardon me. I'm draining fast, honey. Don't think it rude if I lie down."

"Of course not."

Olivia coughed, thick mucus crackled in her chest. "There's a lot more to this than I have time for, so I'll give you the quick version while I still have the energy. Your daddy and I had been dating for a good bit when he started opening up about his past. He used to tell me all kinds of things. He'd usually start ranting when he was drinking, so I never knew exactly what to make of it. Mostly it was a lot of tears and a lot "of slurred words, but I read between the lines enough to know what had happened between him and your mama. He used to talk about things your mama had done to you and him. Some were so awful, he couldn't tell me what they were. I knew she ran around on him. He wasn't shy about telling me so. But then he always used to say that he'd never forgive himself, or her. There was a lot more to that, I know, but he never really explained. If he got real drunk, he'd start rattling off names…all men, and Frank was always one of them."

Olivia waited a beat. "Listen, Laura. I'm not sure if I'm helping or hurting, but if you're not feeling right about your daughter being alone with those people, maybe, if you're feeling up to it, you can talk your doctor into letting you leave early. The things your daddy did tell me your mama did…" Olivia's voice trailed off. She frowned. "They were so terrible, I couldn't imagine what the things were he couldn't bring himself to talk about. Maybe none of this adds up, and I'm awfully sorry if I'm just stirring the pot. But your daddy…his face…when he'd start talking about Frank. I don't know. He thought the man was the devil himself."

In the silence that followed, in which both women kept their eyes trained on each other, something passed between them. An understanding as clear and potent as if it had been shouted over a loudspeaker. Olivia didn't need to confess that there was more she couldn't bring herself to say, because the truth sat right there, in her eyes. And that was enough for Laura. Knowing her father had felt the same about Frank was enough to get her up and out of the hospital.

"Go get her," Olivia finally said. "Don't leave her there."

Adrenaline fired every cell in Laura's body to life. A sudden, eerie sense of *déjà vu* hit her. Olivia's words were an omen.

Laura pressed the call button. "You said you don't know Frank well, but can you tell me anything about him?" She pressed it again, harder.

"Not much. But I never thought highly of the man. Especially after all that business with his fiancée and son. You can't help but learn some things about a person when you live in a small town."

Laura mashed her thumb into the button. "Fiancée and son?"

"That's right. It was years ago. Hell, decades. His fiancée up and left him. Even left her baby boy with him. No one knew why, but no one really ever met the girl. I saw her a couple times, but she was real quiet, never introduced herself. I didn't even know she was with Frank until after she left him. After that, he sent his baby away to live with some family a few counties away. Least that was the story."

"Shit." Laura threw the call button on the bed. "I had no idea he had a kid."

"Odd ducks, those two," Olivia said. "But Frank…I never liked him. And then everything your daddy went on about. What kind of man intrudes on another man's family like that? And during a time like that?"

"A time like what?" Laura's red eyes stood out against her pale skin.

"A time like war. You don't bark up a woman's tree while her husband's off fighting for his country."

"Jesus," Laura said. "That far back? I assumed my mother had cheated on my father with Frank, but…" So that's where all the old family friend nonsense had come from. She felt a dark familiarity seep into her flesh. "How is it that my father has been dead for ten years, yet somehow we feel the exact same way about the same man? What could that mean? And where the hell's the nurse?" Laura ripped off the tape holding her IV in place.

Olivia raised her eyebrows. "Somehow you do know, or you wouldn't be running outta here like a bat outta hell."

When Laura heard those words, she froze in place. Finally, she slowly turned around, looked at Olivia. She thought about her father's reports, about the alleged suicide, about all the lies, about Frank…and about…

The nurse burst through the door, standing face-to-face with Laura. "Ms. Hallow, please be more patient. I was on my way. You need to get back in bed."

Laura reached her arm out. "Take it out."

"Ms. Hallow!" Blood was beginning to pool around the site. "The doctor was held up, but he'll be in here shortly. I need you to get back in bed, now."

When the nurse tried to walk around her, Laura stood in her way, trying to hide her unsteadiness. "Take it out. I feel fine. I'm leaving tonight, with or without Dr. Murray's approval."

"You're being unreasonable." The nurse's voice carried around the room, this time with warning. "Get back to—"

"If I need to yank this out myself"—Laura grabbed the IV—"I'll do it. Or you can help. Either way, I'm leaving."

"This is…." The nurse's lips thinned. "Fine. I'll get Dr. Murray. Just please sit down and wait, will you? He needs to discharge you. I can't. Not without losing my job."

"Fine," Laura said. "But I don't have a car. Someone needs to call Jackie Brenner and tell her to come get me."

~

Jackie and Laura walked out of the hospital and into the cold air. The sun had already set, leaving ambient streaks of orange and purple across the sky. Laura pulled her arms into her chest, huddling against the wind as they walked to the car. The cold brought life to her increasingly dizzy head, clearing the last bits of the medication, but the uneasy whooshing in her brain and the wobble to her legs stood as a reminder of Dr. Murray's warning. He let her leave under one condition: she had to rest. She was severely anemic, and if she pushed herself, she was bound to crash.

~

Laura talked fast, bringing Jackie up to speed. "It's just too coincidental, isn't it?"

Jackie made a fast turn out of the parking lot. "It can't be a coincidence. I think you're making the right call by getting Danlyn."

Laura wiped tears off her cheeks. "How could I have left her with them? You offered to get her. How could I have said no?"

Jackie reached over, and with one hand gripped Laura's shoulder. "Listen. I'm gonna give you a dose of tough love. You can break down later, but you need to stay strong right now. And for the love of God, stop beating yourself up. You did what you thought was best by waiting to get her. That's really all you could've done."

"You're right. I need to get my head straight. I have no idea what my mother's going to do when I get there. What would I do without you, Jackie?"

"Eh. That's what I'm here for." Jackie put both hands back on the steering wheel, gripping it tight. "And I'm coming with you, so don't argue. We can get your car tomorrow."

"My mother's going to lose her shit. Maybe you shouldn't."

"That's all the more reason I should be there. You feel like hell, and I'm willing to bet she'll see that coming a mile away. You really want to walk in there at a disadvantage? Besides, you can't drive right now."

"It'll be even worse if she sees you."

"Then I'll stay in the car and wait. At least I'll be there if you need me."

"What about Steven?"

"What about him?"

"He's gonna be pissed when he finds out I brought you out here."

"Laura Hallow," Jackie shouted. "Would you please shut up and relax? You're done battling all of this alone. Your mother, Frank, all this shit. So pipe down and take the help. And don't worry about Steven. It's not like your mother's going to murder us. She's nasty, but her reach only goes so far. Fuck her." Jackie paused. "What? What's wrong?"

"I love you. That's all."

Jackie smiled, so bright and wide that it almost lit up the car. "Good. You should."

Laura watched the last of the color drain from the sky. The closer they got to Hallows' Farm, the darker it became, and then Laura thought about Olivia again. "I feel like I'm about to walk into a nightmare, Jackie." She felt the way the road changed under the tires and knew without having to look that they were nearing the house.

Jackie slowly turned left onto the driveway and grabbed Laura's hand. "It only feels that way. It's gonna be okay."

Laura's heart raced, her head felt too light, like a balloon on a string.

The farmhouse was hidden in a shroud of darkness, but Laura could just make out the truck.

"Shit."

"What?"

"There." Laura pointed at the side of the house. "Frank's truck. I was hoping he wouldn't be here."

Jackie turned off the headlights, then came to a stop near the front of the house, hidden behind some trees. "You sure you don't want me to come in? I think I should."

"I'm sure. Just wait here. I'll be quick."

Chapter 25

Laura walked to the front door and quietly unlocked it. Her heart went *thud-thud-thud*. She pushed on the door with one finger, and a slight groan crept from its hinges. Only darkness awaited her on the other side.

The cold brass doorknob slipped out from under her fingers as she shut the door. She reached out into the darkness, bracing against the round table in the foyer. Standing perfectly still, she listened. But there wasn't even a whisper. And it was too early for bed. Where was everyone?

She took a few steps forward, reaching the wall across from the staircase, and slid one foot in front of the stairs while grabbing the banister. Gently raising one foot, she placed her weight onto the first step. She waited for the creaking of the hardwood under her foot. A muffled *pop* rang out, then silence.

Laura's heartbeat filled her ears. She held tightly on to the banister and slowly, quietly made her way up the stairs, thinking she'd find Danlyn awake in her room. But as she reached the top of the stairs, she saw no light coming from under Danlyn's bedroom door. But Vivian's light was on, her door shut.

Laura steadied herself, testing her balance. She let go of the banister, but every step she took required more energy than the last.

Something was very wrong.

She hurried up the last two steps, and that was when she heard it. Danlyn was yelling, pleading. Her voice was muffled and distant. But then it was clear.

"I want to go!"

Laura turned in the direction of her voice and flung Vivian's door open. The room was empty. Danlyn's voice again, clearer this time.

"I don't want to!"

Vivian's bathroom. Laura heard another voice. Frank's. Rage shot through her body like a bolt of electricity. She charged the door, knocking it open, sending the doorknob through the wall.

"What in the..." Laura screamed. Her eyes darted around the bathroom as she tried to register what she was seeing. "Jesus Christ!"

Frank spun around, startled.

"Go, Danlyn!" Laura yelled. "Get out of here!"

Vivian sat in the bath, naked, her shoulders hunched over, silently watching Laura.

Danlyn was still leaning against the wall, as far away from Frank as she could get. Frank was knelt down beside the bathtub, soapy rag still in hand.

"What in the hell's going on?" Laura's voice came out in a thunderous roar that cut Frank's ferocity in half. He dropped the rag into the water, and Danlyn ran to Laura.

"He told me I had to start helping more, with you being gone," Danlyn said, throwing herself into Laura's body. "I didn't want to come in here, Mom. I swear."

"What did he do to you?"

"Nothing. I just didn't want to help."

"Go get your things," Laura instructed, still zeroed in on Frank. "We're getting out of here."

When Danlyn ran to her room, Laura yanked the towel off the wall beside her and threw it at Vivian. "What the hell were you thinking?" She waited for someone to answer, but they only stared at her with dumbstruck expressions. "Someone better start talking. What the hell was going on in here?"

Vivian stood up, wrapped the towel around her body. "Danlyn told you. Nothing happened. I was just taking a bath. You're overreacting."

Laura placed her face in front of her mother's. The hate radiating off Laura was palpable. The fierce look in her eyes and the growl in her throat forced Vivian a step back until her calves hit the side of the tub.

"Someone better answer me, or God help me…" Laura heaved like a bloodthirsty lion. "What the *fuck* was going on in here?"

No one moved an inch. Laura froze, incapacitated by the hate she felt for these two people. It wasn't until Vivian moved to the right and stepped one foot outside the tub that Laura realized Frank was up and walking out of the bathroom. Laura turned, peeled after him, shouting at him to get out.

She ran down the stairs, on his heels, and into the living room, another scream readied in her lungs when he abruptly spun around, slamming his chest into hers, pressing her into the wall.

"I'm not goin' anywhere," he growled in her ear.

"Get the fuck out now, or—"

Frank grabbed her arms, squeezing like a vise, and drew her into him. She clawed at his forearms, trying to free herself, but he was stronger, and her body was too weak for any fight.

"Get the fuck off me," she grunted, but her words and her fight only seemed to encourage him, as evidenced by his mischievous smile.

With every bit of energy Laura exerted, he gained more control, yanking her here and pushing her there. All Laura could do was struggle for her next breath. Jackie would hear her, if she could just catch her breath and scream loud enough. But she couldn't draw in enough air to make it count, and the rain now pounding on the roof would surely mask her feeble cries for help.

Frank dug his fingers deep into any part of her body he could find. He threw her sideways, shoving her into the side of the fireplace, and pressed his body into hers so hard that even shallow breaths felt impossible. Laura writhed underneath his weight, fighting with every fiber of her body. As he leaned in closer and she felt his body responding to her, a gurgling scream escaped her just before Frank pressed his mouth against hers.

Laura twisted, tried to lunge her weight forward, but Frank knocked her back, allowing him the chance to pin her head against the wall. He grabbed her neck with one strong hand, keeping her from veering left or right. She was quickly losing the strength to even stand.

Then he shoved his weight into her hips and chest. With her head forced back, he pressed his mouth against hers again. With his other hand, he frantically groped at her sides, prying at her clothes.

Laura's strength had bled out, her body felt like dead weight. She could do nothing but sink into him, allowing him to sandwich her against the wall. Her eyes began to cloud with brilliant lights and her lungs burned. There were no more cards to play. All that was left was to fight just as dirty.

When Laura settled into his arms, Frank leaned his head back with a smile. Laura relaxed her lips, allowing them to open. Frank hesitated for a moment, then kissed her softly. All Laura could do was silently scream at herself not to close her mouth, even when her throat tightened against his foul taste.

She finally felt his body loosen, his arms go a bit slack, and he slowly took his hand off her neck, reaching down to her breasts. He didn't fight when Laura grabbed a hold of each side of his face, pulling his mouth firmly against hers. Again and again, his tongue worked in and out. Laura opened her mouth wider, now holding firm to his jaw, gaining the most leverage possible. When she knew she had him, she drove her teeth into his tongue.

An animalistic cry ripped from Frank's lungs. He grabbed Laura's face, prying her mouth from his while throwing his weight back.

Laura could taste blood in her mouth. She'd hurt him. She'd bought time to get away.

Frank reeled backward, grabbing his mouth. "What the fuck is wrong with you?"

Laura ran for the staircase, but before she could reach the first step, Frank's hands were around her waist. He yanked her back, her head hurtled into his chin. A loud *crack* rang from his jaw, and he grumbled again, moaning in pain.

Laura kicked behind her, at his groin, his knees, at anything she could reach. "Jackie! Help!" she tried to yell, but her throat was raw and her voice didn't travel beyond the house. Frank reached around, pressed his hand over her mouth, but Laura bit, thrashing like a rabid dog.

"Let my mom go!"

Laura saw Danlyn standing at the top of the stairs, terror plastered on her face. "Stay there, Danlyn," she ordered. "Don't—" Frank pulled her back again.

Danlyn clasped her hands over her mouth.

"Don't come down here," Laura yelled.

"It's all right." Frank struggled to hold on to her. "Your mama's just havin' a little upset. I'm keepin' her from hittin' me again."

"Liar," Danlyn shouted. "Let her go!"

Vivian finally joined Danlyn, watching the spectacle from the top of the stairs. "Stop it now, Frank!" she said.

When Frank smiled, the blood coating his chin and lips gave him a deranged look. "Viv, come on. Laura just got a little rowdy and I had to—"

"Bullshit," Laura spat. "Get your hands off me, you sick fuck."

Vivian glared at him. "Let her go."

Frank threw Laura across the foyer. She bent over, drawing in deep breaths, working to get oxygen back into her body.

"What the hell are you sayin'?" Frank shouted. "You think this is my fault?"

Vivian walked halfway down the stairs, ushering Danlyn in front of her. "We're not doing this here, Frank."

Frank flung an open hand toward Laura. "It's her fault. It's always been her fault. You know that, Viv."

Laura stood up, fighting against gravity. "You attacked me, you son of a bitch."

Frank pretended not to hear her. "I'm tryin' to keep us together. This…this is all her fault."

Laura took a wobbly step toward him. "What the hell does that mean?"

Vivian's voice rose well above everyone else's. "No more, Frank. That's enough."

Frank walked to the stairs, resting one hand on the banister. "Viv, Sugar…"

Vivian brought her fists up, shaking them. "No!"

"Jesus Christ." Frank slapped his hand on the banister, causing it to shake. "Has that tumor eaten away so much of your brain that you can't see the truth anymore? Laura's comin' between our family again. It's like it always was. She came in between you and me before, now she's tryin' to do it again."

"Out," Vivian demanded, her lungs full of fire. She pointed at the door.

The blood beginning to dry on Frank's lips cracked when he smiled at Laura. His eerie expression worked its way under her skin. On his way to the door, he stopped next to her, whispering in her ear, "I guess some things never change."

The hair on Laura's arms stood on end. A dozen thoughts flashed through her mind in rapid succession.

Your daddy thought he was the devil himself.

Frank opened the front door, turned around. "I'll come back to check on you later, Viv."

Laura whipped her head around, waiting for her mother's response. Surely she'd tell him never to come back. Instead she said, "I'll call you later."

Laura's heart took its final step towards hardening completely for the woman who had given her life, but had done nothing since but slowly take it away. It was a mother's job to protect her child, no matter how old they were. But Vivian had sealed the hate she felt for her daughter in granite.

Laura jumped when Frank slammed the door behind him. She looked up at Danlyn. "Get your bags and let's go."

Danlyn ran past Vivian, who was still bracing herself against the banister.

"You can't leave," Vivian told her.

Laura walked to the foot of the stairs. "Are you kidding? We're not staying here. We're leaving, and we'll never come back. That's a promise." Laura yanked the house key from her jacket pocket and threw it down.

"You don't have a say in this, Vivian. You had your chance to be a mother, but you didn't want the job. In fact, you degraded it in every way possible." Laura looked up into her mother's eyes. "You didn't have to love me. You didn't even have to raise me. You could've washed your hands of everything. All those times you threatened to kill yourself, you could have just done it. I didn't ask to be born. You chose to have me, and then you spent every day of your life making clear how much you couldn't stand me. I wasn't a part of you. Isn't that what you always said? I was William's daughter, and you hated me for it."

Laura barked out a laugh. "Your feelings, your opinions, they mean nothing. You have no right to tell me what to do now. I can only imagine what might've happened had I not come back tonight, or why your boyfriend tried to have his way with me, in your house. Something you seem unfazed by. But I know I'll never get answers from you, you decrepit bitch. As far as you're concerned, be thankful I didn't rip your heart out of your chest when I found Danlyn in there with you and Frank. Put you out of your fucking misery."

"I don't need you," Vivian said. "You've been a burden on my soul since the day you entered this world. I cried the day you were born. I cried for everything I had lost, for my miserable future with you and that disgraceful father of yours. I never needed you. I will live and die never needing you. Frank will be back. You can't push him away. And we will be a family, but you'll not be a part of that. Danlyn will, though. So long as I'm standing, you'll not take her from me. You're a drunk. You're no proper mother. And after what you did tonight…" Vivian's dark eyes narrowed. "Seducing Frank, trying to finally break us apart."

Maternal instinct bubbled to life in Laura. It was like a monster had broken from its confines and was climbing through her gut, up into her chest, latching on to the soft tissue of her lungs, spilling its powerful venom into her blood. If protecting Danlyn meant resorting to a finality there was no coming back from, so be it.

Laura looked down at her hands. They were so still—they suddenly felt so strong. She wondered if these hands were capable of such violence, and then she looked into her mother's eyes and knew. They were.

She slowly walked up the stairs, stopping on the step just below Vivian, searching her eyes for a gap through which her words would penetrate. "You and Frank can rot in your own hell together. But if you try to stop me from leaving with Danlyn, that'll be the last thing you'll do on this Earth."

Vivian lips twitched. "Frank's been more of a father to you than William ever was."

Such desperation. Laura almost pitied her. "Come on, Danlyn," she hollered.

Vivian's eyes reddened, she curled over the banister. "He was here for us after your father left us."

"My father never left us. He was fighting in a war, and Frank moved in on his family."

"Frank was here for—"

"Shut your stupid mouth! I'm warning you, Vivian, don't say those words to me again. Frank's a sick, perverse son of a bitch, and he'll be lucky if I don't turn him in."

Every inch of Vivian's skin turned blotchy. Her eyes were crazed.

Danlyn came running down the stairs with the bags in her hands.

"Jackie's waiting outside," Laura told her, taking a couple of the heavy bags. "Go get in the car."

As they rushed down the stairs and hurried to the front door, Vivian let out an unearthly shriek that seemed to rattle the whole house. Danlyn and Laura stopped dead in their tracks and turned around. Danlyn dropped the bags, clasping her hands over her ears.

Vivian's face seemed to bulge, ready to burst. She screamed, "You get out of my house, Laura. And don't dream of ever coming back. But you will not take my daughter from me!" Vivian clamped her hand over her mouth.

"Jesus," Laura gasped. Her eyes slowly shifted to Vivian. "How could you?"

Terror-struck, Laura looked at Danlyn and saw that her hands were no longer over her ears but were hanging limp at her sides. She stared at Laura, as though waiting for something; anything that would tell her that what Vivian just said wasn't true.

Laura tried to take Danlyn's hand, but she moved away in slow motion as her grandmother's words sank in.

"Please, Danlyn," Laura said. "Let me explain."

But Danlyn remained silent, only looking at the two of them with a horrified expression.

"Danlyn, listen to me," Laura tried again. "Please listen."

Vivian leaned over the banister, holding on to the railing. "Dear God," she mumbled. "I didn't mean to. It just..."

"Come on, Danlyn." Laura wasn't giving up. "Look at me. I'm so sorry." But as she watched her little sister's eyes narrow with pain and betrayal, she knew. Danlyn wasn't ready to listen. Her world had just been turned inside out, and nothing she said right now could pull her from this nightmare.

The front door slowly opened and Jackie peeked her head around it. "Is everything okay? I was waiting for Frank to leave before coming in, but he sat in his truck for a—"

"Take Danlyn to the car," Laura said. "I'll be right there."

"Of course." Jackie quickly scooped up Danlyn's bags in one arm and wrapped the other around Danlyn. "Come on, sweetie. We'll go warm up in the car."

As Jackie walked her out the front door, Danlyn looked over her shoulder at Vivian, her expression heartbreaking, wretched.

Laura bent down and grabbed the remaining bags, trembling from head to toe. "God forgive you, Vivian. Because I never will."

Chapter 26

Jackie pulled into the driveway, killed the engine. Danlyn was already running through the front door when Jackie and Laura got out of the car.

"What the hell happened over there?" Jackie asked, grabbing the bags from the back seat.

Laura fell back against the car, too stunned to cry.

"Never mind." Jackie laced her arm through Laura's and gave her a gentle tug. "Let's just get you inside."

"I don't know what to say to her, Jackie. Everything that just happened…I don't know how to make it better."

"Whatever it is, just give Danlyn some time. She'll come around."

"I don't know if she will. Not this time. This was too…"

Steven walked out the front door, wearing a stern look. "I've been worried sick," he said. "And what's wrong with Danlyn? She locked herself in the guest room. You said you were just going to the hospital, Jackie."

Jackie handed him the bags while giving him a look that said it wasn't time for a lecture. "Laura got out of the hospital early so she could get Danlyn. Things got... I don't know. They obviously didn't go well."

"You all right?" Steven asked Laura.

"No." Her voice sounded far away. "Nothing's all right."

"What is that?" Steven peered through the darkness, straining to see what was smeared all over her light blue sweater.

Laura crossed her arms over her chest without looking down. She didn't want to see it.

Jackie leaned in, squinting. "God, Laura! Is that blood? I didn't even see that earlier. Where's that from? Are you hurt?"

Laura wiped at the stains. Stains that would last forever. "It's not my blood."

Jackie put her hands around her shoulder, escorting her in the house. "Holy fuck." Jackie's eyes widened. "Your neck."

Brought to a sudden halt, Steven dropped the bags. "Who did this?" He lowered his voice. "It was Frank, wasn't it? Your mother couldn't have caused all this."

"Yes," Laura whispered.

Jackie looked around. "Danlyn's still in the room?"

Steven nodded once, unable to speak through his anger.

"Good." Jackie sat Laura down on the sofa. "I'll go get Danlyn settled in for bed. Then we'll look you over and clean you up."

Steven kneeled in front of Laura. As gently as he could, he held her face in his hands. "Let me get a closer look." He slowly lifted her chin, inspecting the bruises forming on her neck.

Laura could feel his hands trembling against her skin, could see his face strain with anger.

He spoke softly. "Let's roll up your sleeves a little."

There were welts and red blotches all over her wrists. As he pushed her sleeves higher, some of the bruises were already turning blue.

"Did he hurt you anywhere else?"

"No."

"This is all Frank's blood? You sure you weren't bleeding?"

"I'm sure."

Jackie shut the guest-room door, rushing back to Laura's side. "How bad is it?"

"I see a lot of bruising," Steven said. "But it doesn't look like anything's broken. It's not her blood."

Laura unzipped her sweater and pulled it off, groaning as she worked her muscles.

"You need to tell us what happened," Jackie said.

"Frank tried to… Nothing happened. I didn't let anything happen. I didn't even feel all this." Laura looked at her arms. "He was too strong. I had to—" she saw the look on Steven's face. "I didn't kill him, if that's what you're thinking. I bit him. He wasn't letting go, and I never could've fought him off, so I bit him."

Steven grabbed hold of Laura's hands. "You did what you needed to do to protect yourself. I'm proud of you."

"He's right," Jackie said. "And now you and Danlyn never have to go back there. It's over. But we should take you back to the hospital. Just to make sure you're okay. We can probably just talk to the police there."

"No." Laura tensed. "No police. No hospital."

"You need to get checked out. And of course we need to call the police. You can't let Frank get away with this," Steven said.

"I'm not going back to the hospital."

"Laura, you're being—"

"I'm not leaving Danlyn. I'm not hurt. Bruised, but not hurt. I'll be fine. And I'm not calling the police. I can't call them."

"You're joking, right?" Steven asked.

Laura closed her eyes, slowly exhaling. How had the words come so easily to her mother? How had they just spilled out, like they didn't carry the weight of the world behind them?

"Listen," Laura said. "I can't call the police. I also can't explain everything to you until I have a chance to talk to Danlyn. But I can't call because…I don't want them taking Danlyn from me."

"Why would that happen?" Jackie asked. "Because of what you told me earlier in the hospital? They can't do that, Laura."

"No, not because of that."

"Why then?"

Laura wasn't ready to hear words she'd never before uttered. Words she'd sworn never to speak.

"Because Danlyn's not"—the words tried to hide behind her sealed lips—"she's not my daughter. She's my sister."

Jackie blinked several times, and Steven's face went blank, like he'd not heard anything at all, but Laura saw the way he swayed, as subtle as it was.

"I'm sorry," he finally said. "But you're…" He pointed toward the guest room. "Danlyn's not…" His forehead creased. "She's not yours?"

Laura looked away. She didn't want to see Steven's expression. After all, this lie had defined his life as much as hers. "No. Vivian's her mother. That's why I can't call the police. If I send the police over there, for all I know my mom will tell them I kidnapped her, and they'll take her away from "me. Could you imagine, after all this, Danlyn being thrown back in that house with those people?"

"Jesus Christ," Jackie finally said. "I'm just... Your sister? After all this time, she's your sister?" Her mouth gaped open. "Holy shit. That poor thing. That's why Danlyn's so upset. You told her?"

"God, no. Vivian told her. The woman's completely lost her mind." Laura paused, finally feeling tears in her eyes. "You should've seen Danlyn's face...the pain. I didn't know what to say. That's what happened right before you walked in, Jackie."

Jackie looked back toward the guest room. "She didn't say anything at all?"

"No. I can't imagine what she's feeling. But I can't risk her being taken away. Do you see now why you can't call the police?"

Steven started pacing back and forth, pinching the bridge of his nose.

"I'm sorry for... I didn't want to lie to you guys," Laura said. "And Steven, I..."

He looked back at Laura, his expression still one of confusion. "None of it was true? Everything that happened...back then...it was all a lie?"

"Yes."

He opened his mouth, stuttered. "Never mind. Doesn't matter. So what's your plan? Just let Frank get away with this?"

"My plan is to nail his ass, and my mother's, too. That's the only way I can guarantee they never get their hands on Danlyn. But I have to prove what happened."

"Prove what? You've got proof all over your body."

"Prove that they had something to do with my father's death."

"Laura, seriously?"

"Listen. I saw it the other day. They were hiding something. I hadn't put the pieces together then, but it was there. At first, I convinced myself I was losing it. But not now. I know they were involved. I'm certain of it."

Steven came to a stop in front of her. "I can't even wrap my head around how you've figured that one out. But let's just say your theory is right. How're you going to prove anything, and what if you're wrong and the only thing that comes from this is you getting hurt again? Or worse, you're right about Frank, and the lunatic decides you're too much trouble to have around? What then? What would happen to Danlyn? She'd still get stuck with them."

"He's right," Jackie said, sitting down beside her. "You need to let it go."

"Exactly. Look at you." Steven nodded towards her. "I don't know if this guy's a murderer, but he's obviously crazy. Do you really wanna piss him off even more?"

They didn't understand, but Laura desperately wanted them to. Whether Steven and Jackie knew it or not, they were the only people she had left. She and Danlyn needed them, because they loved her and she loved them and if she lost them now, she and Danlyn would have nothing.

"I know you both care about me and that's the reason you feel so strongly about this, but I need you to try to understand." Laura grabbed Jackie's hand. "William wasn't just my father, he was Danlyn's father, too. I know he was an alcoholic, but he loved Danlyn and me more than life itself. I'll always hate myself for not speaking to him the day he died. I was just so angry with him for not standing up for me and Danlyn. I hated both of my parents for what they did, but I know my father was trying his best. I just…I have to make sense out of his death. More than that, if I don't do something to stop her, my mother "will always have the upper hand. She'll always have the ability to call the police and tell them Danlyn's hers. I can't live looking over my shoulder, and neither can Danlyn. As many times as Frank has talked about us being a family and how nothing will break us apart, I know he won't let this go. Neither will Vivian." Laura's shoulders slumped. "I came back here to make a better life for my children. I can't lose Danlyn now, too. I won't, because she deserves a chance. I have no idea how I'm going to do it, but I'll find some way to stop them. After tonight, and after what Olivia told me, I know I'm right."

"Olivia?" Steven asked.

"Laura met this woman in the hospital who was dating William before he died," Jackie said. "Apparently William thought Frank was Satan incarnate."

After a moment, Laura said, "I know he and Vivian had a hand in my father's death. I'd bet my life on it. Every time I mentioned my father or insisted that he hadn't killed himself, she and Frank would start acting strange. Nervous, actually. They're covering something." Laura paused. "Maybe Jackie told you what I shared with her yesterday, Steven?"

"She told me."

"Then you know I have more regrets than I have any right to. I've done things I will never forgive myself for. I can't run away from this. If I leave here, if I leave without honoring my father, without ensuring Danlyn's safety, that'll be another regret I can't bear to live with. I owe him this, you guys. I owe this to myself. But more than anyone, I owe it to that little girl in there, whose world just completely fell apart. They can't get their hands on her. Especially not after what they were doing with her."

"Doing with her?" Jackie asked.

"When we got there, I found them upstairs in the bathroom. All three of them." Laura's rage crept back up. "Vivian was in the bath and Frank was, I don't know, I think he was washing her back. But Danlyn was in there, leaning against the wall. She said Frank told her she had to help bathe Vivian. Sick fucking bastard. Danlyn was begging him to let her go. She said nothing happened, but..."

Steven's lips thinned, his nostrils flared. "I'm gonna kill him. I'll fucking kill him."

"And what?" Jackie shot off the sofa. "Get thrown in prison? That piece of shit deserves what's coming to him, but no one's killing anyone. We're turning his ass in."

Laura felt the weight of their anger on her shoulders.

"Someone has to do something," Steven said.

Laura's voice rose. "No one's doing anything. Steven, you're not touching the guy. I'm not letting you go to jail on my account. And Jackie, you're not calling the cops. They arrest me for kidnapping, that means Frank gets what he wants. I told you, I'm gonna nail their asses. I just need a little time. But no one does a damn thing right now."

Jackie and Laura watched in a nervous silence as Steven stormed out of the room.

When he returned, Jackie's eyes widened. "What the hell are you doing with the gun, Steven?"

He tossed the box of ammunition on the chair. "Calm down. You know it's in the house. You just don't like seeing it."

"No. I don't like why I'm seeing it. What're you doing?"

"I'm not going after Frank. But Laura's right about him, and you three won't be sitting ducks." He laid the revolver down on the kitchen table. "I'm not going to stand here and tell you this is a good idea, Laura. But if there's something to "find—something you can use to permanently get these people out of your lives—let's find it."

When Jackie's mouth opened, Steven raised his hand. "Stop, Jackie. I'm worried, too. But are you going to tell Laura that you can't understand her position? Cops aren't always the answer. I wish they were, but in this case, Laura might really lose Danlyn. So I'm going to sit here tonight, just in case that asshole pays us a visit. In the morning, we'll figure something out. But like Laura said, no good decisions can be made tonight. We're all too wound up."

"Laura could tell the cops what they were doing with Danlyn, and Danlyn can confirm—"

"Jacks, it's still Danlyn and Laura's word against theirs." He sat down at the table, opened the box of ammunition. "And with Laura's past"—he shot Laura an apologetic look—"they might not believe her story."

"Steven," Jackie scolded him.

"He's right," Laura said. "On every mark. I'm not credible. Not in their eyes." She watched as Steven loaded the gun. Five quiet slaps. "But we can't stay here. I won't put you two in this position."

Steven set the gun down. "All due respect, you're an idiot, Laura."

Despite herself, Jackie burst out laughing.

"What the hell does that mean?" Laura asked.

"Awe, come on now," Jackie said. "I love you, but it's true."

Laura's lips parted, but she made no sound.

Steven said, "You can feel as guilty as you want, but leaving… Yeah, you aren't going anywhere."

Jackie rested her hand on Laura's shoulder. "I told you at the hospital that you were going to stay here and not argue.

"Now you get to deal with Steven. Apparently he's running the show. Armed and all."

Steven rolled his eyes. "Laura, what I'm saying is that if I were in your shoes, I wouldn't stop until those people were put away, either. I'd also hope that my friends would stick by me, even if that meant being brutally honest with me. You're using your heart instead of your head. You've gotta be pragmatic here."

He ran his hands through his hair, stretched. He was doing a good job at looking calm, but Laura detected a definite edge to his voice. "For now, everyone needs to get some rest. Laura, our home is yours now, so anything you need or want, don't hesitate."

Pride always tasted bitter going down, but her friends weren't wrong, not even about her being an idiot. They just forgot to add prideful to that description.

"I don't want you two in danger. Seeing you go to such lengths…it's just…"

"It's fine," Steven said.

Jackie took Laura's hand in her own. "Let's get you cleaned up. I'll help you out of those clothes."

Laura followed her, then paused and looked over her shoulder. A single tear fell from the tip of her chin. Her lips parted as she searched for the right words. But before she could speak, Steven said, "You're welcome, Laura." And just like that, she felt the shattered pieces of her soul begin to fuse back together, never to be perfect—always scarred and tattered—but in one piece.

~

When Jackie shut the bathroom door, Laura shared her plan. "I'm going to the hospital tomorrow. I think Olivia knows more."

"Not alone, you're not."

"Jackie, I need time with Danlyn. I'll be careful. We're a mile from the hospital. We'll be okay."

"I'll think about it," Jackie said. "Either way, we'll figure it out, one step at a time.

~

When Steven heard the water turn on, he picked the gun up, turning it over, peering at the trigger. Maybe Laura's words had just soaked in too deep; maybe he couldn't find logic when all there was to see were bruises and welts and violent handprints all over Laura's body. He didn't much care what the reasons were. He knew she was right. He hated that he knew it. But that changed exactly nothing.

He slipped the gun back into the waistband of his jeans and stood up, checking each window and lock. When he sat back down, he stared at the front door. "Give me any reason to blow your fucking head off, you piece of shit."

Chapter 27

Frank drove home in a daze, his blood pressure soaring, his mind gripped in fury. He barely remembered leaving Vivian's, and had even less recollection of drinking the quarter-bottle of whiskey in the cab of his truck and then arriving at his own front door.

He went into his kitchen, flung open every cupboard, searching high and low for the bottle of Old Crow he'd hidden months ago. The bottle was somewhere, but every cupboard turned up empty, and with every letdown, he slammed another door closed, sending shudders through the hollow floor under his boots. Not that it took much. Sometimes when the wind picked up, his doublewide trailer felt like it might leap from the ground, right off the small hill it sat upon and into the vast, empty land around it. It was only because the way he built the foundation under and around it that he never found his house tangled in a pile of trees. But tonight, he felt like he could pick it up off its base and hurl it into the heavens.

He stood in front of the small window set above the kitchen sink. The black sky was dotted with the kind of brilliant stars and radiant moon that always followed a rainstorm. He drew in a breath, wincing at the pain in his tongue.

"Come on, you old bastard. Think."

He squinted, just making out a line of trees in the moonlight, off in the distance, around the perimeter of his trailer. He was so isolated, so far away from anyone that he could scream at God and no one would ever hear him. So he did. Gripping the sides of the sink, he yelled so loud that it momentarily deafened him. His biceps bulged, jagged, sinewy muscles popped from his forearms. His arteries throbbed under his flesh, like snakes, coiling around his throat. He pounded his fist into the kitchen counter, kicked at the bottom cupboards, and he yelled and yelled until he felt most of his anger drain from his body.

He bent forward, resting his weight on the counter. Every heavy breath came with a wheeze. Dammit, he even sounded old. He pushed off the counter, rocked back on his heels. "Where the hell would I have hid it?" And he would have done just that: hid it, even though Vivian hadn't come near his trailer since William was alive.

"Son of a bitch." He looked up, finally remembering. "Gotcha."

He stood high on his toes, reaching above the top cupboard, into the small space above them, where most women would place cute decorative teacups. But not Frank. That was where cigarettes and whiskey ended up when he was too drunk to find a better place for them.

He scraped his hand back and forth until he felt the cold glass slide under his hand. His eager fingers clamped around the bottle, and he gently pulled it over. He twisted off the cap, threw it on the floor. Things were looking better already. When he walked to the sofa, bottle in hand, he sat down and heard a *clunk* from under the springs of the cushion. He slowly ran his hand over the cushion beside him. Just thinking about what was hidden under there, within the frame of the sofa, made him smile. Getting up and pulling the sofa off the wall seemed too great a feat, but maybe he'd treat himself tonight. After everything that had happened, a little self-soothing was certainly in order.

He brought the bottle to his mouth, tipping his head back, methodically pulling in the liquid fire. He didn't care that it burned like hell. He drank until he heard the dreadful slapping back and forth of liquid within the neck of the bottle that meant he hadn't paced himself. But again, he didn't care, because the hot sting of the liquor on his gashed tongue was a devilishly alluring reminder of Laura's good fight, and it felt real and painful and sweet.

He stood up, walked to the edge of the sofa. The windows on each side of it cast rays of moonlight through the curtains and onto the floor next to him. He wedged the toe of his boot behind the back of the sofa and the wall it sat against and used his leg to push it out a few feet. His heart was racing like a horse behind the gates, and he grabbed the bottle, suckling at the last drops while looking down at the small space behind the sofa. The trailer was eerily quiet, aside from the sound of the toe of his boot playing with the loose flap of fabric on the backboard of the sofa. He could almost hear the buzzing of his anticipation as he pulled it open, exposing a dark cavity. Maybe he wouldn't need another bottle after all. What was in that box was stronger than any drink he'd ever had.

He tipped the bottle back again, forgetting it was empty, and chucked it on the floor. He bent down, yanked the small wooden box out from under the flap of fabric. His hands shook and his mind raced and his legs were growing unsteady, so he hurried back and sat down. Blood rushed to his limbs, making his fingers and toes tingle and his brain go fuzzy. So rarely did he give himself permission to look through the box that had been hidden under his sofa for decades. Most of the time, it hurt too much. Shed too much light on what he had lost. But not tonight. Tonight he would allow himself to feel the full capacity of his desires. Tonight he would get lost in his memories. Tonight—even if it were only in his mind—he would fulfill himself.

He set his hand on top of the box, but he was shaking so much that his fingers only fumbled around the edge of the lid. He clasped the corner, but before he could manage to lift a single item from it, his heart quickened and his body responded too eagerly. He panted, trying to stop himself from ruining what the night still had in store. He gripped the side of the sofa, tried to think of nothing at all, but his senses were too raw. His body jerked forward.

"Shit. Shit."

He couldn't catch his breath.

"Shit."

He smiled.

When his body finally came down from the high and his mind followed behind, he leaned over and picked the box back up, this time with still hands and calmer thoughts. It was as if a decade had been shaved from his body. His limbs felt easy and his heart pawed at his ribs, begging for more. When he opened the lid, he pulled one item out, brushed it with his fingers. He pulled out another, and another, until the coffee table was littered with his dark treasures.

He peered down into the box. Barely visible through the moonlight, atop a pile of postcards, was his most prized possession. His heart tightened, and all the years of living rushed back into his body, making him ache.

He settled then and there that he'd stop at nothing to keep what he loved. He knew what he wanted, and God have mercy on anyone who tried to stop him.

Chapter 28

Jackie tossed and turned, too preoccupied with thoughts of Laura and her *sister* in the other room, and her husband, sitting at the table with a gun in his hand. She ran her hand across Steven's side of the bed. The sheets were cool and lonely. She looked up at the clock. Three thirty. Grunting, she grabbed Steven's pillow, pressed it over her face. No sleep for the weary tonight.

Jackie crept out of bed and opened the door, tiptoeing past the guest room and into the living room, remembering Steven telling her not to get up and walk around the house. Damn gun. And damn Frank. This was all his doing.

She peeked her head around the corner and saw Steven sitting at the table with a book in his hands.

"Psst," she hissed. "It's me."

Steven nearly reached for the gun when his tired brain registered the voice. "Jackie, I told you not to get up and walk around."

"You look tired. Can I come out there? You're not gonna shoot me, are you?"

"Real funny. Get out here."

Jackie cinched her robe tight around her waist and leaned into Steven's outstretched arms. "Why don't you come to bed? I'm sure nothing's going to happen."

Steven wrapped his arms around her waist, pulling her tightly into him. He kissed her stomach, she kissed the top of his head.

"I've lasted this long," he told her. "A few more hours won't kill me."

She lifted his chin up with one finger. "In a few hours you're going to be spent."

"Still won't kill me."

"Know what your problem is?"

Steven patted the chair next to him. "Sit down and tell me all about it, you lovely creature."

She brushed her hand over her worn robe. "Lovely creature? You are tired, Stevey-Boy." She sat down, pulling her knees to her chest, wiggling her cold toes on the edge of the chair. Steven leaned forward, rubbed them.

"So what's my problem, Jacks?"

"You think you're nineteen years old still. Pulling an all-nighter before work."

He leaned back. A big, tired grin spread across his face, making him look even more handsome. "What're you trying to say? That I'm old?"

Jackie wiggled her toes in his hands. "If you need me to explain it to you, then yes, you are." She craned her neck around, looking into the living room, tapping her finger on her chin. "Hmm... I know I placed your cane somewhere, but where..."

Steven leaned forward, kissing her passionately. "I love you, Jackie."

Jackie brushed her hand across his stubbly cheek. "You okay, sweetie?"

"I'm fine. I'm just loving you right now."

Jackie rested her head on his shoulder. "I love you, too. Even if you need to shave."

"I'm going for a Grizzly Adams kind of thing. You don't approve?"

Her laugh was short-lived. "All this is crazy, isn't it?"

"'Crazy' would be an understatement. What the hell kind of crap luck do you have to have to get stuck with Vivian as your mother? Even William, I mean… Why stay with Vivian? I just can't imagine subjecting any child to her."

Jackie shrugged. "We've both been wondering that since high school. Who knows why he stuck around as long as he did. And now knowing that Danlyn is William and Vivian's daughter… I still can't wrap my head around it."

"Tell me about it. You could've knocked me over with a feather."

Jackie frowned, looking at him curiously.

"What is it, Jacks?"

"It's just…how does that make you feel?"

The sides of Steven's mouth drew down. "No different than it makes you feel, I guess."

"Yeah. But Laura getting pregnant was the reason you two broke up. You thought she cheated on you. I know how much you loved her. How can you not feel something more after finding out that the entire reason you broke up was complete shit?" She looked down at the floor. "I guess what I'm asking is…would we be sitting here together, married, in our house, if you had known back then what you know now?"

The look on Steven's face was so pained, Jackie immediately felt bad for asking, but she wasn't willing to have more sleepless nights in the future. These questions needed answering.

"Look at me," he told her. "I was shocked when Laura told us, and I'd be a liar if I said a thousand realizations didn't hit me. But here's the thing. You know that I believe things happen for a reason. Maybe I don't understand some of them. I certainly don't understand why Laura and Danlyn have to go through all this, but there's gotta be a reason. Maybe that's just what I tell myself when things happen that make no sense." He yawned, shook his head fast. "I'm tired, and I'm rambling. The important thing for you to know—because I knew you'd be thinking about all this—is that I love Laura like family. Always have, always will. But I fell out of love with her, Jacks, and I fell in love with you. You're the woman I want to be with. You know that. I'm more in love with you now than I was the day we got married. I don't regret a damn thing."

Jackie smiled. "I'm not doubting how you feel about me. I just want to know how you're coping with this. You were heartbroken back then. What you thought Laura did crushed you."

"It did. And it hurts knowing I held so much against her for so many years, because of a lie, but I can't do anything about that now. I can't blame myself, and I certainly can't blame her. I still feel the same way I always have, and you know what that is, Jackie. Without things happening the way they did, you and I would never have been us."

"That's true," Jackie agreed. "You know everything she told me in the hospital? About the drinking?"

"What about it?"

"Well, at the time, I didn't know Danlyn was her sister. Kind of changes things, doesn't it?"

Steven thought about it. "I guess. Not that it makes it okay, but…shit. After everything her parents did to her, and then to get shackled with raising a baby without a pot to piss in. What was William expecting?"

A long silence passed between them, and then Jackie stood up, looking down at the gun. "Are you really worried about all this? Obviously you have to be, to pull that out and stay up all night."

Steven followed her eyes. "I guess I panicked a little. I probably shouldn't have pulled that out when I did. I wasn't trying to scare you guys or make a show. I was pissed off, seeing Laura bruised up like that. Then hearing about the stuff with Danlyn. They know where we live, and they know you were there, Jackie. I was working on autopilot. Sorry I spooked you."

"I get all that. But that doesn't answer my question."

"I'm not scared for us. I'd tell you if I was. But I don't have a good feeling about Frank and Vivian. I think Laura's right. And I already know you think I'm nuts, so don't lay into me."

"I wasn't going to. I wanna see that asshole pay, whether he did anything to William or not." She wrapped her arms around herself.

"I don't know," Steven said. "The oddball stuff with her father's death records, and all this bullshit with Frank. Apparently no one's ever thought highly of the guy. Maybe there's a reason for that. Then again, maybe it's almost four in the morning and I've not slept." He stood up. "Come on. You need to get some sleep."

Jackie wound her arms around his neck. "God, I love you."

Steven kissed her neck, leaving her skin covered with goose bumps. "Just promise me you won't get in the middle of things, Jackie."

She nodded against his chest.

"No. Look at me and say it. We're involved enough, and I don't need you putting yourself in danger. You've seen what that man is capable of. It's already taken everything in me not to do something about it. But if he ever laid a hand on you, I'd kill him, Jackie. I swear, I'd kill him."

Jackie looked up into his eyes. "You have my word."

Chapter 29

Laura lay in bed, unable to sleep. Her neck throbbed and her arms ached, but mostly her heart broke for Danlyn. Despite being in the same bed, it felt like a world lay between them. She wished there was some way to ease Danlyn's suffering, but only time could heal this wound.

Laura watched her sister sleep in the soft glow of the moonlight. She saw the curvature of her sweet face, listened to her gentle breaths. Laura's heart seized. She wanted to hold Danlyn in her arms and love away all the pain, but she didn't know what role to play now. Was she a mother? Sister? Or an enemy? She didn't know how to be a sister. All she knew how to be was a mother, and even at that, she'd failed. Now the pieces of their lives were scattered about, left in every place they had lived, in every dirty motel room, in Vivian's home. How would Laura ever find them all and glue them back together?

The hours rolled on, and when the room brightened with the morning sun, Laura sat up, pushing aside the heavy comforter.

"Danlyn," she spoke softly. "It's time to get up." Laura sniffed the air. "I think Jackie cooked sausage. Your favorite." She waited. "Okay." She crept her legs over the side of the bed, forcing her aching body up and into the cold air. "I'll let you sleep, but if you're awake, I really need you to get ready." Laura closed the door behind her, content to give Danlyn space.

In the kitchen, Laura could hear Steven and Jackie talking. She poked her head around the wall and saw Steven sitting at the small breakfast nook, looking dreadful. But he still managed an enthusiastic smile when he saw her.

"Hey, hon. How'd you sleep?" Jackie asked. Before she let Laura answer, she started inspecting the bruises on her neck. "Are you in a lot of pain? Where's Danlyn?"

"She's still sleeping. That or she doesn't want to come out. My neck's pretty stiff, but I'm all right. Can I help with breakfast?"

"Yeah. Eat it."

"It smells great," Laura told her. "But I'm not really—"

"I wasn't asking. You're eating. We can do it the easy way or the hard way. It's up to you."

"What's the hard way?"

Jackie pinched Laura's nose. "You see. It's just like a dog. I plug your nose and that's when I stick eggs down your throat and wait for you to swallow."

Laura slapped her hand away. "You're too nice to do that. Even to a dog."

"No," Steven said. "She's really not. Did I mention I don't like radishes?"

"So," Laura said, her smile fading, "you didn't really stay up all night, did you, Steven?"

"Eh…you know." He looked and sounded half-awake.

"Yes, he did," Jackie said. "Which is why he's taking a vacation day. It's supposed to storm later. He doesn't need to fall asleep behind the wheel and drive into a tree." Steven rolled his eyes. "It's true, Steven. It's supposed to be a bad one."

"Well. That's my cue to start building the ark," Steven said, getting up and dragging himself to the dining room with his coffee. "I'll be waiting for my breakfast, woman."

Jackie slapped his butt as he walked by. "Pour rat poison in your food is what I'll do…talk to me that way."

"Bring it on, little lady. I'm not scared."

Laura grabbed the silverware while Jackie stacked what must have been half a dozen eggs on her plate. Laura didn't argue. They made a plate for Danlyn, just in case she joined them, and brought the food to the table, where Steven sat, rubbing his chest.

"You keep trying to be funny, you're gonna hurt yourself," Jackie told him, then bent down and planted a kiss squarely on his nose. "You're a moron, Steven. And I love you. Now eat." Jackie looked in the direction of the guest room. "Should I go get her?"

"No," Laura told her. "Let's give her time."

Once they sat down, Jackie eyed Laura from across the table. "So, how're you feeling about, you know, everything?"

Laura took a bite of toast but didn't know if she could swallow it. "Well, I'm feeling all-around pretty damn hopeless. I still have no job, no idea what I'm gonna do. I'm covered in bruises, and all I want to do is sleep it all away. But what's bothering me the most is that Danlyn might hate me forever. She's got a pretty good reason to."

"Yeah, but she won't," Jackie said. "She just needs to process all this. Hell, I'm still in shock. Plus, she had to find out that Vivian—of all people—is her mother."

Laura's eyebrows rose. "Ain't that the truth. It was hard for me, too. My mother always said I was a colicky baby. Cried all the time. But I was just coming to grips with her being my mother."

Steven tried not to laugh out his food. Jackie held her hand over her heart. "I'm so proud, Laura. I knew that smartass was still in there somewhere."

Laura picked up her fork, shrugged. "Gotta laugh, or I'll go crazy."

"That's right," Jackie said, then smiled at something behind Laura. "Good morning, sweetie."

Laura slowly turned around and saw her sister standing behind her, shoulders slouched, eyes puffy from crying. "Danlyn!" Laura got up, wrapped one arm around her shoulder. Danlyn nudged past her.

Jackie gave Laura a reassuring look. "You hungry?" she asked Danlyn.

"Dig in," Steven told her. "We have loads of food."

Danlyn pulled out a chair and sat down in front of a plate full of food. "Thank you, *Jackie*," she said, avoiding Laura's side of the table.

Laura watched Danlyn scoop hash browns up with her fork and drop them back down, making several piles on her plate. No way her little sister was going to break bread with the enemy.

"I'm going to get ready," Laura announced. "And Danlyn, you don't have to say anything, but I need you to get ready when you're finished."

~

"Can't even tell a storm's coming," Laura said, peering out the windshield. "Not even a cloud in the sky."

Danlyn sighed.

"It's cold, though. Don't you think?" Laura asked. Danlyn turned away.

"You turn any farther, you're just going to end up facing me again."

"I don't know why I couldn't stay with Jackie. I didn't want to come with you."

"I know." Laura was so tired. "But I need you with me right now."

"Why?" Danlyn snapped.

"Because. I just do."

Danlyn rolled her eyes and finally looked at her sister, only to give her the nastiest look she could muster. "I hate being with you. I wish you'd let me out of the car. I'd rather walk back to Jackie's."

"Well, that's progress. You're actually looking at me. I'll take it."

Danlyn made a guttural noise, turned back around. "Where are we going, anyway?"

"To the hospital. You can sit outside the room, if you'd like."

"Why are we going there?" Danlyn tried covering her curiosity with resentment.

"Can I be honest with you, or would you rather not know?"

Danlyn nearly looked at her again. "I don't want you to lie to me." Her voice broke. "I don't want you to lie to me about anything, ever again."

Laura hoped this was an opportunity to clear even a fragment of the air. "Okay. I'll be completely honest with you. I'll never, ever lie to you again. I give you my word."

Danlyn's eyes slowly crept over. She looked at Laura's hands. After a pause, she asked, "So, who are we going to see?" Her voice was small but hadn't lost its bitterness.

Laura squinted, focusing on the road ahead. "We're going to see a woman. Her name's Olivia."

"Who's she?"

"She dated my father." Laura waited a moment. How was she supposed to refer to William? Her father? Their father? "I met her when I was in the hospital."

Laura's heart quickly sank into her stomach. Danlyn didn't know about the baby. Dear God. When did the bad news end?

She reached over, touching Danlyn's shoulder. "I have to tell you something else."

Danlyn looked back out the window and began crying. "I know why you were in the hospital."

Laura's mind buzzed with anger. She could spot Vivian's work a mile away.

"*They* told me."

"God. I'm sorry, Danlyn. I wish I had been the one to tell you. I wanted to be. Please believe me. I didn't ask them to tell you. I never even spoke to them while I was in the hospital."

Danlyn had been dealing with so much more than Laura knew. How was she still able to stand and talk and breathe? Laura didn't think she could ever be that brave.

"I know," Danlyn finally said. "They wouldn't let me see you." The more Danlyn cried, the harder she strained to hide her face.

"I wanted to see you, too," Laura said. "You were the only good thing I had to think about in there. That's why I left early, "to get back to you. To try to keep what happened from happening."

Laura came to an empty four-way stop. She sat for a moment, hoping Danlyn might turn around. She might not believe her words, but if Danlyn would just look at her, she'd see the truth in Laura's eyes. Another car pulled up behind them and Laura pulled forward, down the side road and into the hospital parking lot.

Danlyn wiped tears from her cheeks while looking around. "This is where you were?"

"This is the place." Laura pulled in front of a parking space. "Think we'll fit? I'm not used to driving something this big. I don't wanna ding Jackie's car."

Danlyn surveyed the space in front of them. "I guess."

"Help me out? Look out the window and make sure I'm not about to scrape the other car."

Danlyn leaned over, pressing her nose against the cold glass.

There was ample room, but Laura needed to pull Danlyn out of her shell before it was too late.

"You're okay over here," Danlyn said, fogging the window with every word, apparently forgetting for a moment how upset she was.

Laura smiled. "What would I do without you?" She put the car in park, pulled out the key. "You okay with coming in the room with me? Or would you rather wait in the hallway?"

"Hallway."

"All right." Laura grabbed the door handle, then stopped. "I promised you that I'd always be honest with you."

Danlyn silently stared ahead.

"Can you promise me that you'll be honest with me about something?"

"I've always told the truth. I don't lie to you." Danlyn's voice was icy.

Laura wiped her moist palms on her jeans. "Last night, in the bathroom, are you *sure* nothing happened?"

That got Danlyn's attention. She whipped around, finally looking at her. "Did you tell them?"

Laura shrunk into her seat, floored by Danlyn's temper. "Who? Steven and Jackie?"

"Obviously!"

"Yes, I did."

Laura held her breath while Danlyn slammed herself back into the seat.

"I don't know what happened. But whether you think you hate me right now or not, you have to tell me if someone did something to you. Did Frank touch you?"

Danlyn's anger was replaced with absolute disgust. "No! Ew! I told you what happened. Frank washed her back, and he told me to watch so I'd know how to do it."

"You know you can always tell me. None of this is—"

"I think I'd know if he did something gross. It's not like you were a good mom or anything, but you always warned me about stuff like that." Danlyn hesitated, her cheeks flushed. "With all the guys we lived with."

"You're right, Danlyn. I screwed up in so many ways, we both couldn't count them. I don't mind you calling me out, but I hope you understand why I needed to ask. Walking in that bathroom and seeing all of you in there… I had to know."

Danlyn's face finally softened a bit. "I know why you asked. I get it. It's not like I don't know that Frank's weird or whatever. I begged him and Grandma…" She faltered, "Vivian…not to make me go in there with them, but she didn't say anything, and Frank just kept pushing. He wouldn't stop "laughing at me, like I was the freak for not wanting to be in there. But nothing else happened."

For the first time all day, Danlyn turned back into the sweet girl she'd always been, and when she next spoke, Laura could see desperation in her eyes.

"I really did tell him no. I tried not to go in the bathroom. I swear, I really—"

"Danlyn, I believe you. You don't ever have to convince me that you tried to do the right thing. Like I said, none of this was your fault, and don't you dare tell yourself it was. You weren't the adult in that house. They were. It was their job to watch out for you. You did absolutely nothing wrong. You got that?"

"Okay," Danlyn said, her face turning stony again. "Is that all?"

"Yes." Laura finally took a deep breath. "That's all."

And just like that, Danlyn went back to pretending Laura didn't exist.

Chapter 30

Laura eyed the empty bed she had been in just hours ago. She couldn't think about that now. She stood in front of the pink curtain, pulled it back. Olivia was holding a worn copy of a book with a half-dressed cowboy on the cover.

"Hey there!" Olivia said, looking over the top of her book. "You're back." She pulled herself up, pointed next to her. "Pull up a chair, honey."

Laura sat down, careful not to send another muscle into spasm. "You don't mind me visiting like this, do you?"

Olivia let out a hearty laugh that sounded more like a cough. "You never have to ask if I want visitors." She chucked the book to the foot of the bed. "It's either that crap or a good talk. I'll take the talk any day."

"That looks like some first-rate material they're giving you to read in here," Laura said.

"Just some junk another patient left behind. Guess the nurses figure an old, lonely woman like me can't get enough romance. Terrible things, those books. I can tell you right now "that no cowboy ever romped with me in the hay…by candlelight, no less."

"Same here," Laura quietly laughed. "Sounds like a fire hazard, if you ask me."

Olivia held her chest. "Oh, oh, oh. I'm gonna have a heart attack. But don't stop. It feels good to laugh." She offered a lopsided smile. "But I'm guessing you didn't come here for a good time. Did you fetch your little one last night?"

"I did."

Olivia laid her head back. "From the looks of you, I'm guessing it didn't go so well?"

"Not at all." The turtleneck hiding Laura's bruises suddenly felt too tight. "But I can't thank you enough for telling me to go. Had it not been for you, God knows what would've happened."

"Your little one, she's okay? You're okay?"

"Yeah. Nothing that won't heal." Laura hoped.

"I guess I understand why you wouldn't want to bring her here. Probably a little strange, me being the mistress and all."

"She's waiting in the hallway. One of the nurses said she'd keep an eye on her for me." Laura frowned. "And what do you mean 'mistress'?"

"Me, honey. I'm the mistress. Or I was."

"Well, I don't think of you that way. It's not like my father was with my mother when you met."

Olivia's eyebrows gathered together. "No. But he was still a married man, and I was very much the mistress. At least that's how everyone else saw me. I heard talk." She shrugged. "Screw 'em, is what I always said. Your daddy never saw me that way, either, and that's all that mattered."

"What do you mean, he was married?" Laura asked. "They were divorced."

"No, they weren't, honey. Your daddy certainly wanted a divorce, but it never happened. Surely your mama told you that?"

Laura felt all the guilt of the last decade settle back in its place of comfort, right upon her shoulders. "I left right after my father died. We hadn't spoke the last year of his life, and I certainly never spoke to my mother. I just assumed they divorced. I should've guessed, though. My mother and her supposed religious beliefs."

Questions filled the tired space between Laura's ears. If Vivian wanted to be with Frank, why not divorce William? He hadn't been a wealthy man, and the farm wasn't even his. Rose had left everything to Vivian. There was no financial gain in staying married to him. On the other hand, there was no financial gain in killing him, either.

Laura shook the thoughts away. "Anyway, I certainly don't think of you as the mistress, for what it's worth."

"Thanks, sweetie. You're a good egg, just like your daddy. You seem like two peas in a pod."

Laura felt her heart open. For so long, she'd been the only woman to speak fondly of William Hallow. But here was Olivia, smiling at the thought of his memory.

"You really loved him," Olivia said. "I can tell by the way you talk about him.

Laura nodded. "That's actually what I'm here for. For my father. I'm trying to make sense of all this, but I don't know who to turn to."

"I figured as much." Olivia sat up a little straighter. "I don't know that I can help, but I'm more than willing to try. I'm afraid I didn't know your daddy all that long, but I'll do my best."

Laura clasped her hands in front of her. "Where were you when my father died? I mean, did you see him that day?"

"No. But I saw him the evening before, and I talked to him on the telephone the day he died."

"I got copies of his death certificate and the coroner's report. I know you weren't together long, but did he seem suicidal to you?"

Olivia rolled her eyes. "I heard that version. No, I hadn't known him long, but it never sat well with me. Seemed a little too convenient. But who was I to question anything? I was just the other woman. I knew my place."

Laura felt a cold spindle of needles run the length of her spine.

"Convenient? What do you mean?"

Olivia looked away.

"Please, Olivia. I need to know."

"Ah hell, honey. You've obviously been in the dark for too long. I'm not certain of anything I'm saying, but I opened up this can of worms yesterday, so I'll give you my opinion. But I could be wrong."

Laura leaned in.

"Your daddy called me the day he died. I don't know when for sure, but I was getting ready to make my supper, so it had to be around four. He was frantic. I'd never heard him that way before. He'd been trying to reach you like crazy."

Now Laura looked away.

"He said he drove out to your mama's place to ask if she knew where else you might be. I can't tell you what happened for sure, but Frank was there, and it got pretty ugly."

It was suddenly too hot in the room.

"He had something real important to tell you. I guess he told your mama that, too." Olivia's hand was back on her chest.

"It's just my two cents, but I don't think William killed himself. He loved you and your little girl so much. He was always talking about making things right. That seemed to be the most important thing to him. He never would've taken himself away from you girls without doing that. Made no damn sense at all."

Laura felt exposed. Surely Olivia could sense her shame and smell the guilt dripping off her skin.

"Olivia, I know I asked you before, but is there anything else you can tell me about Frank? Even if it seems too small to count?"

"I got lots of opinions about lots of folks. Once you've been around a while, it's something you just can't help. I could say I'm shooting blind here, but I'm usually right. I've got good instincts about people." Olivia squared her small shoulders. "Ah, damn. You really want to hear what I think?"

Laura silently waited.

"I think I don't trust Frank as far as I can throw him. I think it's strange that your daddy went out there and gave him and your mama a piece of his mind and told them he needed to finally clear some things up with you, and then, that same night, he died. He would've given his life for the chance to talk to you. I never told anyone this, but William asked me to marry him, just as soon as Vivian signed the divorce papers. Your daddy wasn't a man with nothing to live for. Why, before that day, he'd gone a good three months without drinking. He was setting things straight. He wouldn't have ended it all."

Laura expected to feel more. More anger, more emotion, more fear, but Olivia's words didn't feel like news at all. It was as if Laura knew all these details already, deep down, in her marrow. Her intuition had been screaming at her from the moment she read her father's records. Olivia's words only reaffirmed what her subconscious knew.

Laura just needed to keep breathing and start knocking down walls, one at a time. But the first wall would be the hardest; how could she prove anything? Right now, everything she felt and everything Olivia said was speculation, and speculation wasn't worth a damn thing.

"Maybe…" Laura hesitated. "Maybe I'm nuts, but I can't help but think that Frank was involved in my father's death. But I also don't understand any of it." Her eyes narrowed. "Less than two months ago, when I came back and met Frank, he was a complete stranger to me, yet my mother insists I've known him all my life. She even credits him for picking up William's slack when he was in Korea. I have no memory of any of this, though. I mean, my father knew Frank, my mother obviously knows him, so why don't I remember him? It's all a big blank spot in my mind"

Olivia raised her head. "What about his journals?"

Laura froze. "Journals?"

"Yeah. Your father's."

"My dad kept a journal?"

"God, yes. Quite a few of them. He had these hardcover books in his place, a whole row of them sitting on the bottom of a bookshelf. Said he started them in Korea."

"I had no idea. I never saw my dad write, ever."

Olivia shrugged. "There had to be half a dozen, at least. If you can track those down, maybe you'll find something. I know he was still writing in them the last week he died. I visited him unannounced one day. He answered the door with a pen in his hand, and I saw one of those books lying open on his table. I didn't ask about it, but he offered. Said he'd been keeping a journal ever since the war, in case he didn't make it home to you and Vivian."

Laura's shock drifted away, making room for rage. "My mother," she said. "She took them. I'd bet my life she took them."

"That would make sense. Since they never divorced, I'm sure she got all his things. Actually, I know she got at least some of it. I was having a pretty tough time afterwards and used to walk by his old place. About a week after, I saw your mama coming out of the building. I didn't see Frank. Just her. I only noticed because it was strange seeing her out at all. She had some bags in her hand. I don't figure you can ask her about his journals?"

"Ask my mother? No. She'd burn them before ever admitting they exist. That's assuming she hasn't already." Laura heard her own words play back in her head, her chest tightened. "Damn her! What the hell right does she have?"

Olivia's chest cracked with another current of coughs. Her lips were tinged blue.

"I'm sorry," Laura said. "I've got no right barging in here, venting my problems on you."

"Honey," Olivia smirked. "I'll let you in on a little secret. I don't scare easy, so don't fret about me. I'm glad to see a little fire under your ass. You've been sitting here looking like a beaten dog for the last fifteen minutes. Get that damn tail out from between your legs, 'cause you're gonna need some piss and vinegar in your veins if you plan on getting through life. There are plenty of Vivian Hallows in this world, and even worse, if you can imagine. You can't stay afraid of her forever."

Laura was too angry to cry. "How do I find them?" she asked, and then she heard it, the beaten dog—starved of love and punished for its mere existence.

Olivia tilted her head. "You all right, sweetie?"

"Yeah. Just realizing how right you are…about me and my dad. Vivian's always had power over us. Still does."

"Only because you're giving it to her. She only has as much power as you allow. She's like the boogeyman under the bed. I'm not saying she's not mean, but she's only as strong as you make her out to be. You're stronger, though, Laura. You just don't see it."

"I don't know about that."

Olivia looked deep in thought. "My daddy was mean, like a bull. Used to hit me and my brothers. They were never that afraid of him, but I was. Funny thing is, they ended up just like him, but I didn't. In the end, you could say I was stronger, even though I was always so afraid. Sometimes that fear is a good thing, because it means you hate the source of that fear so much that you never end up like it. You're afraid of your mama because she's different than you, but that doesn't make her stronger."

Laura got up, sat on the edge of the bed, and took one of Olivia's frail hands in her own. She looked at the woman whom her father had loved, whom he had wanted to spend the rest of his days with, and all she could think of was how very much she wished she'd met Olivia sooner.

"You really do remind me of your daddy," Olivia said.

"I've heard that before. Only it sounded a little different." Laura's face brightened. "I like your way better."

"I'm sorry I can't help more, Laura. But I'm awfully glad I met you. I feel like I've known you for a long time. I heard so much about you. All wonderful. Your daddy loved you so much."

"Thank you for loving my father, Olivia. For being there for him."

"No need to thank me, sweetie. I still regret that I never got to thank William for loving me back. But meeting you...it kind of feels like I got to make my peace." Olivia held her arms out. "Now what do you say to giving me a hug?"

"I'd like that."

The strength drained from Laura's arms and she sank into Olivia's chest, allowing herself to forget for a moment that everything was falling apart, because she knew this might be the closest she'd ever come to knowing a mother's love.

~

Danlyn and Laura sat in the booth at the diner where Laura's car was still parked. Danlyn silently ate her macaroni and cheese, still in no mood to talk, and all Laura could do was think about Olivia and William, of their unfinished love, and of journals, filled with secrets about the past. Laura sipped her coffee, willing the pieces together. They were all there, waiting to be arranged, but maybe she'd never figure it out because her brain was still running on fumes and her sister still wouldn't look at her and that took her mind away from what she needed to focus on.

He thought Frank was the devil himself.

What had happened the day William went out to Hallows' Farm? Had her father known his life was in danger? Was that why he was so desperate to reach her?

Danlyn's voice broke through Laura's concentration. "What's going on?"

"What?" Laura asked.

"You look weird."

"I'm just thinking."

"About what?" Danlyn still sounded aloof, but just as she could see through Laura's expression, Laura could read through her failed attempt at carelessness.

"Trying to figure something out. That's all."

Danlyn rolled her eyes. "I'm not stupid, you know. I know something's going on."

"Danlyn, if there's one thing I know about you, it's that you are not stupid."

"Then why are you treating me like a baby? After last night, and…" For all her forcefulness, it was clear Danlyn wasn't ready to talk about everything that had happened.

"Listen." Laura leaned in. "I'm not keeping things from you because I think you're stupid. I'm not hiding anything from you. I promise. What I am doing is giving you time to deal with everything without pouring more crap on top of it. When it's time, I'll tell you. When I actually know everything, I'll tell you. But for now, you don't need to worry about me and what I'm thinking about. Just worry about you. When you're ready to talk, I'm here."

"Well, I'm not ready."

"Okay." Laura tried to ease the moment with an agreeable tone. "There is one thing I need from you, though."

Danlyn gave her a bland expression. "What?"

"Today is Vivian's appointment, right? I wouldn't have brought it up, but it's important."

Danlyn looked back at her half-eaten plate of food. "Uh-huh."

"Are you absolutely positive?"

"I said yes."

"What time? And I need you to be certain."

Danlyn took a deep breath and spoke briskly. "On the days when she has an appointment, we get up at six. We pray "from six to six-twenty. From six-twenty to seven, I read aloud from the Bible."

Now Laura rolled her eyes.

"From seven to eight, we do math. From eight to nine, I practice grammar. From nine to ten, I read whatever boring history book she makes me read. From ten to eleven, I do—"

"Science," Laura said, helping her get to the point.

"No! She doesn't believe in science. She told me so the first day we did school."

Laura placed her palms together and set her elbows on the table, steepling her fingers. "Fine. So when does she usually see the doctor?"

Danlyn picked her spoon back up, spun it in her fingers. "Not till later in the day. Usually around five."

Laura subtly glanced at the clock perched above the entrance to the bathrooms. "Okay, kid. Eat your lunch. I've gotta get Jackie's car back to her. She still has to bring us back to get our car."

Danlyn scooped up a large pile of macaroni and cheese and shoved it in her mouth. She dropped the spoon on the plate, sending a splattering of cheese across the table and onto Laura's shirt.

"Sorry, Mom. I mean..." Danlyn looked away, her eyes glossed over.

Laura reached across the table. "It's okay. You don't have to act different with me."

"How am I not supposed to act different?"

Laura waited for an answer to come, but when one didn't, she said, "I have no idea, but I know we'll figure it out. That's all I can promise you. We'll get past this because we love each other. We're family."

Danlyn didn't say *I love you* back, but moved her hand so Laura couldn't reach it. She pushed her plate across the table. "You hungry? I'm not."

"That's okay," Laura said. "I'll eat later."

Danlyn pulled the plate back, picked up another huge bite.

"Thought you weren't hungry?" Laura asked.

"You need to eat, too."

Laura smiled.

"Whatever," Danlyn said, turning her face away, trying to hide her own awkward, crooked smile. The most beautiful smile Laura had ever seen.

Chapter 31

Laura pulled back into the Brenners' driveway under a heavy cloak of dark clouds. Electricity buzzed through the air, like a current of anticipation. As Laura knocked on the door, she could feel the eerie pull of the storm all around her.

Jackie opened the door. "Hey, you two. How'd things go?"

Laura walked past her, shivering. "It was revealing. I'll tell you later. Sorry I took so long. I got Danlyn some lunch."

"No problem." Jackie tossed the rag in her hands over her shoulder. "How about you, young lady? How was lunch?" Jackie almost looked away when she saw the sour look on Danlyn's face.

"It was fine," Laura said. She watched Jackie turn all the locks on the door and give it a good tug. "Where's Steven?"

"Getting some sleep. Had to threaten his life to get him to bed. He worries too much."

Laura felt another pang of guilt.

"So what's the plan?" Jackie asked. "You wanna get your car now?"

Avoiding the truth without having to outright lie would require the kind of creative thinking Laura didn't have energy for. "Yeah. I was thinking sooner than later. I've got an errand to run."

"Okay." Jackie grabbed the rag off her shoulder. "Just let me finish up in the kitchen. I haven't put the roast in yet, so it would be better to go now."

"We'll go wait outside. I don't want to wake Steven," Laura said, really just wanting to avoid talking about her mystery errand, which proved pointless because when Jackie met them out front a few minutes later, she asked, "By the way, where're you going?"

"Nowhere special. Like I said, it's just an errand."

"I got that part. But where?"

The knot in Laura's gut returned with a vengeance. Danlyn turned around, full attention on Laura, and Jackie paused, staring her down. It was time to take the bull by the horns, even if it bucked and screamed and demanded she not go.

"I won't lie to either of you, but I also won't argue with you. When I get back, I'll tell you."

Jackie shook her head. "Nuh-uh. Whatever it is you think you're doing, you're not."

Laura had been ready for Jackie's reaction, and it wasn't going to stop her, but what she didn't expect were the tears in her sister's eyes.

"You're going out there, aren't you?" Danlyn said, lips trembling. "That's why you asked about her appointment."

Laura hesitated, then gave in. "Yes. I am," she told Danlyn, then looked at Jackie. "One step at a time, right? Isn't that what you said?" She felt a little low for using Jackie's words to justify her actions, but that didn't negate their validity.

Jackie put one hand on her hip and let out a huff of air from her tightly pinched lips. "That's not what I meant, Laura. I didn't say to put yourself in danger."

"I'm not putting myself in danger. They won't even be there. There's just something I need to find, and I'll tell you about it later. But it's important, Jackie. As in, might-be-the-key-to-everything important."

Jackie stepped back, unable to argue but unwilling to approve. Her face twisted as she struggled with Laura's words. "Damn it, Laura."

"I've got to, Jackie. Sorry."

Danlyn suddenly grabbed Laura's hand. "Please don't go back there. Please. I'll go tell Steven, and he won't let you go. I'll call Vivian. I'll tell her what you're doing."

"Listen to me, Danlyn. I'm going to be fine. I'll get in there after I know they're gone, and I'll be out before they get back. I know I've not given you much reason to believe me, but you have to this time. This is very important. Will you trust me?"

Laura looked up at Jackie, who still refused to take a step toward the car. "I need both of you to trust me. One way or the other, I'm doing this. And Danlyn, I need you to stay here with Jackie. I need to know that you're safe. And I'll be safe, too. I've got no desire to get caught. This is the last time. Okay? Can you do that? Because I can't be safe out there if I have to worry about you doing something that could get me in trouble."

Danlyn closed her eyes tight. Tears rolled down the lines of her downturned lips. "Okay."

Laura grabbed Danlyn, holding her tightly to her chest, taking in the sweet smell of her hair. "God, I love you, kid. I love you so, so much. There's nothing I wouldn't do for you. Nothing in this whole world."

Danlyn hid her face in Laura's chest, and though her words were broken and muffled, Laura heard them, and they filled her heart with the all the strength she needed. "I love you more."

Laura whispered back, "Impossible, kid."

"That's all well and good," Jackie said. "But you're still an ass, Laura."

Laura turned around. "Can you please try to understand?"

"I do, but…" she sighed. "I know there's nothing I can say to stop you. What do I tell Steven?"

"Nothing. There's no way in hell he'll let me go." Laura already felt guilty for asking Jackie to lie for her, but this lie was necessary. "He'll drive out there. If you tell him, he'll follow me there, and if we get caught, he'll be stuck in the middle of it. But I won't get caught if I'm alone."

"I'll think about it," Jackie said, wearing a scorned expression.

Laura reached her arms out, smiled. "You want one, too?"

"Want what?"

"A hug."

"I'm pissed at you, Laura. I don't really want to hug you right now."

Laura dropped her arms. "I'm doing the best I can, Jackie."

"For the record, just so we're clear, I'm against this, Laura. I think you're being bullheaded and stupid."

"I understand," Laura said, grinning. "I wouldn't have it any other way."

Jackie's lips finally turned up, the dimple on her left cheek deepened.

"For the record, and just so we're clear," Laura said, "I love you."

Now Jackie did hug Laura. She grabbed her ponytail, giving it a good yank. "I love you, too, stupid."

Chapter 32

Vivian was sitting in front of the fireplace, still wearing her robe when Frank walked through the front door. She didn't acknowledge his presence. Even when he bent down, inspecting her, she didn't move.

"Haven't even showered?" He sniffed her hair, stepped back. "You look like shit, ol' girl. You been sittin' here all night?" He waved his hand in front of her face. "Hello. Anyone in there?" A snap of the fingers. "Cut it out, Vivian! Can't let a little scuffle knock you on your ass."

Vivian finally blinked. "What did you say?" her voice thick with sleepiness.

"I said you can't let a little hiccup kick your ass. Why didn't you sleep?"

"She took her."

"'Course she did. She was pissed."

"You're okay with this?" Vivian was sounding more alive.

Frank didn't answer. He scraped a match along the stone siding of the fireplace. The noise grated on Vivian's eardrums like a viper's hiss. "Stop it!" She held her hands to her ears. "Stop that blasted sound!" Through her hands, Frank's muffled laugh tore at her mind, banging off the sides of her skull. She saw how delighted he was with himself and nearly leapt at him. He loved tormenting her. The more rise he got out of her, the more he teased.

"How can you laugh at a time like this?"

Frank threw the lit match in the fireplace. "A time like what?"

"This is serious, Frank. Danlyn's gone. And after what Laura saw, who knows what she might do. And you...you were in a panic the other night. Why the sudden turnaround?"

"Because this isn't such a big deal. They'll be back."

"They're not coming back. I assure you."

"Let's just say"—Frank rubbed his hands together, smiling like a mischievous child—"that I took out a bit of an insurance policy."

Vivian eyed him suspiciously. "A what?"

"Laura will realize she's got nowhere else to go. It was one thing when she was eighteen and thought she could take on the world, but now she knows better. I made sure of that."

Vivian shot off the sofa. Her head was on fire, pounding with an intensity that would've knocked most men off their feet. "They will never come back, mark my words."

"How do you know? How the hell are you so certain?"

"Because I told Danlyn. She knows, Frank."

Frank's eyes honed in on hers. His eyebrows lowered so that it looked like he had two dark caverns for eyes. His voice was so low, Vivian could feel it reverberate in her chest. "Told her what exactly?"

Vivian faltered, stepped back, eyes glued to the lines of his face and how they made him look villainous. "Not *that*!"

His lip curled up. "Not what?"

"Nothing about you. And it was an accident. I didn't mean to say anything."

He came closer. "What did you tell her, Vivian?"

She could feel his spittle land on her face when he screamed her name. "That Danlyn's mine," she yelled back. "That I'm her mother. I told Laura not to take her, but she wouldn't listen, and I got so angry, and—"

He placed his finger on her lips. "That's all you said?"

"Right hand to God, yes."

Frank didn't move. He searched her eyes, and when he finally took a step back, she asked, "Are you mad at me?"

"Mad? No." He stretched his jaw, cracked his neck. "It's about time that girl knows who brought her into this world. Maybe she'll have a little more respect for you now."

"I don't think that's how she felt. She looked…" Vivian searched for the right word, but her weary mind kept it at bay.

"Angry? So what? She's a kid. She'll get over it."

"No." Vivian shook her head. "She didn't look angry. She looked terrified."

"Vivi-Vivi." He grabbed her shoulder, moved her back to the sofa. "You never were good with emotions. You shook her up, I'm sure, but you're her mama. She can't just walk away from that."

Vivian's chin started to quiver.

Frank cocked his head to the side. "Good Lord. I've never seen you this way. You've really worked yourself up." He frowned. "Don't go breakin' on me now. I need you around, ol' girl."

Vivian couldn't afford to think about why he needed her anymore. What her purpose was to him. If she did, she'd find herself back in the darkest room in her mind. The one with no windows or doors or means of escape. The one Frank had barely managed to pull her out of after William moved out.

"I guess I'm scared, or maybe really mad," she told him. "I can't tell the difference. But I'll be damned if Laura takes her from me."

Frank had a way of getting what he wanted out of Vivian, and she knew it. He sat beside her, kissed her left hand, then her right. "I love you," he whispered, then kissed her cheeks and her lips.

For the first time in her entire life, Vivian felt a fire burn in her body, spreading an alluring heat to her hands and fingers, legs and toes, and then to her head, where it took her away, upon a sweet mist of heightened senses. She didn't even fight it.

"Don't you worry. They'll be back," Frank spoke softly into her ear. "They won't get very far without any money. That's the insurance policy I told you about." He kissed the edge of her ear. "Laura probably hasn't noticed yet, but she'll scuttle on back when she does."

"What?" she pushed him away. "Why would you do that? I don't want to keep Laura from leaving. I don't want her back here. Not in my home, not even in Rome. You said we would be a family. You, me, and Danlyn. Not Laura."

"You're not hearin' yourself. That's your daughter you're talkin' about." Frank's voice gained momentum. "They both are. When they come back here, and they will come back, you won't turn Laura away. You hear me?"

Frank's words nestled in Vivian's mind, eating away at her, sending her jealousy soaring, squelching the life from every fiber of her body. If feeling was what it meant to be human, to be alive, Vivian wanted no part of it. Let the damn tumor take from her the life that filled her lungs and the rancid emotion that now plagued her mind.

Frank centered himself in front of her and spoke with a cold certainty that made his smile look out of place. "If anyone will be to blame for breakin' this family apart, it'll be you. You remember that, Vivian. You destroy this, you and me…we'll be havin' a whole other discussion."

"I can't listen to this anymore. I'm going to be sick," Vivian said. She flew off the sofa and ran into the bathroom next to the kitchen, slamming the door behind her.

~

Frank hoisted Vivian into the truck and set a bowl on her lap. He walked around to the driver's side and got in. "You sure you don't want to cancel?"

"No," she said. "You might not be able to take me if we have to reschedule, and he's giving me a new medication today. It's supposed to help with my symptoms."

Frank slapped the steering wheel. "This is stupid, Viv. You've been pukin' all day. I'll just call and let 'em know we can't make it."

Vivian glared at him sideways. "You weren't there last night. You didn't see me. I wasn't in control. Since they can't cut this evil thing out of my head, I have to try whatever they can give me, or God knows what I'll say next."

Without another word, Frank started the truck, floored the gas. By the time he reached the road, Vivian had her head hanging over the bowl. All he could do was hold his breath, try not to notice what was happening next to him, and get to town as quickly as possible. So he turned onto the road like a bat out of hell, not even noticing that behind him, hidden behind some trees and bushes, sat Laura's car.

Chapter 33

Laura ran around to the back of the house, into the acres of barren farmland behind it. Large plumes of dirt rose up around her. But she wouldn't stop, even though dust filled her lungs and her heart raced unnervingly fast.

She spotted the tiny basement window that crept just above the earth and slid on her knees in front of it. With any luck, the lock would still be broken. But even then, it wouldn't be easy. Half the window was buried beneath the earth, leaving a small space for her to fit through, and she couldn't see through the years of caked-on dirt to see what might be blocking it from the other side. She placed her palms on the farthest end of the window and pulled. The window creaked, but it didn't give. She pulled harder this time, but her hands only slid off the dirt.

The sky was nearly black now, pregnant with an unsettling green undertone. Laura felt cold drizzle fall on her nose and reached above her, just getting her hands damp. When she pressed them back onto the window, her skin clung to the glass and the window slid back, rickety and hesitant, moaning along the way.

"One step at a time," she whispered.

She hung her feet through the window, then she lay back, sliding further into the dark basement. She grabbed the brick siding surrounding the window, holding on tight, waiting for the drop. Searching with her feet, she felt for anything to stand or land on, but there was nothing. She took a deep breath and exhaled, narrowing her ribcage. Moment of truth. If she didn't fit—or worse, got stuck—this would mark the end of the road. But when her chest narrowed, gravity pulled her down until she fell freely to the basement floor, slapping her head on the wall behind her and landing firmly on her tailbone. But there was no time to think about pain. She reached up, felt for the string dangling from the ceiling. *Snap.* The lone light bulb above her flooded the room in a dingy glow. She looked at her watch. "Shit." Four forty-five. If Vivian's appointment was at five o'clock, that left her forty-five minutes. An hour, if she was lucky. If she wasn't back at the Brenners' by six, Jackie said she'd send out the hounds. Too little time to tear through a large, two-story farmhouse.

The rain was coming more steadily now. Laura closed the basement window, leaving it open just a hair, and looked around the room. There wasn't much. There were two small shelves on the wall opposite the window. The wall to the right of that one had a few boxes piled against it. To her left was a stack of chairs and broken furniture. Beside the furniture was the staircase leading up to the kitchen.

She slid in front of the bookshelves, running her fingers along the bridge of each book, searching for non-descript, hardcover journals. That wasn't much to go on. She scanned them, found nothing but old textbooks. Next bookshelf was the same. She ran to the boxes and tore one open. Inside was a pile of papers, books, Bibles. God, how many did one woman need? The next box was full of miscellaneous items: a blender, silverware, ladles. The last box housed fabric, tons of it, in modest shades fit for the Amish. Still no journals. "Dammit!" She stacked the boxes back in the corner.

On the other wall were two boxes. One labeled "Christmas," the other "School Supplies." Were her father's secrets lurking next to a manger, or under a pile of pencils? She pulled back the top flaps. Everything was as it was labeled, so she sloppily closed each box, stacking them in order. She put her hands on her hips, took a few deep breaths, staring at the stairs ascending into the darkness above. Grabbing the string from the ceiling, she yanked, and when the room went black, the air felt colder and the night full of horrible possibilities.

She wiped her sweaty palms on her jeans, nibbled her lip. "You can do this." She placed her foot on the lowest step. It felt like walking into a grave, like the house might swallow her up and never let her go. "One damn step at a time." She thought of Frank, of what he'd done to her, and of Danlyn and what might have happened had she not come back the other night. "Now!" she whispered, and bounded up the stairs, feet crashing thunderously on each step. When she felt the cold doorknob under her fingers, she slowly turned it, opening the door just a crack.

Vivian and Frank weren't there. She had watched them leave. But that didn't stop her imagination from placing them right behind the door. This was it. Once in, she had to move, and move fast. There was no going back until the job was done. She squeezed her eyes shut, pushed the door open. When it squeaked to a stop, she opened one eye, then the other. All that awaited her was an empty room and the sound of rain dancing on the roof.

Before she knew what direction to head in, she was running as fast as her feet could carry her. She stopped in front of the stairs, looked up. The attic. She leapt up the stairs, taking two at a time. The thumping of her feet on the hollow wood rang out along with the thunder rolling in over the mountains. When she met the top landing, she grabbed the string and clasp above her, and the extendable ladder from the attic came down. Laura flew up the ladder. When she pulled it up and closed it behind her, a momentary ease washed over her. She was safe and hidden—for the moment.

The lone window, like an eye looking out from the attic, gave too little light to work with. Laura could see flickers of lightning in the distance, setting off a mild strobe effect. She tottered along the slats separating the flooring. Her father's old shelf was in the corner, tucked away where Vivian must have hid it—out of sight, out of mind. She could just make out its shape. Outlines of objects: screwdrivers, saws, empty cans filled with bolts and screws, and what she thought must be a measuring tape stood out in the dull light. Just behind an empty bucket sat a flashlight. She grabbed it, nudging her thumb under the switch. Dead. She slapped it against her palm, tried again. This time, a faint glow radiated from the end, but whatever life was still in the batteries wasn't going to last long. That was okay. She didn't have long, and she couldn't risk Frank pulling into the driveway and spotting the flicker of a flashlight.

Now she could see how many boxes lined the walls. There were too many. She looked at the farthest corner, in the southwest side of the attic. It was as good a place to start as any. She held the flashlight in her mouth, biting down on cold metal that tasted like coins. She lined three boxes in front of her, paying no attention to the labels. She tore back the lids, sending random items up into the air behind her. First one down and nothing, so she threw everything back in and started on the next. Nothing there, either. She bent over the third box, and a furious crack of thunder tore through the attic, rattling the floor beneath her feet. Her heart palpitated, sending a tingling sensation to her arms and legs. She bit down firmly on the flashlight. Third box was open. Stuffed animals, more linens, old dresses. She put everything back and moved on to the next batch.

On the adjacent wall sat another stack of boxes. She leapt over the slats, nearly falling. The thunder was getting louder, the lightning zigged and zagged out the windows behind her. She pulled the boxes down, placed them in front of her. First one: blankets. Second: photo albums. Third: a projector and loose slides. Lightning struck so close, the attic filled with a neon-blue light, and Laura waited, bracing for the blow of thunder. It shook the floor, and rain slapped at the window, sending hissing wind through the cracks. She looked at her watch. Five fifteen. She was losing time.

She stood up, kicking each box over at breakneck-speed. The fourth box was heavy, and when she tipped it on its side, a shriek caught in her throat as she watched books slowly slide out. Her heart quickened, she started to sweat. She got down on her knees, clawing at the books, spreading them out in front of her. A brilliant glow of lightning splashed across the floor, shedding light on the covers. "Shit. No!"

She recognized all of them, every cover, every author. She'd read them all. They had kept her company on so many long days and even lonelier nights when she was a young girl. But now, all they did was fill her with emptiness. As she piled each book back in the box, her hopes fell to the floor, lost among the dust and dirt and all the wrong books with the wrong covers and wrong authors.

Thunder, lightning, and rain played outside, like an obscene band. Was that a truck Laura heard, lost in the manic melody? She flew from the floor, turning off the flashlight, and looked out the window. Thunder boomed and echoed with the angry promise of destruction, but it was just a big dog with a loud bark and no bite. What Laura feared was an old green truck, with a rusted bumper and white-wall tires. That dog had bite.

The light slipped through the window in a hysterical sequence. Blue-and-white strobes flashed, creating eerie shadows that swooned across the walls, and a powerful unease hit Laura. She had to fight the urge to flee, leaving the possibility of undiscovered journals behind. There was no truck, no one in front of the house, unless the headlights were lost in the dazzling lightshow. Laura could only hope that with the rain coming down in buckets, Frank wouldn't park around the house. He'd park right out front, giving Vivian a straight shot to the front door.

With a strength fueled by pure adrenaline, Laura got back to work, throwing the boxes back into a stack. Last was a set of boxes on the other side of the room. Her arms worked so fast that her brain struggled to keep up with them. More stuffed animals went flying, clothing tossed over her head, papers floated through the air, household goods littered the floor. She heaved and searched and hoped. When her fingers touched the bottom of the last box, her anticipation mutated, rearranging into unadulterated fear. She'd come here for nothing, and now…

She looked at her watch. Five twenty-five. She was never going to make it back on time. It didn't matter if everything was back in its place. She shoved the items back in the box, chucked them along the wall. She'd have to use the flashlight one more time. Corner to corner, ceiling to floor, she aimed the timid beam of light around the room, looking for another possible hiding place.

"More junk," she said, and then covered her mouth. They could be listening. They could be right below her, on the stairs, or on the landing. Frank could be reaching up to pull the cord to the attic door down.

Laura sat the flashlight down, twisted her head around. She stared at the floor, where the ladder lay. Her peripheral vision blurred, making the ladder the sole figure in the room. More light zipped along the room. Was the door moving, or was it an optical illusion? She held her breath, listening to her beating heart. Thunder growled, the attic window rattled in its frame.

"Oh, God," she whispered. The flashlight. She'd set it on end, aimed at the ceiling, without realizing it. Dust circling the room hovered in the beam of light, making it dense. If they were pulling in the driveway, they'd surely see it. She shoved the flashlight into her jacket, pulled the switch down, then ran back to the window and looked out over a dark, murky world where questions waited and threats lived in unforeseen places. The rain poured down so heavily she could barely see through the strands of water dripping down the pane of glass. There was no truck, but that didn't stop the eerie crawling of her skin.

~

Vivian braced Frank's arm as he walked her back to the truck through the rain. When he slammed the door behind her, he narrowly missed her ankle. He didn't much care.

When he got in the driver's seat, he could feel Vivian's eyes on him.

"What?" he barked.

"I'm sorry. I didn't know it was just the flu."

Frank flung the bowl onto her lap. "You should've. Come all the way out here for nothin'. It's just like he said, you turn everything into cancer. You puke, must be the cancer. Can't hold your tongue, must be the cancer." He leaned forward, wiping his wet forehead while starting the engine. "Next time, find someone else to take you. I'm not gettin' yelled at by your doctor again. Bringin' you in with a fever, around all those sick people. I said we should've canceled."

He just wanted to get Vivian home and in bed so that he could get away from her and back to the simplicity of his own four walls. But she was never going to let him go. She was growing needier by the day, clinging to his side like a lap dog. The fact that he had stock in her life made it all the more unbearable. He couldn't walk away. She held the keys to the future he'd been dreaming of for much of his life. He had more strings attached to the woman than a damn puppet.

"If you're gonna be sick, roll the window down and stick your head out," he ordered.

"I'm not doing this to upset you. I can't help it."

Frank put the truck in reverse, pulled out of the parking lot. "Doesn't make any difference. I can't take it. If I have to smell it anymore, I'm gonna be sick, too."

"You're going to leave me alone tonight, aren't you?" Vivian asked.

The desperation in her voice made him want to slap her, but he swallowed his anger. "Would you stop sayin' that? I'm here, ain't I?"

"You'll stay with me tonight, then? You don't have to sleep in bed with me. You can take the sofa."

Frank slammed on the brakes at the four-way stop. Shit. The sofa. His sofa. He'd been so drunk the night before, he'd forgotten to move it back against the wall. "I...uh. I need to run back to my place first. Then I'll come back."

"Please stay with me." Vivian sounded no less desperate.

"Fine. Just...try to hold it in for the next twenty minutes. Then you'll be home. Can you manage that?"

"Yes."

Frank looked at the bowl on her lap, then back at Vivian's miserable expression. "Screw it. Let's make it ten."

He floored the gas.

Chapter 34

Laura did a quick search of the upstairs hall closet. She didn't think she'd find the journals there. Same with Vivian's room. There was no way her mother was sleeping in a room with any part of William Hallow in it. She ran down the hallway, then stopped. "My God." Rose's room. The door had been unlocked the other day.

Laura stood in front of her grandmother's old door. The thunder rumbled outside, like two children throwing giant jacks and unleashing a macabre laugh. Another splatter of light bathed the wall, coming down the hallway from Vivian's bedroom window. Laura looked at her watch but couldn't make out the hands. She was playing Russian roulette, and the player before her had fired an empty round.

When she turned the knob, she heard the unlatching of the lock. Time to enter the belly of the beast. She opened the door and slipped in, closing it behind her. The smell hit her first, followed by the uncanny sense that something far worse had happened in this room. Something she couldn't remember, but was very much present for.

Laura ran to the dresser and bent down, pulling each drawer open. Trails followed behind her fast-moving arms, and the flash from the lightning bounced off the mirror above her. Startling blow after blow belted from the sky, but she was getting used to it. So used to it that she feared she might not hear footsteps or slamming doors.

Every drawer came up empty, with the exception of one long piece of lace, neatly folded inside. She spun around, looked under the bed. All that awaited her was darkness. Another sequence of flashes covered the room in light as she ran to the armoire. She flung the doors open, almost screaming in frustration. An old, wispy dress hung from the middle of the rack, gently swaying. It dangled there, mocking Laura for all her fruitless efforts. She reached up into the top shelf of the armoire and pulled down two wool sweaters. She thrust them back and stood on her toes, sliding her hand along the top of the armoire. There was something there. A single book. Too big to be a journal. When she pulled it down, her heart sank. A photo album. "Dammit." But what was in there? Vivian had never been one for photos. She didn't have a single photo framed in the house, aside from the one of Rose.

Laura stood in front of the window, letting the light shine on the cover. Inside were black-and-white photos of Laura when she was little. Too little for her to remember. She flipped over another page and found more photos of herself, only she was a little older, maybe two years old. She recognized the room, the furniture. It was their living room, only who was the baby cradled in her tiny arms? She flipped another page and again found more pictures of her with the same baby. Page after page went flying as she tried to recall a single detail.

Laura slammed the album shut, threw it back on top of the armoire. She turned around, looking from left to right. There was nothing left to search. No closets, no nooks or crannies. But there was something in the room, tempting her memory, and the longer she stayed in there, the stronger her fear became. Not of Frank or Vivian coming home, but of what truths the room had to offer. The walls were slithering to life, breathing in her sanity. She quickly crossed the room and pulled the door open, blindly walking into the hallway, not thinking about what might be beyond it at the bottom of the stairs.

Chapter 35

Frank quickly parked the truck in front of the house just as Vivian started making that awful gurgling sound again.

"You're ten feet from the front door, Viv. I'll go unlock it. Just hold it in."

He ran up the steps and slid the key into the lock, giving the door a push, letting it open on its own. Then he turned around and ran back to the truck through the rain. "Let's get you inside, Viv."

Chapter 36

When Laura ran down the stairs and reached the bottom, a gust of wind rushed past her, causing loose strands of her hair to float around her face. Her mouth fell open, her head drained of blood. The door was open. They were home. She could hear Frank yelling outside. Then—like a living nightmare—she saw their shadows on the hardwood floor as they came toward the front door.

Laura's brain screamed to move. She tore through the kitchen, afraid to even breathe, in case they heard her. She turned the knob on the basement door and slipped behind it, shutting it just in time to hear Frank's voice and see the kitchen light come on. Laura stood there, feet from him, paralyzed by fear. Surely he'd open the door any minute and toss her down into the basement where he could do with her as he wished. For all Laura knew, they were standing face-to-face, separated only by a thin slab of wood. Then she heard his boots on the floor, thudding toward the sink. Time to move. Time to breathe. Time to get out.

She tiptoed down the stairs and hid in the corner under the bottom of the staircase. The cement wall was cold when she leaned against it, and the dirt under her feet kicked up, encasing her face in a cloud of musky earth. She pressed her hand firmly against her mouth and leaned all her weight against the wall while trying to pull air in through her closed fingers. Heaving and straining in tiny gasps, her heart was working too hard, and every couple seconds she felt a sickening flutter in her chest.

She strained her ears, listening to the sounds above her. Frank was still talking, then Vivian's voice followed, but Laura couldn't make out a word, only the thumping of their feet. Or was that a knock at the door? Dear God. Was it Jackie, or the cops?

The air in the basement was too thick. Laura panted, climbing her way into an anxiety attack. She twisted her head around the staircase, tilting her ear up toward the door. Frank yelled, "I'm coming, Viv. Just a second." Then the pipes behind the wall banged with a loud *pop*, and Laura nearly screamed.

The pipes…the bath. Vivian was taking her bath.

Laura inched closer to the window while listening to Frank walk across the floor, out of the kitchen. She turned around, sliding the window back at a snail's pace. In one powerful flood of adrenaline, she hoisted herself up and through it. Pulling half her body out of the basement, she felt rain on her head. The temperature of her body soared, as if her blood was boiling, and the cold rain felt foreign on her skin. Still, she'd never been more thankful for the dose of cold air that pricked her lungs with life, pushing her into higher gear. She was going to make it, and the exhilaration was enough to fill her arms and legs with momentary strength.

The ground was muddy and slick. Laura slipped, got up, slipped again, got back up. She tore off into the open fields surrounding the house. She ran fast and hard, and when she thought she might collapse, she ran even faster. All she had to do was get to the car, and so she pushed and pushed until the car's hood came into view.

Fumbling with the keys, she nearly dropped them in the mud. She fell into the seat, floundered with the ignition. When she felt the key slide into place and turned it, the engine made a putting sound. Then it went silent.

"Fuck! Oh, fuck!"

Another *put-put-put*.

"Not now. You can't!"

Foot slamming on the gas pedal, tears filled her eyes as the weight of the evening's disappointments added up. No journals, no discoveries, aside from those photos—those damn photos, still nagging at her— and now this.

"Please," she moaned. But the engine still wouldn't comply.

~

Laura had only been walking along the side of the road for ten minutes when headlights appeared in front of her. The rain had let up some, but the night was too dark and the clouds too thick to make anything out. The car ahead was slowing, veering into the other lane in front of her. She didn't have enough energy to care anymore, or to run the other way, through hills and rocks and trees. Her mind could do no more, and her legs had given all they had.

The car came to a stop. The driver got out, running toward her. It wasn't until she was face-to-face with him that she realized who it was.

"Are you kidding me?" Steven yelled. "Are you out of your mind?"

Laura didn't answer. She simply collapsed into his arms.

Chapter 37

Jackie looked over her shoulder at the clock, her dinner left untouched. Danlyn sat across the table from her, unable to eat, as well.

"They'll be back soon. Don't worry," Jackie told her. She reached over, patted her hand. "Why don't you try just a bite?"

Danlyn put the fork in her mouth, working a bite of a potato into the side of her cheek. "What if they caught her?"

Jackie's forehead creased. "If they're not back by—"

The front door opened and Laura and Steven walked in. Danlyn whirled around so fast she almost knocked her plate on the floor.

Jackie leapt from her chair. "What on earth were you doing?" She rushed to Laura. "You know how worried we were?"

Steven slammed the door shut, threw his keys on the end table. "You're as much to blame as she is, Jackie. I can't believe you'd let her go out there. And for what?" He looked at Laura. "She didn't find them."

"Find what?" Jackie asked.

"She didn't tell you why she went there?" Steven asked.

"No. She said she'd tell me later." Jackie scanned the length of Laura's body. "So…why did you go? And why the hell are you covered in mud?"

Laura looked at the muddy prints left from her shoes. "Sorry, Jacks."

"I don't care about the floor. What on earth happened?"

Steven shook his head. "She crawled through the basement window."

"It was the only way in," Laura told them. "I was still in the house when they came home."

"Holy sh—"

"They didn't catch me."

Laura was so tired. All she wanted was a hot shower and clean clothes. But from the look on Jackie's face, she wasn't going anywhere. She was going to stand right there until she talked.

"I got away, but then my car wouldn't start. Thank God Steven was there."

"That still doesn't explain what was so important that you had to go out there."

"Journals," Steven said.

Jackie shot him a confused look. "Journals?"

He nodded toward Laura. "Ask her."

Laura leaned against the wall next to the door, still trying to get warm. "Olivia told me my father kept all these journals. He started them when he was in Korea." She winced. The acid still tearing through her muscles was brutal. "I guess he wrote in them all the time."

"Okay." Jackie finally uncrossed her arms. "So you went looking for them?"

"That day, when my dad kept calling your house…when he couldn't get ahold of me, he drove out to my mother's to ask where I might be, and Frank was there. I guess things got *interesting*."

Jackie frowned.

"My father told Vivian and Frank that he had something important to tell me. Then he and Frank got into it. And Olivia never believed the reports, either."

"So, she thinks…?" Jackie asked. When Laura nodded, Jackie looked back at Steven.

"She told me everything on the drive back," he said. "And to think, if you'd just told me, I would've helped you, Laura. At least I could have gone with you."

"Are you nuts?" Jackie asked. "It's not bad enough that Laura's risking her safety. Now you're willing to do the same?"

"You two are the ones who concocted this stupid plan," he said. "No one thought to let me in on it. You wouldn't have told me where she was if I hadn't threatened to call the police. But regardless, you've got to admit that this is all pretty compelling."

If looks could kill, Steven would have been a dead man.

"What happened to everything you said last night?" Jackie asked him.

Steven looked at the table where Danlyn sat, not eating but watching them intently.

Danlyn threw her fork down on the plate, then stood up.

Laura shoved off the wall, suddenly awake. "Danlyn, don't act—"

"No," Danlyn shouted back. "I'm tired of everyone talking about things but not telling me anything. You're all doing it. I know you're keeping secrets. I'm sick of it."

She stomped off toward the room. Before the door slammed shut, she yelled, "You promised you wouldn't keep things from me."

Steven looked around. "Um…did I say something?"

Laura exhaled. "No. But it's time I told her everything."

Chapter 38

Laura rested her forehead on the guest-room door and closed her eyes. The day William told her she was going to be a sister was one of the worst days on Hallows' Farm. Laura could still remember it so clearly. There was no laughter, no proud smiles. Just silence and tears and empty liquor bottles all over the porch. And blood.

It was three months into Laura's senior year, and instead of desperation, she felt hope. The days ahead, after graduation, came with the promise of freedom, and maybe, finally, happiness. She and Steven were more in love than ever, and while Jackie was a year behind them in school, they were inseparable. The only time Laura wasn't with them was when she missed school because her father was too drunk to care for himself and Vivian had locked herself away. But those days were coming to an end. Once she graduated, she was going to escape, even if that meant leaving her father behind.

The day that marked the beginning of Laura's end started out like any other. Steven held her hand and walked her home after school, kissing her goodbye at the entrance to the driveway before leaving for his job at the old textile plant. It was supposed to be temporary. At least that's what Steven and Laura always said. They were both going to go to college somewhere far away, live out their dreams, become professionals. Laura a vet, Steven a surgeon.

Laura kicked rocks along the drive, lost in a blissful future that would never come to fruition. She turned the corner, holding her books to her chest, and veered around the large elm tree in front of the house. Then she heard the scuffling of shoes on the front porch and the *bang* of a glass bottle falling to the ground. William was swerving on his feet and tripped down the stairs, landing on his knees in the dirt. There was something on his hands. Something bright. Something like death.

Laura dropped her books and ran to him. "Where's the blood from, Dad? What happened?"

William held his head in his bloody hands and rocked back and forth, quietly groaning.

"Are you hurt?" Laura asked.

William tried to speak but his words caught in his chest, and only muffled cries slipped from his drooling lips.

"Is it her? Did she hurt you? Did she hurt herself?" Laura got up, horrified she'd find her mother bleeding from her wrists.

"Don't go," William begged through his tears. "Your mother will be fine."

Laura looked into his bloodshot eyes. "What's going on, Dad? You're scaring me."

William wiped his face with his large hands, leaving behind trails of blood.

The harsh stench of alcohol on his breath made Laura cringe. "Jesus. How much this time? Did you fall again? Is that why you're bleeding?"

"She tried to k-kill it."

"Kill what? I don't understand."

"Your mother's pregnant. I came home and saw the hanger on the floor in our bathroom."

Laura's body gave out, she fell to her knees. Vivian…pregnant. She looked again at his bloody hands, and her chest swelled with a scream that she didn't let escape. "I didn't even know she —"

"She didn't want you to know." William cleared his throat. "She didn't want anyone knowing. Still doesn't." He sniffed hard. "You know how your mother's been worse lately? Well, we've known about it for a few months. She didn't want it. Said she was gonna kill herself and the baby. But I didn't believe her. I swear, I didn't think she was gonna do it."

After that day, Vivian never left Rose's room. It was a while before William and Laura figured out that she hadn't managed to abort the baby. When Laura brought food to her, she saw the change in her belly, growing week after week.

Foolish or not, William had been so happy. He actually thought when Vivian saw their baby's precious face, she'd have a change of heart. "She was just too young when she had you," he told Laura once. "She's forty-one now. Maybe she'll handle everything better."

But he was wrong.

Vivian didn't speak anymore, didn't move, aside from trips to the bathroom, and she'd practically stopped eating. William drank more and more as the pregnancy progressed. He promised Laura that when the baby was born he'd stop for good. Always for good.

Laura spent months playing nurse to both her parents while still marking off the days till her sentence was over, never stopping to recognize the whisper in her ear, telling her that once her baby brother or sister was born, she wouldn't be able to walk away.

Laura's visits with Steven and Jackie became scarce, and her grades started dropping for the first time in her school career. Towards the end of the pregnancy, Vivian was nearly catatonic, requiring feedings, baths, dressings. William spent most days as a functioning alcoholic, going to work each morning only to come home already drunk. He'd spend hours crying on Laura's shoulder, and when he wasn't crying, he slept.

It took everything Laura had not to fall in line with her parents, depressed and slobbering in her own self-pity. But she somehow moved forward, fighting through each day, working hard for herself and her family, and she kept her mother's pregnancy a secret, even when Jackie prodded or Steven wanted to know why he never saw her anymore. Once, when she thought Steven had reached the end of his rope, tired of the excuses she made, she almost told him. For years after, she wondered what would have come of them had she been honest with him that day. But those thoughts settled with time, drowned at the bottom of every drink she poured for herself.

Laura felt tears on her cheeks and opened her eyes. She should've been more prepared. She wanted to be. But the time had come, and Danlyn needed the truth. Not the whole truth, of course. Laura didn't know what the whole truth would do to her. When Mommy tries to snuff the life from your little body before you've even had a chance to breathe, that could maim your mind beyond repair. Then Laura thought of her own baby. A baby she would have given her life for. A baby she still hadn't mourned the loss of. A baby whose blood, Laura felt, was on her hands. Life was cruel, and there was no rewind button, nor was there a way to patch the gaping hole in her heart. But there was this moment, here and now. There was Danlyn, still young, still vulnerable, still in need of a mother and a protector. And here Laura was, finally ready to provide those things. She opened the door.

Danlyn sat on the bed, legs crisscrossed in front of her.

"Can I talk to you?" Laura asked.

Danlyn rolled her eyes. "Why?"

"I want you to know what happened with Vivian. Why you never knew the truth about her."

"Really?" Danlyn suddenly looked pale.

"Really." Laura sat at the foot of the bed. "I'm trying to figure out the best way to explain everything to you." She gently rolled her fingers over the blanket, her eyebrows knitted together. "I've been a horrible mother, Danlyn. I never knew how to be a mom. That's no excuse, but I had no idea how to raise you. You've seen Vivian. I didn't exactly learn from the best. But I know that I hurt you, and I'll never forgive myself for that. I don't expect you to, either. I took everything out on you, and I'm so sorry. From the bottom of my heart, I'm so incredibly sorry, Danlyn. I know you're angry with me, and you have every right to be, but I'm hoping you'll understand a little more after I explain things to you."

"I talked to Jackie," Danlyn said, playing with a loose string on the comforter. "She said you told her everything. Like, about the things you did. How you were with me. She also said I shouldn't be upset with you about what Vivian told me, because you love me, and you were only trying to keep me safe.

"And how you're doing all this stuff, like going out there tonight, because you want me with you." The lines on Danlyn's young face deepened. "Is that stuff true? You want me with you?"

"Yes. More than anything in this world. That's all I want. Do you want that?"

"I want you to tell me everything first. I want to know why you never told me I'm not your..." Danlyn still couldn't say it.

"I understand. I'll tell you everything I know. And you're going to have questions. I know you will, because I do, too. But I don't have all the answers, Danlyn. All I can tell you is my side of things. Why other people made the decisions they made, I'll never know."

"Okay." Danlyn tensed.

Laura shifted, cleared her throat. "Vivian was pregnant with you during my last year in high school. I didn't even know she was pregnant until she had a breakdown. A bad breakdown. I came home from school one day and saw my dad...our dad sitting on the front porch. He was hysterical. Vivian lost it that day. Just snapped. She said she couldn't have another baby. She never wanted me and never liked being a mother and just couldn't do it again. And our dad..." Laura hesitated. "Well, what you've heard about his drinking is true. He was an alcoholic." Laura took a deep breath. "No one else knew Vivian was pregnant, and I wasn't allowed to tell anyone. I stopped seeing my friends, took care of her all the time, took care of Dad. I barely graduated. That's when Steven and I were going to leave Rome. That was the plan, anyway."

Danlyn squinted. "You and Steven? Jackie's Steven?"

"Yeah. We were dating. Had been for a long time, actually. But when I told him I couldn't leave, things changed. I couldn't "tell him I was busy caring for my pregnant mother and that was why I never saw him or Jackie anymore. I also couldn't tell him why I wasn't going to move away with him."

"Why didn't you want to move away with him?" Danlyn looked so innocent, so naive.

"I wasn't going to leave you. I wanted to be a good sister, and I knew you were going to need me around."

Danlyn couldn't hide the smile on her face, but her eyes looked sad.

"And it was a good thing, because the week after graduation, you were born. Just like I told you, in Rose's room. I was there. Well…not in the room, but I was waiting in the hallway, right outside the door, and then I heard you cry. A good cry, I remember thinking. Strong. It felt like an eternity before I got to meet you. When Dad finally opened the door, he had you in his arms."

Laura made a sound, something between a laugh and a cry. The memories were so near the surface, still so vivid and lovely. The first time she held Danlyn in her arms. The smell of her hair. Her tiny fingers and the way they wrapped around hers.

"When Dad handed you to me, the world just stopped. You were the most amazing thing I'd ever seen. Standing in that house, where good things never happened, I experienced the most happiness I'd ever known. You were the most beautiful thing in the world. I just couldn't have imagined that anything could be so sweet. Dad bent down and whispered in my ear, 'That's Danlyn. Your little sister. I picked the name you liked.' And just like that, you had me, kid." Laura wiped a tear away, but now she was smiling, so genuine and unbridled that it seemed to reach Danlyn.

"I wish I could lend you that memory, Danlyn. So you could see how loved you were and are. And Dad…my Lord. I'd "never seen him glow like that. For the first time, the sadness in his eyes wasn't there. It just vanished. He beamed. He loved you so much. I used to watch him hold you, the way he cradled you, sang to you, made funny faces at you. For a while after, he didn't even drink anymore. He just"—she shrugged—"lived for us."

"What about her?" Danlyn asked. "Did she love me like you and…our dad?"

Laura's smile faded. "She couldn't do it, Danlyn. And this is the part I can't explain. No matter how I try to explain things, you'll never understand why Vivian couldn't be your mom, or mine. It's crazy and insane and it shouldn't be possible for a mother to not love her children, but it is. When it comes to mothers, we got the short end of the stick, by no fault of our own. We were just dealt a really crappy hand."

"Did you take me away because she wasn't a good mom?"

"No. I wouldn't have done that. Not to our father. He loved you too much."

"What happened, then?"

"A few weeks after you were born, I went to Jackie's, just to hang out. When I got home, Vivian and William were standing in the living room with all my things on the floor in front of the fireplace. The minute I walked through the door, I could smell whiskey. I looked at Dad and knew. He was drunk for the first time since you were born. And Vivian, she just stood there, looking at me like the last year hadn't happened."

"What were they doing?"

"I figured Vivian wanted me out. What else could explain all of my things being packed up? Well, they had a big fight about me leaving. Vivian wanted me out, Dad wanted her out. But she wasn't going anywhere, and he didn't want her around you because she was so messed up. That's all I knew. Even "now, I don't know what prompted everything that day. Part of me was relieved because I knew I wouldn't have to live with my mother anymore. But then I thought about you, and I panicked. What would happen to you? Who would care for you? I asked where you were. That's all I could say. 'Where's Danlyn? Where's Danlyn?' When no one answered, I tried to go find you, but Vivian wouldn't let me past her. Then something in the luggage caught my eye. There were a few suitcases, some bags. Just next to the last suitcase, I saw this brand-new baby carrier, and there you were, curled up in it, asleep. I just stared at Dad...so confused. He was shaking so bad. I yelled at him to talk to me, but he couldn't. I still remember the look in his eyes. And Vivian...she was always a monster, but that day, she looked possessed. God, it scared me. Then she told me exactly what to do. 'No one will know the difference. You'll tell them you hid the pregnancy and that she's yours. You'll never speak a word of this to anyone.' I tried arguing. I begged and cried. Then Dad went back in the kitchen and I never saw him again. Ever. Vivian started throwing our things in the fireplace. I was screaming for her to stop, but she just kept on. I had no money, nothing at all, and I knew I couldn't afford to lose anything, so I grabbed you and a couple bags and headed for the porch. Little did I know Dad had gone into the kitchen to call Jackie's parents. He didn't tell them anything. Just asked them to come get me. When Jackie and her mom showed up, Vivian came out, handed me some money. Said it was plenty, and that she never wanted to see me again. I got in the car and told Jackie and her parents what I was supposed to tell them. And that was that."

Danlyn's eyes were huge. "You went through all that because of me? It's my fault."

Laura leaned over, gently holding her by the shoulders. "Don't you ever feel guilty. Not for anything. You were the "greatest thing that ever happened to me. I was just too young and scared to be the mother you deserved. But you were a gift, Danlyn. All the years of drinking and being mad as hell, it wasn't because of you. It was because of me and my guilt."

Danlyn's voice trembled. "But you gave up everything for me. You didn't get to do anything you wanted to do, and everyone thought you lied."

"No. I didn't give anything up for you. You had to give everything up for me. You gave up having any kind of decent mother. You gave up a real childhood. And you didn't even have a choice in the matter. Being your mother, caring for you, it didn't force me to give anything up. *I* didn't handle it well because *I* was too screwed up. Coming from Vivian's home, having an alcoholic father who I felt betrayed me...that's what screwed me up. But I can't even blame them. It was my responsibility to pull myself up and be a good mother to you. I let my childhood hold me back." Laura held Danlyn's chin gently in her hands. "Tell me you believe me, Danlyn. Because you can't blame yourself. I couldn't handle that. Not after everything I've put you through."

Danlyn nodded, giant tears streaming down her cheeks.

"You were the only good thing in my life. You still are. And I know I blamed you, Danlyn. I know I said I wouldn't be where I was in life if it hadn't been for you, but I was lying. I put myself there. I was too much like our father, and I made myself a drunk, and I kept myself in that role. That, and that alone, is why I was in so many bad spots. Worst of all, I pulled you down with me. But you've always been the one joy in my life. And come hell or high water, I'll stick by your side until the day I'm gone. Nothing will take you away from me. Not drinking. Not Vivian. Not Frank. Nothing. Do you understand me?"

"Yes."

"And do you believe me?"

"Yes," she said again, and threw her arms around Laura, tucking her head in her neck, holding on as if her life depended on it.

"I love you, Danlyn. With all my heart."

"I love you," Danlyn said. Then she looked up into her eyes. "I don't want any other mom. You're my mom."

Laura pulled Danlyn's head to her chest and wept, rocking her back and forth, wondering if Danlyn could feel that her heart had grown ten times bigger. "I'll always be your mom. Always, my sweet girl."

"And she can't make me live with her, can she?" Danlyn asked.

The prospect sounded all the more terrifying coming from Danlyn's lips.

"Absolutely not. I'll do anything to make sure that doesn't happen." Laura tightened her grip on her. "That's why I went out there. I need to find something that'll keep that from ever happening."

"Mom?" Danlyn pulled back, wiped her nose. "I know you're still not telling me things. I can tell by the way you and Jackie and Steven talk. But what if I could help?"

"Your job isn't to worry about this stuff. You leave it to me, and I'll worry about it for the both of us."

"But what if I saw something that could help?"

"Why? Did something happen?"

"You were looking for something in Vivian's house?"

"Yeah. I was looking for books. William's journals. Why?"

Danlyn squinted, as if trying to recall exactly what she had seen. "The other day, Frank came by and did something in the attic. I could hear him up there because I was in your old room.

"When he left, he didn't see me looking out the window. He was holding a big box. I don't know what was in it, but it looked heavy…the way he was holding it."

"When was this?"

"The day you were in the hospital."

"Jesus," Laura whispered. "They're at Frank's."

Chapter 39

"Frank." Vivian reached down, blindly searching for the bowl on the floor. "Frank!" She could hear his boots slamming down with each step as he made his way upstairs.

"What?"

"Bowl. Please."

"You could've got your ass out of bed and grabbed it, Viv." He bent down, taking his time, dragging out each nauseating moment.

"Ple…ase," Vivian begged. A tiny dribble of vomit seeped from the corner of her mouth. She yanked the bowl out of his hands and leaned over, purging her dinner.

"Call me when you're done," he said. "I'll be downstairs."

"No." She spat into the bowl. "Stay."

"What is it you need now?" Frank leaned against the doorframe. He wouldn't look at her.

Vivian fell back into the pillows, panting. "I'm dying. You can say this is a bug, but I know it's not. It's cancer, masquerading as something else. I know why it's happening "now. Why I'm dying. It's because I want to be around. For all the years I didn't care if I died, now I know there's nothing sweet about it. It's agonizing, Frank. Every dreadful step toward it."

"For Christ's sake! You're not dyin'. You're sick."

"I've got cancer, Frank. What do you call that? Living?" She pulled the covers up under her chin. "I'm dying," she murmured through chattering teeth.

Frank walked around the bed, pressed his hand to her forehead. "See. You're burnin' the hell up. You're just sick. Why're you actin' like this? It isn't like you."

"Like what?" Vivian could play at this game.

"Needy. You won't let me leave. You're havin' a fit over Danlyn. This isn't you."

"It's different now. I didn't see it before, but now I do. I never meant to tell Danlyn, but now that she knows, I want to start over with you."

The truth was there, on his face, if she could just bring herself to look at him. But what if what she saw wasn't the same? If he didn't want her anymore...

"Tell me you want that, too, Frank."

"I've made clear what I want."

Vivian made a sound deep in her throat.

"You gonna puke again?"

Her face twisted with anger. "No. I'm just disgusted with you. Laura's not a part of me, and I'm not a part of her. Blood or not. I see her face and I see William's. I hear her voice and I hear William's. She looks at me the same way he did."

"What the hell's gotten into you? You've always been as rock-solid as they come, but now, I walk through the door and have no idea what the hell's gonna come out of your mouth. I don't know how to deal with you, Viv."

Vivian bolted up. Screw the spinning in her head. Screw Frank. If she vomited again, she'd aim for his boots. "I don't like it any more than you do, Frank. I don't want to feel these things. I used to be strong. But not as strong as you gave me credit for. You know about my depressions, but you don't know how far I sank. You don't know about the cutting, how I wondered if William and Laura noticed how close I'd come to ending it all. Not that they would've cared. But once William left, I didn't need to make myself bleed just to remind myself that I was alive. That it hadn't all been a bad dream. You rescued me, for the second time, Frank. But I feel it again, like something stirring in me. You look at me the same way William did. With pity. And you talk and talk and talk of Laura."

Frank could only stare at her with a blank expression. Someone had replaced Vivian with this complex creature. One no one could control. Not even Frank.

"I've never before cared about much of anything but you," Vivian said. "But for once in my life, I'm scared. Scared of losing everything. You…Danlyn. All of it scares me senseless. Most of all, Laura scares me. She can't leave anything alone. She's as bad as William, and you see where it got him. She'll meet the same fate if she doesn't learn."

Frank lunged at her. She fell back. He plowed his fists down into the pillow on each side of her head. "You'll have to spell that out for me," he growled.

Vivian clutched the sheet, her skin broke out in a cold sweat. "I just meant that…she'll have a bottle back in her hand by next week, if she doesn't already."

Frank cocked his head sideways, his lips curled back. "The drinking? You sure that's what this is about? Because that sounded like a threat to me."

"No. That's all I meant." A tear rolled down Vivian's cheek. She could have turned away. She probably should have. But then she saw Frank's eyes, the way they softened.

"Damn, ol' girl." His voice smoothed, like black silk. "There's somethin' I ain't used to seein'. What're you cryin' for?"

"I don't want to be alone. But you're sick of me."

He leaned back and laughed, then plopped down next to her and bent over, yanking his boots off. "Is this your plan? Make me feel bad so I'll stay? You don't need to reel me in, Viv. Have I ever left you? Even when *he* came home, the big war hero, I didn't walk away."

"I'm not trying to make you feel guilty." But those words sounded untrue, even to her.

Frank got up, walked to the dresser. "Whatever you say, Viv." He grabbed his pajamas and headed to the bathroom. "I'm gonna wash up."

~

Frank rummaged through the medicine cabinet. How the hell a woman dying of brain cancer didn't have more medication, he didn't know.

He searched the few bottles kept under the sink. Cough syrup. That would put her on her ass. That was if she didn't puke it up first.

He slammed the cabinet shut, looked at his watch. Eight-fifteen.

Chapter 40

Laura sped through the living room on her way to the kitchen. "Can I use your phone?"

Jackie sprang up from the kitchen table. "What's wrong? How'd it go in there?"

"Phone, Jackie. Can I use it?" Laura didn't wait for an answer. She was already in the kitchen, Jackie and Steven trailing behind.

"What're you doing?" Jackie asked. "You have that look."

"I don't know where he lives," Laura said. She picked up the phone, dialed information. "Yes. Do you have a listing for a Frank Roland, in Rome, Georgia?"

Jackie shot a hard look back at Steven. "Stop her!" she whispered.

Laura covered her free ear with her hand. "What do you mean there's no Frank Roland?" She didn't have time for this. "Well, try again."

Jackie slapped her finger down on the receiver, ending the call.

"What're you doing?" Laura snapped, trying to nudge Jackie out of the way. "I need his address."

"No. I draw the line here."

"Danlyn just told me she saw Frank leave with a box the other day."

"So?"

"He took something from my mother's house, Jackie. She said it looked heavy, like it could've been books. And why the hell isn't there a listing for..." She tried for the phone once more—Jackie blocked her again.

"You're not thinking straight. You barely got out of your mother's house, and now you want to break into his? Are you a lunatic?"

Laura's voice rose. "A lunatic? No, Jackie. A lunatic would just sit here, waiting for those pieces of shit to take Danlyn. *That's* lunacy. Frank's got the journals. I know it. One way or another, I'm going. Even if I have to walk to a payphone and to his house."

"You need to think for a minute," Steven said.

Jackie turned around, glaring at him. "And what're you so calm for? Are you not hearing what I'm hearing?"

"I'm not arguing about this," Laura said, storming out of the kitchen. Nothing was going to stop her. "I'll wait till Danlyn's out of the shower and asleep. Then I'm gone."

Laura walked to the front door, picked up her wet jacket. "Shit." She reached in the pocket, just now remembering that her father's autopsy reports were in there. She had been reading them while waiting for Frank and Vivian to leave. Holding them by her fingertips, she moved them from side to side, letting them dry. She could see Jackie and Steven watching her. Steven was whispering something in Jackie's ear.

"What are those?" Jackie asked.

"My father's…" Laura just now noticed how they both wore the same relaxed expression. Where had their fight gone? "My father's autopsy reports. Just don't tell Danlyn where I've gone if she wakes up. Okay?" When neither of them responded, Laura said, "Hello?"

"You can't go," Steven told her.

"What're you going to do, tie me up?"

"No. I mean you literally can't go. I don't know where you got the name Roland, but that's not Frank's last name. You're not going to find his house, so knock yourself out. Use the phone, if you think it'll do any good."

Laura's brain went blank; the papers fell from her hand. She bent down to scoop them up, but her fingers were still cold and slow. "What's his name?" she asked. "You obviously know it." When Steven didn't speak, Laura froze, staring at him fiercely.

"If I'm right," Laura said, "if he took those journals, ask yourself why. What's in them that they don't want me to see? What if this is my one shot to nail their asses? Think about it."

Steven bent down, offering Laura an apologetic smile. He picked the papers off the floor, holding them out to her, but she wouldn't take them, wouldn't move.

"I'm sorry," he said sincerely. "I wish there was another way." He looked down at the papers. "But there's—" His voice broke off, his eyes focused. He blinked several times. Before Laura could ask what was wrong, he rushed into the kitchen, picking up the phone.

"What're you doing?" Jackie asked him.

He put the phone to his ear, punched in three numbers.

"What in the hell are you doing?" Jackie again.

Steven spoke fast into the phone. "I need an address for Frank Day, or maybe Franklin Day, in Rome, Georgia."

Jackie spun around and looked at Laura. Laura's jaw had gone slack, her eyes glossed over.

"What is it?" Jackie asked. "What's going on?"

"Jesus," Laura whispered. "They're related?"

"Who's related? Will someone please tell me what's going on?"

Steven hung up the phone and handed Jackie the autopsy report. "The name. Look at it."

Jackie scanned the paper, shaking her head. "What am I looking for?"

Steven pointed to the name of the second examiner.

"Benjamin Day?" Jackie asked. "I don't…" She looked back at Steven, then at the paper. "But…" Her eyebrows rose.

Steven took the paper back, handed it to Laura. "The second autopsy report," he said to Jackie, "was done by a Benjamin Day. That's Frank's last name. I wouldn't have known, except that one of his new contractors did business with us. Wrote Frank's name on the slip." Steven looked back at Laura. "Roland's his middle name, according to the operator."

"His son." Laura didn't sound like herself.

"Son?" Steven asked.

"Olivia…she told me Frank had a son and a fiancée. She left him with the baby. Olivia said Frank sent his son to live with family a couple counties over. How much you wanna bet Frank's got a son named Benjamin? It all makes sense. The reports, the bullshit cause of death. It makes perfect sense."

Steven tore the sheet with Frank's address on it off the pad on the wall. "I'll go with you, Laura."

Jackie turned on her heels with daggers in her eyes. "No, you won't! What the hell's wrong with you? The both of you?"

"She's right," Laura said. "You're not coming with me. No way I'm letting you do that." Laura tried grabbing the paper in Steven's hand, but he was too quick.

"I've made up my mind." He lifted the paper high in the air. "That's it. And Jackie, do you need any more proof?"

"Obviously not." Jackie pointed at the window. "But you're not going out there, breaking into some psycho's house. Just call the cops."

"We can't." He grabbed the paper, holding it in front of Jackie. "They're not just going to arrest Frank because of this one piece of paper, and that won't keep Vivian from getting Danlyn back. We need more proof." He folded the papers back up, shoved them in his back pocket. He lowered his voice. "What if they do take Danlyn, Jackie? Knowing what we know now, how're you going to feel about seeing Danlyn around town with that man? Can you live with that?"

"You were just telling her earlier how stupid it was to break into Vivian's. Where did sensible Steven go?"

"I needed proof. Now I've got it. Now answer my question?"

Laura could see Jackie's resolve wavering. Steven wasn't giving her any choice.

"Don't worry," Laura said to her. "Steven's not coming with me."

Jackie shook her head. "I don't want *either* of you going, especially now that we know how dangerous he is."

"All the more reason to go," Steven said.

Laura broke in again. "Steven, you're not—"

"Enough!" Steven reined in his volume. "I'm not arguing with either of you. It's decided. Just tell me he's sleeping at your mother's tonight, Laura."

Laura knew if she answered, that would seal the deal, but the look on Steven's face told her he'd go, even if Frank were home. "Yes. He'll probably sleep at my mother's. But..."

Jackie's face went blank, her eyes slowly fell to the floor. She seemed to be searching for another solution. "You could both get—"

"Into Frank's house and back out, all without getting caught," Steven said, grabbing his keys off the counter. "Worst-case scenario, we walk away without having found anything. Best case, Laura finds something she can use against them."

"No," Jackie said. "Worst-case scenario is Frank finds you two in his house and..." She hesitated; her shoulders sank as she sighed. "But...no. I can't live with seeing Danlyn with them."

Laura turned, heading out of the kitchen. Steven was out of his mind if he thought he was coming along.

"Forgetting something?" Steven asked, jiggling the set of keys in his hand. "You can't walk that far. Frank's a ways out there." He shoved the keys back in his pocket. "I failed you once, Laura. I wasn't there when you needed me. But not this time."

"Two hours," Jackie said. "And write the address down for me. Two hours and I call the cops. I swear to God, Steven, I'll do it."

He looked at the clock. It was eight forty. "No good. Give us three hours."

"Two," Jackie countered.

Steven grabbed the pen. "I'll give you the address, but you'll give us three hours. You jump the gun and send the cops, they'll catch us in his house, and then we're definitely stuck in jail."

But Jackie wasn't giving in this time. "Two." Then she looked over Steven's shoulder at Laura.

Laura didn't want them to see her cry, didn't want them to see that she'd given in. That she was willing to let them risk so much.

"Say good night to Danlyn," Jackie told Laura. "But don't you dare give anything away. I'll be a wreck as it is. I don't need her in a panic, too. And Laura"—Jackie folded her arms around her shoulders, hugging her tight—"you find what you need and settle this shit once and for all." Jackie kissed her on the cheek. "I love you."

Laura closed her eyes. "I love you, too."

Laura heard the shower turn off and the bathroom door open. She walked out of the kitchen, leaving Jackie and Steven to whisper their goodbyes.

"Danlyn." She put on a smile. "You ready for bed?"

Chapter 41

Laura looked out the window, watching the trees and brush along the two-lane road rush by in a blur of dark shadows. "Start slowing down."

"I remember." Steven took his foot off the gas and turned off the headlights.

Laura could just make out the mad spark in his eyes from the dull glow of the clock radio on the dashboard. "You scared?"

He came to a stop just before the entrance to the driveway. "Would you think less of me if I was?"

She shook her head. "No. I am, too."

He brought the car to a stop. "Get a good look. I want to make sure he's still here."

Laura squinted, searching through the sea of bare branches that kept Vivian's house well hidden.

"There," she pointed. "His truck's still in front of the house."

Steven tapped on the clock. "It's nine. Gives us twenty minutes to get there, little less than an hour inside, and thirty minutes to get back." He pulled back onto the dark lane and brought the car up to speed. Then well past it.

"I still can't believe I'm letting you do this," Laura said.

Steven laughed. "*Letting* me? You didn't *let* me do anything. I wanted to. You couldn't have stopped me."

Laura hesitated. "I need you to know how sorry I am…for lying to you back then."

"Don't worry about it." He gripped the wheel tight. "Water under the bridge. You've got nothing to apologize for. Vivian's to blame. Besides, had you told me the truth back then, we might be doing something completely different tonight. You might be knitting a sweater—I'd be shining my bowling trophies. But we certainly wouldn't be starting a new career as criminal masterminds."

Laura would have otherwise laughed. But tonight wasn't meant for such things. "You should probably wait to call us masterminds until we've gotten inside. I don't know how we're going to get in."

"We'll see when we get there. Guess I hung out with the wrong kids in high school. Probably could've picked up some good burglar skills." If it wasn't for the subtle tremble in his voice, he might have convinced Laura that he was enjoying this.

"Over this hill is a big valley." Steven nodded at the road ahead.

"I remember," Laura said. "I've been out here."

"Probably not as far out as Frank's place is. Guy's living in no-man's-land." When they crested the top of the hill, Steven pointed. "There's the valley. He's out there. Way out there."

Laura grabbed her stomach, leaned forward. "I'm gonna be sick."

"No you're not."

"Yes, I am."

"Well," he floored the gas. "You're gonna have to suck it up, 'cause we've got just enough time before my wife calls the cops and gets our asses thrown in the hoosegow."

~

Steven veered off the lane, turning onto the small dirt road that led to Frank's front door. "Big trailer," he said, holding tight to the wheel as they bumped over rocks and holes and finally came to a stop roughly twenty feet from the trailer. "If we get stuck, we're in trouble." He turned the car off but left the keys in the ignition and flung the door open. "Okay, let's do this." But Laura didn't move. "Come on."

She stared at the trailer.

"Laura?"

"They're not here. There's no attic. No basement. Nowhere to hide them." Her voice shook. "It's not worth it."

Steven leaned across her, opened her door. "This whole damn place is a hiding spot. You grew up here and even you've never been out here. I know your mother's agoraphobic ass never hauls her cookies all the way out here. The guy thinks he's got nothing to worry about. Probably has them lined up on a shelf inside." He grabbed her hand. "Let's get this party started."

"I'm gonna throw up, Steven."

Steven got out of the car and walked around to her door, pulling her out by the arm. "You already said that, so either do it or shut up. Either way, we're getting in that trailer, if I have to drag you in."

"I'm scared."

Steven gave her another good yank. "Well, I'm not."

"You're a shitty liar."

"Laura, just think, you already broke in to your mother's house alone. Now you've got me."

When he pulled her to her feet, Laura bent over and vomited into the mud.

Steven grabbed her ponytail just before it fell in front of her mouth. "Big showoff. I gave you two options. You could've just shut up."

Laura spat, wiped her mouth with the back of her jacket. She breathed deeply, spat again. "Okay…I think I'm ready now."

"Good." He grabbed her hand and ran to the front of the trailer. "Just don't puke on the welcome mat. That's an automatic ten-point deduction."

"This isn't funny," she said, her feet scrambling behind her as they ran.

"You're right." Steven tugged on the front door. It held fast. "But if I don't take my mind off it, I'll be throwing up right next to you." He tugged on the two windows next to the front door. "Dammit!" He pulled again, but they held firm. "New plan. Come on."

They ran around the perimeter of the trailer, pushing and pulling on windows, even trying their luck with a credit card, and when they were done with that, they did it again.

"Fuck," Steven yelled. "He's got this place locked down."

Laura propped her hands on her hips, pacing a small path in the mud while panting and shivering. "We can break a window if we have to. He can't prove it was us."

Steven shook his head. "That's last-resort stuff."

"Steven, we've been trying locks and windows for fifteen minutes. That gives us an hour and fifteen minutes before Jackie calls the cops. And she'll do it. You know she will."

Steven snapped his fingers. "Follow me." He ran around to the back of the trailer again, pulling a small flashlight out of his pocket. "Come hold this." He handed Laura the flashlight. "Aim it under the trailer."

"Where're you going?"

"Under there." He pointed at a small gap under the trailer. "Point it where I tell you to. Sometimes these things have a latch door built into the floor. I'm going to need both hands, if there is one." He took his jacket off, handing it to her, then got to his knees and slid under the trailer, head up, lying on his back. "Just shine the light under and up. I need you to get as low as you can."

Laura got to her stomach and lay on the ground with her head cocked sideways. She turned the flashlight on, aiming it above his head. "Is that good?"

"Yep. Just move the light with me."

Laura shivered against the semi-frozen ground and watched him disappear into the cramped, dark space. She could just make out the bottom of his shoes.

"Can you still see?"

Steven shouted, "Angle it up." He slithered to the center of the trailer. "Okay, moving to the left."

Laura followed him with the light.

"Keep it right there. Steady. Good. Now tilt the light up a little...just a hair."

"See anything?" she asked.

"Holy shit!"

Laura startled. "What?"

"Well, without some kind of zoologist, I can't tell if it's a spider or a really hairy baby."

Laura slapped the ground. "You scared the shit out of me. Come on!"

"Light, Laura."

"Sorry." She laid her head back down, tilted the light above him.

A minute later, the walls of the trailer rattled, a thunderous *clap*.

"What the hell was that?" Laura yelled. Another round of blows broke up the quiet night. "Steven? You okay?"

"Come on, fucker." He slammed his fists into metal, again and again.

"Steven?" Laura called, but then she heard the sound of metal squeaking.

"Got it!" he said. "It's the bathroom. Meet me at the front door."

Laura watched his feet disappear from view as he crawled into the trailer. Her stomach seized again as she hurtled toward the front door. "Oh shit, oh shit, oh shit." Her brain zapped with newfound energy, and she peeled around the corner, almost slipping in the mud.

"Come on," she heard Steven call from the front door.

"I'm coming."

When she reached the door, he pulled her inside. "We only have an hour to get back."

"Aw, shit," she said.

"Aw shit's right. Let's go."

Laura moved deeper into the small living room that opened into the kitchen and dining room. There was a small sofa, a coffee table, one end table. No bookshelf. "It's so empty," she said. "And dark."

Steven turned the light on over the range. "Wow." From the kitchen he could see all the adjoining rooms. "You're right. This place hardly looks lived in. Makes it easier on us, I guess. Let's start in the rooms. There's probably only two. I'll take one, you take the other. Use the flashlight if you need to."

Laura entered the first room, which sat directly across from the other. "Looks like the master."

"Yep. This one's pretty much empty," Steven said. "No bed."

She scanned the room and, through the darkness, saw bits and pieces of what made up Frank's personal space. Where he slept. Where he undressed. An eerie chill ran down the back of her legs.

Steven turned the light on in the other room, flooding part of the master in just enough light.

Laura bent down, immediately opening the dresser drawers. She moved quickly, lifting up clothes, sifting through socks and boxer shorts. Nothing in the dressers. "Anything in there?" she yelled.

"Not really. Just keep moving."

Next she searched under his bed. "Who doesn't have at least one thing under their bed?"

"I'd say there's probably more in that room than there is in here. I'm already done. I'll start on the kitchen."

Laura opened the one drawer in the nightstand. That was empty, too, unless you counted the small pile of dirty magazines. She patted the top of the bed down, lifted up the pillows, reached between the mattress and box spring. Her chest tightened. She wasn't as nervous as she was angry, and as each corner and drawer came up empty, her temper flared with thoughts of her mother's fireplace and burning stacks of journals.

She turned, facing the closet door, not knowing how she could possibly know the journals wouldn't be in there, but she did, and when she opened the door and pulled the string above her head, the truth exposed itself, empty and bare.

Immaculately organized boots and clothes were lined up in perfect order. When she slid the shirts and pants to the side, the smell of Frank's cologne smacked her hard. She recoiled. "All his shit's at my mother's. There's nothing in here."

She looked up at the top shelf. There were a few small items: two belt buckles, a pocketknife, a small box. She pulled the box down, opened the lid. There was a stack of photos, most of which were of Vivian, some bills, and...

"What the...?" she shouted. "Are you fucking kidding me?"

Steven ran into the room. "What? What'd you find?"

Laura held up an envelope. "My money. This is my money, from my suitcase. He must've taken it while I was in the hospital. Look! That's my writing! I had a little money left in my purse. I didn't even notice this was—"

"Put it back."

"What?"

"Put it back. He'll know we were here, Laura. You can't take it."

"But I—"

"We need to hurry up. I'm sorry, but we've gotta go."

Laura didn't move.

"Now, Laura!"

"Fine." She slammed the lid down, put the box back, money still inside. "Dammit. They're not here. They destroyed them."

Steven grabbed her hand, pulling her into the living room. "Don't think that way. We're not done yet."

Laura bit down on her lip. Her eyes stung with tears. "Jesus, Steven. Danlyn said he put the box in his truck. What if it's still in there? What if this whole damn time they've been in his truck? I could've been less than twenty feet from them earlier. I'm such an idiot."

"You didn't know, and you're only an idiot if you get us caught. Let's just finish here, then you can peek through the windows in his truck on the way home, if we have time. We've only got forty-five minutes to get back."

"You sure you looked everywhere?" she asked.

"I'm sure. This place is small. It wasn't hard."

"The kitchen cupboards?"

"Done," he said.

"On the top of the cupboards?"

"There, too." He sounded more agitated with every question.

"Shit. Fridge?"

"Yes, Laura. Fridge. Freezer. Cupboards. Everywhere. There're no journals."

Laura looked around the living room, rubbing her forehead. Her instincts had been all wrong. This whole night was based off one box, in one man's hands, and at a time when she hadn't even been there to see it. Danlyn could have been wrong.

Laura sank to her knees without an ounce of hope to keep her moving, letting herself cry even though Steven had said not to.

"Come on." Steven pulled her up. "I've gotta get some rags from the trunk and clean the mud off the floor, and you need to look around this room."

She stood on wobbly legs, wiping her eyes, smearing dirt on her face. "Okay." She looked behind her. "But move the sofa back before we leave. I don't want to forget."

Steven stepped aside, allowing the light from the range to shine on the sofa. "I didn't move it off the wall." He looked down into the small space behind it.

"You sure?"

"Absolutely. Hand me the flashlight. There's something back here." He grabbed the light, aimed it down. "The fabric, it's torn." He bent down, pulling up the loose flap on the back of the sofa. Reaching in, he pulled out the small box. "It's too small to hold books, but whatever it is, Frank clearly doesn't want anyone seeing it. Shit." He glanced at his watch. "You wanna see what's in it?"

Laura felt a burning in her stomach. She nodded, then sat down next to him on the floor. They stared at the box, like an animal might leap out.

Steven lifted the lid, peering inside. On the very top sat two envelopes. He picked them up, turning them over. One was thick. The corners were bent, the paper aged, but the faded script on the front could just be made out. He nervously glanced at Laura.

"What?" she asked.

"It's got your name on it."

She searched his eyes for understanding, for some small pebble of comprehension.

The paper felt cold when Steven laid it in her hands. It was strange and mysterious yet somehow familiar. She closely inspected the name scribbled on it, and her face twisted. "This is my father's writing."

She slowly peeled the back open and pulled out several sheets of paper. "It's a letter to me, from my dad." She held it out to Steven with shaky hands. "Read it."

"We don't have time for—"

"Please, Steven."

He sighed, then held the pages up in the faint light.

My Dearest Laura,

I've been trying to reach you, but Mrs. Landy says you're not home. I know why you don't want to talk to me. Your mother and I did something awful to you and your sister, and I know you can't forgive me. Hell, I can't forgive myself. But I need you to hear me out. There are things I need you to understand so that if I'm not around, you're not left wondering. What I'm hoping is that this letter helps you understand things about your mother and me. I never should have kept these things from you, but I didn't know how to say them. All I knew was that I never wanted to see you broken the way I was, but I guess I broke your heart anyway. But if you don't mind humoring your old man, I ask that you read this letter. Not all of it will be easy to read. Some of it will cut deep, honey. But you need to hear it.

The day you were born was the greatest day of my life. You were the most beautiful thing I'd ever seen, like God had sent down one of his angels just for me. I was blessed to have a few months with you before I had to leave. Those were some of the best months of my life, Laura. You were such an angelic baby. Never cried or complained. You were lovely. It broke my heart to leave you. If I'd been wiser, I wouldn't have, but the storm wiped out every crop we had, and money wasn't coming in. The Army seemed as good a place as any. I couldn't be home, but I could send money to you and your mother. During those times, we were living hand to mouth, and feeding you and Vivian was more important than my selfishness, so I shipped out.

Your mother used to write to me when I was over there. She never wrote much, but I loved getting those letters. She even sent a photo of you once. I still have it in my wallet, even now. I cherished that photo. It got me through a lot of bad times.

When I got word that your grandmother died, I knew Vivian wouldn't handle it well. I felt so guilty being away and not helping. That's when your mother stopped writing as much. It seemed like an eternity between letters. I knew how hard times were for her, but I swear to you, I had no idea how ill she was, or I'd have swum across the ocean to get home to you.

I sent home my paychecks, but things were still so tight. That's when your mother started tutoring local children for extra money. It wasn't much, but you two were doing okay. I learned later that that was when Vivian started taking in boarders for extra income. As you know, a couple years later I got shot. I didn't even care that I'd never walk well again. I just wanted to get home to you. By that time, I wasn't getting letters from Vivian anymore. I wrote to her all the time, but I never got word back. I was worried out of my mind. It had been six months since her last letter and I had no one else to check in on her. My aunt and uncle had passed and your grandmother was gone. I thought about writing another letter to let her know I was on my way home, but I was going to get back before my letter would, so I just came home without any notice.

I remember getting off the train and calling a taxi. I tried to call your mother, but no one answered. I didn't know what I would find when I got back, but I had a feeling you two would be gone. That was my worst fear. Looking back on it, that would've been better than what I did find.

I got home real late that night, and when the taxi pulled up to the drive, I hobbled right out of the car. I was so scared and excited that I didn't give the driver a chance to drive me down to the house. Your mother never heard me coming. When I got to the house, I saw a car parked out front. I'd never seen it before. If I hadn't been scared before, I certainly was then. To be honest, I thought your mother had taken up with another man. It made sense, with her not writing and all.

I walked into the house and all the lights were off, so I crept up the stairs to our room. That's when I heard a man's voice coming from Rose's old room, and I knew exactly what I was hearing. Even now, I find it almost impossible to write about. Every time I relive it, I feel like I might go out of my mind. I used to tell myself it was just a dream. That none of it happened. Then I drank a lot, trying to numb myself, but it was always waiting for me on the other side.

I thought, here I'd come home from war, and my wife was cheating on me right under my nose. I walked in the room, ready for a fight. I was just so damn angry. I felt so betrayed. But when I opened the door, my heart climbed into my throat.
You were on the bed, Laura. Just a tiny thing. You were only three years old. An innocent baby.

Steven looked up from the letter. "I don't think I can read this."

Laura would have grabbed the letter from him if she could have willed her arms to move, but instead she felt disoriented, full of a kind of dread she'd never known. "Keep going."

Steven looked back at the letter. The papers crinkled in his shaky fingers.

> *You were naked, on the bed, and there was a man lying next to you. It was a man I'd never seen before. He had no clothes on, and he was touching you. Touching my little girl. Your mother was just sitting there in the rocking chair, watching from the corner.*
>
> *My heart broke. The man that I was, he just broke. Here was my world, my little baby girl, being abused, and the woman who was meant to protect her was allowing it.*

"No more," Steven said, looking sickened.

"Keep reading." Laura's voice was low, breathy, and came with a warning. "Was it him? Was it Frank?"

> *Your mother nearly jumped out of her skin when she saw me. It took a minute for her to recognize my face. She got up and threw herself at the door, but I grabbed her and threw her across the room. I wanted to kill both of them, Laura. And I could have. Your mother went flying into the wall, and the guy made a run for it. Tried to run right past me and through the door, but I was seeing red. I'd never known a feeling like that before. Never knew I was capable of such hatred.*

I grabbed him by the neck and squeezed. He fought me, even got my hands off his neck for a second. He screamed a couple times, 'She let me do it. She let me.'

I got a better grip on him and squeezed both my hands around his neck. Your mother was screaming at me, trying to get off the floor, and you were screaming from the bed. I don't know if I meant to do it or not. It was like my body was possessed, just completely taken over, like the devil had crawled into my mind and had taken control of my body. I squeezed until there was no more life in him.

Vivian stared at me for a while. She got up and just stood there, didn't say a word. She was glaring at me like I was the bad guy, like she hated me. Then I ran at her. I grabbed her neck and I squeezed again. I swear, to this day, I think I would have killed her. I squeezed and squeezed, but then she started fighting. I remember the look in her eyes, and I got scared. It was the first time since I'd met her that I saw emotion in them. I saw the fear of God, and all I could think was that I didn't want this to be the last memory I had of your mother. I didn't want that memory seared into your mind, either. So I let her go. I couldn't finish it.

I threw her back on the floor. You were watching me, looking at me like I was this big, scary stranger. I started screaming, asking how many and for how long. Vivian started crying, saying there were two other men, but she swore to God she couldn't remember their names. But I knew better. She rattled on about needing the money, about how you two weren't making it, and these men were paying her. I remember reaching back and planting my fist in her face. That was the first and only time I ever hit a woman. After that, she said she was sick, that she wasn't right in her mind. Then she swore it would never happen again, now that I was home. I ran into her closet and started throwing her things on the floor. Told her to get out and never come back. I was going to raise you alone, and she'd never see you again. I made one big mistake though, Laura.

Vivian looked me right in the eye with the most wicked look I'd ever seen. She said she'd never leave, and I couldn't make her. She had watched me kill a man, and that was all she needed. She said she'd call the police and tell them what I'd done, and then I'd never see you again. I thought for sure the law would be on my side, but Vivian said it would be my word against hers. She also said you wouldn't be able to back up my story, which was true. You never spoke, Laura. For the longest time after that, you never spoke. I always prayed that you'd wake up one day and be able to tell the police what happened, but that day never came. By the time you started talking, I just assumed you didn't remember any of it. And after long enough, I prayed that you wouldn't remember it.

I didn't know what to do after that. Your mother had me up against a wall. She could have had me thrown in jail. I could have left, but I wasn't going to leave you. That was all I knew. I needed to be there to watch out for you.

In the weeks and months that followed, words can't say what things were like. Vivian did as she usually did and locked herself away. It took months before you would let me hold you, but I slowly gained your trust. I still remember the first time you called me Daddy and held my hand. I wanted to take you and run away, baby girl. I wanted to keep her away from you, but she had me in a bind, and every time I asked who else touched you, she'd deny knowing any names, and she never failed to threaten me. So I stayed at home, I watched over you, and after years, I forgave your mother, but I never forgot. I knew how sick she was. Sicker than you ever could remember. But not one day went by when I didn't regret not finishing them both off. I've never told another soul that, but I'm telling you. If I had been a man, if I had been a good father, I wouldn't have held back that day. The only good that came from your mother living is that Danlyn's here.

Years went by and you know the rest. Your mother and I never talked about what happened. I heard gossip sometimes. Heard names and talk of different men who stayed here. I never knew what to believe. I think I know, though, Laura. I think I know who one of the other men was, and that's part of the reason I'm writing to you. I don't know what's going to happen with you and Danlyn, and I can't imagine you ever going back home, but I need you to stay away from your mother's.

A few years after everything happened, I started hearing the name Frank. I heard that he stayed at our house while I was gone. I had myself convinced that this man had touched you. When I worked up the courage to ask your mother about him, she looked at me like she wanted to cut my throat. I kept asking if he ever laid a hand on you, and she swore up and down that he hadn't. She said he was just a friend. I thought that was strange, coming from her, but she said he was there for her in my absence, and that nothing ever happened. When I pushed the issue, she snapped. She started crying and screaming, and I knew something wasn't right. I told her I'd kill him, and she threatened me again. Made it clear I'd be out of the picture. She was so crazed that day, I didn't put it past her. I knew she meant business. But I

also knew something wasn't right. Your mother's reaction said it
all.

I messed up today. I know Frank's been at your mother's
place a lot since I left. When I couldn't reach you earlier, I drove
out there. She wouldn't pick up the phone when I called, so I got
in the car without thinking, and when I got there, Frank was
there. When I saw him, it was like everything from that night
came back. I wanted to kill him.

I asked where I could find you, but Vivian had no idea.
Said she wouldn't know. Then Frank got angry. He wanted to
know why I needed to find you and Danlyn so bad. I didn't
much appreciate him questioning me about my own daughters,
and I let my mouth run on. I told both of them I was going to tell
you everything. I said we'd kept Vivian's secrets too long, and
that it was time you knew, so that you and Danlyn would never
come back around her and Frank.

Frank looked like his blood turned to ice water. I thought
he was going to hit me, but Vivian got between us. He made his
threats, but I'm not too worried about that. Your mother made
her typical threat, too. About turning me in. I told her this time
was different. I don't care anymore. You deserve the truth, and if
that means me going to prison, so be it.

Baby girl, I didn't want to tell you this in a letter. I wanted
to sit down in person, but I can't seem to reach you. I'm sorry for
everything, Laura. I've ruined your life, and I don't know how
you can forgive me, but I'm asking that you please do. I never
wanted anything but your absolute happiness. I went and took
pity on Vivian when I should have taken you away from her, I
loved her when I shouldn't have, and I started believing her when

she told me that everything that happened was my fault because I left you two alone. I heard it so many times. Then I started drinking. I didn't know how to handle my pain, and I hurt you in the end. Strapping you down with a baby was one of the worst things. You never knew, but the day you came home and found all your things on the floor, the day you left with your sister, I came home and found your mother holding a pillow over Danlyn's face. I fought with her, and then she destroyed me all over again. Told me that it was my fault she tried to kill her, because no baby deserved a father like me. She said she wasn't going to raise her, no matter what. I must have begged enough because that's when she said you'd take her. I was so desperate, I just went along with it.

The truth is, your mother and I never should have had children. We were both unfit to raise them. The day we gave you your sister, I knew no child could survive Vivian, and I was too much of a coward to fight her anymore. I'll go to my grave regretting that I didn't take you away, that I didn't protect you. You may not believe this, but it was never from a lack of love. You and Danlyn are my universe. I love you so much. I can barely breathe under the weight of what your mother and I have done, and what I allowed. I've hurt you too much. The worst part is that I didn't protect you. But I'm trying to now. I need you to stay away from your mother and Frank. I need you to keep Danlyn away.

You will always be my special girl, my best little pal. Your daddy loves you, Laura. And little Danlyn, too.

I'll be sorry for the rest of my life.

Love,
Your father, William

Steven opened his mouth to speak, but Laura lunged at the box.

"What're you doing, Laura?"

Her hands were flying, her fingers racing. She turned the box over, spilling everything out on the floor.

"Laura, talk to me."

But she'd lost touch with all parameters of sanity.

"Laura," he tried again, unable to reach her. She ripped at the pile of photos and letters.

There were random photos of people. Children and women. But nothing that stood out. Laura's breaths escaped her in deep growls. She wanted to cry, to scream, to let out every ounce of pain, but she couldn't. Not yet.

"Laura," Steven grabbed her hands, but her rage made her stronger.

She tore his fingers off hers, screaming, "Stop it!" Tears flooded her eyes. "Don't touch me!"

Steven sat back, open-mouthed.

Laura had an eerie feeling she knew exactly what she was looking for. Something was pouring over the rim, memories were floating to the surface. She lifted up the empty box, looking closely at the bottom. There was one last envelope. It was small and blended in with the wood. She peeled it off the bottom, tore the back open.

Steven peered down at her hands, and when she pulled out a few small photos, he grimaced. "Jesus fucking Christ."

Laura sat motionless, staring at the photos of her and Frank, together, in Rose's room, neither wearing any clothes. Everything slowed, like the world had stopped spinning. She thought again of the fall trees, stripped so clean, and how she had felt a kinship with them. Now the weight of Frank's sins permeated her flesh, her soul. They drenched her in filth so heavy she couldn't breathe. And then it happened. Her mind took its first step into a mad world where rules didn't exist and where she could smell only the decay of her childhood. Steven's words drowned into the silence around her. Even his presence seemed to fade away. There was only hate—pure and seething and alive inside her. And there was Vivian and Frank and the rifle William had kept in the hallway closet in her mother's house.

Final snap.

Laura moved.

~

She grabbed her father's letter off the floor, the photos still gripped in her fingers. She turned sideways and leapt at the front door, sending it flying open.

Steven chased after her, but she was moving like a demon.

"Laura, wait!"

He ran and ran but only saw her feet as she peeled around the corner of the trailer. Then he slipped when he hit a moist patch of earth.

"Please, Laura. Wait!"

He got back on his feet, but she was already in the driver's seat. The taillights came on, momentarily blinding him. He threw himself at the car, hitting the taillight. He felt his way to the front window and leaned into it, panting for air. "Wait a damn minute," he gasped, pulling at the door, but the car was moving too fast.

Laura floored the gas pedal, sending rocks and mud into his face.

"Laura, it's too dangerous," he shouted.

But the distance between them only grew.

Chapter 42

Jackie kept herself busy by wearing a path into the kitchen floor and biting her nails down to stubs. She stopped in front of the window, pulling back the curtains. No headlights coming up the street; not even the sound of an engine.

"Shit." She chewed on another nail and only stopped when she tasted blood. "That's it."

Early or not, she was calling the cops. She picked up the phone and dialed.

"Nine-one-one, what's your emergency?"

Jackie thought fast. "My husband is stranded out on"— she looked at the pad Steven had scribbled the address on— "Cipritch Road. He called and said he was trying to get his engine started, and some man let him use his phone. I guess the guy was acting strange. It's been a while, and I haven't heard anything from him. Can an officer take a drive out there and make sure my husband and our friend are okay?"

"You want us to check up on your husband, who broke down on the side of the road?"

"Well, yes. Can you do that?"

"Ma'am, if we went looking for every man who had car trouble, we'd never get to the actual emergencies. I'd recommend your husband find a good mechanic." The operator laughed. Raspy. A smoker.

Jackie pressed the phone to her mouth, lowered her voice. "The 'actual emergencies'? This is Rome. Nothing ever happens here. Now, are you telling me you're refusing to go check on my husband and friend, even though I'm worried for their safety?"

The woman hacked into the phone.

"Hello?" Jackie was getting angry.

"Calm down, ma'am. Now how long ago did your husband call you?"

"About two and a half hours ago," Jackie lied, but it was worth it if it got them moving. "And it's a forty-minute drive home, at most."

"And he gave you the address?"

"Yes. Like I told you, he said the guy was acting odd. He wanted me to know where he was."

"Fine. Give me the address and I'll send an officer out to look around."

Chapter 43

The speedometer reached seventy. The rain started pouring down again. The driveway was just ahead, and when Laura slammed on the brakes and the car screeched—barely slowing down enough for a safe turn—she didn't even notice the headlights off in the distance, from the police car coming in the opposite direction.

She crept down the driveway and stopped in front of the house. Shoving the photos in her pocket, she sprang from the car and ran to the basement window that now flew open with ease.

Feet first, knees next, one drop.

Laura was in.

The darkness didn't bother her this time. She felt for the stairs and took each step, quiet and lithe. The kitchen was dark, too. That was good. They must be sleeping.

Laura crept to the hallway closet, opposite the stairs. She quietly opened it and felt around the back wall, behind jackets and umbrellas. Her fingers gripped the top of the barrel, and she heaved it up and out, freeing the forgotten carbine rifle from the tangle of junk. Hoisting it up and into her hands, she remembered the first time her father had taught her how to use it.

"Please, Dad," she whispered. "Say it's still loaded." And it was. This was one thing she could thank William's forgetful, drunken state for. His irresponsibility was her gain—and Frank's loss.

She turned around, one foot landing softly on the first step. Even her breathing was steady. The photos and her father's letter rustled in her pocket, burning a hole through her mind, turning her heart to stone. Her need for justice and self-preservation stood up, out of the shadows and onto the main stage, ready for their long-awaited performance.

Laura peered up into the darkness above, pointing the barrel in front of her. Another step, and her heart finally boomed. It was getting louder, stronger. Next step. *BOOM-BOOM-BOOM.*

And then she flew.

She tore around the banister, turning into Vivian's bedroom door, slamming her body against it like a two-ton truck. The door burst open, cracking and echoing through the house. A slat of wood from the doorframe flew off, rattling to a stop on the hardwood floor.

Vivian and Frank shot up in bed, glassy-eyed but alert from the sudden clatter. Laura stood at the foot of the bed, holding the rifle in one hand while pulling the pictures from her pocket with the other. She threw the photos on the bed. Both hands back on the rifle, she aimed the barrel at Frank's chest.

"How could you?" Laura said. "Your own child?"

The faint moonlight through the window shone on the photos, and Vivian's face turned severe when she saw them.

"How?" Laura screamed, holding firm to the rifle, but a hairline fracture threatened her resolve.

The photos sat there, as full of poison as a black widow. Vivian reached out, touching one with the tip of her finger. Her mouth fell open. She yanked her hand back, tucking it into her chest.

Frank slowly pulled the blanket off his legs, lifting himself out of the bed. "Come on, Laura," he said with a soft voice. "We all know you're not gonna use that. Just put the gun down."

"Shut up, you vile piece of shit!" Laura's hands started trembling, her chin quivered. "You touched me. You hurt me. Fucking pedophiles. Both of you."

Frank picked up one of the photos, looked at it thoughtfully. "Just put the rifle down. You're not shootin' anyone." He tossed the picture back on the bed.

Laura raised the barrel, pointing it straight at his head. "Stay there. Stay right fucking there or I'll blow your fucking head off!"

Frank froze next to the bed, brought his hands up. "Come on." He nodded toward the rifle. "It's probably not even loaded."

"Who's Benjamin Day? That your son, Frank? He changed my father's reports, didn't he?"

That seemed to finally break through Frank's cool exterior.

"Didn't he?" she screamed louder.

Frank remained silent.

"You two are murderers. Child molesters and murderers. Why'd you do it? Why'd you kill my father?"

Frank stood firm; he wasn't going down without a fight. Vivian sat there, white as a ghost, lifeless.

"Mom, answer me!"

Vivian blinked twice. She leaned over a fraction of an inch, whispering something to Frank.

He whispered back, and when he took a step toward Laura, he seemed to glide effortlessly.

"Stay back. I mean it," Laura ordered. She readied the rifle, took a step backward. Her loss. His gain. She forced herself to stay put, trying to sound in control. "Why'd you kill him? Because he was going to tell me everything?"

"That's a question you need to ask your mama."

Vivian's eyes snapped to life. "Shut up, Frank."

Frank slowly reached for the rifle. "Put the gun down." His voice was gentle, barely there.

Laura stepped back, revolted.

"I won't hurt you, Laura. Don't you remember anything? I loved you, and you loved me. God, the way you used to hold on to me."

"You fucking monster," Laura cried. "Get back!"

But he did no such thing.

"Don't be afraid of me," he said, narrowing the distance between them. "It's always been about you. All these years, all the waiting, it was for you. Don't you see?"

Vivian sprang to her knees. "Don't say those things!"

"Shut your mouth, Vivian," Frank yelled over his shoulder. He looked back at Laura. "I love you."

"I hate you," Laura said. One more step back and Laura felt the wall behind her. She was cornered. "I hope you rot in Hell." Her pulse whooshed in her ears, lights danced in her eyes. "What did he ever do to you, you bastard?"

Frank's chest puffed up, his face turned hard. His voice worked like a saw, ripping through the air. "He took my child from me."

"No!" Vivian said. "No more!"

Laura's eyes darted from Vivian to Frank. Her arms shook. She almost dropped the rifle. "What?" she whispered.

Vivian begged, "Frank, don't."

"My family!" Frank exploded. "He took everything from me. If I'd finished him off sooner"—he pressed his chest against the barrel, closing the only gap Laura had left— "everything would've been different."

"It's not true," Vivian shrieked, springing from the foot of the bed. Coming from behind, she drove her fingernails into Frank's face, clawing at his eyes.

He spun around and pushed her hard, sending her flying into the bed.

"How could you?" Vivian cried. "How could you say those things?"

Vivian tried to get up, but Frank shoved his palm into her forehead, knocking her back again. "Sit the fuck down."

Before Laura could make a move, Vivian shot back up, hurling her weight at Frank. Laura tried to move past them, but they were a jumbled mess, forcing her back into the wall. She told herself to shoot. The target didn't matter. But they were crowding the barrel, knocking it here and there.

Vivian's fists came pounding down on Frank's head, all the years of subdued lunacy seemed to be pouring out with every strike. She dug at his face again, sinking one nail into his cheek, right below his eye. Frank roared, then grabbed hold of her hair, smashing his fist into her face, sending Vivian hurtling backward on her skull, making a sound like a melon splitting open.

Frank dropped to her side. "Viv?" He shook her hard. "Vivian?"

This was it. An opening. Laura held the gun to her chest and ran out the door, turning the corner as Frank tore after her.

Laura had only made it a few steps down when he pulled her hair and her head snapped back. Her upper body went plummeting back into his chest, and the rifle fired into the ceiling above their heads. Startled, Frank slipped, losing his grip on her hair. Laura reeled forward, ready to throw herself down the remaining steps, but he yanked her back again, ripping hair from her scalp.

"Stop fighting me," he grunted, but Laura yanked harder, giving no thought to the burning pain in her scalp. She pulled and pulled, but with every bit of effort, he got a better grip. She screamed as loud as her lungs allowed, though there was no one to hear. If she could just get the rifle aimed behind her, but the angle was too awkward. She kicked behind her, and when that didn't work, she shoved the barrel back, aiming for his face. She hit something hard and heard a *crack*. Frank growled, grabbed her ears, using them for leverage. When he pulled her up, her back arched, and he wrapped his hands around her neck, pulling her into his chest again.

As Frank squeezed the air from her lungs, Laura reached back, clawing at anything, but her strength drained and her mind went fuzzy. He bent his neck forward, breathing heavily into her ear, "Stop fightin' and I'll let go."

The words made no sense. Laura could hear them, but they sounded foreign.

Frank was struggling to keep her upright. When she yanked and twisted, he nearly lost his balance and went hurtling with her toward the bottom of the stairs. "Stop fightin'!"

Laura felt the way her body swayed, and how Frank's swayed with it every time she flung her chest forward. She was getting too heavy for him. She leaned forward, bent over at the waist. In the dark, Frank couldn't tell what she was doing, but he felt the movement and tried to counterbalance it.

"Fuck!" he yelled.

Again, she flung forward, using all the momentum. His grip was loosening, his strength waning. But so was hers.

The last thing Laura felt before they went hurtling toward the bottom of the stairs was the rifle slipping from her hands.

~

Laura was aware of the awkward angle of her body and the cold floor beneath her. Her nose filled with a strange smell, and her head felt far away. When she tried to lift her arms and legs, the message seemed to stop at her neck. Panic pierced her insides, finally reeling her back into the moment. Her surroundings were coming into focus, everything snapped into proper order. Frank…the gun…her mother's crushed skull. Frank. Where was Frank?

Laura's head was turned to the left. She could see the front door and the glass panels in it, and shadows from the branches just beyond the front of the house. Bright moonlight now passed through them, making skeletal shadows prance across the floor. A heavy wind blew outside.

She lifted her head, just barely. The room spun. When she tried turning her neck to look behind her, where she thought Frank must have rolled off her after she broke his fall, the numbness in her arms and legs slowly faded away, replaced with a prickling sensation. She tried her legs again. They worked, and her arms, too. Then the prickling transformed into a vibrant heat that poured throughout her body as her blood fiercely pumped.

She pulled herself up on all fours, hanging her head to the floor. The pain was something amazing, but the fear was greater. She looked again at the front door, at the branches playing peek-a-boo. It was so close, if she could just reach the doorknob.

One foot on the ground, then the other, but gravity had other plans. Her legs collapsed as the room tilted. Again, she tried. She pulled her weight up with all her might and pushed off the floor, taking one rickety step toward the door, but then something caught her eye. Moonlight poured in from the kitchen window behind her, spilling out into the foyer, where she stood. A dark, bulbous shadow appeared at the bottom of the beam of moonlight, ascending up and up, transforming into a head, then shoulders. Laura took a fast, topsy-turvy step toward the door before swaying to the side.

"No," she whimpered through a bloody, swollen lip. She threw herself at the door, twisting at the lock, but her fingers were still numb. She could feel Frank closing in on her. "Help!"

Frank wrapped his arms around her, pulled her back. Her neck arched high into the air, cutting off her scream.

"If you don't stop all that hollerin', I'll snap your fuckin' neck like a twig." He gripped her neck with one hand. "You got that?"

Laura tried nodding, but her neck wouldn't move in his hand, and when she fought against him, her spine felt like it was wrapped in barbed wire. "Yes," she mumbled.

"Good." He moved his hands under her arms, leaning her into him.

Laura was vividly aware of everything now: his smell, his touch, the way his heart beat against her back. She looked around the room, past Frank's shoulder, and saw the outline of the rifle on the floor at the bottom of the stairs. He hadn't grabbed it. He wasn't going to kill her—yet. Then Laura felt them moving away from the door. Her feet scuttled under her as she tried gripping the floor with the soles of her shoes, but the spinning in her head made it pointless. Her movements were several steps behind her thoughts and were scrambling to catch up.

"No," she tried to scream while bringing up her fist, but she only punched at air.

Frank moved her deeper into the family room. "What'd I tell you about actin' that way, Laura?"

"Let me..." She brought her fist up again, weak and pathetic feeling even to her, but she felt his face beneath her fingers and slashed at his eye. "Let me go."

"Dammit." Frank threw her down on the sofa and landed on her so fast she didn't know what hit her. He pinned her arms down, screamed into her face. Saliva splattered her eyes and nose. "Fuck you."

"Get off," she screamed back. "Help!"

Frank's palm came down hard on her cheek. Her mouth clamped shut. Laura kicked her legs and thrust her hips wildly into his groin, like a drowning child, thrashing with no real aim. But her bucking and fighting couldn't touch Frank's eighty-pound advantage. All it did was slow him down and make her head spin more.

He sent another fist into the side of her face and gripped her thighs, sliding her off the sofa, smacking her head on the floor. He climbed on top of her, pinned her hands above her head, and spread her knees with his own. "You can fight all you want, Laura, but that fall's gonna catch up with you eventually."

Laura didn't have another scream left in her. Her lungs felt like they were made of concrete. Frank slid a hand down to her chest, yanked at the zipper on her jacket. Laura freed one hand, punched his shoulder, his face, his chest, but each blow was weaker than the last. Then her jacket was open, and the cold air hit her skin when Frank ripped her blouse open. Buttons went flying into the air around them. She grabbed her shirt, tried to close it, but Frank's fist came again, fast. The hit brought life back into her lungs, and she begged for God to save her. Frank only laughed.

Laura squeezed her eyes shut, yanking her head back when she felt Frank's lips on her chest. He sucked at her skin, drawing in small folds of flesh. She punched his head, but it was only foreplay to him. He slammed her hands down, softly bit the skin of her nipple through her bra. Laura's eyes filled with tears, her throat tightened, and with each quick whimper, Frank's excited breathing filled her ears.

"Please stop," she pleaded. Only every time she opened her mouth to cry out for help, he pressed his lips over hers.

She twisted her head left and right, dodging him, but she was growing more disoriented.

Frank slipped his tongue between her trembling lips, then quickly pulled away. He quietly laughed. "Forgot you like to bite." He moved his mouth back to her breasts, tugging, pulling, caressing. Laura cried, clenched, fought. Then her vision went black and her head gently rolled to the side. Her eyes closed.

~

Frank smiled at the shadowy figure on the floor. He lightly brushed his fingers along Laura's neck. "Thatta girl. Just relax."

He ran his hands down her body with the eagerness of a starving man. The softness of her flesh under his fingertips sent his mind to another planet. "Just take it slow." He wanted to relish this.

His finger rolled around her bellybutton and came to a stop at the top of her pants. He fiddled with the button, working it in his fingers, then the zipper. He grabbed both sides of the denim and ripped it apart the rest of the way, exposing the light fabric of Laura's underwear. He reached his hand beneath the cotton, too shaky with anticipation. And Laura...she was laying all wrong, if he was going to get her jeans off.

He got on his knees, pulling his boxers beneath his buttocks, exposing himself. He grabbed Laura's pants by the waist and pulled, trying to peel them past her hips. It still wasn't working. And it was too dark—he couldn't see well. He hoisted her hips up, pulling and pulling, finally making a little progress. He gave one last good yank, sending a searing pain through Laura's injured lower back, and she cried out with an earth-shattering scream so startling that he dropped her.

Frank now saw that the ember slowly burning in her had just grown into a blaze.

The real fight began.

Frank rushed forward, leaned on her.

Laura gripped the floor beneath her, twisting like an alligator. She kicked and punched with purpose. She bit with strength and screamed like a banshee. Her palm met his eye; his fists met her face. Her knee cracked his ribs; his slap sent her head spinning. She gasped, clenching her teeth against the pain, spat more venom.

He scrounged for her, his arms scrambling. She kicked more, punched more, ripped her nails through his flesh more, and when she wasn't doing that, she lunged back, ripping her body from beneath his. But he pinned her back down and sat on her stomach, holding tightly to her fists. Every time she bucked, he fell back.

"*Fuck you,*" she roared.

He took the risk and let go of her fist. The punch came hard, and Laura's neck bolted back. She brought her arms up, grabbed his bottom lip, yanking so hard that she felt her fingernails penetrate the lumpy tissue.

He screamed, sucking in his torn lip, and leaned forward, grabbing her head, squeezing. Laura brought a knee up, slammed it into his groin. Now his cries blended with hers. She used his moment of weakness and scooted back, positioning herself right under the window. Her lungs opened and she screamed for help again.

~

Heavy plumes of mist billowed around Steven's face. The night was too cold, the road too long. He coughed, fighting to take another breath.

After a while, the trees all started to look the same, along with the turns and curves in the road. There was no telling how long he'd been running, but it felt like hours. The big hill had been the worst. After that, downhill felt like a treat, but what followed was more darkness—an endless maze of empty lanes in the middle of nowhere. But he had to push, even if his lungs felt like they were made of steel, because somewhere, just a few miles beyond the vast trees, a nightmare was unfolding.

When there wasn't any strength left in his legs, he saw Laura's face, the bruises on her neck, the way her eyes looked when she found those pictures. Those damn pictures.

He pushed harder, one foot in front of the other. If Laura didn't find Frank first, he would, and Lord have mercy on him, because Steven wouldn't.

"Seven…six miles. Can't be much more than that," Steven panted. Wishful thinking. He needed to run faster.

Headlights? Steven stopped, dragging his feet to the edge of the road. He covered his eyes against the glare and waved his other hand around. "Stop!" Maybe it was Laura. Maybe it was Frank. He didn't much care. "Stop!"

He bent over and grabbed his knees, coughing while watching the car come closer and then stop. Then the car door opened.

"Steven Brenner? That you? What're you doin' all the way out here?"

Steven knew that voice. He nearly collapsed with relief. "Thank you, Jackie," he whispered, staggering to the police officer. "Officer Teady"—Steven grabbed his shoulder, still badly out of breath—"we need to get to Hallows' Farm. Now."

Chapter 44

Laura could scream all she wanted. "No one's going to hear you," Frank snarled, gripping her shoulders tightly in his hands.

She screamed anyway, kicking her knee up and into his tailbone.

"Motherfucker," Frank's voice rang out.

Laura's fear was nowhere to be found. She was fighting like a beast—nothing but snarling teeth and ferocity.

She blindly reached up, yanked. If she could just get the curtains in her hands, she could rip them down and use the large metal rod, but another punch came fast, right into her stomach. Her mind flooded with pictures. She saw Danlyn's face.

I promised you I'd be safe.

She pulled hard on the bottom of the curtain and felt curtain rings fall on her face. Metal clanked on the floor beside her. She squirmed under Frank as she saw him reach for the rod.

I promised you I'd make it up to you.

Her arms scrambled, entangling in his. She could hear the metal pole scraping on the floor, and Frank's labored breathing above her. Any minute, that pole was going to come flying down into her face.

Frank grabbed the rod, reared back, and brought it down hard.

Laura reeled to the side, narrowly dodging the lethal blow. She tried prying the rod from his hands.

"You bitch!" Frank spat on her face. His body came back up, torso high, arms in the air, armed with the rod. He shouldn't have dropped his guard.

Laura drew her arm back, packing her fist like a stone. She heard the air leave Frank's lungs when she hammered her fist between his legs and he fell sideways, dropping the rod and grabbing his groin. He curled into the fetal position while mumbling something Laura couldn't understand.

If Laura's past had taught her anything, it was that monsters didn't give up easily. She grabbed the pole and got to her knees, but Frank's foot shot out and drove into her hip. Something snapped loudly and Laura fell back, writhing in pain.

Frank leapt on her, slamming his forehead into hers. She grabbed his face, dug her thumbs into his eyes. They felt like hard olives as her thumb sank right into the spongy center of one.

"Jesus," her voice soared, horrified by her own brutal will to survive.

His head cranked back, he grabbed his face. "I'm gonna kill you!" He brought both his hands together and laced his fingers, lifting his nestled fists into the air.

Laura, pinned between his knees, tried to wiggle out, but her hip fought her and acid shot into her legs. The pain was too severe. This was it. Frank's face was the last thing she'd see before she died.

I love you, Danlyn.

Laura turned away, closing her eyes against the final blow. He'd make a mess of her, right here in front of the fireplace.

Fitting end to a sad life.

She could hear the hissing wind from his rushing fists and the way his weight adjusted on top of her, all the momentum flying forward. The monstrous *boom* that followed was deafening.

The floor rattled beneath Laura. A gunshot. She smelled gunpowder. Where were his fists? Where was her horrible ending? Her eyes shot open.

Frank looked down at her, his face smooth, jaw limp. His torso swayed, and a dollop of blood seeped from each side of his mouth. Something warm coated the floor around Laura. It was slimy and thick, and the smell mingled with the gunpowder—something like roasted iron.

Frank fell to the floor, his bloody mouth pressed against her ear. Laura grunted, using all her strength to push him off while trying to see through the dark.

Where was the gun? Where was the shooter?

"Steven?" she called.

She heard a clicking sound, a tiny movement. Neck swiveling, eyes searching, she rushed to her feet, swayed, then widened her stance.

"Steven?"

But the silence and darkness around her swallowed her up, sending her right into the gates of hell.

"Who's there?"

A scuffle came from the other side of the room, in front of the stairs. Laura strained her eyes and saw something there...a shape, white and billowy and streaked with something dark.

She's not dead. Jesus, she's not dead.

Footsteps dragged across the floor, and Laura watched the billowy figure slowly move toward her. She reached for the small lamp on the table next to the sofa and turned it on. A dim light spread throughout the room, and in front of her, like a horror movie come to life, Vivian stood, rifle in hand, blood coating her disfigured face. The whites of her eyes stood out in contrast, sharp and wretched. The eyes of the devil.

Laura pressed her hand to her mouth, cowering. A rush of saliva pooled in the space under her tongue. She took a step to the side, almost slipping in the island of blood surrounding Frank. In the dim light, the blood looked black, like the floor had fallen out, leaving Frank's body suspended in air.

Laura's mind worked like rusty gears, trying to take in the scene. The blood on her hands, in her hair, on her clothes. She jumped almost halfway across the room, toward the front door, crying out in pain. But the door was still too far away, and Vivian was still trailing behind. The bottom of her long, white nightgown swept through the blood, spreading it around like paint on a canvas. The rifle dangled at her side.

"Mom...what're you doing?" Laura stopped moving. She put her hands up.

Vivian staggered. Her eyes fluttered, then focused.

Laura tried not to think about how her mother's nose seemed to sit in a different place. She slowly moved back, edging toward the door. And then Vivian's eyes locked in on her feet.

"Don't move," Vivian ordered.

"Mom, just let me go."

Vivian looked back at Frank's body. She moved in slow motion, seemingly trying to register what she'd just done.

"I'm going to open the door," Laura told her, taking another small step back.

"No," Vivian snapped. "Look what you've done."

Laura looked at Frank's body. "I didn't—"

"You couldn't just let me have him." Vivian tilted her head to the side. "Why wouldn't you let me have him?"

"Why did you take away my father?" Laura was senseless with fear—tempting a madwoman with a gun. Before she could stop herself, she said, "What happened to my father? Tell me."

"I don't know." Vivian's eyes looked black now.

"Yes you do. What happened?"

Vivian nearly stumbled but kept her focus. "William was going to take everything from me."

"What did Frank do to him?"

"Nothing. Frank didn't do it!"

"Yes he did," Laura shouted back, all logic leaving her.

"No. My son did."

That brought Laura up short. "What?"

"Benjamin. Benjamin's my son. I lost him because *he* came home."

"No." Laura shook her head. "You're crazy."

"You don't even remember your own brother. He loved you, Laura. He adored you. You were inseparable the whole year he lived here, and you don't even remember him."

"This is just another lie." Then Laura remembered the photos of her with the baby.

"It's not a lie. Frank wasn't going to let your father near his son, so he took him away from me and let him live with that whore. I didn't even get to know my boy because your father came back. And you..." Vivian looked deranged. "After I had

"Benjamin, I wasn't enough for Frank anymore. But *you* were. You always were...from the very beginning. You took him from me, but I got him back. After you left, I had everything. But then your father came out here that day, looking for you, threatening us, threatening Frank. Well...I wasn't going to lose Frank again. Benjamin wasn't going to let that happen. Some children respect their parents. Not you, you black-hearted bitch. But Ben did. He protected me and Frank."

"I don't believe you. Frank did it. He killed my—"

"No, Laura! Benjamin went to your father's. *He* brought your father the bottle of whiskey. It was supposed to be easy, and it was...getting your father drunk. But he couldn't just leave with Benjamin, like he was supposed to. He had to put up a fight. Even when Benjamin told him you needed him, and offered to take him to you, your father couldn't do what he was told. All the records, your father's body, it wasn't supposed to happen in Rome. If it hadn't, you never would've known. But even in death, William won't let me be."

"You used me to reel in my father?" Laura's eyes smoldered, her chest pumped. There she stood, covered in someone else's blood, facing what would certainly be her own death, but nothing mattered anymore. "You're fucking evil, Vivian."

Laughter was the last thing Laura expected, but there it was, pouring from Vivian's lips, flowing with a stench of insanity. "You and your father never loved me. Frank was the only one. He loved me. But then he loved you. He waited for you to love him back. I should have been enough, but it was always going to be you."

"How could you do it? How could you let him touch me?" Laura cried. "What...after Frank, you realized I might be a "profit, so you offered your little girl up on a platter. Is that it? How many?"

Vivian offered nothing.

"Being sick has always been your excuse. Sick people commit depraved acts all the time. But this? Even for you…" Laura took another small step back. "You used me to reel in that piece of filth."

Laura's mouth burned with the truth, her words felt like fire. She needed to rid herself of them before they burned her alive.

"Dad was right. You never should've had children. You were the mistake, Vivian. Not me. You hated me because you hate yourself."

"Frank loved you enough for the both of us. I didn't need to."

"You call that love? Molesting a child, and having your"— the thought was still miles away from Laura's comprehension— "your *son* murder my father?"

"He loved…" Vivian's words trailed off into a hum. She smiled, slowly swaying from side to side, in some morbid dance. A gust of wind creaked through the windows, and the walls seemed to sway around her. The house came to life, moving with her, dancing with her, feeding energy into her.

Laura slid one foot back, then the other. She couldn't breathe under the weight of the house. She kept her eyes on the rifle and slipped her hand back, feeling for the door. Five feet to go. She yearned for the cold brass under her fingers, never wanting anything so bad, because that cold touch meant survival. Survival for her and Danlyn. Then she felt it. She hadn't meant to turn her head, to look down at the knob, breaking Vivian's trance.

Time's up.

She twisted the knob, but the door was still locked. Vivian cocked the rifle, aimed the barrel at her head. Laura froze, hands locked in place, air suspended in her lungs.

"Stop," Vivian said. "Turn around."

Laura did as she was told. Vivian took a step back but kept the rifle aimed with precision. "Danlyn's going to be so heartbroken when she hears about you, Laura. But I'll be here. She'll always have me."

"You're insane." Laura's voice shook so badly, she almost couldn't speak. "She'll never believe you."

"Maybe not. But she'll have no choice."

Vivian took one last step back. She teetered, trying to balance herself, but Frank's blood carried her back, and she went down with a *thud*, sending blood flying up around her. She wriggled like a fish on a hook, trying to free herself.

Laura spun around, feverishly twisted at the lock. Vivian pulled herself onto her knees while sending a bullet soaring over Laura's head. Laura dropped down, hunching in front of the door. She reached up, searching for the lock when she heard the bolt of the rifle again. Vivian pulled herself up by the table in the foyer, barrel aimed back on Laura.

Laura grabbed each side of her head, as though her hands could shield her from a bullet. "Don't shoot, Mom. Please don't do this."

"Frank wasn't going to have you"—a crippling wave of tears broke Vivian's voice—"and neither will Danlyn." She pressed her cheek to the rifle. "You killed Frank." The barrel started to shake. "You destroyed everything."

"I didn't," Laura whimpered. She huddled against the door, face hidden, eyes squeezed shut. "I swear, I didn't..." A scream was building in her throat.

"You couldn't just let us be happy, Laura."

"P-please, Mom, don't!"

~

The officer picked up the radio. "Shots fired. I repeat, shots fired off of Gail Road, on Hallows' Farm. Requesting backup."

Steven pointed at the driveway. "There!"

"Sit back," the officer shouted. He took the turn fast, and Steven flew back against the seat. They sped down the drive; mud splattered the windows. Officer Teady had one hand on his weapon, one on the wheel.

"Hurry," Steven yelled.

The officer stopped outside the front door and ran out, slamming the door behind him, locking Steven inside.

"Police!" The door rattled with each blow of Officer Teady's fist. "Open up!"

~

Laura's heart plummeted. The police were right there, so close. But it didn't matter. Vivian remained oblivious to the pounding on the door.

"Just open the door," Laura cried. "You were protecting me. You can tell them that. They won't arrest you. But if you kill me, they'll take you away." Laura was playing into her mother's fears, if there was anyone home anymore. "You haven't done anything wrong yet," she lied. "Please, Mom." Tears poured down Laura's cheeks as she begged for her life.

The barrel swung wildly, but still in the vicinity of Laura's head. "Shut up," Vivian shouted. "Stop talking!"

"You don't want to live with this on your shoulders, too," Laura tried, but even as she said it, she knew her words had fallen on deaf ears. This was the ultimate, the most unconscionable thing a mother could do, and as she looked up and met the barrel's one dark eye, Laura felt it: finality, her mother's last act of hatred. Vivian would end it all, because her all was over, splayed on the floor, bleeding to death.

Vivian rushed at Laura, pressing the rifle into her forehead. "I have to," she whispered.

"No!" Laura grabbed for the barrel, but Vivian sprang back.

"It's over."

"No!"

"I'm sorry, Laura."

Laura's bloodcurdling scream blended in with the thunderous snapping of wood as Officer Teady kicked the door open, sending Laura toppling over. Vivian's arms shot up, rifle still in hand, eyes bulging from their sockets. Laura sealed her body to the floor, legs down, arms down, head out of range.

The headlights from the car pierced the darkness and shone on Vivian's bloody, pulped face. The pungent smell of blood hung heavily in the air.

"Holy fuck." The officer aimed his gun at Vivian. Vivian aimed the rifle at him. "Drop the weapon," he ordered. "Drop it and put your hands up."

Laura could just see the officer's face. Instinct drove him, but he looked panicked. He was going to have to mean it if they were to come out of this alive.

"Drop the weapon. Do what I say and we'll figure all this out."

The officer was wavering. Laura crawled a little closer, whispered, "She'll do it. She'll shoot."

He centered his aim on Vivian's head. There was a new resolve in his voice. "Drop the weapon, now!"

The light from the car hit Laura's eyes, calling her like a siren—the sweet promise of escape. She could hear the officer screaming at her to stay put, but his voice washed out.

"She's going to kill you," Laura heard herself whisper, but the office wasn't looking at her. He was looking at the old woman, bracing the rifle like a trained soldier.

"Drop the weapon or I'll shoot," he shouted.

But Vivian knew, just like Laura, that Officer Teady wouldn't be using his weapon tonight.

Laura's movements caught Vivian's attention. She looked at Laura, Laura looked back at her. Vivian's tears stopped and she stared eerily at her daughter. She propped the butt of the rifle on the floor, aiming the barrel up toward the ceiling.

"Stop!" Officer Teady widened his stance. "Raise your hands! No! Stop! Stop, stop, stop!"

Laura understood at once. She sprang from the floor, almost knocking the officer back out the door. Arms out, leaping across the small space, she reached out for Vivian, screaming, "Don't."

Vivian bent over and wrapped her lips around the barrel, eyes strained up, locked on Laura's.

Laura and Officer Teady screamed in unison, long and drawn out.

Everything moved in slow motion. Along with Laura, the officer lunged at Vivian. They were arm's length away, and the world around them morphed into a lazy underwater scene; arms and legs moving like gossamer dreams. Their voices tuned out, their cries ceased to exist. And then all Laura could hear was the gunshot, echoing for miles.

The three of them collided, falling down like pillars, Vivian first, then Laura, then Officer Teady. The residual echo slowly faded away like soft thunder. Death had an odor, and it crept up Laura's nose, rising up from her mother's shattered body beneath her, sealing its place in her memory. The officer leapt off the two of them, gasping. He wrapped his hands around Laura's torso, trying to pull her off Vivian. He was yelling something Laura couldn't understand. But she wasn't letting him move her.

Everything was still a million miles away—the officer, the screaming, the howling sirens in the distance, the house—leaving Laura and Vivian alone, hunter and prey, victim and abuser, mother and daughter. Laura cradled her mother's mangled head in her arms.

"She's dead."

Laura's voice was only just there.

"It's over."

Chapter 45

I hate this drive, sitting in a rental car that smells like old smoke, driving along a highway that won't lead me anywhere but to a living hell. And what are those stains all over the passenger's seat? Whatever. It's probably best I don't know.

It's raining again. It rained the last time I came here. Guess it's fitting, really. The sky matches my mood. Not that I'm always this way. Sometimes I'm a regular peach. But not here, and certainly not now.

Hands on the wheel at ten and two, eyes focused, tires peeling down the freeway, brain locked in on memories I wish I could forget. I wonder if I'll make it in the door this time. Last time I didn't. I got to the gate, pulled out my identification, and damn near broke down. I flew back home and called my sister. Cried into the phone for three hours. This time's different, though. Or at least I hope it is.

I remember this freeway. I remember driving on it the day we left Rome. Things were a little different then, and sometimes I think I can't possibly be that same girl. When I see my own reflection, I see a stranger, I see someone else's eyes, hair, nose. I see lots of things that leave me questioning my identity. But I don't see Danlyn Hallow. Not the way I used to. The day Laura and I left Rome, I left behind my childhood, or what was left of it…if I ever really had one in the first place. I also left behind the only people I had come to know as family. Steven and Jackie. We keep in touch, but it doesn't feel like enough.

I was pissed off when we left. Hell, I was more than pissed. Don't get me wrong, I wanted to leave. I just didn't want to leave them. But I also knew why we had to go. Not too many people could shack up in the same town where their mom polished herself off with a pop and a bang. Callous-sounding, I know. But in my defense, it's not like Vivian ever won a place in my heart. Or even tried. I really didn't know the woman, my mother. That part never stops being weird. To this day I don't know what box to put Vivian in. For a while, after we left, I didn't know what box to put Laura in, either. But in time, I managed to think of her as Mom. I needed to, really, and for a long time she stayed Mom. It wasn't until I went through my rebellious teens that her being Mom stopped being convenient and her being sister started making sense. Truth is, I'll always put Laura in both boxes. When I need a mom, she's there. When I need a sister, she's there. But not Vivian. She'll always be this obscure nightmare that doesn't add up to anything, yet defines everything.

It took a while for Laura to tell me what happened that night on Hallows' Farm. She and Jackie and Steven tried to hide it. We stayed with them for a few weeks after all hell broke loose. They hid papers, turned off the local news. They did what they could. I heard trickles of news, and I knew Vivian was gone, but the unrated version wasn't released for some time. Mostly those weeks were just really confusing. Everything was like a roller coaster, except it didn't stop or slow down. Cops were around a lot. Detectives came by. Then the lawyers came in. The Brenners' house became a revolving door for all sorts of people, and my sister was always coming and going, meeting with this person or that person, crying and crying. I think she cried for a month straight. I don't remember her saying a word to any of us for a solid week, at least. If it hadn't been for Jackie, I'd have lost my mind.

I'll never forget the day Ron Gallivan came to the door. Real slick-looking lawyer, chomping at the bit. What for, I wasn't sure, but come to find out that Hallows' Farm was worth a pretty penny, and my sister was the beneficiary of everything. The house, the land, the money, and the horrible memories that came along with it. Lucky girl, eh? With Frank out of the picture, everything went to her.

Of course Laura wanted nothing to do with the house or the land. Good thing Ron Gallivan represented an eager buyer—some guy who'd apparently been hounding Vivian for years. The buyer was in no mood to haggle, my sister was in no mood to care. They settled quickly and we were on our way, all the way to Seattle. My sister wanted to get as far away as she could, but she wasn't brave enough to risk Alaska. We settled in a little house, just north of Seattle, nestled right next to a scenic lake. It was nice, good schools, friendly neighbors. Laura put herself through school, and after two years of community college, she got a job at a local vet clinic. Wasn't much money, but she was happy. We always had our cushion to fall back on, too. As for me, things weren't so easy.

For a long while after we left Rome, I couldn't leave Laura's side. I freaked out if I couldn't see her, panicked when she dropped me off at school. Then things began escalating. I started probing, and when no answers were given, I became resentful and went back to hating my sister. Even when she dated a few nice guys along the way, I managed to drive them out. It's a miracle I didn't drive her back to drinking. That's how horrible I was. Then she met another nice guy, James Bettley. He was different. I couldn't scare him off, but he also didn't give me enough wiggle room to be the bitch on wheels I had become. He loved her so much, and he was good for her. I would never have admitted it then, but I loved him for it. I appreciated the smile he put on her face and the happiness he brought to our home.

It grew increasingly more difficult to hide my joy over our seemingly normal home. James was the first real father figure I'd ever had, and Laura had a healthy relationship for the first time in her life. It was good. They were good. And then they got married. But even with all that, questions nagged at me— took up permanent residence in my mind. Drove me crazy as hell. Here I was, a teenage girl, changing and growing and becoming a woman, yet I had no plotted course for my life. I felt like a cube that everyone was trying to fit into a round hole. Everyone's life was getting on, but I was lost in limbo.

It wasn't until my sister broke down one night that I grew the hell up. I'd been giving her shit by the truckload. Question after question, I hounded her. I didn't want the past to be finished for her, because her peace meant closure, but I didn't have closure, and I knew she wasn't telling me everything. "I don't know, Danlyn. I don't have the answers," was what she always said, then she'd tell me it was all going to be okay. Only that answer wasn't good enough for me. I thought it was bullshit, so I pressed her, hard, called her a liar. I ripped every scar wide open, exposing the battered woman beneath my sister's shiny, new veneer.

She got drunk that night—piss-poor drunk—and her new husband was right there to see it. I made sure of that. Then I hated myself for it. I watched her cry and beat herself up. I saw her hope slip away, as though it had never been there to begin with. Look how powerful I was. I could bring down the person who loved me most. Yeah, I felt real powerful…for about two minutes. Then I broke, too. I never knew I could feel like such a piece of shit. I hated that feeling, and hated myself for causing my sister so much pain.

That night, we had a come-to-Jesus talk. I asked for the thousandth time why, why, why? She cried and swore to me for the thousandth time that she didn't know, didn't know, didn't know. She was so far gone, I finally believed her. Surely I would've pulled any secrets out of her, had she been harboring them. After that, things changed, I changed, and my sister never drank again. But that also had something to do with the bun brewing in the oven.

Little Michael Bettley was born on a sunny Tuesday morning, weighing in at a healthy eight pounds, six ounces—cute as a button and wielding the power of healing. I was the proud aunt, so in love. My sister was the doting mother, hovering and watching and protecting, and James was your regular father of the year. A little too normal for my taste, but I'd seen the alternative, and I didn't want any.

I got my grades up. Even shocked the hell out of myself by graduating with honors. I kept my nose clean but gave my sister just enough trouble to properly fill the role of little sister but not enough to push her over the edge. Especially not with Michael around. Things got a lot better, and then my mom turned into my sister, and my sister turned into my friend. I still had lots of questions and lots of anger, but I stopped directing them at the wrong person, which is why I'm driving down this damn road right now.

I went to college, floundered for a year or so, not knowing what the hell I wanted. First I was going to be a painter. Laura's incessant eye rolls took care of that. I hadn't much progressed past stick figures. Then I was going to be a flight attendant, which came with the added bonus of dropping out of college, but that time, James took care of it. Sat me down and squared me away. Or more like bribed me into staying in school for one more year. "Give it a try. It means so much to your sister."

I was pissed, as usual, but then I was thankful. Six months into my sophomore year, it hit me. I wanted to help people, but I didn't want to wipe their asses and mop up their vomit, so I took on all the shrink jokes, put a down payment on a comfortable couch, and set my sights on psychology. Laura and James had nothing bad to say. They could see how passionate I was, and they supported me all the way, even when that meant more tuition fees and classes and books. My sister had fought for my happiness when I was younger, and she made every bit of room for it when I was older.

Another year into college and my passion fizzled. School counselors talked at me, my sister reamed my ass a few hundred times. But they didn't get it. The idea of listening to married couples bicker all day was like a really slow form of suicide. I didn't want that. I wanted something meatier, something with more substance. I went to my sister's for Sunday night dinner, and over a plate of meatloaf and green bean casserole, she made a random joke that would define my future. I walked into the main campus office on a Monday morning and told my counselor what I'd decided. "My sister said I'm up to my ears in deranged family members, so why not focus there?" Only I didn't want to deal with the scum of the earth, either. I was a kid who'd faced monsters, and while I may not be the most maternal creature in the world, experience like mine can't be bought. Child psychology. It was music to my ears. If through my twisted childhood I could help one lost kid...well, you know the rest. It'd all be absolutely worth it.

I busted my ass and graduated, again with honors. Blew the socks right off the dean by graduating as the valedictorian. He said he always knew I had it in me. Yeah, right. That asshole had dismissed me whenever I opened my mouth, but that was okay. I was a big girl, going into the big world, where people brown-nose and blow steam up each other's rear ends like a year-round sport. He shook my hand, I moved my tassel over, and *c'est la vie*—goodbye college.

That's where I'm at now, in the interim, searching for the right place to use my skills. Okay, that's not true. I'm searching for a place where they won't discredit me the minute I walk into an interview because I'm inexperienced. I actually had someone tell me they liked their wine aged. Here I am, sitting on my fancy diploma, with no job and lots of bills. My sister and James covered as much as they could financially, but I bled the college well dry. Then came the bachelor apartment and my beat-up sedan back home. But at least I know what the stains on those seats are from. As for my career, I guess that's what internships are for. But first things first.

Time to get off the freeway and make the drive to the gate. My hands are shaking, my upper lip's sweating. You'd think I'd be better prepared for this, after all these years, but I feel like a child again. I'm afraid. And to think that I actually thought this would help me grow, personally and professionally. I'm a fool.

I pull up to the gate and hand them my ID. I've done this before, and I'm ready for all the questions. Answer them right and you win a round-trip visit to a cinderblock hell. The men nod, open the gate. I'm through.

Once inside, I'm directed to a wall of a man. He looks like a pit bull with a human head. I sign in, get my badge, and am sent to another waiting dock. The place is a maze, and why the hell shouldn't it be. But it's making me even more nervous, and I know I look nervous, too. The stark fluorescent lights make me feel like I'm in some extraterrestrial probe shop.

Another guard joins us and tells me to follow him. He walks ahead of me, Pit Bull behind me. They actually make me feel safer, which is good, because I might need someone to catch me from falling when I pass the hell out. Pathetic. My hands are completely wet, and my purse keeps sliding off my shoulder. *Stupid.* A purse makes you look weak. Tough women never wear purses.

The guards walk me down a long hallway and unlock another door, through which we enter, and then they lock it behind us. The door in front of us opens and we walk into a room with tall walls, more bright lights, cement floors, and a long row of metal stools fastened to the floor. In front of each stool is a thick slab of Plexiglas separated by narrow panels to give visitors the illusion of privacy. Pit bull points, "Sit there."

The glass in front of me is smeared with lipstick. Some lovesick moron who fell for the wrong man. Makes me wonder about all the sad stories exchanged in this room.

Pit bull walks away, telling me it'll be a minute. The other guard stands back against the wall, hands behind his back, face straight. He's not making me feel safe anymore.

I turn back around, eyes glued on the officer on the other side of the glass, there to keep the rowdy murderers and rapists in line. I hear the unlatching of a door and all the beeps that go with it in a place like this. My throat tightens, and I'm suddenly thankful I'm not usually a crier. That doesn't mean I don't look scared, though.

The other guard walks in, followed by a man in a navy-blue jumpsuit, wrists bound by cuffs, ankles shackled. The other guard behind the glass moves forward, assisting. The door locks behind them.

"Here." The guard motions to the man in blue, and then he moves aside, giving me my first look into a face that's haunted me every day. A face I never wanted to see again.

His hair's gone. He's shorter, or maybe I'm just taller. His skin's mottled and covered with age spots, and his hands and arms are frail and thin, like chicken legs. When he sits down and looks at me, it takes everything not to look away. There's a smile there, I can see it in his eyes, but it never finds its way to his lips. I see why. His teeth are brown with decay. Some are missing. I lean in and can't help but to squint. It's almost unfathomable that this old man has been the keeper of my worst dreams. He's so weak, but that doesn't matter, because it's not his physical strength that scares me. It's his secrets.

Now I can't look away, even if I wanted to. My eyes are glued to him, and his on me.

His voice croaks with the rasp of age. "I know you're not here to see me. After all these years, you're lookin' for the same thing she is."

"No," I tell him. My sister has her demons, and I know she tried like hell to get him to finally tell her where they were. She wrote him a dozen letters over the years, begging for a little compassion.

I look at him, muster up all the courage I can, and say, "I'm not looking for long-lost journals—"

"You're lookin' for Benjamin, then. But I've told your sister I'm not talkin'. My son sacrificed everything for me. I'm not givin' him up. From the day that boy was born, I've watched out for him. I got him away from your mother when she was too messed up to take care of him, I kept him away from that drunk husband of hers, and I sent him away when I knew I couldn't raise him, even though it nearly killed me. So if you're here for his whereabouts, just go."

I'd love to know where the spawn of Satan is holed up. Sneaky son of a bitch has led law enforcement on a wild goose chase for years. But that's also not what I'm here for. I have to get ready to hear the words come out of my mouth, because this time there might be an answer waiting at the other end. An answer Laura could never give me all those years I screamed at her and made her cry.

"I'm not here for journals or information about your son. I'm here because I want to ask something about me."

I have to look him straight in the eye, because I'm hoping to see doubt, some kind of uncertainty that I can hold on to, and I don't want to miss it. And then I hear myself ask, "Are you my father, Frank?"

There it is, my question, out of the box I shoved it in after high school, never letting it out. It just played hide and seek in my mind. I hold my breath and look in his eyes.

"Ah, baby girl," he says. Tears fill his eyes, but not mine. There is no uncertainty in his voice, no hesitation at all. My composure drops somewhere on the floor and scurries away, hiding under a bed in a cell, like a scared cat, refusing to come out.

He puts his hand on the glass. I pull back.

"Yes, Danlyn, I'm your daddy. You wanna know why I didn't fight for you, why I let your sister take you."

"No." Now I'm furious. I want to spit nails straight through the glass.

"Your mama didn't tell me you were mine until after Laura left town with you when you were a baby, or I wouldn't have let it happen." He says it like that's going to make me feel all warm and gooey. Instead, I want to kill him.

"I wanted to tell you when you and your sister came back, and I was goin' to, when the time was right."

I stand up, clutching my purse to my chest like a shield, and all my plans fly out the window. I can't even muster the courage to request the DNA test I hoped would prove that Frank wasn't really my father. For fourteen years, I thought I wanted proof. Now the thought of Frank's blood running through my veins makes me want to high dive into an empty pool. I don't want tangible proof. I just want to forget the last five minutes ever happened. I've got a long plane ride home and tears to finally cry when I get there.

As I walk away, I hear Frank say, "He's always wanted to meet you."

I turn around but can't look at him anymore, and I can't speak.

"Your brother, Danlyn. He's always wanted to get to know you."

I can't take another minute of this Dahmer family bullshit. I need to get out, now.

I walk to the door and wait for Pit Bull to let me out of the visiting room when I hear Frank say something that I'm afraid will follow me for the rest of my life.

"Your brother's closer than you think, Danlyn. You'll meet him soon."

Acknowledgements
I'd like to thank my two lovely editors, Ashley Davis (A.K.A. Mistress of Collegiate Badassery) and Keri Knutson (who not only helped me bring this book to the next level, but who created one hell of a cover). I know I kept your heads hopping, ladies, but you pushed me to be better, and that's one of the greatest gifts someone can be given. Thank you.
I'd also like to thank everyone who helped me along the way. Your support means a great deal to me, and I'll never forget it. Tim Marquitz of Ragnarok Publications and Grant Handgis of Brother Coyote Publications, you're awesome. To all my friends who've supported me over the years, I wouldn't trade you for the world.
Last, but certainly not least, to all my readers: Thank you for giving this book a chance and spending your precious time reading it. You're the best.

About the Author

Sloane Kady is first a mother, wife, and dedicated military spouse. Then comes all the fun with words. As an artist and lover of all things macabre, she finds inspiration in the darkest of corners and finds beauty in honesty, even when it's undiluted and bleeding and so raw that you want to look away. Honesty was the first breath of life for Irreparable Deeds, Sloane Kady's first novel. If Kady promises anything, it's to never shy away from the truth.

When Kady's not writing, she spends every moment possible with her husband and their lovely daughters. For those who know her personally, you know that the occasional, spontaneous round of pine tree-sniffing isn't out of the question. Late at night, when other writers are burning the midnight oil, you can be sure to find this horror-loving, suspense-writing, potty-mouthed, tattooed novelist fast asleep in her comfiest pajamas. After all, not all dark, twisted souls are terribly exciting. But rest assured, she'll hold off on the tree-sniffing long enough to pour herself into her next novel.

Stay up to date with Sloane Kady at www.sloanekady.com.

"We are the granddaughters of the witches you weren't able to burn."

— Unknown

www.ingramcontent.com/pod-product-compliance
Lightning Source LLC
Chambersburg PA
CBHW030359180626
46812CB00005B/1847

* 9 7 8 0 9 8 6 2 7 9 0 0 3 *